"MOON MADNESS," SHE WHISPERED.

Cade's answering smile was disbelieving. "You really think that's all it is?"

"What else could it be?" Jessica replied, knowing it was a lie. It was Brad and her changing feelings for him. It was Cade and the disturbing emotions he was beginning to arouse in her.

"It could be that I've been wanting to kiss you like that for the past two days," Cade said. "And it could be that you've been wanting me to."

"I have to get back to the house," she murmured. "My article's still waiting to be written."

"You can't run away from this, Jessica," he warned. "It's too late. And if it's any consolation, I'll remind you that although you're thinking of Brad now, he probably isn't thinking of you. I know how likable he is, but he'll never make you happy. Just remember that I won't become involved in a triangle. I will wait because I want you, but I'm sure you know that. I'll wait—for a while. . . ."

NEVER LOOK BACK

Donna Kimel Vitek

A CANDLELIGHT ECSTASY SUPREME™

Published by
Dell Publishing Co., Inc.
1 Dag Hammarskjold Plaza
New York, New York 10017

ISBN: 0–440–16279–3

Printed in the United States of America
First printing—December 1983

To Our Readers:

Candlelight Ecstasy is delighted to announce the start of a brand new series—Ecstasy Supremes! Now you can enjoy a romance series unlike all the others—longer and more exciting, filled with more passion, adventure, and intrigue. The stories you've been waiting for.

In months to come we look forward to presenting books by many of your favorite authors and the very finest work from new authors of romantic fiction as well. As always, we are striving to present the unique, absorbing love stories that you enjoy most—the very best love has to offer.

Breathtaking and unforgettable, Ecstasy Supremes will follow in the great romantic tradition you've come to expect *only* from Candlelight Ecstasy.

Your suggestions and comments are always welcome. Please let us hear from you.

Sincerely,

The Editors
Candlelight Romances
1 Dag Hammarskjold Plaza
New York, New York, 10017

CHAPTER ONE

Jessica Grayson took the last place in line at a ticket counter in Atlanta's international airport. After putting her luggage down on the floor beside her, she turned to her assistant, Lynn Bennett, and handed her a set of keys. "Since I'll be out of town anyhow, this is the perfect time to get the car serviced. I've already told them at the garage that it seems to need a complete tune-up and a front-end alignment, but you should probably remind the mechanic of that anyway. And you're sure you don't mind picking the car up when it's ready and leaving it at my house?"

"Heavens, no," Lynn answered enthusiastically. "I'd never pass up a chance to drive something nicer than that old rattletrap of mine. Why else do you think I was so eager to come out to the airport with you and drive the Chevrolet back to the garage?"

Jessica smiled. "I thought you volunteered just to get out of the office for a few hours."

"Hmm, that too. I have to admit I don't mind getting away from work for a while," Lynn said with an unabashed grin, then glanced at the leather briefcase Jessica carried. "And speaking of getting away from work, why don't you just leave what you have in there behind?"

"Wish I could but I can't." Jessica patted the side of the case. "I have in here the lead article for February's issue of *Georgia*. Unfortunately it came in past deadline and it's too long. Before

I get back here in ten days, I have to cut it somehow without chopping it to pieces."

"But you shouldn't have to work during vacation."

"Can't be helped this time. I'd hand it back to the author for cutting, but I can't locate him. I suspect he's living out one of his fantasies and hitchhiking across Europe right now."

"Oh well, since it has to be done, at least you'll be doing it in a fantastic place," Lynn said, wearing a cheery smile once again. "I've heard Bermuda is really beautiful. And it should still be warm there even though it is nearly October. Don't you think?"

"Um-hmm, should be," Jessica responded rather abstractedly, stepping forward as the line shortened and moving her luggage along with her. Then she looked back at her assistant with a smile. "Actually, when Brad called yesterday, he said it was very warm there, almost balmy for this late in the season."

"Ooh, I envy you so much," Lynn sighed, a faraway dreamy look appearing in her brown eyes. "Aren't you practically out of your mind with excitement?"

"I wouldn't go so far as to say that," Jessica replied wryly. "But I am happy to be taking a vacation. I've been needing one for a while."

"Oh sure, the vacation's nice; Bermuda's terrific, but that's not exactly what I meant. I meant your head must be spinning with the thought that you're going to be on a lovely island ten whole days and nights with *Brad Taylor.* Do you know how many women in the world would give anything to be able to take your place?"

"I imagine there might be quite a few of them," Jessica murmured, fond indulgence lighting her features. "Brad's popularity has soared in the past year. It's really amazing."

"Amazing? It's more than that. It's phenomenal. But then, Brad Taylor's a phenomenal man," Lynn announced, gesturing exuberantly and staying close to Jessica's side as the line moved forward again. Her animated expression revealed a suddenly uncontrollable curiosity as she added, "I've never asked before—

I thought maybe I shouldn't, but now I can't resist. What's Brad Taylor really like, Jess?"

Tilting her head slightly to one side, Jessica thought a moment. "Oh, Brad's sweet and tremendously charming when he wants to be. And there's something of a little boy in him. He's . . ." She tossed up her hands. "I don't know exactly how to describe him to you. Brad's just Brad."

"Oh, my Lord. How can you say, *'Brad's just Brad'*?" Lynn mimicked comically, her tone incredulous. "Surely you can tell me something more than that. After all, he's—"

"You're forgetting I've known Brad nearly all my life," Jessica explained good-naturedly while moving to the head of the line and placing her luggage on the scale beside the agent. "Really, to me he's the same person now that he's always been. It wouldn't make much sense for me to suddenly be in awe of him."

"How can you not be? The man's become a hot Hollywood star overnight, and everyone's talking about how tremendously talented he is. Even if you have known him forever, you have to be a little impressed when he's called the new Al Pacino."

"I doubt anyone ever becomes a star overnight, Lynn. Brad certainly didn't. He struggled along for several years, but nobody really noticed him until he got that part in last year's biggest movie hit," Jessica said, then gave her assistant a mischievous smile. "And it's probably a good thing Brad didn't hear you compare him to Al Pacino, not that he'd mind the comparison talent-wise. I'm sure he'd appreciate that. But he'd also be compelled to tell you he is definitely taller than Al."

"Al! You call him Al? Don't tell me you actually know him too?"

"No. No, no, I've never met Al Pacino. I think Brad has, but since I've only seen him three times in the past year, I'm not up on all his new acquaintances."

"Oh. I thought maybe . . . Oh well, I wasn't really comparing Brad Taylor to Al Pacino," Lynn said hastily, controlling her enthusiasm to some extent. "There is a very slight physical

11

resemblance, but mainly I meant that Brad projects himself as intensely on screen as Pacino. In real life is he that intense?"

"Intense?" Murmuring her thanks to the agent who returned her ticket along with baggage checks and a boarding pass, Jessica walked away from the counter while shrugging in answer to Lynn's question. "I wouldn't call Brad intense. His acting is. But he's . . . oh, Brad's just . . ."

"Yes, yes, I know what you're going to say: 'Brad's just Brad.' But I still don't believe it," Lynn cut in with a merry little chuckle, glancing at her own wristwatch when she noticed Jessica checking hers. She looked back up hopefully. "You have nearly forty minutes before your flight. Let's go have coffee. Okay?"

"Thanks, but I think I'll just go on to the boarding lounge." Jessica wrinkled her nose. "And besides, much as I hate being a spoilsport, I want you to get back to the office. You need to straighten out that problem with production by this afternoon if possible."

"Slave driver." Lynn pretended to grumble but was unable to suppress a smile as the two of them strolled back to the airport's east entrance, where they stopped. She gave Jessica an endearing, somewhat sheepish look. "I hate to ask, Jess, since you've already gotten me an autographed picture of Brad. . . . But do you think you could possibly get me another one?"

"For your sister?"

"You know I don't have a sister. It's for me."

"I think I can do better than an autographed picture. I'll ask Brad to write you a personal note. How would you like that?"

"I think I may faint," Lynn breathed, dramatically pressing the back of her hand against her forehead as if in a swoon. "If I could show my friends a personal note from Brad Taylor himself, they'd all be green with envy."

"I'm not sure I understand why. Brad's not a god; he's just a man."

"I wonder if you'll still be saying that when you get back from

12

Bermuda ten days from now," Lynn countered provocatively. "You just haven't seen enough of him lately."

"A situation I'm about to remedy by going along to the boarding lounge while you start back for the office," Jessica said, adjusting the strap of her tote back across her right shoulder. "I'll get Brad to write you a note, and you call me if there's any problem at work you can't handle. If I don't hear from you, then I'll see you a week from Thursday."

"Just have a great time," Lynn commanded fondly, then waved back over her shoulder as she and Jessica walked away in opposite directions.

Ten minutes later Cade Hunter glanced up from his reading to look across the boarding lounge just as Jessica Grayson entered, vaguely and disturbingly familiar. A puzzled frown creased his brow before his photographic memory geared up and he recognized the young woman as Jessica Grayson. His black eyes lighted with interest and some surprise, although he recalled now that Taylor had mentioned she would be taking this flight with him from Atlanta to Bermuda. Yet he had still not expected her to look very much like the woman he had seen in the photograph in Brad's house in Bermuda last week. Considering Brad's apparent taste in women, it hadn't seemed likely he was engaged to a lady with such a refreshingly honest expression, and Cade had decided some trick of light in the photographer's studio accounted for the image projected. But he had been completely wrong, because here was Jessica Grayson in the flesh and she looked exactly like her picture.

Cade sat up straighter in the molded fiberglass chair, allowing his gaze to follow Jessica as she walked across the lounge. Not exquisitely beautiful but lovely in a very natural way with her short feathery blond hair and wide clear eyes that were an intriguing cornflower blue, she drew admiring looks from most of the surrounding men. For several long moments Cade continued to watch her, then neatly folded his newspaper, laid it on the chair beside him, and stood. He walked across the lounge.

"Miss Grayson?"

The deeply melodious masculine voice claimed Jessica's attention just as she was about to take a seat. Hesitating, she looked up at the tall dark-haired man beside her, giving him a polite but questioning smile.

"Yes, I'm Jessica Grayson," she acknowledged, a hint of an attractive lilt in her quiet voice. "But I don't believe I know who you are. Have we met?"

Smiling and shaking his head, Cade casually reached for Jessica's tote bag when she lowered the strap from her shoulder. He placed it along with his own briefcase at the end of the row of seats, waved her into a chair, and sat down beside her. "No, we've never met. I'm Cade Hunter and I've just recently taken on the handling of Brad Taylor's business affairs."

"Oh yes, I remember the name," Jessica said, with a genuinely friendly smile that brought a soft warm glow to her sapphire eyes as she extended her hand to shake his. "Brad told me he was thinking of getting your firm to handle his finances. He was especially pleased you're based in Atlanta, his hometown, since he had been warned not to center his entire life around that Hollywood scene."

"In his present position, it probably would be easy for him to get caught up in that sort of exclusive life-style," Cade agreed, his expression thoughtful, his tone lowering slightly. "He certainly doesn't want to start believing his own publicity and considering himself one of the 'beautiful people.'"

"They do seem to lead pretty superficial lives, don't they?" Jessica murmured, frankly surveying Cade Hunter, then tilting her head to one side inquiringly. "Since we've never met, how . . . did you know who I was when I walked in here?"

"Simple explanation. I was in Bermuda last week and saw your photograph at Brad's house."

"You saw Brad just last week? How was he? How did he look?"

"He looked fine to me. Why? Is there some reason he shouldn't have?"

"No, not really," Jessica conceded, smiling wryly at herself. "It's just that I haven't seen Brad for over four months and I know he's been working long hours on this picture in Bermuda. I was a little worried that he might be run-down."

"Not that I noticed. He looked perfectly healthy to me."

"I'm relieved to hear it. Brad tends to push himself too hard sometimes. But he did tell me Bermuda is very relaxing," Jessica said rather wistfully. "I hope it is because I'd like to spend the next ten days doing as little as possible. It's been a long time since I had my last vacation, and I had to do a great deal of fast talking to get this time off."

Watching her attentively, Cade relaxed in his chair, stretching his long legs out in front of him. "Vacation from what? What do you do?"

"I'm the feature editor of a regional magazine published in Atlanta. It's called, aptly enough, *Georgia*. Maybe you've heard of it."

"Haven't missed a monthly issue in two or three years. I have a subscription," Cade replied honestly. "An excellent informative magazine. I enjoy reading it."

"You're just the kind of man I love to meet," Jessica told him, amusement combining with professional pride to dance in her eyes. "Compliment the magazine and you've won me as a friend for life."

"You obviously love your work."

She nodded. "I enjoy it very much, although it's hectic most of the time. And during the past two months it's been especially demanding. Our managing editor has been on sick leave and I've had to assume most of her duties but, fortunately, she's getting better and should be back at work within a month."

Cade slowly examined Jessica's face. "Aren't you a little young to assume the duties of a managing editor?"

"I'm twenty-six, the same age as Brad."

"You look much younger than he does."

"Maybe he just looks old for his age," she suggested offhandedly as she returned his appraising gaze.

In his early thirties, Cade Hunter was an attractive man, though not exactly classically handsome. His features were finely carved but were a little too strongly defined for mere prettiness, and it was character and intelligence that his sunbronzed face more noticeably conveyed. Tall, slim, superbly fit, he looked like the kind of man who would be as comfortable in old faded cutoff jeans as he seemed to be in the pinstripe charcoal-gray suit he was now wearing. And his coal-black eyes, both keenly perceptive and friendly, commanded interest. When Jessica's gaze met his, she responded to his friendliness with another smile.

"You obviously enjoy Bermuda, since you were just there last week and are already going back again," she commented conversationally. "Or is this merely a necessary business trip."

."Not strictly. I'm sure I'll have a great deal of free time to relax between business discussions with Brad," Cade said, elbows propped on the armrests, his chin resting on long steepled fingers. And as his eyes held Jessica's, his expression seemed to become both speculative and more serious. "By the way, I don't suppose Brad mentioned to you that he invited me to stay at the house this trip?"

"As a matter of fact, he didn't."

"If it's a problem . . ."

"Oh, no. No problem," Jessica hastened to say and meant it. Actually, she almost felt relieved that Cade would be Brad's houseguest because, at the moment, she wasn't at all sure how this visit was going to work out. The last time she had seen Brad, for a weekend four months ago, nothing had seemed quite right somehow. She had felt strongly that something was wrong, that something had changed between them, and that some of the closeness they had shared before had been lost. Since then she hadn't been able to rid herself of nagging doubts, which was her prime reason for going to Bermuda. She had to know if there was, indeed, something amiss in their relationship or if she had simply been suffering from an overactive imagination the last time she had seen him. Yet she could hardly consider herself the overly imaginative type, and that realization invariably brought her back to square one again—perhaps their relationship was changing. Maybe his new life-style was altering his personality to some extent; yet she supposed he could have simply been indulging in a temporarily frivolous mood. But right now she didn't know what to think. All she knew for certain was that she needed the next ten days to gauge Brad's behavior. Perhaps with Cade as a houseguest she would be able to view Brad more objectively. The way he related to other people as well as to herself would give her a better perspective. And maybe, just maybe, she would decide he hadn't really changed one bit. All these thoughts raced through her head as she dismissed Cade's reservations about staying at the house with the toss of one hand. "You certainly won't inconvenience me by accepting Brad's invitation. Please don't think any more about it."

"All right," he agreed. "Anyway, I think some of Brad's other guests from last week are still with him."

Something indefinable in Cade's tone compelled Jessica to ask, "Is that your way of warning me that my vacation might not be as quiet and peaceful as I had hoped?"

"It's a possibility."

"Who are his other guests?"

"A couple of them are members of the cast."

"Well, I can't really say I'm surprised," she said, hiding vague disappointment behind a droll little grin. "Brad's never liked being alone; the more people around, the merrier."

Cade said nothing until several moments later when an intercom speaker emitted a burst of static then a nearly indistinguishable message. Lifting Jessica's tote bag and his briefcase easily in one hand, he rose to his feet. "We might as well board the plane now. I'll carry this on for you. First class?"

Nodding, she got up to walk with him across the lounge,

17

removing her ticket and boarding pass from the side pocket of her purse. "I'm in seat Four-B. How about you?"

Reaching a lean, tanned hand inside his coat, Cade took a small blue envelope from the inside pocket. He glanced at it. "Two-E."

"Oh, that's a shame, but we'll get to talk again while we're in Bermuda. And I'm glad you introduced yourself, Mr. Hunter."

"Cade."

"All right, Cade, and everyone calls me Jess."

Stopping at the end of the short line of passengers, Cade looked down at her. "Jess?" he inquired quietly, a tiny smile of denial moving his chiseled mouth. "No, that doesn't really seem to fit you. I prefer Jessica, if you don't mind."

"Frankly, I'd welcome it," she confessed wryly. "I've always liked Jessica better. But Brad started calling me Jess when we were very small children, and it's stuck since then. Now, everybody calls me that."

"Except me," he countered, indicating with a gesture that she precede through the covered boarding ramp and onto the plane.

Twenty minutes after takeoff, Jessica sat gazing out the window at the soft blanket of fluffy white clouds that stretched out beneath the plane, seemingly into eternity. Although she was allowing her thoughts to wander along pleasant paths, an eerie sensation that made her feel she was being watched soon began skittering up and down her spine. She turned her head and saw Cade Hunter standing in the aisle.

Still caught up in her daydreams to some extent, she smiled rather mystically at him. "Oh, hi, Mr. Hunt . . . Sorry. *Cade.*"

"A no-show?" he asked, indicating the unoccupied aisle seat next to her own.

"Must be. It's been empty since we boarded."

"Then if you don't mind, I'll join you. We can have a drink together."

"I'd like that," she said sincerely, welcoming his company with more eagerness than he could know. Flying, especially

18

alone, frightened her, not obsessively but just enough to make her exceedingly uncomfortable from takeoff to landing unless she was able to lose herself in fantasies, forgetting where she really was. Her small fear was a secret, one she had never shared with anyone and never intended to share. Yet she couldn't suppress a somewhat grateful smile when Cade lowered himself into the seat beside her because she knew simply talking to him would take some of the edge off her uneasiness.

As it turned out, Cade helped her to forget her fear completely, at least for a while. Conversation with such an informed, intelligent man was highly enjoyable and stimulating. He was interested as well as interesting, and while Jessica sipped ginger ale and he nursed his Scotch, they exchanged ideas and opinions of various subjects with an openness that made it seem they had known each other longer than a mere couple of hours.

"Tell me about your work, Cade," Jessica prompted during a brief, natural lull in conversation. "Handling other people's money must be quite a responsibility."

"It's challenging, especially when a client comes to us with his finances in a shambles like Brad did."

A tiny frown nicked Jessica's brow. "Brad?"

Capturing and holding her puzzled gaze, Cade hesitated a few seconds, then raised and lowered his broad shoulders in a slight shrug. "Since you're Brad's fiancée, you must know that he's run through practically all the money he's made this past year and he's also in a little trouble with the IRS for not paying his quarterly taxes. It's nothing that can't be straightened out, though."

"He has mentioned he was having some trouble handling his own finances, but he didn't say anything about the IRS."

"As I said, that can be straightened out. He's not in really serious trouble. He's simply delinquent in paying his taxes, as many other taxpayers are every year. The IRS is used to that."

"I suppose they are," Jessica agreed, dismissing financial matters to go on to something more personal which warranted an explanation. She smiled faintly at Cade. "I'd rather you didn't refer to me as Brad's fiancée because our engagement is not at all official. We don't think it should be until he's really firmly established in his career."

Cade raised his darkly slashed brows. "Oh? And whose decision was that?"

Some odd little nuance in his deep voice made her feel rather defensive. Her chin came up a fraction of an inch. "Isn't that a pretty personal question?"

"Yes," he admitted flatly. "And you don't have to answer it if there's some reason you don't want to."

"I just can't imagine why you're interested in knowing."

"It never hurts to learn as much as possible about a client."

"Well, since it's no secret anyway . . . It was my idea to keep the engagement unofficial, and Brad agreed that might be better at this stage in his career."

Regarding her closely, Cade inclined his head in a brief nod. "I see. But it doesn't really matter if your engagement is official or unofficial. Since you and Brad expect to get married someday, maybe you should try to convince him that he must become more responsible where money's concerned. He can't go on spending everything he makes on expensive cars and . . . entertainment before he's taken care of all his necessary expenses. If you tell him that, he might listen."

"I'm sure he will; he always has. I'll talk to him," Jessica promised. Then as a silence fell between them and lengthened, she turned her head to look out the window, suddenly feeling a bit tired again. At last she closed her eyes against the sun's golden glare.

A feathery touch along her cheek awakened her later, and she opened her eyes as Cade's hand was moving away from her face.

"We'll be landing soon," he explained softly. "You have to fasten your seat belt now."

A dreamy smile was her only response.

"Jessica, you're still half-asleep. Here, let me," he murmured, leaning toward her to deftly snap the seat belt around her.

His knuckles lightly grazed the waistband of her navy skirt. Raising her head, she found his face closer to hers. Her clear blue eyes met the dusky coal darkness of his, and she saw in the depths a faint flicker of new light. She wasn't naive. With the slight quickening of her heartbeat she knew that an awareness had been awakened, an awareness that was exciting, especially because he shared it. Her reaction neither shocked nor dismayed her; her response to Cade was understandable. She often met men she found very sensuously attractive and knew they were attracted to her too. It was of no consequence except to add a little spice to life. As she looked at Cade, a tiny smile touched her softly shaped lips.

"Thanks for the help. I'm awake now," she said quietly and the moment ended.

Less than a minute later, hearing the hydraulic whine of the plane wheels coming down, Jessica tensed. Her mouth went suddenly dry, and she took a deep, hopefully calming breath while staring directly ahead at the back of the seat in front of her. And when Cade's left hand covered her right as it curved over the end of the armrest in a tight clinging grip, she turned to look at him and recognized understanding. She grimaced.

"Oh, I'm all right. Silly, isn't it?"

His answering smile was kind. "We all have our little fears, Jessica."

"What's yours then?"

"Women," he replied, keeping a straight face. "That's why I'm not married."

Laughing softly, she shook her head. "I don't believe that lie for a minute. Don't you have any *real* fears?"

"A very commonplace one. I avoid dark confined spaces like the plague," he said, his dark gaze narrowing, seeming to convey seriousness. "Claustrophobia. I'm not even particularly happy riding in small elevators."

"Have any idea what caused it?"

"My sister. When I was five and she was seven she locked me in a closet for swiping a candy bar she'd been saving," he replied with a wry forgiving smile. "I can't say I blame her. I did eat it. And besides, she only made me stay in the closet for a couple of minutes. But that was long enough for me."

"Isn't it amazing how such a small incident can trigger a fear that lasts into adulthood?" Jessica mused aloud. And their conversation continued until the landing wheels abruptly bounced against the runway, then settled down in a smooth slowing roll toward a terminal building. The flight was ending safely, and Jessica began to eye Cade with some suspicion. "Do you really even have a sister?"

"Of course. Her name's Barbara," he told her. "She's thirty-four and married with two children."

"All right. I'll put my question another way: are you really claustrophobic? Or is it possible you concocted that story just to take my mind off landing?"

"Jessica," he admonished softly, the expression on his lean, tanned face inscrutable. "Would I lie to you?"

She had no idea, but it actually didn't matter if he had been lying or not. Landing was the most fearful part of any flight for her, and if it took someone telling tall tales to help her through it, she didn't mind hearing them. As the plane slowed to a full stop, she slipped her hand from beneath the comforting pressure of Cade's and unfastened her seat belt.

Following behind a line of passengers who had scurried to gather their possessions, Jessica preceded Cade to an exit. Together, they walked across the sun-washed tarmac into the terminal, where it took several seconds for her eyes to adjust to the dimmer light. Then, noticing a sudden profusion of softly exclaimed whispers, she turned and saw Brad coming her way, an entourage of people in his wake.

Jessica smiled and waved, happy to see him and relieved he looked so glowingly healthy. Darkly tanned, his brown hair

22

lightened by the sun, he resembled a young Greek god as he strolled toward her. She noticed with fond amusement that he was clad in cream slacks, a cream shirt unbuttoned halfway down his chest, and worn leather deck shoes, the uniform of the supercasual. She started forward to meet him and found a familiar warmth in the arms that embraced her and in the faint scent of cologne that lay lightly on his skin.

"Jess, I thought you'd never get here," Brad muttered, squeezing her against him. "And how's my baby doing?"

Her smile was her answer as she pulled back slightly to receive his kiss and return it. Then Brad's lips left hers and he turned her toward the friends who had tagged after him, introducing her to them quickly, paying no attention to the terminal full of celebrity watchers staring at him.

"We're throwing a party tonight to welcome you to Bermuda," he told Jessica. "At the house I rented. How's that sound to you, Jess?"

"Fine, Brad; that sounds fine. Oh, I am glad to see you," she said earnestly, slipping an arm around his waist as he draped his across her shoulders and squeezed her close to his side. Then she glanced past him and found Cade Hunter a few feet away watching the scene with great interest. Her eyes met his directly. She smiled and was pleased when he responded with a slow lazy smile of his own. Yet she was vaguely aware of a strange, niggling tension deep within her, a tension she had some trouble dismissing.

CHAPTER TWO

Bright, scattered stars studded the black bowl of the sky. The half-moon's golden light shimmered on the arcing strand of pale sand in front of the beach house and gilded the gently undulating surface of the sea. It was past midnight and the party had wound down. The silence of the night was broken only occasionally now by the muted sound of voices from the driveway and from the sibilant whispering of a gentle breeze as it rustled the slender long leaves of the surrounding palm trees.

Seeking a breath of fresh air before sleep, Cade stepped out onto the side terrace and saw Jessica curled up in a chaise longue, gazing as if mesmerized at the rolling waves breaking in phosphorescent sprays of foam on the beach. He stood still a moment, looking at her, liking the way the soft glow from strategically placed lamps silvered her shining hair and limned her slim enchantingly curved body in a tracery of light. She was alone and he walked on silent feet across the marble tiles toward her.

When the long shadow fell across Jessica she turned her head, looked up, and smiled. "Oh, hi, Cade," she greeted him softly, not minding at all that he interrupted her solitude. Shifting her position, she tucked her long legs closer beside her and waved him toward the end of the chaise longue. "Sit down and enjoy this magnificent view for a while."

Accepting her invitation in silence, he settled himself comfortably near the end of the chaise and glanced momentarily at the ocean before turning his attention wholly to her again. In her rose-colored dress with scooped neck, fitted bodice, and softly shirred skirt, she attracted him strongly yet in a subtle, almost subdued way, and he allowed his gaze to wander slowly over her. If she was aware of his appraisal, however, she offered no sign. Traces of her smile still lingered on her soft mouth and shone warmly in her luminous blue eyes.

"Why all alone out here?" he asked after another few moments of total quiet. "Where's Brad disappeared to?"

"He and Christina walked the director to his car. They wanted to talk to him about a scene they're shooting tomorrow," Jessica answered, then lowered her voice to a rather conspiratorial whisper. "You wouldn't happen to recall the director's name, would you? I met so many people tonight that I've forgotten it, and I guess it would be very undiplomatic of me not to know what to call the director of Brad's movie."

"You wouldn't want to bruise his ego, no," Cade agreed dryly. "The last name's Cameron. As for his first name, your guess is as good as mine."

"Cameron, Cameron," Jessica muttered mainly to herself, then snapped her fingers. "Now I remember. It's C. Z. Cameron." Giving Cade a grateful smile, she filed that tidbit of information away in her mind before looking back out over the ocean stretching endlessly to the dark horizon. She sighed, but not unhappily. "You know, I think I could almost sit out here and watch the waves tumble in all night."

"Maybe you'd better leave that for some other night," Cade countered wryly, watching her try to conceal a yawn behind one hand. He moved closer to her, reached out, and brushed the edge of a thumb over the faint violet crescent that shadowed the skin beneath her left eye. "I think you're very tired, Jessica."

"Yes, I am," she admitted, as he immediately lowered his hand again after only the briefest of touches. "But I'm planning to go to bed as soon as I can say good-night to Brad. He should be along soon. After all, he needs sleep too. I think he has to be on the set practically by dawn in the morning." After stifling another yawn then following it with a self-amused apology, she suddenly shivered when the breeze picked up. Rubbing her arms briskly, she started to move off the chaise. "But I think I will get something to throw around my shoulders while I wait for him, if you'll excuse me, Cade."

"Take my coat," he suggested. "I have long sleeves and won't miss it."

Nodding agreement and murmuring her thanks, she watched as he shed his gray jacket, but even as she started to reach out to take it from him, he leaned closer to drape it over her shoulders. He drew it around her, and as he did, his hands feathered against her bare upper arms, lingered, then curved lightly around them.

"You do feel chilled," he said quietly.

His palms rotating lightly against her felt pleasant and relaxing. Yet more than that, she knew in an instant. The touch of his warm flesh on the cooler surface of her skin warmed her throughout, and although she was exceedingly tired, his hands were conveying more than a desire to give comfort while her own response came from more than a need to be comforted. Without pausing to think about it, she drew back slightly, causing him to release her and the tension that had seemed to flare between them abated swiftly, leaving her wondering if it had ever truly existed except in her weary brain.

With a half smile, she drew his jacket more snugly around her. "That's better. I'm feeling warmer already."

Cade nodded, then turned his head at the sound of footfalls on the terrace. He watched as Brad came around the corner of the house and strolled toward them.

"Ah, Jess, there you are," Brad said with a pleased smile, coming to her and stroking her smooth shiny hair. His hand dropped down to squeeze her shoulder. "Sorry I was so long, but Christie and I wanted some changes made in one of the scenes we shoot tomorrow, and C.Z. was a little hard to convince. But he finally decided to do it our way." Including Cade in the

26

explanation, he nodded a greeting. "Thanks for keeping Jess company while she was waiting."

"Anytime," Cade replied flatly, rising lithely from the chaise. He looked back down at Jessica, a bland unreadable expression on his dark face. "It's been a long day, so if you'll both excuse me, I think I'll turn in. Good-night, Jessica. Brad."

"Good-night, Cade," she called after him as he strode away.

When he had disappeared into the house, Brad dropped down on the edge of the chair close to Jessica and rested a hand on her right thigh just above her knee. "Hope you don't mind my inviting Hunter to stay here."

"Why should I mind? Cade's an intelligent, interesting man. I enjoy talking to him."

"Good. I figured I might as well ask him to stay, since I have these other houseguests. Christie was all set to get a suite in a hotel when the lease on the house she was renting ran out, but I had more than enough room here to take her in. And speaking of Christie, what do you think of her, Jess?"

"I like her," Jessica said in all sincerity while smiling at his excited chatter. "She's very friendly and seems to be one of those genuine free spirits."

"Oh, she's that all right. But she's also a damned fine actress; she really is," Brad declared, then gave her one of his most endearing smiles and dismissed that subject with a flick of his wrist. "But enough about her and everybody else. Let's talk about something much more important. Have you missed me?"

Leaning forward, Jessica pressed a light kiss against his lips and then drew back to comb her fingers through the shock of hair that had fallen down across his forehead. "Don't I always miss you?" she asked, affection warming her eyes as she looked at him. "But you could call me more often. Mom and Dad are always asking if I've heard from you. They've given up on hearing from you directly."

"Guess it doesn't seem like I appreciate all they've done for me, does it? But I do, Jess," he assured her. "I hope they know that."

She nodded. "I'm sure they do, Brad."

"As for calling you, I've tried, but you're hardly ever at home anymore in the evenings," he complained. "I've told you how many times I've called and got no answer."

"And I've explained to you why I wasn't home," she reminded him. "Peg's been out sick for two months, and besides doing my own work, I've had to keep up with hers as best I can. I'm just hoping she gets back to the office in the next few weeks because I'm really beat."

"You don't have to go on that way, Jess," Brad murmured, lifting his hands up to clasp her waist. "If you'd just quit that job, move in with me, and let me take care of you . . ."

"You know I love my work, Brad. It's exhausting sometimes, but I'd be lost without it," she said with conviction. "Besides, I don't think I'd like being a 'kept woman.'"

"Then you could get a job on a magazine in California," he persisted beguilingly. "I wouldn't care if you did that."

"And maybe I will look into some editorial positions out there. Later, when we've set a definite date."

"I'm ready to set a definite date right now."

"Are you, Brad? I don't think so." Shaking her head, she gave him a small smile, though her heart was suddenly heavy with the realization that the idea of marrying him had lost much of its appeal. Yet the timing was all wrong for her to admit that; she was simply too tired to begin what would have to be a long serious discussion, one which was sure to be emotionally wearing. Soon, very soon, she would talk to him, but not right now, so she offered an excuse for her answer that was actually a truth anyhow. "I know you, and you're so wrapped up in the way your career's taken off that you don't have much time for anything else. Besides, there's no rush anyway."

"I guess you're right; there's no hurry," he conceded, then a sudden animation spread over his handsome face and he playfully grabbed both her hands, tugging at them. "Hey, come on, let's go for a walk along the beach."

"I'd like to, but how about a rain check? Let's do it tomorrow night when I've had a chance to rest up a little," Jessica suggested gently. "I've been working late for the past two weeks to try to get ahead on my work so I could come see you, and I'm incredibly tired. If we went for a walk, I think I'd fall asleep on my feet."

"My poor sweet baby," he commiserated, nuzzling her neck with kisses. "But I wanted to tell you about this movie, Jess. It's going to turn out to be a smash hit; I can just feel it. The role I'm playing is so powerful and the most challenging of my career, Jess. Did I tell you I'm playing an independent fisherman who's drawn into a situation where he's pitted against a network of drug smugglers? I mean, that's a losing proposition, isn't it? But this guy just won't quit. He's scared but he never gives up the fight for a minute."

"I know. You sent me a copy of the script," she said with a warm smile for his enthusiasm. "It's a fantastic part for you, and I'm so happy you got it, because you're right—this movie looks like it could be a real hit."

"Oh yeah, yeah, it has to be!" Brad nodded vehemently. "Especially since we've convinced C.Z. to make some changes that turn this into a really class film. For instance . . ."

Not bored but horrendously sleepy, Jessica fought back yet another yawn, which suddenly died in her throat when she heard the clatter of rapid footsteps on the marble tiles.

"Brad, Brad. Oh, there you are," a musical feminine voice called. Christina Myerly, clad in a faded silk kimono and flopping heelless slippers that clunked with every step, dashed across the terrace, then stopped short, uttering a self-derisive curse. "Oh, Jess is with you. I'm sorry. I didn't mean to intrude. I just hoped we could read over our lines for that scene tomorrow since we've made those changes in it. But that's okay; we can do it in the morning. I'll go back to my—"

29

"You don't have to, Christina. Stay," Jessica insisted, swinging her legs off the chaise with a nod and a smile for the other woman. "Go over the lines with Brad. You're really not intruding because I'm going to bed now anyhow or I'll fall asleep right here where I'm sitting."

"Jess," Brad murmured so quietly only she could hear. "Are you sure you don't mind?"

"I really don't, Brad, honest," she reassured him, brushing a kiss across his cheek, then rising wearily to her feet. She reached down to smooth his hair back off his forehead again and smiled very sleepily. "I'll be better company tomorrow, after I've had some rest. Then we'll go for that walk on the beach and talk. All right?"

When he nodded agreeably, Jessica started for the house but halted when Christina stepped in front of her, tall and as reed-slender as a model. Exotically beautiful with natural raven-black hair swinging around her shoulders, she tapped a rolled up script against the palm of one hand.

"Thanks for letting me borrow Brad for a while, Jess," she said, then grimaced rather comically. "I didn't mean to run you off, but I do want to go over these lines with Brad so we can show C.Z. that the scene's much better the way we want to do it. He's such a pompous old goat, and I can't wait to prove that somebody besides him can have good ideas occasionally."

Jessica laughed. "He did seem like a pompous little man."

"A legend in his own mind, no less," Christina pronounced dryly. "Then you can see why I want to go over these lines with Brad?"

"Of course I do. You're really not running me off, Christina."

"Call me Christie, please. Christina's too formal for me."

"All right. Then, good-night, Christie. See you tomorrow, Brad," Jessica called back over her shoulder, then left them alone to plot their conspiracy against C.Z. Acting was an insecure career, and wondering if Christie and Brad would always feel compelled to be proving something to somebody, Jessica continued across the terrace toward the house. Wrapping the coat about her shoulders closer around her, she detected the very faint lime fragrance of Cade's after-shave that clung to it and smiled to herself. Obviously money management as a career didn't induce insecurities in him because he certainly appeared to be a man who wouldn't often feel the need to prove anything to anyone else. He seemed to know exactly who he was, what he wanted, and where he was going—a thoroughly confident man.

As it turned out, Jessica saw very little of Brad during the following two days. A series of scenes were being shot aboard the fishing boat off Bermuda's south coast, and there simply wasn't enough room for visitors to watch the filming. Jessica didn't mind, however. She was more than content to putter around the house or go down to the beach for a swim in water that was decidedly cool but not too cold. And she also had Cade to keep her company. Although he had brought work to the island with him and was often on the phone to Atlanta and New York, he had free time, which he spent with Jessica. While this was her first visit to Bermuda, he was familiar with local points of interest and proved to be a relaxed and relaxing, unhurried tour guide. And wherever they went, Jessica was enthralled with the glorious profusion of scarlet hibiscus and the varicolored oleanders that perfumed the gentle breezes.

Jessica and Cade spent most of their second afternoon in the quaint old township of St. George. They had a leisurely drink on the wharf before he took her to a few of the finest shops where he asked her help in choosing a birthday gift for his mother, and she bought fine lamb's-wool sweaters for both her parents and flacons of heady French perfume for Lynn and Peg. It was a wonderful day with swimming and playing on the beach in the morning then shopping half the afternoon away, and Jessica was beginning to feel more her old self again, rested, relaxed, and ready to enjoy the quiet evening Brad had promised they would have, which would finally give her a chance to talk seriously to him.

But Brad disappointed her. After rushing through the dinner she had prepared, he announced that there was yet another party they had to attend that evening.

Jessica nearly winced. Alone with him in the living room, curled up at one end of the white crushed-velvet sofa, she looked hopefully at him. "Do we have to go to this one?" she asked quietly. "There was the party you had Wednesday night to welcome me here, then the one the crew threw last night at the hotel. If we go to this one, that's three parties in three nights. Couldn't we just miss it?"

"I can't do that, Jess" was Brad's answer, though he gestured half apologetically. "When most of the cast and crew will be at a party, I can't refuse to go. I'm the star of this movie, and they might think I imagine I'm above all of them. I sure don't want to get a reputation for being a prima donna. Besides, the party tonight is at C.Z.'s, and he won't like it if I don't show up."

Jessica sighed softly. "Well, I like parties, but three in three nights is a bit much for me," she told him, not adding that last night's party especially had nearly bored her to tears besides thwarting her efforts to talk to him.

Listening to constant chitchat about fast foreign cars, the high cost of living in Malibu, and the very-very, too-too chic shops on Rodeo Drive hadn't exactly thrilled her. And she was surprised Brad could tolerate incessant discussions of such trivialities night after night. He was certainly accustomed to more scintillating, pertinent conversation than that. Yet, she supposed he knew what was best for his career. She gave him a resigned smile. "If you think you should go, then I guess you should. But I'll pass. I'm not in a mood for another party, and since I've rested up, I can start working on that article for the magazine that I brought with me."

"Oh, come on, Jess, I want you to go with me," Brad cajoled. "You don't really want to stay here and work anyhow. Do you?"

32

"The work has to be done sometime. I don't mind getting a start on it tonight."

"You're saying you're not going with me then?" he asked, some irritation audible in his voice and visible in his face. "You'd rather stay here and work than be with me?"

"I'd rather be with you . . . but not at another party," she explained calmly, touching his hand. "We don't get much of a chance to talk to each other at them anyhow, and I do need to talk to you."

"But at least we can see each other across the room, and that's better than nothing, since we've had hardly any time together since you got here," Brad said. "You can't be having a very nice vacation."

"But I am," she assured him, and it was true. "I needed rest and a break from constant work, and I'm getting that. I'm not sorry I came, Brad, because I had to see you."

"Then prove it," he challenged, smiling sexily, misunderstanding what she meant. "Come with me to the party, okay, baby?"

She shook her head. "I'd like for you to stay here."

Brad hesitated, then turned his head when he heard the beeping of a car horn from the driveway. "That's Christie. She's waiting for me . . . us. She has to go tonight too. I have to go now, baby," he muttered hastily, bending down to plant a hard, quick kiss on Jessica's lips. He straightened, turned, and strode away, adding, "But I won't stay long. I'll be back in a couple of hours or less."

Jessica wondered about that. Disappointed, she watched him leave, suspecting he would stay until the party ended if he believed that was what was expected of him. Barely able to bite back a frustrated oath, she got up and left the room.

An hour later she abandoned the article she was editing in favor of some fresh air. She walked outside and found Cade standing at the edge of the lamplit terrace, thumbs hooked over the back pockets of his trousers as he gazed out at the foaming

33

surf. Hearing her, he turned to watch her approach, raising his dark brows.

"I didn't realize you were here," he said when she stopped beside him. "I thought you'd gone with Brad and Christie."

"To the party? No. I decided I could afford to skip this one. Why didn't you go though? Brad said he'd asked you."

"I had some work I wanted to do."

"So did I. But mainly, I just didn't want to go," Jessica admitted with a rueful smile. "I was in the mood for a quiet evening, and I tried to persuade Brad to stay here. But he felt he had to go. I just wonder how long he can go on doing exactly what he thinks is expected of him without burning himself out."

Cade looked down at her, his piercing black eyes seeming to plumb the depths of hers. "Jessica," he murmured gently. "Brad may be living the way he does because that's precisely what he wants to do."

"He may think he does right now, but six months ago he wouldn't have," she said, meeting his gaze, solemnity shadowing her delicate features. "He's changed even more since I saw him last. If you'd known him before, you'd understand what I mean. Brad's never felt he absolutely had to be one of the 'in crowd' before, but now, it seems he does. And he and I need to talk about that."

"Adjusting to instant fame and fortune isn't easy," Cade reminded her, even as he wondered what the hell he was doing defending the man who wanted the same woman he himself wanted. And Cade did want Jessica; their time together during the past two days had proved that beyond all doubt. She was intriguing, lovely, intelligent, and real. He suspected beneath that quiet exterior there was a secret woman capable of intense fiery emotion. That suspicion enhanced her appeal, and since, to him, she and Brad seemed so totally unsuited for each other ... But she had to fully recognize and accept that fact for herself, hopefully in a way that would cause the least amount of pain. Cade sensed she was beginning to experience some doubts about

34

Brad; he had seen the pensive rather unhappy expression that occasionally came over her face and had wanted more than once to draw her to him and kiss that unhappiness away. Yet he hadn't; he couldn't do that. Brad was his client, and though they weren't close, they were friends. Besides, as importantly, Jessica had to resolve her problem on her own and make a clean break with Brad. Cade didn't want it any other way, and until she was able to do that, he could wait.

Still, as he stood beside her in the moonlight that shimmered over her silky flaxen hair, he responded strongly to the open honesty in her clear blue eyes. Once again he wanted to bring her into his arm but didn't. Instead, he simply brushed the back of his hand across her cheek for a brief instant while adding, "Brad's not used to all the attention he's been getting recently, and he's caught up in the glamor of it."

"I know, but it can't last forever. Brad's basically a sensible person, and I'm sure he'll eventually settle down," Jessica said hopefully. "Maybe very soon now."

"Maybe. Or maybe he'll choose to go on living in the fast lane."

"God, I hope not," she muttered fervently. She hated the thought of Brad succumbing permanently to such superficiality. "If he does, I don't know what might happen."

"Let's walk," Cade quickly suggested, cupping her elbow in one large hand. As she fell into step beside him, he guided her from the terrace to the white limestone path that led toward the beach. She drew in a slow deep breath of the cool night air, and he looked down at her. "Where did you meet Brad?"

"His grandmother lived next door to us in Marietta, and after his parents were killed in a car accident, he moved in with her. We were both about two years old at the time, so it seems to me now that he was just always there. He spent a great deal of time at our house," she murmured reminiscently, wondering with some deep sadness how their closeness that had survived so many years was recently fraying very badly around the edges.

Then she pushed such disturbing thoughts to the back of her mind and continued, "My parents sort of unofficially adopted Brad because I was an only child and they'd always wanted a son. Besides, Brad seemed to need them, since he'd lost his parents. His grandmother loved him, but he needed a relationship with younger adults. So he and I grew up together, then started dating in high school. I guess you could call me the typical girl next door."

"Never typical. No girl like you ever lived next door to me while I was growing up," Cade stated drolly, then decided it was time to put an end to Brad as a topic of discussion. When they stepped onto the beach and Jessica's espadrilles sank in the thick cooling sand, he released her elbow to catch her hand lightly in his. "Tell me more about your work. What were you doing tonight before you came outside?"

During the following twenty minutes or so, Jessica and Cade discussed their respective careers and in the end agreed there was no business anywhere that didn't have its share of disadvantages as well as its advantages. As they laughed together about one of his more troublesome clients, a man who never liked to make an investment unless his own horoscope and those of his three ex-wives seemed to favor it, Jessica watched Cade's face, noticing the crinkles that appeared at the corners of his eyes and the small indentations that carved into his lean cheeks beside his mouth. And suddenly she was enormously glad he had been on the terrace earlier when she had come out for fresh air because, in actuality, she had begun to feel very lonely in her room and in no way in the mood to spend her entire evening cutting an overlong article.

For a long while conversation ceased and they walked in silence along the beach bordered by gently swaying palm trees. But at last Jessica tired of her heels sinking deep in the sand with every step she took and, tightening her hand around Cade's to keep her balance, she bent down to slip off one espadrille then the other.

36

"The sand's much cooler than it was this morning," she said but dug her toes down into it nevertheless. With a happy smile, she shifted her eyes toward the breaking waves, then looked back up at Cade again and slipped her hand from his, gaily announcing, "I'm going wading."

He caught her arm. "Maybe you shouldn't. The water gets chilly at night," he advised, his dark gaze intent upon her upturned face. "You don't want to spend the rest of your vacation sniffling and sneezing."

"No problem. I take Vitamin C," she teased and slipped away from him to run lightly down the beach into wet sand. Feeling amazingly adventurous, she watched eagerly as the incoming waves crested, broke, then swirled up around her ankles in soft, warm whirlpools of foam. The sand being sucked away from beneath her feet tickled her soles, and she was laughing lightly when she beckoned to Cade. "Come on in. It's really warmer than I thought it would be," she called, then watched with delight as he stepped out of his shoes, rolled his trouser legs up to his knees, and strode into the surf to join her.

Emboldened by his participation, she held up her skirt and waded farther out until the water was lapping midway up her thighs. For a moment she challenged the ocean, dared the onrushing waves to catch her, but knowing the indifferent tide's fascinating regularity, she was ready to jump back to safety to avoid being drenched to the waist. At the last possible moment, while the wave rolling toward her began to crest white, she dashed back toward the beach, laughing as Cade caught her in strong arms.

Instinctively she pulled away, but he wouldn't release her completely. His hands still spanned her waist, holding her fast, and her laughter died in her throat with the inaudible catching of her breath. Scarcely aware of the water running in rivulets down her legs or the salt-softened frothy surf eddying around her ankles, she stood practically transfixed by Cade's narrowing gaze. Her heart raced as suddenly the night seemed to change, to become something entirely different from what it had been. The cascading rush of the ocean surging over the beach nearly mesmerized her with its constant primitive beat, and the only other sound she heard was the secret whispers of stirring palm leaves. A caressing breeze, lightly scented by fragrant oleanders, drifted over them, and the moonlight chased shadows on the sand. And Jessica was unable to look away from Cade.

His hands tightened gently around her. He drew her slowly and inexorably toward him.

"No," she whispered breathlessly, but to no avail. And when he caught her small chin between thumb and forefinger to lift her face then leaned down his dark head, she could utter no further words of protest. Although his lips scarcely grazed her own, she felt their firm shape and seductive warmth. Her heart was skittering madly now, and as a sweet anticipation rushed through her veins, catching her off guard with its very intensity, she slipped free from his light grip, meaning to escape him and her own crazy response to that one tiny kiss.

But Cade allowed no escape. Catching her wrist when she started to turn away, he pulled her closer. "Jessica, come here," he commanded softly, an appealing huskiness in his deep voice as he reached out to run his fingers through her fair, silken smooth hair. Then surveying her face as if to gauge her reaction, he floated the ball of his thumb along the gentle curve of her slender neck down into the hollow at the base of her throat.

By merely taking a backward step, Jessica could have taken complete control of the situation by simply ending it. But she didn't take that step; at that moment it never occurred to her to do so. A normal young woman with all the normal needs, she found pleasure in Cade's caress, a pleasure she really didn't want to deny herself. Feeling took precedence over rational thought, and as sensations of delight danced on her skin wherever he touched, she nearly trembled, without the will to drag her gaze from his.

"You're so lovely," he murmured, exploring her upturned

face with pleasantly rough-textured fingertips, lightly tracing the line of her jaw, the curve of her lips, and the contouring shape of high cheekbones. He touched her eyebrows, the dashing pulsebeat at her temples, and the straight line of her small nose, then lowered his head and followed the trail his fingers had blazed with searching lips.

Jessica felt as if she might never breathe deeply again. The heat emanating from Cade's long lean body combined with the fire flaring up inside her enveloped her in a warmth she didn't want to relinquish. As her soft swift breathing quickened again, she detected the clean male scent of him combining with faint traces of lime after-shave. Thrill after pulsating thrill of desire scampered through her as Cade kissed her eyelids, the hollows beneath her ears, and her hair. His warm breath stirred the soft tendrils at her neck and tingled against her scalp. An irrepressible shiver ran over her, and she swayed slightly toward him, her heart leaping with excitement when muscular arms slipped around her. Perhaps during the past two days she had begun to like and respect Cade too much to withstand an expert seduction like this because she was succumbing, surrendering, to a hypnotic force far more powerful than her present will to resist. She liked Cade, liked what he was doing to her, and liked how he was making her feel. And she had to touch him.

Beckoned by a promise of ever-increasing sensual delight, she moved closer to him and laid her hands upon his arms, exhilarated when she felt the swift tautening of his muscles beneath her fingertips. Alive with exquisite sensation and breathtaking anticipation, she waited, waited for the touch of his lips on her own again, and when it came at last, hers parted in a soft, warm invitation that he accepted with a barely leashed urgency. Sensing his tight control over himself, Jessica understood the smouldering fires of passion that burned just beneath the surface in him and was suddenly intrigued by the very possibility that those fires might blaze and threaten to consume them both. As if caught up in a vivid dream where time was suspended, she couldn't think;

39

she could only experience feelings that were ages old and as natural as the mighty throbbing beat of the ocean. The need to touch and be touched overpowered all others. Her fingers tightly clutching his shirt-sleeves slowly relaxed while his firm seeking lips played over hers, testing their tender softness, tasting honeyed sweetness, and exerting an ever-increasing pressure that ranged from persuasive coaxing to heady, hardening demand.

Cade nibbled at the full curve of her lower lip and, tugging gently, opened her mouth beneath his. Jessica made a soft pleased sound that rose in her throat to mingle with his warm minty breath as she swept trembling hands up across his broad shoulders to curve around the strong column of his neck.

Cade cradled the back of her head in one hand, his long fingers entwining in her hair, and although he had to know that her kisses were his for the taking, he pulled back slightly. Disappointment, keen and stiletto sharp, stabbed through her. She opened her eyes and saw the dangerous glint of reflected moonlight in the black depths of his as he looked down at her, intently searching her face as if he expected to find an answer to some unspoken question there, searching as if he needed to know all the secrets of her very soul. A feeling of utter vulnerability washed over her. Her widening blue eyes were caught by the flaring light in his. She tensed.

"Cade, you . . ."

"You're such a delight, Jessica," he murmured, his tone as caressing as the fingertips outlining the bow shape of her mouth touched first one corner then the other again and again until her breathing was revealingly quick and shallow. His thumb feathered over her chin, moving with a gentle tugging pressure while he coaxingly whispered, "Relax."

"I . . . can't," she muttered, her tension growing rather than easing. Awash with confusion, she shook her head. "It's . . ."

"Brad. I know," Cade assured her softly, stroking her hair. "And I know you have a difficult decision to make about him.

40

Jessica, I didn't mean for this to happen tonight. I'm sorry. But I'm lonely and a man and you're . . ."

As if he couldn't help himself, he touched his lips to hers once more, and the kiss that was initially almost comforting became in a brief instant so much more. His mouth took possession of hers again, kindling wildfires in her that spread from the very core of her being and made her sway closer to him. Then she found herself returning his kisses, her parted lips sweetly exploring the curved sensuous shape of his, rewarding his insistence and thereby encouraging more of the same. Like him, she was unable to pull away. Wildly pleasurable sensations played over her, and her heart commenced an out-of-control trip-hammer beat when Cade widened his stance and gathered her with swift compelling urgency against him. Warm, femininely acquiescent, she moved within the tightening circle of his arms, quivering inwardly at the enticing pressure of his hard, muscular chest against her breasts. Yet, when his hands began to move caressingly down her back, common sense reasserted itself, and she dragged her lips from his.

"*No.* This is insane because I *do* have problems to resolve and I don't think I can handle any added complications right now," she uttered quietly, resting her forehead against Cade's shoulder for an instant, trying to regain control over her heart rate and accelerated breathing. After a second she tilted her head back to look up at him, glad it wasn't light enough for him to see the heightened color she felt warming her cheeks. She wanted to appear more self-assured than she felt, more in control of a situation that had been rapidly veering toward dangerous zones. And, because she could still sense the danger pulsating like electricity between them, threatening to flare again and engulf them both, she reached behind her, easing away the large hand curved into the small of her back. When it dropped away, she felt she had backed away from the edge of a precipice and was able to muster a tiny, tremulous smile. Shaking her head, she whispered, "Moon-madness."

41

The answering smile that moved Cade's hard mouth was disbelieving and highly disruptive. "You really think that's all it was?"

"It must be," she replied, though it was a lie, and she knew in her heart it was much more. It was Brad and her changing feelings for him. It was Cade and the disturbing emotions he was beginning to arouse in her. And perhaps more important, it was the strong attraction that was developing between them that had made tonight practically inevitable. Moon-madness had little to do with what had just occurred, yet she was incapable of admitting that to Cade, and she shrugged. "What else could it be?"

"It could be that I've been wanting to kiss you like that for the past two days," he said, touching her face, his expression somber. "And it could be that you've been wanting to kiss me like that too. If so, maybe you'd better start thinking about why."

Jessica opened her mouth as if to object, but no words were forthcoming because she had no answer for him. Right then, she was unsure about what she was feeling or what she had felt during the two days she had spent in his company. She was unsure of almost everything except the importance of returning to the calming sanctuary of her room, where she could sort out her emotions and think reasonably about Brad, about Cade, and about herself. Averting her bemused gaze from Cade's lean face, she stared down at the sand while her left hand moved rather uncertainly.

"I have to get back to the house now," she murmured, by some miracle managing to steady her voice. "My article's still waiting."

"You can't run away from this, Jessica," Cade warned softly. With one long stride he diminished the distance she had put between them, one finger lifting her chin. "It's too late to run away now. And if it's any consolation, I'll remind you that although you're thinking about Brad right now, he probably isn't thinking about you. I know him, and likable as he is, he'll never

42

be able to make you happy. Just remember I won't become involved in a triangle. I will wait—for a while—because I want you, but I'm sure you know that."

She knew. Yet the sound of his low-timbred voice speaking the evocative words aloud sent shivers coursing along her spine, and she caught her lower lip between her teeth. Cade wanted her. But why? Because of something intrinsic in her that he was drawn to? (Could he even know her that well after only two days?) Or did he want her merely because, unofficially at least, she belonged to Brad? There were men who wanted women simply because they belonged to someone else. Was it possible Cade was one of them? Jessica had no earthly idea. At the moment she was too confused to try to analyze her own emotions, much less his, and longing for solitude, she turned away from him, murmuring, "I'm going back now."

"I'll go with you."

Woodenly nodding agreement, she waded out of the churning surf, then was barely aware of the gritty sand that clung to her wet feet as she walked across the beach to pick up her shoes in one hand. But she was overwhelmingly aware of Cade, who, after retrieving his own shoes, fell silently in step beside her as they walked back toward the house. Surreptitiously, she glanced out of the corners of her eyes at him and was unable to ignore the burst of tension and excitement that instantaneously quickened her heartbeat. Life can take the strangest turns sometimes, and it was ironic that her first walk along a moonlit Bermuda beach hadn't been with Brad. Yet, even more ironic was the fact that she was almost glad she had taken that walk with Cade instead, despite the fact it had left her feeling more bewildered than she had ever felt before in her entire life.

CHAPTER THREE

Brad had changed much more than Jessica had even suspected the last time they had been together. And, after five days in Bermuda, she was beginning to realize the difference in him might not be just temporary. He seemed quite content with his fast new life-style, despite its superficiality, and thus far she had found no real opportunity to talk to him about the obvious effect stardom was having on his personality and their relationship. Since the night he had gone alone to C.Z.'s party, he had stayed home in the evenings, but mainly because Cade insisted they get to work trying to put his financial affairs in order.

On Monday night, while Cade familiarized Brad with a few high yield investment possibilities, Jessica read a book in the living room. In the chair across from her, Christie flipped through the pages of a glossy fashion magazine, pausing occasionally to show Jessica an outfit or a pair of shoes that had caught her fancy. Both women looked up when Cade and Brad left the small adjacent study, still discussing finances as they walked across the living room.

"I would like to go ahead and buy that Ferrari I mentioned," Brad declared. "There must be some way we can work it out."

"I wouldn't advise it right now. Maybe in a few months," Cade told him flatly, then dropped the entire matter. "Have you decided yet which charity or charities you want to contribute to?"

Shaking his head, Brad dropped down into a low-slung easy

chair and grinned. "Before this year I made so little money acting I was more qualified to accept charity than to give it, so I don't know which ones to choose."

"What about the Salvation Army?" Jessica suggested, closing her book on one finger to keep her place. "They put contributions to very good use."

"A fine idea," Cade agreed, joining her on the sofa. "And there are many other worthwhile organizations. I'll list a few of them, Brad, and you can select the ones that interest you."

"I just made a large contribution to my guru," Christie piped up with an excited gesture "Well, he's not exactly a guru. In fact, he doesn't like to be called that. He says he's a simple philosopher, but he's more than that to me. He's given me a lot of good advice in the past six months. You should meet him, Brad. You might want to donate some money to help him with his work too."

"Better let me look into that first, Brad," Cade said, a nononsense expression on his lean face. "I'm sure you'd want to know your donation was being used for a good cause, and of course, there's a good possibility that contributions to this man wouldn't be tax-exempt."

"Oh, I'm sure they are," Christie said, but soon was eyeing Cade with some doubt. "Don't you think?"

"I really don't know," he answered, his smile gentle, almost indulgent. "That's a question you should take up with your accountant or whoever you have managing your money."

"Well, I did have an accountant, but we just didn't see eye to eye at all, so I finally dropped him last month. I haven't had a chance to find anyone to replace him yet."

"I think you might want to do that as soon as possible."

"Then what about you?" Christie suggested enthusiastically, nodding at Cade. "I'd certainly trust you to handle my finances."

"I appreciate the offer, but I'm not taking on any new clients right now," he said. "But I can give you the names of some very competent people, if you'd like me to."

45

"All right."

"Maybe Cade just doesn't want to get involved with you and your guru," Brad suggested teasingly, and when Christie poked the tip of her tongue out at him in response, everyone laughed. Then Brad looked around the room, a certain restlessness in his eyes, and suddenly slapped his hands against his thighs. "I have an idea. Christie, let's take Jess and Cade to that little nightclub we found near Hamilton. It's a nice place, Jess; you'll like it. Won't she Christie?"

"Oh, sure," his lovely co-star agreed. "It's one of my favorite places. Soft lights, dancing. Let's do go. All of us. All right?"

Cade was agreeable and Jessica was too. Dancing would be fun, and besides, since arriving on the island, she had only attended private parties. She couldn't return to the States without sampling some of Bermuda's public nightlife.

Less than twenty minutes later they were past the airport and across the causeway. The narrow winding road that led to Hamilton was at one point carved through a tower of solid limestone, and as they passed through there, Jessica gazed up at the sheer rock faces, finding them far more ominous at night than they had seemed the day Cade had brought her this way. About a half mile farther along, they stopped at the nightclub, a sprawling, dazzling white limestone building accented by black shutters at the windows and looking more like a private home than a public establishment. Secluded in lush green foliage on three sides, it was poised at the rocky shoreline overlooking the ocean and a crescent of sandy beach.

Jessica was impressed, no less so when the four of them went inside. A long mahogany bar curved around one corner of the spacious but cozy room, and small round tables encircled a highly polished dance floor which continued out onto a side balcony. Seeing Brad's expectant gaze, Jessica smiled and started to speak, but before she could express her appreciation of the subdued but elegant decor, several patrons had spotted him and

Christie, and were up out of their chairs on their way toward them. Soon they were surrounded.

"It's not easy being a star," Jessica commented wryly, smiling at Cade when he lightly gripped her elbow to direct her away from the chattering mob. When they reached an empty table, he held her chair and she sat down, slipping her powder-blue mohair shawl from around her shoulders. She glanced back toward the crowd but could only make out the top of Brad's head near the center. She gave Cade a somewhat resigned smile. "Think they'll ever get away?"

"In time. We'll have a drink while we wait for them," he said, deciding, and beckoned a nearby waiter to order her usual white wine and Scotch and water for himself. When the man had gone, he sat back in his chair and simply looked at her.

To Jessica, his intense examination of her face seemed to go on for a very long time. It was almost as if he was about to say something, but as the seconds crept by without his speaking, an uneasiness mounted in her until finally she shifted uncomfortably in her chair.

"I got the impression that you were looking forward to dancing," he at last said perceptively. Getting up, he came around the table to take her by the hand. "Dance with me, Jessica."

Her heart felt as if it did a crazy little somersault, and she hesitated, looking up at him towering over her. Since that night on the beach, nothing further had happened between them. Although they still spent part of every day exploring Bermuda together while Brad was working, Cade hadn't touched her again, but he was touching her now, his thumb moving in slow light circles over the back of her hand. It would be sheer folly to agree to dance with him; she knew that, but as he gently yet relentlessly pulled her to her feet and into his arms, she went like a moth drawn to flame. Her pulses pounded and she held herself stiffly until slowly the strong arms around her and the warmth of him reassured her in some strange way. She relaxed, slipping her arms up to his shoulders as his tightened almost imperceptibly around her narrow waist.

Closing her eyes, losing herself in the slow exotic tempo of the music provided by a small live band, Jessica followed Cade's lead easily as they moved out on the dimly illuminated balcony beneath the far-flung stars in the black sky. The sweet fragrance of late-blooming flowers perfumed the night. And as they began to merely sway together to the sensuous beat, she found her head was resting in the hollow of his right shoulder. She took in a deep shuddering breath while a comforting sense of inevitability flowed over her. For the past few days she had imagined that what had happened between Cade and her on the beach had been a one-time occurrence already forgotten by him. Now, she knew he hadn't forgotten. Held gently against him, she could feel the sexual tension between them, electrically charged and irresistible. And when he suddenly stopped moving to cup her face in both his hands, she looked up at him, a faint bewitching smile curving her lips.

"Jessica," he whispered huskily, enfolding her in his arms which tightened around her involuntarily as she pressed against him, feeling she could never be close enough. The supremely masculine, unyielding firmness of his body heightened her awareness of her own femininity, and as her growing desire intensified his, his intensified hers in a seemingly endless spiraling of emotion. After several poignant spellbinding moments, Cade released her only to lead her a few steps into the shadows beneath an overhanging branch of a sprawling hibiscus shrub. Immediately gathering her to him once more, he looked down, dark eyes wandering over her face, then imprisoning hers, causing her breath to catch. She had never felt more alive nor more attuned to her own physical needs than she did in that moment. She longed for his touch, and when he brushed back her hair then cradled her delicate jaw in one large hand, she lifted trembling fingers to trace the taut tendons of his sun-browned neck.

She saw the sudden tightening of his chiseled features, heard

48

his gruff tortured whispering of her name, and her eyes fluttered shut when firm lips grazed her right temple, hesitated, but never feathered down across her porcelain cheek toward her mouth. He wanted to kiss her, she knew, as much as she wanted to be kissed, and when he simply drew her nearer instead, scarcely bridled mutual longing became almost like a tangible thing between them, coiling in her like an overwound spring. It wasn't nearly enough to move with him to the slow beat of the music, but right now she knew that was all she could have of him and couldn't force herself to pull away. Eyes shut, the crescents of her lashes lying lightly on her creamy skin, she swayed in his embrace until she began to slowly become aware of approaching voices.

Beneath the seclusive canopy of the hibiscus branch, she was sure she and Cade couldn't be seen, and she was greatly tempted for several longs moments to again lose herself in what she was sharing with him. Yet, it was too late. The voices had broken the spell, and she was being dragged back toward reality against her will. At last she ceased moving, then stepped back out of his strong secure arms into the pale light that dappled the balcony. She turned away.

A hand descended heavily on her right shoulder, and she went very still. Finally, she had to look back at Cade, managing to produce a weak smile. She shook her head. "We've done it again," she said as flippantly as possible, but her voice was somewhat strained. "It's all too crazy, Cade."

He stepped closer while turning her sideways to face him. Removing his hand from her shoulder, he stood simply observing her face for a number of seconds that seemed to her to be endless. She wanted to look away but found she couldn't, as if the very intensity of his gaze held her in a hypnotic trance. Yet her thought processes were so hopelessly jumbled she couldn't understand whatever it was his coal-dark eyes might have been telling her. The expression in the fathomless depths was inexplicable, and she couldn't define it. But then a hint of a tender smile played over his lips, and she felt suddenly safe and enfolded in an invisible but wonderfully comforting warmth.

"Jessica," he began softly. "This—"

"Hey, Jess, I've been looking for you," Brad called out. "You too, Cade."

Impatience at Brad for intruding at that particular moment flared up in Jessica. She struggled to suppress it and finally succeeded, but when she saw Cade's jaw tighten to a near-stony hardness, she thought for an instant he was going to send Brad away so he could finish what he had been about to say. But when he didn't, she wasn't at all sure whether she was sorry or relieved.

"I'll go find Christie," Cade said calmly as Brad joined them. "Is she waiting at the table?"

"Just left her there. Jess and I'll be with you in a minute," Brad replied. And when Cade had walked away, he turned to give Jessica a remorseful yet hopeful smile. He took her hand. "You're upset with me, aren't you, baby? Look, I'm sorry we got separated right after we walked through the door of this place, but you know how it is," he said, lifting his shoulders in a resigned shrug. "Fans are fans, and I like to be friendly and give autographs. I can't tell them to buzz off, can I?"

"Of course not. I understand perfectly," Jessica told him while easing her hand from between both of his. "I'm not that upset because we got separated tonight. I'm much more concerned because I've been trying to talk to you for days and you never give me a chance. I'm telling you again, Brad—we absolutely have to discuss some serious matters very soon."

"Oh?" He frowned. "If it's so urgent, why weren't you waiting for me at the table inside instead of coming out here?"

"For one thing, I didn't know when you were going to join us . . . if ever. And besides, Cade asked me to dance."

"Well, now you have me to dance with you," Brad announced, moving closer. "And try not to be mad at me, baby, even though

I haven't been able to spend much time with you since you got here."

"No. You haven't" was her straightforward answer. "I knew when I came that you had to work while I was here, but I did think we'd have most of the evenings together. But it hasn't worked out that way, and we're going to have to talk about why it hasn't."

"No need to talk, Jess. Everything's going to be different from now on," he promised rashly, gripping her arms to pull her to him. A winning smile appeared on his face. "We'll spend all the evenings alone for the rest of the time you're here, and we'll have as many serious discussions as you want to have. I'll make sure we do. You'll see."

Jessica had her doubts about that but didn't voice them. This was really neither the proper time nor place to try to talk to Brad. Cade and Christie were with them, and a nightclub wasn't very conducive to serious conversation anyhow. But she planned to seize an opportunity soon to have that talk with him; she had to. They had to discuss the change in him and the change in their relationship . . . because it had changed, even more than she had suspected four months ago. And she was overwhelmingly aware of that fact when Brad clasped her to him and covered her lips with his. He was kissing her, but it was Cade she was thinking about.

The next morning Jessica slipped out of the house early. She went out onto the terrace and settled herself on the chaise longue facing the beach. Staring off in the distance, she nibbled at a toasted English muffin, plain, and sipped cautiously at the steaming coffee in a bone china cup. Usually she had breakfast with Cade, but not today. She was deliberately avoiding seeing him this morning in order to give herself a better chance to think because she knew only too well that when he was with her all her common sense seemed to fly right out the window. And that was exactly what she had to think about, that and, naturally, Brad.

They had grown away from each other, and there was no getting away from that fact. Brad's new life-style, which he seemed happy with, didn't appeal to her in the least, and she suspected her life-style would no longer satisfy him—a very important difference that she could see even more clearly now than she had been able to the last time she'd been with him.

As far as Cade was concerned, Jessica was bewildered. She would have almost liked to have believed that all she felt for him was lust, pure and simple. Yet, that wasn't true, and deep in her heart she knew it. He was of course a very sensuous man, and her physical attraction to him was powerful, more powerful than her attraction to Brad had ever been. But her feelings were more complex than that, which was what concerned her most. She liked him too much, respected him too much, and seemed to be becoming too emotionally involved too fast, considering the fact that she had no idea what his feelings were. And how could she analyze them when she still had Brad to contend with? . . .

But what *did* Cade want from her? It had occurred to her that he might only want her because Brad did, but that seemed too unhealthy a motive, so she considered the possibility that he wanted no more than a brief sexual encounter, which was all some men did want, but Cade simply didn't impress her as that kind of man either. Yet she didn't really know him. But there had been times during the past several days when she had felt much closer to Cade than she did to Brad. Then again, Brad seemed something of a stranger to her these days, so that sort of logic meant nothing.

Such indecisive thoughts whirled round and round in her head as she finished half the English muffin and nearly all the coffee. After placing the dishes and snowy linen napkin on the glass-topped table beside the chaise, she lay back and gazed up at the brooding gray sky. It was an overcast day, but the air was sultry hot, and the tumbling mass of clouds overhead seemed to foretell rain, possibly in the very near future. Jessica's lips twisted in wry amusement. Unsettling weather would certainly correspond to her mood.

For the next few minutes she lay staring up at the roiling cloud banks, lost in thought until she heard Cade's footsteps on the terrace tiles. She stiffened momentarily, then forced herself to relax as much as possible, though the edge of her teeth sank down into her lower lip while she waited for him to reach her.

"Morning," he greeted her quietly, stopping by the chaise. "Penny for your thoughts."

"You'd be paying too much for them." Smiling wryly, she looked up at him, wishing he didn't have to look so damnably attractive and virile. Clad in khaki slacks and a cream sweater that accentuated his bronzed skin, dark hair, and black eyes, he exuded a subtle yet potent masculinity that could cause most female hearts to flutter. Jessica was hardly an exception. Her heartbeat had already quickened, but she ignored it and lazily moved one hand. "I really wasn't thinking about much at all, just woolgathering, mostly."

"Good. Since you're lying around doing nothing, you're not too busy to help me," he announced, bending down to catch hold of both her hands and starting to pull her up off the chaise. "Come on, you're drafted."

"Drafted? To do what?"

"Typing. I have a couple of important letters I have to send out today, and it won't take you any time to do them for me."

"Oh no," she protested, hanging back, laughing up at him. "I'm on vacation. Remember? Besides, you can type them yourself. I know you can. I heard you using the electric typewriter in the study just the other day."

"But I'm out of practice, very rusty. It might take me hours to do what you can get done in twenty minutes."

"Hours, Cade?" she questioned with good-natured skepticism. "Aren't you exaggerating just a little?"

"Would I exaggerate about something like this?" he asked,

pretending to be wounded by her suspicion but making no attempt to mask the amused light in his eyes. He sighed. "Ah well, if you refuse to help me . . ."

"All right, all right, I wouldn't want you to spend the rest of the day hunting and pecking at the typewriter," she agreed at last, rising lissomely to her feet and giving him a cheeky grin. "I'll help you. I wouldn't be able to stand the guilt if I didn't."

"I thought appealing to your conscience would do the trick," he murmured, then hurried her into the house before giving her any chance to change her mind and back out of the agreement.

Less than a half hour later both letters had been typed, and while Cade added his signature to them, Jessica addressed the respective envelopes. When she finished, she leaned back in the swivel chair behind the desk in the study and announced nonchalantly, "Oh I forgot to mention that I charge by the page."

"In lieu of money, how about accepting lunch as payment?" he bargained, tapping the sealed envelopes against the palm of one hand. "I'll drive into St. George now and get these in the mail, then come back here and meet you on the beach. After we have a swim, I'll take you to any restaurant you want. Deal?"

"Deal," she agreed without hesitation, unwilling to refuse him since they had lunched together every day this week anyhow. If she said no to him now, he might think she was afraid to be with him because of what had happened between them last night. That wasn't precisely true. It was herself she worried about. Her response to him was so powerful that he made her feel more vulnerable than anyone else ever had, yet she decided that with a little extra self-discipline she could get over feeling like that. She had to try anyhow or spend the remainder of her vacation making up excuses not to be with him, and she wasn't willing to do that. Besides, he was complicating her basic problem—dealing with Brad.

While Cade drove to St. George, Jessica put on her rose-colored maillot swimsuit and matching wrap skirt, then went to the beach. Several people were already swimming, and she watched them toss a beach ball back and forth while she spread a wide blanket on the sand about a hundred yards from the spot they had laid out their towels. She sat down, stretched her legs out, and leaned back on her hands, staring contentedly at the crystal clear ocean. Although the overcast day seemed to darken the hue of the sapphire blue water and made the rolling waves appear a bit more ominous, she was still eager to get out in it. Despite the cover of clouds it was a balmy day, and she lifted her hair off her nape to allow the breeze to cool her skin. To pass time while waiting for Cade, she brought a book out of her bag but had only read a couple of pages when he appeared. Jessica looked up from her book. As if by their own volition, her blue eyes traveled in somewhat bemused fascination over long, darkly tanned muscular legs, past lean hips clad in black swimming briefs, and broad chest covered by the tan polo shirt, the shirt Cade suddenly stripped off over his head as he dropped down on the blanket with the lithe easy grace of a big powerful cat.

"Don't sit down. I can't wait any longer to go in the water," Jessica merrily told him, scampering to her feet and running down the beach into the creamy surf that lapped at the sand.

After swimming for a while, Jessica's arms and legs began to tire, so she flipped over onto her back to float in the surprisingly placid surface beyond the breaking waves where the water rocked her with gently undulating movements. Relaxed, her eyes closed, she put all thoughts out of her mind, and it was some time later when she heard Cade calling her name. She lowered her feet and began to tread water, aware for the first time that she had drifted some distance from shore.

Cade swam toward her, his long powerful strokes slicing cleanly through the water, and judging from the glimpses she had of his face, his expression was thunderous. Yet, by the time he reached her, his lean face and dark eyes only conveyed minor irritation.

"Unless you plan to float back to the States, I think you'd better stay closer to the beach," he muttered, somewhat winded as he tread water beside her. "Trying to rescue you from drowning doesn't sound like a great adventure to me."

"I'm sorry, Cade. I didn't realize . . ."

"I don't think it's wise for you to swim alone," he interrupted rather impatiently. "What if I hadn't been watching you?"

"But I knew you were."

"Trusting little soul, aren't you?" he asked softly, but with no hint of contempt in his deep voice. "How could you have possibly been sure that I was watching out for you?"

"Why shouldn't you have been? I always watch out for you when you swim out farther than I do," she answered simply. "It's just something people do for each other."

A small irrepressible smile gentled his features. "I'm not about to try to argue with logic like that," he conceded. "Let's just swim back now before we both have to float all the way home."

On the beach once more several minutes later, Jessica shivered under the cold spray of the outdoor shower which washed the sticky salt water from her hair and skin. Then while Cade took his turn, she dried off as best she could with a thick fluffy towel. When he joined her on the blanket, she had run a comb through her hair, and wispy tendrils were already drying at her temples and her nape. Propped on her elbows, she tilted her head back to look at the sky.

"Those clouds are getting grayer," she commented. "And I think the breeze has picked up a little. It's going to rain."

"It may do more than that. I caught the weather on the car radio when I drove into St. George. There's a tropical storm moving in from the south," Cade said quite calmly, scooping sand up in one hand then allowing it to sift away between his fingers. "They expect it to hit here late tomorrow night or the next day if it continues on the same course."

Jessica's eyes widened slightly. "Do they think it might develop into a hurricane?"

Looking at her, he shook his head. "The weather caster said

they didn't expect it to, but it'll still be a fairly severe storm nevertheless."

"Luckily I'm not as afraid of storms as I am of airplanes," Jessica said, poking fun at her own unreasonable fear. "In fact, I think there's something almost exhilarating about storms. They're so uncontrollable and dramatic. Of course, I've never been caught out in a bad one. I'm sure it's easy to think a storm is exciting, even beautiful, if you're safe inside where it's cozy."

"That does make a difference."

"Definitely," she murmured but glanced back at the house Brad was renting. "But I wonder how safe it is, even inside, this close to the ocean. I've never been on an island during a tropical storm."

"It can be unpleasant, but Bermuda has been here a long time," Cade said reassuringly. "I'm sure it'll be here after this storm passes, though it probably will cause some property damage."

"Maybe it'll veer out to open sea and not hit here at all," she said hopefully, combing her fingers through her drying hair to fluff it.

Spun gold. Even without the sun shining on it, her hair looked like spun gold, glowing with highlights. Watching as she turned onto her stomach to begin probing in the sand for tiny shells, a daily habit, Cade reached out to tuck a wayward strand back behind her left ear, feeling the enticing silken texture of it between his fingers.

Jessica turned her head to smile at him, hoping he had no way of knowing her breath had caught deep in her throat simply because his fingertips had feathered over the top of her ear. She wished she could gain some control over her responses to him, but beginning to doubt seriously she was ever going to, she resumed her search for shells. Smiling to herself when she discovered a minuscule unbroken one that was lemon-yellow and knobby surfaced, she placed it carefully in the shallow depression she had made in the blanket beside her, then began brushing one finger through the sand again.

"You mentioned gardening is one of your hobbies," Cade broke the silence a few minutes later, "but you didn't tell me you collect seashells too."

She shook her head. "These aren't for a collection. They're mementoes. When I get home, I'll put them all in a small, clear glass bottle, and whenever I see them, I'll think of Bermuda."

"Simple things make you very happy, don't they? Many women would want to take souvenirs home that were much more extravagant than a bottleful of small seashells."

"Whoa, now, don't go making a flower child out of me," she protested laughingly. "If you recall, I'll also be taking home a mohair shawl and a gold necklace that I bought here. I do like simple things, but I have to admit it's still nice to get some of the things money can buy once in a while."

Cade smiled. "Are you always so honest?"

"Usually, but only because I realized years ago that I couldn't lie worth a damn," she quipped. But her expression became more serious as she turned onto her side, leaned on one elbow, and rested her head in her hand, looking at him. "What about you, Cade? You told me photography was something of a hobby. Any others? Any collections?"

"No collections, except for my photographs. But occasionally, I take a trek up to the mountains to hunt unusual rocks."

"There. You see? There's nothing much more basic than a rock, so you obviously like simple things too. What others do you like?"

"Peanut butter cookies," he replied wryly but truthfully. "I still visit my grandmother whenever I can, not only because I enjoy seeing her but also because I'm always hoping she'll bake up a batch. And she usually does."

"Umm, peanut butter cookies; I love them," Jessica said. "I learned to bake them in Girl Scouts and made so many one summer that my father swore we had to own stock in the peanut butter company."

"Maybe you'll bake some for me sometime," Cade suggested, smiling. "I could tell you if yours are as good as my grandmother's."

"Ha. I'm no fool. I'd never have a chance in a contest like that because one of nature's basic laws is: *every*thing always tastes better at Grandma's house."

Cade laughed softly. "I've never thought about it that way before, but I guess you're right. I've even tried making the cookies myself, following my grandmother's recipe to the letter. They turned out all right but just never tasted as good as hers do."

"Then I rest my case. Now you understand why no one with any sense at all gets involved in a bake-off against anybody's grandmother." Amusement softly shone in Jessica's azure eyes. "You'll have to find someone else to bake for you. I decline the invitation."

"I'm sure there must be some way to change your mind."

" 'Fraid not."

"Don't be so sure of that, Jessica. I don't give up easily."

She grinned. "Determined, aren't you?"

"Very. And willing to be patient, if necessary, to finally get what I want," Cade murmured, his words sounding like a promise as he captured and held her gaze. "You understand that?"

She did indeed and her smile faded slightly. Suddenly, the very cadence of his deep-timbred voice had altered, and she realized that baking no longer had anything at all to do with this conversation. There had been an undertone in Cade's words that made his statement far more personal, almost intimate, and now a compelling excitement plus more than a little uncertainty fluttered in the pit of her stomach. She had no doubts he could be a determined man, perhaps nearly ruthless, in his pursuit of whatever he wanted, and that mere thought was enough to practically take her breath away. Why did he want *her*? If only for a casual sexual interlude, she would have to fight all his powers of persuasion to avoid that sort of involvement. But if he were interested in a more meaningful relationship . . . She pressed her fingertips against her forehead, hoping to reassemble thoughts that certainly needed much reassembling because she really shouldn't be thinking this way at all until she had dealt with Brad. But the mystery of Cade's true motivation nagged relentlessly at her. Looking at him directly, she wished she could somehow read his thoughts, but those dusky coal eyes were mere dark impenetrable insolvable puzzles, and his expression told her nothing. Perplexed, her heart beating too rapidly for comfort, she started to turn to resume her search for shells, but when Cade moved to gently curve one hand around her waist, she was immediately still, her pulses racing as a wild heat coursed through her veins.

He whispered her name.

And glancing beyond him, she saw that their fellow swimmers had gone, leaving them alone on the deserted beach, which now seemed a too private and potentially dangerous place. His touch was too pleasurable, and confused as she felt, she needed to escape it fast or risk reaching a point where she might begin to ardently encourage his caresses.

"How about that lunch you owe me?" she said, the words tumbling a bit too quickly from her mouth. "I guess we should go back to the house so I can start getting ready to go."

An endearing smile of understanding lifted the corners of Cade's mouth. He removed his hand but not without some obvious reluctance.

Feeling his gaze on her, Jessica got up to tie her skirt loosely around her waist, but that task was not as simple as it should have been because her hands were unusually shaky. And it did nothing at all for her equilibrium to know he was closely watching every move she made. She couldn't recall having felt this self-conscious since adolescence, and it was only after Cade began folding the beach blanket that she was able to draw a truly normal breath.

Together they walked back to the house beneath a sky aswirl with darkening gray clouds. The air, balmy as it had been earlier, seemed even heavier now, and wondering when the storm approaching from a distance would begin to make the ocean itself heavy with high choppy waves, Jessica stepped onto the terrace with Cade. Entering the house through the laundry room, they deposited their towels in a hamper. When Cade had tucked the neatly folded blanket, which he had shaken free of sand, back in its proper place on a shelf, he followed Jessica across the kitchen along a wide corridor to the east wing where the bedrooms were located.

She stopped at her open doorway, transferred the straps of her straw beach bag from one hand to the other, then smiled somewhat tentatively at him. "It should take me only a half hour or so to get ready," she said, stepping across the threshold. "But we have plenty of time anyway, don't you think?"

"Plenty. In fact, it's far too early to even think about having lunch, and you know that. You're just trying to run away again." The same understanding smile he had given her on the beach reappeared on his sensuously shaped lips, and he stepped toward her, shaking his head. "But this time I'm not going to let you get away, Jessica. I can't."

Her heart seemed to leap up into her throat, then to plummet back down to commence a thunderous beat as he advanced in one long stride into her room, then pushed the door closed behind him, shutting the two of them inside together while quite effectively shutting the rest of the world out. Suddenly his very height and the breadth of his bare sunbronzed shoulders seemed to somehow diminish the size of the room, and Jessica felt rather trapped, but amazingly enough, the feeling was not entirely unpleasant. A rushing excitement battled with a basic need to protect herself from what she knew could possibly cause her much emotional pain. As those conflicting emotions warred for supremacy, she stood as though transfixed, unable to decide how to react. The pale light of the overcast day shone through the opened windows to bathe the room in a mystical gray. Her pupils widened, adjusting to the dimmer indoor illumination and darkening her eyes to deep pools of navy blue that reflected some of the uncertainty she felt.

But there was no uncertainty in the black depths of Cade's. He stepped in front of her. Gently, he uncurled her slender fingers from around the straps of the beach bag, took it from her, then tossed it aside onto the chair next to him. Lifting his hands, he ran them over the golden cap of her hair, smiling tenderly when she took a swift tremulous breath.

There was an instant when she could have rebuffed him, yet she allowed it to pass and was at once irrevocably lost in the moment, in him. His touch, when his hands cupped her slender neck, was electric, and the tingling burning sensations that scampered over every inch of her skin made her feel gloriously alive. Impaled by his piercing gaze, she reached out to feather her palms over his naked hair-roughened chest. She heard his quick intake of breath, felt his muscles constrict to corded steel-hardness with her caress, and a faint smile played over her lovely mouth, a smile that was somewhat shy but also sensuous.

"Jessica," he whispered, catching her chin in one cupped hand, his fingertips stroking the arch of her eyebrows, brushing the tips of thick lashes, and tracing the high-boned contours of her cheeks. Watching her as if to gauge her response to his provocative tactile exploration of her features, he too smiled sensuously as her lips parted.

Jessica recognized the hint of triumph in his smile, but that recognition did nothing to defuse the needs rising within her. Instead, her longing for his touch to continue mounted steadily, becoming stronger with each passing second, and accompanying it came the overwhelming yearning to go on touching him too. His smooth bronzed skin and heated firm flesh invited her caresses. Her hands drifted in slow circular motions over his broad, subtly muscled chest.

It seemed a moment of discovery, a tantalizing promise of a

sweet beginning. Unhurried, Cade plied her with spellbinding patience and sure, masterful strokes. Imprisoning her bemused gaze, he at first did nothing more than continue his searching quest of her upturned face, as if he were committing its very structure and texture to memory. Pleasantly roughened male fingertips glided with feather-lightness over creamy skin, bringing every nerve ending to keen sensory receptivity. And by the time he lightly touched the corners of her mouth, then drew one long finger across her lips, she was breathlessly awaiting his kiss.

Yet when he gripped her arms to draw her to him and lowered his dark head, his own warm lips sought not hers but her temples, the curve of her delicate jaw, and the slight enticing hollows in her cheeks. Jessica began to tremble as dangerous weakening warmth invaded her limbs. Her eyes had fluttered shut and her slowly released breath was a whisper when she stretched up on tiptoe to curve her arms around his shoulders and tilted her head to one side, inviting the hot nibbling kisses he scattered along her neck. His warm breath tickled inside her left ear as he closed his teeth gently on the tender lobe of flesh. Rushing, fire-tipped arrows of delight shot through her. She swayed closer, her fingers entwining in his thick hair. And when he cradled the back of her head in one hand while the tip of his tongue teased first one corner of her mouth then the other again and again, she could stand to wait no longer.

"*Cade,*" she gasped, her lips seeking and finding his.

His arms went around her then but did not yet bring her tightly against him. As if intent on arousing her desire to a fever pitch, he played with her, caressing her lips only lightly with his, probing the fine flesh and bone structure of her spine with feathering fingertips that kindled fires on her skin even through the clinging fabric of her swimsuit.

His obvious attempt to seduce her was devastatingly effective. Jessica cared about nothing except being closer to him. She moved sinuously in the circle of his arms, her slender shapely

63

body brushing against the firmer lineation of his, and his response was immediate and intense.

With a deep muffled groan he crushed her against him, one arm tightening round her waist while his other hand swept over her silken hair down to curve around the back of her neck. His hardening lips took hers, parting them, and opening her mouth, the tip of his tongue slipping within to taste her honeyed sweetness. And when her own tongue welcomed the intimate invasion of his, he widened his stance, arching her to him.

Jessica wrapped her arms around his neck, holding him tightly. The compelling heat of his flesh seemed to permeate her skin and warm her to her very bones, to the innermost core of her being. It was so right to be embracing him and embraced by him in the cool pale gray seclusion of her room. As if she had been waiting all her life for this particular moment with this particular man, she was warmly pliant and responsive as the kisses they exchanged deepened and lengthened and became more intense. Her heart was beating crazily; her breathing was becoming as ragged as his while their lips came together then parted time and time again, as if they hungered insatiably for each other. She had never before felt as wondrously aware of her own femininity as she was feeling now. And it was only when Cade swept her swiftly up in his arms and strode over to gently deposit her on her bed then came down onto the coverlet beside her that she experienced even a millisecond of fearful doubt.

Gazing up at him as he leaned upon one elbow over her, seeing the hot glint of passion burning like black fire in his eyes, she moved her head from side to side on the pillow. "Cade, no," she breathed. "Don't."

But her protest was tentative, weak, and it did nothing to deter him. With a slow lazy smile he leaned down, his chest hard against the yielding fullness of her breasts as he possessively claimed her mouth once more.

Her doubt and fear didn't survive the white-hot heat of her carefully stoked desire. And Jessica surrendered to needs more powerful than she had ever known. Moving fluidly, she turned toward Cade, one arm slipping eagerly around his waist as his tightened across her back and he pulled her against him. She rubbed her softly shaped parted lips over his, knowing the effect she was having and reveling in her ability to arouse him in the same way he was so capable of arousing her. Her shapely smooth legs tangled with the long length of his, and she smiled a woman's secret smile at his uncontrollable response. Adrift in sensual delight, her senses spinning when his marauding mouth captured hers, seeming to demand total surrender, she kissed him back, giving of herself to him. And the giving was not only physical. She gave with a wondrous surge of pure emotion.

When Cade released her lips, she murmured a soft involuntary protest, and as her eyes flickered open and she saw the brief flash of triumph in the depths of his, she didn't even mind. He knew how he was affecting her, and she knew he knew. It would be extremely foolish to try to deny it, and right then she didn't feel at all foolish, simply gloriously alive. Cade brushed her straps aside and proceeded to trail a strand of light provocative kisses along the gentle slopes of her creamy shoulders. Rippling waves of keen pleasure raced through her. Her fingertips pressed down convulsively against the corded muscles of his back, and as his lips found the pulse fluttering in her throat, she trembled.

Cade lifted his head, brushed her tousled hair back from her entrancingly rose-tinted cheeks, then grazed the tip of one thumb slowly back and forth over her lips. "I want you, Jessica," he murmured huskily. "But I'm sure you know that."

She nodded. "Yes."

"*Yes.* I've tried to be patient, but I want you more than I've ever wanted any woman in my life. And, Jessica, you want me."

She couldn't respond to that, although she knew deep in her heart what the truthful answer would be. She did want him or believed she did, which amounted to nearly the same thing. But it was beyond her capabilities to voice what she wanted just yet. It was too soon . . . or too unexpected . . . or too . . . Frightening?

Yes, it was in some ways frightening to realize Cade wielded such control over her. Yet in other ways it was intoxicating to realize he did. And she simply lay there beneath his gaze, looking up at him in silence.

He seemed to understand. "Maybe you aren't quite sure yet what it is you want," he whispered roughly. "But you soon will be."

With that breathtaking promise, he covered her lips with his again, exerting a gentle twisting pressure that demanded her response and received it. When she pressed her supple warm body against him, his hands wandered over her, shaping the womanly rounded curves, kneading and massaging her waist, then roaming upward to ease the top of her swimsuit down a couple of inches. His mouth, warm and tender, sought her creamy flesh.

Jessica drew in a sharp breath, but even a fresh burst of oxygen did nothing to help her think clearly, and she felt hopelessly lost. Then Cade was slowly pulling the top of her swimsuit down to drape around her waist, exposing her to his hot searching gaze, and to her amazement, she wanted to do nothing at all to stop him. Scarcely able to breathe, she turned acquiescently onto her back beneath the coaxing hand he curved over her left hipbone. She lay still yet incredibly relaxed considering the circumstances, and through drowsy blue eyes saw Cade's long lingering gaze rove over her. Her body grew hot, or at least it felt as though fire ran though her veins. She felt erotic and daring and very very vulnerable in a most tantalizing way.

"God, you're lovely," Cade said, meeting her wondering gaze.

And seeing the genuine appreciation of loveliness mirrored in his eyes, she *felt* beautiful and desirable and aroused. Before she actually realized what she was doing, she caught both his hands in hers and brought them to her breasts.

"*Jessica,*" he groaned softly, weighing them in his palms, curving his long fingers around the full taut flesh.

"Oh Cade, yes," she whispered, stroking his shoulders while

he traced concentric circles around her breasts, then sought the summits, his fingertips rubbing, brushing, teasing the throbbing roseate peaks erect. She moaned softly. A pulsating emptiness opened deep inside her like an awakening flower, and she was astounded by the sheer force of its clamoring to be filled. She ran her fingers through Cade's hair and caressed the firm edges of his ears as his hands moved over her, continuing to explore the perfect roundness of her breasts.

"Do you know how long I've needed to touch you like this?" he murmured. "And kiss you like this?"

As much as Jessica longed to feel the touch of his lips on her skin, she was afraid of where such intimate caresses might lead, afraid more of herself than of him. Catching his lean face in her hands as he bent down, she sank the edge of her teeth into the curve of her lower lip and slowly shook her head.

"Cade, I . . . I just can't," she explained breathlessly. "All this . . . is happening much too fast."

For a few long spellbinding moments of silence he seemed unwilling to release her, but at last he sat up on the bed and raked his fingers through his hair. Watching as she pulled the swimsuit back up over her, he rose from the bed, then leaned on one hand over her while gently stroking her cheeks with the other. His faint smile was understanding and somewhat teasing when he whispered, "You think it's happening too fast, and I think it's not nearly fast enough. But, as I told you, I can be very patient if I have to be." Straightening, he started across the room, then stopped to look back at her. "Can you still be ready for lunch in half an hour? Or have you changed your mind about going with me?"

"I haven't changed my mind. I'll be ready," was her unhesitating answer. She wanted to be with him, was unwilling to pretend otherwise, and when he nodded, then turned to leave, her eyes followed him.

Without another word or backward glance, he went out. As he pulled the door shut quietly behind him, Jessica hugged her arms across her breasts and nuzzled her cheek in the soft pillow, feeling as if her feverish body retained the imprint of his hands on her skin. She closed her eyes, wondering yet again exactly what Cade wanted and wondering what she might eventually be willing to give if she didn't seize control of this situation right now. But how? She had no idea. No easy answer came to her, and she sighed inwardly. The very question was made even more complex when she thought about Brad and knew deep in her heart that she had never once felt guilty about the kisses and caresses Cade and she had shared. Beyond all doubt Brad no longer played the most important role in her life, and she must talk to him as soon as possible, no matter what she had to do to make him listen. Everything was so very different because now she felt much happier and more alive with Cade than she ever had with Brad.

CHAPTER FOUR

The threatening storm did not veer out to open sea. By seven o'clock the following evening it had encompassed Bermuda in its outer fringes. Driving sheets of rain lashed the island, and the winds that whipped the waves into a white-capped frenzy were expected to reach near-hurricane velocities before the night ended.

In Brad's beach house, Jessica stood at the bay window overlooking the paved driveway, staring up at the swirling twilight sky. Sheet lightning flashed every few seconds, casting an eerie ominous glow on the tossing clouds and making her worriedly gnaw a fingernail. *Where the devil was Brad?* This morning she had told him they must have a long serious discussion, that somehow he had to set aside some time for it, and he had assured her that he would be able to return to the house by early afternoon. Now it was past seven, but he still wasn't back, and the worsening storm was beginning to make her feel rather apprehensive.

She knew that C.Z. had scheduled another scene to be shot aboard the fishing boat for early in the morning. It had been safe then. The ocean had still been relatively calm, but it was far from calm now. From early afternoon on, the waves had risen higher and higher, and even with the house pretty well closed up, she could now hear them crashing against the beach. Twisting a golden tendril of hair round one finger, she restlessly shifted her weight from one foot to the other then back again as an unbidden fear began stirring in her mind. What if shooting the scene had taken longer than expected? What if the boat had been caught up in the edge of the storm? What if, right at that very moment, it was still out on that treacherous ocean, unable to make harbor. Or worse, what if . . .

Jessica shook her head, determined not to let panicky thoughts like that torment her. Yet she was worried. Although she knew her feelings for Brad had changed, she certainly had not stopped caring about him. She had known him forever; he was part of her life, and that was something that could never change. She winced when a jagged streak of lightning split the sky, then was followed closely by booming thunder, heightening her concern about Brad, about Christie, and about C.Z. and the rest of the entire crew and cast, for that matter. She didn't want to allow herself to assume they were still out on the boat in this severe weather, but . . . if they weren't, why weren't Brad and Christie back here yet?

She stared glumly outside, praying for the sight of headlights sweeping across the drive, but the paved space remained mockingly bare and dark except when the lightning flashed. After a couple of endless minutes, she dragged herself away from the window, knowing that watching and waiting wouldn't hasten Brad's return anyhow. Standing in the center of the living room, she stretched out her left arm, and shot back the cuff of her blouse, consulting her wristwatch with a deepening frown. It was past seven thirty now. She glanced at the closed study door. Cade was in there attending to some details in Brad's growing investment portfolio. Suddenly, she was nearly overpowered by the need to be close to him, talk to him, simply see him, and she was tempted to go knock on the door. Yet, she didn't. He was working, and she didn't want to interrupt him. Sighing, she wished she hadn't already finished cutting the article she had brought with her. Working might have diverted her thoughts, but it was too late for that now. The article was ready for the production department. There was nothing more she could do to it.

She wandered over to the glass-topped coffee table, picked up and flipped through one of the glossy magazines Christie had left there, but soon tossed it back down. Too edgy to settle in a chair, she went into the kitchen to check the steaks she was broiling. The dinner she had planned was almost ready, except for the steaks and the vegetables she would steam at the last minute. But it was beginning to look like this would be a meal Cade and she would share alone, a situation she would have undoubtedly favored if the reason for it had been different. Without knowing that Christie and Brad were safe, however, she felt increasingly uneasy.

Close to eight o'clock Cade came into the kitchen. Leaning nonchalantly against the doorjamb, ankles crossed, hands in the pockets of his trousers, he watched as she carefully turned the two-inch steaks, then switched off the broiler.

"I wish Christie and Brad would get here," she murmured, looking over at him. "These steaks are just perfect right now."

"It won't ruin them to sit there a few minutes," Cade declared, catching her by the wrist as she walked past him and reaching behind her to deftly untie the apron she wore. Smiling, he directed her toward the living room. "Come have a drink with me while we wait for them to get here."

Jessica complied but seated herself on the very edge of a sofa cushion while he went to the small built-in bar. When he came back across the room to hand her a glass of white wine, she accepted with murmured thanks, took a tiny sip, and watched solemnly as he settled in a chair across from her.

"I'm worried," she stated at once, troubled blue eyes seeking his. "Brad and Christie should have gotten back by now."

Cade's dark eyebrows rose questioningly. "They've been this late before, haven't they?"

"Yes, but Brad said he'd be back here early this afternoon because they expected rain, and the only scene they could schedule in cloudy weather was the one they were to shoot aboard the fishing boat this morning."

71

"They actually planned to take that boat out today knowing this storm was moving in?" Cade asked, his jaw tightening. "Why the devil were they willing to take an unnecessary chance like that?"

"Because they wanted to shoot this scene when the ocean was rougher than usual. Brad said C.Z. thinks this storm is a godsend."

"I wonder if he still thinks so. It was getting more than just rough out there by late morning, and if they did go out, I imagine C.Z. wishes they hadn't," Cade said with a rueful quirk of his mouth. "Didn't someone mention that he tends to get seasick very easily?"

Jessica couldn't suppress a faint answering smile. C. Z. Cameron was such a pretentious, mean-spirited, and thoroughly unlikable man that she couldn't feel much sympathy for him. Besides, he should never have risked taking cast and crew out on a boat in such violent weather anyhow. But perhaps it was all right and she was worried about nothing. Certainly Cade's rueful comment about C.Z.'s propensity toward seasickness indicated he wasn't unduly alarmed by this situation. Her spirits lifted a little, and she looked hopefully at him.

"Then you don't think they could be caught out in the storm right now unable to get back in?"

"No. I don't think so, Jessica," Cade replied softly, leaning toward her, resting his elbows on his knees. "I think if they had run into trouble, we would have heard about it by now."

"Yes, you're right," she agreed, knowing he was. Yet, something akin to intuition nagged at her still, making her feel a lingering uneasiness. Trying to ignore it, she set aside the glass of wine and stood. "Well, you must be starved, and I think we should go on with dinner. We can't wait forever for Christie and Brad to get here."

"You don't seem completely reassured," Cade said perceptively, rising to brush the back of his hand over her cheek. "Why don't you go ahead and see to dinner while I give Air Sea Rescue a call."

"I'd thought of doing that. If you think it's a good idea . . ."

"Would it make you feel better if I called them?"

"Maybe it would," she conceded, giving him a grateful little smile. "Thank you, Cade."

"They might not be able to tell me anything, but it can't hurt to try," he said.

And when he turned immediately toward the telephone, Jessica walked back to the kitchen, hoping vaguely that the steaks weren't ruined. They didn't seem to be, and she transferred them from broiler pan to a warming plate after putting the fresh asparagus tips on to steam. She carried the crisp green salads she had prepared into the dining room, and when she returned to the kitchen, Cade was there, the expression on his dark face unreadable. She stopped short.

"What did you find out?" she asked him. "Were they able to tell you anything?"

"Nothing except they've received no distress signals from the *Sea Maiden,* and the man I spoke to said they probably would have if something had gone wrong," he told her, then smiled kindly. "Feel better now?"

She did. Yet . . . "I do feel like they're probably safe, but I still wonder where they could be. Less than half an hour ago I called C.Z.'s house and the hotel where the crew and the rest of the cast are staying, but there was no answer at C.Z.'s, and the desk clerk couldn't locate anyone for me. But I guess it's possible they had to take shelter somewhere, in a cove maybe. Don't you think so?"

"I think they're perfectly safe right now . . . somewhere," was Cade's flat answer as he reached for the bottle of chilled wine she had picked up. "And they've probably already had dinner, which we haven't done, so shall we?"

Smiling, Jessica nodded, then preceded him into the dining room.

Most of her tension eased at least momentarily, her appetite piqued by the aroma of the food she had prepared, she managed to do justice to the meal and also converse intelligently with Cade. Yet, by the time the dishes were cleared from the table, anxiety was mounting in her again. Ten o'clock had come and passed, and after Cade helped her tidy the kitchen and they returned to the living room, she started nibbling her nails again as she strained her ears for the sound of a car pulling into the driveway. Not that she could have heard one if it had. . . . The wind was wailing against the house, rattling the windows in the living room until Cade went to secure the shutters again, which she had opened earlier so she could look out. Rain pounded on the roof, terrace, and drive, and between the shutter slats Jessica could see the explosions of fearsome bright lightning that was almost instantaneously followed by deafening thunderclaps.

On the sofa, hands folded in her lap, she tried to relax while companionably talking to Cade, but it wasn't easy. She couldn't help worrying about Brad. She had always taken it upon herself to worry about him and realized she probably always would. Besides, she worried about Christie too. Carefree and somewhat irresponsible, at times like Brad, she was thoroughly likable nonetheless, and Jessica needed to know that she along with Brad had found safe haven from the storm somewhere. And that need became more acute with every long second that ticked by.

Despite her determination not to act like an alarmist, her involuntary gestures betrayed her anxiety. She began to unnecessarily smooth her skirt or fidget with the collar of her blouse or simply wind a strand of hair round and round one finger. Watching her, seeing worry written on her face once more, Cade got up from his chair, announcing, "I'm calling Air Sea Rescue again."

The line was busy, and it took a couple of minutes for him to get through, but at last he did. Poised on the sofa, Jessica tried to hear what he was saying, but he was on the far side of the room and speaking quietly so his words were indistinguishable.

"Nothing," he said a moment later when he hung up the phone and turned to face her. "No distress signals, no radio messages at all have been received from *Sea Maiden*."

The old axiom "No news is good news," proved true, but only up to a point. While Jessica was relieved that there was no actual confirmation that the *Sea Maiden* was in trouble, the uncertainty of the situation was becoming nearly unbearable. She felt she could no longer sit and wait. There must be something more she could do. Moving swiftly off the sofa, she started toward the phone.

"I'll try to get St. George's Harbor again. I tried earlier but couldn't get through," she said. "Maybe I can now."

But she couldn't. During the following fifteen minutes she ceaselessly dialed the harbor, received a busy signal, then broke the connection and dialed again. Finally, she gave up, frustrated by the persistent, caustic buzz-buzz that sounded in her ear with her every attempt and hounded by an apprehension she couldn't subdue. Sighing heavily, she replaced the receiver in its cradle.

"I'm driving over to the harbor," she decided aloud, her jaw firmly set as she walked toward Cade. "It's the only thing left to do. Maybe the harbor master has received a radio message from them."

"Jessica, you said yourself that they might have taken shelter in a cove somewhere," Cade reminded her quietly, stopping her as she started past him, taking one small hand in both his. "I imagine that's exactly what they did. It's even possible someone's taken them in and they're waiting out the storm in comfort right now."

"I'd like to believe that," Jessica murmured, smiling wanly. "But if they had been taken in, Brad would have called to let me know they're okay. I'm sure he would have."

Cade wasn't at all sure of that but merely suggested, "Maybe he has tried to call and couldn't get through."

"Maybe, but I have no way of knowing that, and I need to *know* something pretty soon. That's why I have to drive over to the harbor, to find out if they've heard any news."

"You're not driving anywhere in this storm," Cade stated flatly. "Chasing all over the island isn't going to help anything."

"It'll help me feel like I'm taking some kind of action," she disagreed, her voice softly urgent. "I have to go. I want to."

"I don't give a damn what you want. You're not going. It's too dangerous, Jessica," Cade uttered, his jaw hardening perceptibly, his tone unyielding. "It's out of the question."

Defiance lifted her chin as indignation sparked in her eyes. "I beg your pardon but you can't . . ."

"I beg yours. You're not going out and that's final."

"You can't tell me what to do. I'm an adult and I do what I damn well please. You have no right ordering me around."

"I do when you're considering doing something this reckless. And useless. If *Sea Maiden* was in the harbor, Brad would be here. But since they obviously didn't dock there, you'll be wasting your time going."

"I have to find that out for myself," she retorted heatedly, then bit back more angry words before they could tumble from her mouth. Sensing a strength of will in Cade that no amount of arguing was likely to wear down, she took a deep calming breath and sought his understanding instead. "Cade, don't you see why I have to go? This not knowing anything is beginning to make me crazy. We have no idea where Brad and Christie are, and I think I have to try to do something to find out."

"All right, Jessica," he relented, his expression gentling somewhat as he intently surveyed her face. "But *you're* not driving over to the harbor. I'll go myself."

"No! I don't expect you to do that. It's my idea. . . ."

"And I'm going to follow through on it," he cut in, releasing her hand to take her shoulders in a firm, commanding grip. "Maybe you're right. Someone at the harbor might be able to give us some news, so I'll go right now."

76

"But Cade, I don't want you to," she exclaimed softly, unwilling to allow her fears, justified as they seemed to be, drive him out into the night in a violent storm like this. A certain supplication darkened her eyes as she gazed up at him. "Really, you don't have to go for me. I'm perfectly capable of driving myself."

"I'm sure you're an excellent driver, but you've never driven here where you have to keep to the left, and I'm sure you're not used to driving in near-hurricane weather," he said, hardness coming back to edge his voice. "So either I go to the harbor or nobody goes. Is that clear?"

"Yes," she muttered reluctantly, though she recognized there was some irrefutable logic in what he said. "But I'll go with you."

He shook his head. "You should stay here in case Brad and Christie come in. We don't want them to get here and find us gone. They might start searching for us while we're searching for them. That's the kind of mix-up we just don't need on a night like this. Right?"

"I guess, but I don't want you to have to drive to the harbor alone either. Maybe we should just forget the whole thing. You stay here."

"No. I think I should go. Even if I can't find out anything about *Sea Maiden,* I can ask someone to try to make radio contact with her," he told her, pressing long fingers over her shoulders reassuringly before releasing them. He turned away. "Better get my raincoat."

Watching him stride toward the bedrooms, Jessica wrapped her arms tightly round her waist, her features drawn with concern. She muttered an oath beneath her breath. Now she wished she had never mentioned going to the harbor. Much as she wanted to know that Brad and Christie were safe, she didn't want Cade out in the shrieking wind and driving rain with lightning striking all around him. He would go, though; he had made his mind up, and she wasn't going to be able to change it.

When Cade quickly returned to the living room, Jessica followed as he walked to the front door while sliding his long arms into the sleeves of a tan raincoat.

"You'd better button that," she suggested softly, reaching up to fasten the first two or three buttons for him while he did the rest. When she finished, however, her hands lingered lightly against his chest and her dark blue eyes sought and held his. "Please be careful, Cade. Promise me you will."

"I'm always careful," he said, stroking his thumbs over the backs of her fingers before he put her hands away from him. "Be back as soon as I can."

Then before she could say another word, he opened the door, and slanted, driven rain peppered into the foyer. As he forcibly yanked the door shut behind him, Jessica sped to open a window and the shutters to watch him cross the driveway. Leaning forward in a gust of wind that doubled over the surrounding palms, he reached the car and got in. Shivering, Jessica never heard the engine start, but in a few seconds headlights flashed on and the car was moving along the drive. Then it was out of sight and Cade was gone and she felt suddenly almost physically ill.

For a long time, an endless time it seemed, Jessica paced back and forth across the living room while the wind rampaged outside and jagged spears of lightning flashed again and again, increasing her tension until she felt every muscle in her was tied in tiny knots. At last she sank down on the sofa and glanced at her watch for the millionth time. Cade had been gone nearly half an hour, and as she wondered if she dared hope he might return very soon, the lights in the house went out.

"Oh no, not that too," she groaned, then sighed with relief as the lights flickered back on again. But within seconds they went out. Then back on, then out, repeatedly, as if a mischievous child were playing with the switches. Soon, Jessica wished they would either go out permanently or stay on permanently, preferably the later. But as they continued their eerie flickering, she carefully made her way to the kitchen where she brought out two hurricane lamps and matches. These she carried to the living room, and as she was putting them down on the coffee table, the telephone began ringing shrilly.

She made a mad dash for it, scooping up the receiver and praying it would be Cade calling . . . of course with news of Christie and Brad. Instead, when she hurriedly said hello, it was Brad who spoke from the other end.

"Hi, Jess, you sound a little out of breath," he began. "I guess you've been a little worried, haven't you? And I'm sorry about . . ."

"Is everyone okay?" she interrupted, relieved that he at least sounded all right but wanting to make sure of it. "Are you? Is Christie?"

"Everybody's fine. We had some trouble getting in, but we managed to make it to the cove below the house C.Z.'s renting about three o'clock. We docked there and . . ."

What did you say?" Jessica asked disbelievingly, thinking she misunderstood him. "I must have heard you wrong. What time did you say you got in?"

"About three, three thirty, somewhere around there. That's what I want to explain. You see, it was . . ."

Jessica heard nothing after he repeated the time. And for a moment, she was too stunned to speak. Angry red color rose in her cheeks. She gripped the receiver so tightly that her knuckles went white while her other hand curled into a small tight fist at her side.

"Damn you. Damn you, Brad," she muttered at last through clenched teeth. "How could you be so thoughtless? You said you would be back here by early afternoon, and it's after eleven now. Do you realize I've been worrying all this time, afraid you and Christie and everyone else had been caught out on that boat in this mess? Why didn't you call me? Where have you been?"

"Aw, come on, Jess, that's what I'm trying to tell you," Brad cut in, his voice too smoothly soothing. "I was just saying that C.Z.'s neighbor invited us over . . ."

"For a party?" she guessed tersely, noticing for the first time the faint sound of babbling voices in the background. "You're at another party, aren't you, Brad? God, I can't believe this. You got so involved in a stupid party that you didn't even bother to call me."

"I did try to call, Jess, honest to God. But the phone's been out."

"But now it's suddenly repaired? Come on, Brad, don't insult my intelligence. I don't believe you."

"But it's true! The phone was dead until just a minute ago. How could you think I wouldn't have called you?"

"Well, even if you did, and I doubt it, why didn't you have someone drive you home when you couldn't get through to me?" she questioned icily. "Didn't it even occur to you that I might be worried?"

"Well yes, but . . . I didn't think you'd want me to go out in this storm if I didn't have to."

"Dammit, Cade's out in this storm right now trying to find out what happened to you. And he went out because I was so worried," she countered, blinking back the hot tears that suddenly filled her eyes. "How do you think that makes me feel, knowing he's out in this hellish mess on a wild-goose chase because of me?"

"Jess, baby, don't worry," Brad responded far too carelessly. "Cade can take care of himself. He'll be all right. You'll see."

"You're impossible. Impossible," she muttered, a strangling constriction clutching her throat. "I'm hanging up. I don't want to talk to you now."

"You really are upset, aren't you?" Brad asked unnecessarily. "Look, Jess, just hold on. I'll get someone to drive me over right now and we can straighten this out."

"Don't bother. As soon as Cade gets back, I'm going to bed. Enjoy your party, Brad, because I don't care to see you tonight. I may not even care to see you tomorrow."

"Jess, you . . ." he began.

But Jessica was in no mood to listen.

CHAPTER FIVE

Willing herself nqt to slam down the receiver, she replaced it noiselessly, then made a low impotent sound deep in her throat as she glared at the phone. The lights flickered once more then came back on and stayed on, but even that improvement did little to soothe her feelings. She was so angry that her fingers seemed to itch with a need to make stinging contact with Brad's face, and if he had been there at that moment, she probably would have slapped him hard and enjoyed doing it. Although she had already realized he had changed, she had expected better than this from him. There was no excuse for the trick he had pulled today, and she wasn't sure even the lifetime of affection and closeness that bound her to him could survive many such strains. And if something were to happen to Cade while he was out in the storm trying to locate Brad . . .

But no! She wouldn't allow herself to think that way. Pressing her lips tightly together, she wearily pushed back the sun-streaked curve of hair that feathered across her forehead while she sank down in the closest available chair to wait for Cade.

Time became an enemy. She checked her watch often, and with every minute that crept by, the icy hand of uncertainty that had taken hold of her heart seemed to squeeze harder. Cade had been gone far too long. Despite the horrendous weather conditions, it shouldn't have taken him well over an hour to make the relatively short trip to St. George's Harbor and back. And the coil of tension in her was so tightly wound she was unable even

81

to seek release in restless pacing. Instead she could only remain immobile in her chair, curled up, arms wrapped around her legs, chin resting on drawn-up knees as she stared longingly at the front door, praying Cade would soon walk through it.

Earlier she had worried about Christie and Brad, but the concern she had felt for them was nothing compared to what she felt for Cade now. More than she had ever wanted anything in her life, she wanted him to be safe and back here again with her, and even her anger toward Brad faded to something akin to indifference. There was no room in her mind for him when her entire being was focused on thoughts of Cade. Closing her eyes, she could see his dark face, his slow lazy smile, and she would have given anything to have been able to reach out and touch him. Somehow, in little more than a week, he had become very important to her, perhaps too important considering she still had no idea if he felt anything more for her than physical desire, or if perhaps he saw her only as a challenge. Despite her uncertainties about him, however, she couldn't alter what she was beginning to *feel* deep in her heart.

Another half hour dragged by as the storm continued its fierce assault on the island, and it was at the moment a particularly brilliant flash of lightning was followed by a sharp pop of thunder that the front door blew open with a crash, causing Jessica to softly cry out. Then, through the gray curtain of rain, Cade dashed into the house, and she practically propelled herself out of her chair toward him, stopping just short of throwing herself into his arms.

"Thank God you're back," she exclaimed quietly, clasping her hands in front of her, watching as he pushed the door closed against an opposing wind. Her eyes dark with concern swept over him, taking in the soaking raincoat that clung to him like a second skin and the rain that glistened in his hair and on his face. When he turned away from the door, she stepped closer to him. "Oh Cade, you're drenched." Chewing her bottom lip, she reached up to swiftly undo the coat's buttons, then after he had peeled it off, took it from him. "I'll get you a towel."

In the kitchen she draped the dripping coat over the back of a chair and hurried out down the long corridor toward the bedrooms where the linen closet was located. Cade followed and, silently taking the towel she held out, pressed it briefly against his face before rubbing it briskly over his head. Damp hair fell forward across his forehead as he moved across the hall into his room, stripping off his wet shirt as he went.

"I'm so glad you're okay," Jessica murmured, following behind him. "I was afraid. . . . You seemed to be gone such a long time, Cade."

"*Sea Maiden* wasn't docked in St. George's Harbor, and the harbor master couldn't raise her on the radio, so I tried to call Hamilton Harbor," he said, dusky coal eyes drifting over her as he draped the towel round his neck. "I couldn't get through. The telephone lines are down over that way, and I had to drive over. Before I left St. George, I tried to call you to tell you where I was going, but this line was busy." He shook his head, gesturing almost apologetically. "The boat isn't docked in Hamilton either, and I don't know any more now than I did when I left here. I'm sorry, Jessica."

"Oh Cade, you have nothing to be sorry about. Brad's the one . . ." she began, her voice taking on a harshness when she said Brad's name. She broke off to start again more calmly, although she dreaded Cade's reaction to what she had to tell him. A pained expression flitted across her face, and she weakly lifted one hand. "When you tried to call here and got a busy signal, I was talking to Brad. He and Christie are all right. Everybody's all right. In fact, I'm sure they all feel just fine since they've been partying at C.Z.'s neighbor's since about three this afternoon." Shaking her head, she took two tentative steps closer to Cade, regret mirrored in her wide blue eyes. "*I'm* the one who's sorry, sorry you had to go out in this horrible storm looking for him when, all along, he was perfectly safe."

83

"And did you ask him why he didn't bother to let you know he was all right?" Cade questioned, advancing toward her, lean hand on equally lean hips, a thunderous scowl appearing on his face. "If you did, what did he have to say for himself? What excuse did he make?"

"He said he couldn't call before because the phone was out and had just been repaired."

"And you believe that?"

"It could be true, I guess . . . But no, I don't believe it," she said with a slight tilt of her chin. "And anyway, even if it is true and he did try to call, he should have gotten someone to bring him here if he couldn't get through. There was no excuse for him letting us sit here and wonder where he was. I told him that—I was so mad I even told him not to bother coming home when he said he was going to. But I can't begin to tell you how I hate that all this happened. I'm so sorry, Cade."

"Forget it. No harm done," he muttered. "And for God's sake, stop apologizing for Brad. That's not your responsibility."

"I feel like it is," she murmured. And she did. She had known Brad forever, and that somehow seemed to make him partially her responsibility. She spread her hands expressively. "What he did today was ridiculously thoughtless, and I *am* sorry he acted that way."

Looking at her, Cade said nothing. His narrowed gaze captured and held hers. Seeing the disillusionment in her face, he wondered if some of his comments to her had helped her realize and accept the fact that the love she felt for Brad was wasted on him because he was no longer the Brad she remembered. Or did she still harbor hopes that he would miraculously become that Brad again? Cade didn't know but thought that her ardent response to him must have made her realize at the very least that her relationship with Brad could never be quite the same again. Surely she understood that or she would never have let Cade touch her, and that fact encouraged him. Although he hadn't at first set out to pressure her into leaving Brad and had wanted her

84

to come to him totally of her own free will, he decided in that instant that he would do almost anything to have her. He wanted her. She fascinated him. He wanted to see those lovely blue eyes alight with passion and glowing with drowsy warmth in the aftermath of lovemaking. He wanted to possess her, body, soul, and mind. And if Brad was too caught up in his new life-style and status to make an effort to hold on to her, that was his loss and hopefully Cade's gain. Yet, if he had to be patient awhile longer, he would be, instinct telling him she wasn't a woman to be rushed. And as his eyes searched the clear honest depths of hers, a slow easy smile at last moved his mouth.

"No more apologies," he commanded softly. "We'll forget tonight ever happened. Deal?"

"Deal," she agreed with an inward sigh of relief as she smiled back at him, then noticed for the first time that even the bottoms of his trouser legs were wringing wet. A tiny frown replaced her smile. "You did get soaked, didn't you? I think you better take all your clothes off."

"Is that an invitation, Jessica?" he murmured, a rather wickedly amused light in his black eyes as he stepped closer. "If it is, I . . ."

"It isn't, you devil," she retorted, laughing softly up at him as she counteracted his step forward by taking one back. "It's merely a suggestion. I think you should get out of those wet clothes if you don't want to catch cold. That's what I meant and you know it." She started to turn toward the door. "In fact, the sooner you get into something dry the better, so I'll go and you can change right now."

"Don't rush off. I can change in here," Cade said, striding into the adjoining bathroom but leaving the door open a few inches as he continued talking. "I noticed the hurricane lamps in the living room. Did the electricity go off while I was gone?"

"Almost. The lights flickered off and on for ten minutes or more but finally decided to stay on, thank heavens," Jessica answered, wandering back across the room. She sat down on the chest at the foot of the bed. "How was it out there, Cade? Very bad?"

"Bad enough. Hamilton is completely without telephone service. Electricity's out in some areas, and there are quite a few trees down. That's one of the reasons I was so long getting back—a tree fell across the main road, blocking traffic both ways. It took us awhile to clear it."

"No wonder you got soaked, if you had to help clear the road," she murmured glumly, still feeling marginally responsible for his venturing out into the storm. Yet even the guilt she felt was immediately forgotten when he came out of the bathroom, clad in a short beige terry robe, his feet bare and his hair still tousled from the brisk rubbing he had given it with the towel. Jessica's heartbeat accelerated as her eyes swept swiftly over him. He was always attractive, but in this state of undress he seemed even more excitingly male, or perhaps seeing him this way simply made her more acutely aware of her own femininity. Perhaps just being alone in his bedroom with him made her far more susceptible to the dizzying aura of masculinity that emanated from him. For whatever reason her rate of breathing had quickened, and she mentally chided herself for her rather weak-kneed reaction to him. After all, she had seen men in bathrobes before, but then again, those men hadn't been Cade. He was different. She liked him too much, was too responsive to his every touch, and the thought of making love with him was becoming more enticing every minute they spent together. As Cade walked across the room toward her, she did not give any indication of how very vulnerable he made her feel.

Sitting back on the chest against the foot of the bed, she smiled naturally and nodded her approval. "There. You look much more comfortable out of those wet things. But maybe you'd like a drink to warm you? I'll go get you one if you like."

"Maybe later, thanks," was his casual reply as he sat down in a nearby easy chair, extending his long legs before him. Propping his elbows on the armrests, he laced his fingers together across his flat abdomen and leaned back against the cushions, apparently totally relaxed despite his recent rather harrowing adventure out into the night. When a particularly violent gust of wind rattled the outside shutters closed over the bedroom windows, he glanced in that direction then back at Jessica again. His smile was teasing. "Well, you said you think storms are exhilarating. Is this one exciting enough?"

"More than a little *too* exciting," she admitted, wrinkling her nose. "What I had in mind was a nice summer thundershower. This storm is going a little too far. I could have done without the experience."

"Shouldn't last much longer. The weather service is predicting it'll move out of the area by morning. In the meantime, at least we're inside where it's safe and cozy."

"You weren't just awhile ago," she murmured, inwardly shivering as once again she considered that he could easily have been hurt while out in the storm. She sighed. "I still feel really terrible about you going out in this for no good reason. Just because I . . ."

"Jessica," he interrupted, his deep voice softly admonishing. "We agreed to forget that happened. Remember?"

"Yes but . . ."

"*Jessica.*"

"All right, all right, it's forgotten." Throwing up her hands in mock surrender, she smiled mischievously. "You certainly are persistent. Do you always have to have things your own way?"

His dark brows lifted. "You don't really know how persistent I can be . . . yet."

The intimation wasn't lost on her—his very tone made his words personal and provocative, but despite the rush of excitement that made her heart beat too fast, she pretended to take his remark at face value. "Oh, I do think I know how strong-willed you can be. You've convinced Brad to make some very wise investments, and that's a major accomplishment, since he's done his best to avoid discussing his finances with you. He hasn't been very cooperative, but you've managed to get through to him anyhow, although I know you've had to stay here longer than you'd planned."

"You really think that's why I've stayed?" he asked, holding her gaze as he slowly leaned forward in his chair. "It isn't, and you must know that. I could have wrapped up business with Brad in three or four days, but I didn't want to. I wanted to stay here, and you're the reason why I have."

Happiness tried to bubble up in her, but she abruptly forestalled it, too unsure of him. She smiled rather dubiously. "Is that the truth, Cade?" she asked lightly. "Or did you just think it might be a nice effective line to hand me?"

His answering laughter was low, rumbling, soft. "How skeptical you are, Jessica."

"Not skeptical, exactly. Simply cautious."

"Or overly cautious."

"Sometimes it's wise to be that way, and this is one of those times because I'm not sure I really know you very well."

"Maybe you know me much better than you realize," he countered. "Don't you feel you've learned a great deal about me in the past few days? I certainly feel I've learned a great deal about you."

"Not too much, I hope," she retorted, grinning. "A woman likes to have some secrets."

"Hmm, but you may not have complete success in that department because you have such honest eyes," Cade said quietly, gazing intently into them. "They're very expressive."

"Oh, but I make it seem that way deliberately," she quipped, with a dismissive toss of one hand. "I only pretend to be an open book. People think they know all about me, but I'm actually a mysterious femme fatale in disguise."

He shook his head. "Not a femme fatale, Jessica. A woman like that is usually brittle, pretentious, and extremely boring. You're far too real and warm to qualify," he said, his deep melodious voice lowering. "Subtle mysteries are much more intriguing, and that's what you are."

"Oh good. I want to be a little mysterious," she said, exaggerating a relieved sigh, needing to keep up the lighthearted banter as the glint of amusement in his dark eyes slowly altered to a smouldering ember-glow that disturbed her considerably. Her heart lurched violently against her breast. For a breathtaking moment she felt hopelessly imprisoned in his gaze, but at last she managed to break that disruptive visual contact and smile casually at him. She sat up straight on the chest. "Well, now that we've decided I'm not a completely transparent person, how about that drink?"

"No, thanks."

She stood. "I'd be happy to get you one before I go to bed."

Reaching out, Cade caught both her hands in his and began to draw her slowly, inexorably toward him, murmuring, "I don't want you to leave yet."

"But it is late," she said steadily, despite the inaudible catching of her breath. "And it has been a long stressful day."

"You won't be able to sleep anyway. The storm alone is enough to keep you awake."

"But . . ."

"Jessica," he whispered coaxingly, pulling her nearer. "Come here."

She held back, moistening dry lips with the tip of her tongue as her heart raced. Gazing down at his face, she tried to think straight but couldn't as affection and physical need seemed to short-circuit all rational mental activity. She shook her head. "Cade, I . . . can't."

"You can." His smile was warming, gentle. "Stay with me all night."

She hesitated, a strange consuming ache plunging through her, making her tremble. She *wanted* to stay with him. How she wanted to spend the long stormy night in his arms, in his bed, giving of herself, taking from him, and soaring to the exquisite peaks of pleasure she knew instinctively they would find together. And when his hands released hers to swiftly span her waist, sweet compulsion carried her onto his lap, into his arms, and her softly shaped parted lips sought his.

"My sweet Jessica, you have to stay now," he groaned roughly, his warm breath filling her throat. His hardening lips exerted a gently twisting pressure on the tender curve of hers, taking possession of her mouth and entering its sweet warmth with lazy probing sweeps of the tip of his tongue.

Jessica moaned, explosive passion flaming up into a searing pillar of fire deep within her and making her melt against him, her supple body hot, pliant, yet eagerly seeking. Trembling as his tongue tasted the veined inner flesh of her cheek, entangling slender fingers in the vital thickness of his hair, she slipped her other hand beneath the lapel of his robe, guiding her fingertips over his hard-muscled heated flesh until she found a flat nipple surrounded by a fine covering of dark hair and felt the aroused nub surge erect beneath her questing touch. She caressed him, played with him until he too was trembling and the compelling hardness of his lips was echoed throughout the length of his body. Yet the aroused masculinity that pressed against her thighs satisfied her only for an instant. Cade's hands, exploring and conquering, wandered over her with dizzying insistence, tracing every enticing curve, probing the satiny texture of creamy skin, and lingering long on soft yet wondrously resilient feminine flesh. And she was swept away in the awesome need for total completion. Emptiness became a chasm inside her, deepening with every thrilling sensation evoked by his masterful caresses.

As the tip of her tongue followed the edge of his, parrying its tenderly invasive thrusts, he held her fast against him, as if he could never bring her close enough. His strong arms were flexed tightly around her, and as her hand skimmed over his hair-roughened chest down to the flat taut surface of his midriff, his lips released hers and braised down over the delicate curving of her slender neck.

"Oh God, you have to stay with me now," he murmured against her smooth skin. "I want you . . . God, I want you. And you want to stay with me."

"*Yes.* Oh, yes," she breathed, detecting the urgent appeal in his husky voice and responding to it. She moved her hands through his hair, fascinated by the clean crisp texture of it. When Cade caught hold of one wrist, turned his head, and his warm mouth grazed into her cupped palm, brushstroking erotic traceries over sensitized skin, she made a soft pleasured sound and feathered fingertips across his tanned face, enamored of the carved contours and planes of his cheeks.

The hand he released once more sought the bare expanse of his chest as he cradled her in one supporting arm and lowered his dark head to trail a strand of nipping burning kisses just beneath the smooth line of her jaw into the hollows under her ears. He captured one tender fleshy lobe between even teeth, then the other, tasting their sweetness with maddening nibbles. Licking white hot flames of desire ran over her. She trembled as exquisite tingling sensations coursed through her and scampered with devastating effect over every inch of her skin, awakening every nerve ending. Her breathing soft, shallow, she brushed the lapels of his robe aside, turned her face into his hot flesh, her parted lips slowly tormentingly circling his shoulder.

"Jessica," he uttered hoarsely, winding a swathe of her hair round one hand while impelling her up closer, harder, against him. Whispering her name endearingly, he kissed the delicate curve of her brows, the pulses drumming in her temples, the thick fringe of her eyelashes, and the smooth fragile skin of her closed eyelids. His heavy yet gentle hand touched her covered breast, lightly massaging and kneading the yielding cushioned flesh, as he whispered, "Do you know how lovely you are?"

"Tell me," she whispered back haltingly, her eyes fluttering open to encounter the scorching passionfire glinting like black diamonds in the secret depths of his. Her faint smile beckoning, she stroked his strong jaw, her fingers stroking his left ear. "I like to hear you tell me. You make me feel beautiful."

"God, you *are* beautiful. An exquisite temptress," he muttered, sweeping oddly shaky fingers over her finely cut features, allowing them to linger with disruptive lightness along her finely cut mouth. "I think I could go on looking at you forever."

"Touch too," she invited, the words out of her mouth before she could stop them. Yet, she didn't care. All that mattered in that moment was him, his warmth, his nearness, the feel of his body, and she felt as if she could surrender eagerly to anything he wanted to do with her. Her luminous blue eyes held his. "I want you to touch me again too."

"Oh, I intend to," he said gruffly, gripping her narrow waist, fanning long strong fingers into the enticing arch at the small of her back. "I may never stop. I love touching you."

". . . love touching you too," she confessed, shapely arms slipping inside his robe completely and curving over his bare broad back. Drawing caressing fingers down the strong ridge of his spine down to its base, she realized with a sudden tremor of excitement that beneath the covering robe he wore nothing else. And the mere realization of his nakedness inflamed her senses, and the danger signals that were set off in her head were consumed in the blazing path of primitive need.

Deliciously warm and weak-limbed, she responded instantly to his large hand that curved over her right hipbone and pressed her back. Through drowsy eyes she watched Cade's lean face as he slowly began unfastening the tiny buttons of her georgette blouse. Raw emotion surged, full and hot, in her chest. If she wasn't in love with him already, she was very close to it. He was everything she had ever wanted in a man: assertive yet incredibly tender, intelligent, warm, passionate, and able to laugh at himself. Overwhelmed by the depths of her feelings for him, she touched his hair, his face, then slowly drew one hand up and down the strong brown column of his neck. Nearly lost in his fiery gaze, she shivered slightly when he opened her blouse and pushed the straps of her bra off her shoulders. Her clothes seemed a bothersome barrier now; she longed for him to strip her of all of them.

In actuality her sheer brief bra was a very ineffective barrier. Cade's hand roamed over the tautly filled cups, fingertips lingering on the peaks. His impassioned gaze wandered over her. And as the supporting arm beneath her arched up slightly and he bent down his head, she took a swift audible breath that was almost a soft gasp and felt a smile curve the lips that moved sensuously into scented shadowed cleavage then followed the slope of one breast. His tongue touched her. She trembled as he drew torturing circles around first one straining tip then its twin, dampening the fabric and clearly defining the darker flesh of her nipples. And when he took one into his mouth with warm drawing pressure, wild sensations rushed through her, piercingly keen.

Her arms tightened around him, her hands gliding feverishly over his naked back, and when he eased off her blouse, she uttered no protest. Even when he slipped her off his lap, rose, and swept her out of the chair up into his arms to carry her across the room, she offered no resistance. He gently sat her down on his bed and settled himself on the edge, hands holding her waist momentarily before skimming around over her back to the hook of her wispy lace bra. He undid it but then simply waited expectantly instead of removing it. And at last, after several poignant moments of silence between them while their eyes met and held, it was Jessica who brushed the straps off her arms. An excessive heat laid siege to her entire body, and her heart hammered frantically in her ears as she unhurriedly peeled off the flimsy garment then allowed it to drift from her fingers down onto the floor beside Cade's feet.

"Enchantress," he said, smiling softly at the faint hint of pink that rose in her cheeks. He moved closer, cupping the weight of ivory peach-tipped breasts in lean sun-browned hands as he kissed her with reassuring tenderness.

"Oh Cade," she whispered breathlessly, thrills rushing through her when his thumbs moved in slow rousing forays over her nipples. Her fingers crumpled the terry fabric of his robe but soon spread open to slip beneath once more, seeking his bare skin. Her parted lips met the firm compelling warmth of his again and again in a series of teasing kisses that made her ache for a rougher taking of her mouth. She swayed toward him, desire evoking an urgently sighed *"Cade."*

A low murmur of satisfaction rumbled up from deep in his throat, and he lowered her gently onto the mattress, his lips hardening on hers, taking their sweetness with spellbinding demand. Yet when Jessica's arms started to go around him, he drew back and sat up, but only to undo the button and lower the zipper of her black skirt.

Her heart leaped. She tensed instinctively.

Cade's smile was tender. He shook his head. "Jessica, relax," he coaxed, easing her skirt down and off completely. "I only want us to do wonderful, pleasurable things together. That's all I want."

What he wanted she wanted, and as his promising words echoed through her consciousness, she realized with sudden clarity that she was not merely close to falling in love with him—she did love him. And it was love that brought her swiftly up into his arms and close against him.

This time when he impelled her back down onto the bed, he came down beside her, lithe and lean and hard-muscled, his long body half covering the slightness of hers, his weight both imprisoning and evocative. Supporting himself on one elbow, he cradled the back of her head in his other hand, turning her face this way and that to rain lingering kisses over her ears, her cheeks, her temples, and the corners of her mouth.

"And what is it you want, Jessica?" he questioned unevenly. "Tell me."

Her eyes flickered open; his beloved face filled her vision, and his broad bending shoulders blocked the light from the lamp on the dresser behind him. Captivated by his searching gaze, mentally acknowledged love now surging up free and pure in her, she could only look up at him, stunned to silence by the sheer magnitude of her feelings.

"Tell me," he persisted, withdrawing his hand from beneath her head to outline the contours of her lips with one fingertip. His gaze narrowed, his dusky coal eyes shattering her soul with hot flickering glints of a man's desire. He lightly gripped her small chin between thumb and forefinger. "Tell me what *you* want, Jessica. Now."

"You. I want you."

"Yes," he muttered, a hint of triumph in his fleeting smile. "Yes, I think you finally do."

Finally. Yes, at last she felt free to admit that to herself and him, but the far-reaching significance of her confession was soon exiled into some oblivious sector of her mind by the persuasive power of his kiss. No coherent train of thought could survive the implosive fire of raging emotions that consumed her, and she gave herself up to the ecstasy of giving her love to him, not in words—not yet—but in the only way she could. She intertwined her arms around his neck, and her mouth opened slightly beneath the marauding strength of his. The tip of her tongue braised his carved lips, and as he shuddered against her and his weight pressed more heavily upon her, she returned his kisses with an ardor that nearly equaled his.

"Jessica, I *need* you," he groaned, his warm breath branding her neck, the pulse in her throat, and the hollow at the base as he drew the edge of one hard hand through the valley between her breasts and down over her bared midriff. His fingers spread open across her flat abdomen, searing her skin even through the fabric of half slip and panties. He whispered against her collarbone, "I need to touch you, taste you. Possess you completely."

Then his lips were on her left breast, seeking the throbbing summit, the touch of his tongue electric as he flicked it gently over and around aroused warm flesh. And her soft moan was almost a delighted whimper when his mouth closed around the rise with gentle pulling pressure.

Utterly lost, adrift in a realm of sensual pleasure, Jessica caught his face in her hands, urging his lips onto hers again. Fingers tangling in his hair, she sought all the superb potent power of his kisses and returned them with abandoned sweetness. The very flesh and bone structure of his magnificent body sent her hands roaming over him. Cade's fingertips slid beneath the waistbands of both her panties and slip, feather-stroking downward over the satiny flatness of her abdomen. Wild pulsating thrills crashed through her, but then she stiffened.

Cade's patient caresses, arousing yet wondrously gentle, made her arch for him to touch her intimately, and she tried to relax again, but couldn't. Unbidden doubts exploded in her brain, nagging at her, affecting her physical response. Passion simmered as she was reminded that she really wasn't sure of Cade. How could she be certain their relationship wasn't simply a working holiday fling for him, a diversion to while away the time while he was away from home? How did she know he wasn't seriously involved with some woman in Atlanta, a woman he might hurry home to without another thought for her after they left Bermuda? How did she know if she would ever see him again after she ended everything with Brad and her time here was over? She didn't know. Those insidious mental questions had no answers, and she only knew she was in love with him, which meant she could be badly hurt if it turned out she meant little or nothing to him. Yet the need for physical completion was awesomely powerful, and though she was tense and plagued by doubts, was unable to deny either herself or him what they both wanted so badly even while her mind prodded her with reminders that she was not ready to make that ultimate commitment.

Cade obviously sensed the turmoil going on within her because after long moments of plying her with caresses and kisses that did little to ease her tension, he whispered huskily, "God,

96

Jessica, don't you know what you're doing to me? My patience has its limits."

"I know. Cade, I'm . . ."

"The timing's wrong again, dammit," he muttered, rolling over away from her onto his back, draping an arm across his eyes. "And I suppose *this* is hardly the appropriate place for it to happen. You'd never feel right about it."

After an instant of initial confusion, she realized what he had meant by that last cryptic statement. *This* was Brad's house, although she had managed to push that thought far back in her mind and close a door on it for a while. But she hadn't talked to Brad about the change in her feelings toward him, and until she did, it wasn't right to be in bed with another man in his house, a man she loved and wanted to make love with. And since Cade was giving her an out, all her doubts surged forth and railed at her to take it, despite her driving need to give herself to him.

She sat up on the bed beside him. Her hand went out and touched his arm, but she pulled it back immediately when she felt his muscle flex tightly beneath her fingers. She caught her upper lip between her teeth. She didn't really want to leave him. Yet she slipped off the far side of the bed, scooped up her blouse and pulled it on, and continued on her way around to retrieve her skirt, shoes, and bra. Standing beside Cade, close enough to touch him, she hesitated.

"Cade," she said softly. "I don't know what to say."

"You don't have to say anything. I understand," he murmured without removing his arm from across his eyes. "We'll talk tomorrow. Go to bed now. Get some sleep."

She went but didn't sleep for quite a long while. Lying alone in her own bed, staring at the ceiling as bright lightning occasionally flashed like neon in her room, she finally reached a decision. If the storm moved on by tomorrow as the weather service predicted and she could get a flight back to the States, she would leave Bermuda. She needed to go home, immerse herself in her work, and find time alone to think. After her confrontation with Brad, she would be emotionally weary but then, only then, could she try to sort out her feelings for Cade. She knew she would need solitude for that, but still, she hated to leave him. Yet if he felt anything at all for her, he would easily be able to locate her when he returned to Atlanta. And if he didn't, then her decision to leave Bermuda would prove to be one of the wisest she had ever made. At the moment she had no idea what would happen but knew it was futile to dwell on any of it now. She would simply have to wait and see what the future brought with it. There was only one certainty in her life—it was time to bring this vacation to an end.

CHAPTER SIX

"Brad, after we've talked, I *am* flying home today," Jessica reiterated firmly the next morning. "I've decided to go, and nothing you say will change my mind."

"Come on, Jess," he persisted, giving her a charming smile while patting her hand. "You're not going to let a storm chase you away."

She sighed. "The storm has nothing to do with my decision. There are other reasons. For one, my vacation time's nearly over anyway, and since I know the work is piling up on my desk back home, I need to get back to it. Besides, after I say what I have to say, there won't be any use staying here two more days anyhow."

Brad's expression clouded a little. "So, you're still upset with me about yesterday. But there's no sense leaving in a huff."

"I'm not leaving in a huff, although you're right in a way—I'm still disappointed in you. What you did was ridiculously inconsiderate. I expected better from you," she said bluntly but without actual rancor, extracting her hand from his to pick up her coffee cup. After taking a slow sip, she leaned forward in her chair, resting folded arms on the dining room table and looking across at Brad, her face solemn. "I'm really not going home because of what happened yesterday. Although that's a part of it, my reasons are much more complex, and we need to have a serious talk."

"We are talking—about you staying here two more days the

way you planned," he countered lightly, leaning back, arms crossed behind his head. "Until we've settled that and you've decided not to leave today, we can't really talk about anything else."

"That is settled, Brad. I'm flying home. My mind's made up," she said patiently, ignoring his irritated frown. When he opened his mouth as if to argue, she lifted a silencing hand and went on, "And we do have to talk. About us. About the way we've grown away from each other. I'm sure you've noticed things aren't the same anymore."

"What the hell are you talking about?" he exclaimed, his handsome face tight as he sat up straight, glowering at her. "Things are the same as far as I'm concerned, and I don't know why you're saying they're not."

"Brad, don't try to fool yourself. You must realize that everything is different between us," she said softly, hoping he wasn't going to make this more difficult than necessary by being unrealistic. "It seemed to be changing four months ago, and I came to Bermuda to be sure. Now I am. It's obvious we no longer have much in common. Our interests aren't the same anymore, and that's mainly what's made our relationship different."

"Different? How? Come on, Jess, will you get serious?"

"I am being very serious, Brad, believe me. Maybe things started changing even before four months ago. I'm not sure, but they probably did. After all, we haven't seen much of each other, especially in the past year, and I think we've just grown apart. That just happens between people sometimes, and it's no one's fault. It's simply something that has to be accepted. I have to admit I never imagined this would happen to us, but now that it has, I can't ignore it, and you can't either."

Staring at her as if unable to believe a word he was hearing, he shook his head. "I knew you were upset last night when I called, but I guess I didn't realize *how* upset. You must be furious with me or else you wouldn't be talking such nonsense."

"I'm not furious and this is certainly not nonsense. You're just not listening to me, Brad," she murmured, directly meeting his challenging gaze. "What we had together before is gone. We've drifted apart. We don't seem to have much to say to each other, and you know it never used to be that way. For years when we were going to different colleges and afterwards, when you went to drama school then started getting small parts to play and I started working in Atlanta, we didn't get to see each other often. But when we did, we spent almost all our time together because we wanted to be with each other. This time and the last time haven't been that way. You've left me alone a lot; you've started acting very inconsiderate, and I haven't felt at all close to you."

"So that's the problem. You've gotten this crazy idea into your head because I haven't been able to spend every minute with you since you came to Bermuda," Brad declared confidently, his expression brightening as he gave her a mildly chiding smile. "But, Jess, love, I did warn you before you came that I'd have to work practically every day because we're behind schedule shooting this film anyway."

"I remember that, but I don't recall your telling me that besides working all day you'd be partying all night every night," Jessica frankly told him, watching the scowl appear on his brow once more. "It's not that you had to work while I was here, Brad. I understand that perfectly. It's your free time I'm talking about. We spent very little of that with each other either, just like the last time we saw each other. Don't you think that's odd? People in love long to be together, alone preferably. But, here especially, we're never really alone and aren't even together all that often. I wasn't willing to go to all the parties you wanted to attend, and you weren't willing to stay here with me. Doesn't that make you think our relationship has changed a great deal?"

"Maybe it just tells us what's wrong with it," Brad retorted, his scowl deepening. "To tell you the truth, Jess, it's not easy for me to be alone with you. Lately, you've acted awfully stand-offish."

"Like I said, I haven't been feeling very close to you, but face the facts, Brad—you really haven't tried to rectify the situation," she reminded him calmly. "You've been too busy going to parties."

"You could have gone to them with me, but you wouldn't. Maybe you're just not all that interested in seeing me get ahead in my career," he suggested rather petulantly. "Maybe you never have been."

"Oh, what rot, Brad," she muttered coolly, eyes narrowing. "You know damned well I've always been excited about your career and tried to encourage you in it. Don't try to pretend I haven't. Your career isn't our problem. It's the way you've let success change you personally and the way it's changed everything for us. You've gotten so wrapped up in your 'peer group' and the partying that . . . Well, to be honest, you don't seem like the same person I used to know."

"There's nothing wrong with going to parties."

"Of course not. But one every night? Aren't you beginning to get bored?"

"Why should I?" he countered sulkily. "I get to mingle with some very important people in this business."

"And gossip with them about fast cars, expensive clothes, and astrological signs," she added flatly. "I was bored with that kind of chatter after only two parties."

"And I thought you'd be impressed by all the famous people you met."

"I was happy to meet them. But I'm not overly impressed by people simply because they're famous. I'm only impressed if they show some depth of character."

Brad leaned forward, staring at her. "You almost sound like you're saying you're not very impressed by me anymore."

"I think it should be obvious I'd be happier if you hadn't changed so much."

"That's strange. There are plenty of people who like me the way I am now and think I'm pretty impressive."

"I know that."

"Millions of them are women," he added, his mouth twisting slightly. "And a lot of them are so impressed they'd take me as a lover, given the chance."

"I know that too," she replied shortly, her lifelong affection for him strained at that moment. "And now, I can imagine you've been to bed with some of them."

"Come on, baby, let's stop this silliness," he said evasively. "I don't want you to be angry. Let me cheer you up."

She heaved a sigh. "I think you're getting too used to women falling at your feet," she suggested tersely. "You're a superstar now, a movie idol who can snap his fingers and get anything he wants. But I can't see you like that. To me, you're still just Brad."

"And that's all I want to be to you, Jess."

"Is it? Really? Wouldn't you rather I be more adoring and fall down on my knees to worship you at the drop of a hat?"

"Well now that you mention it, that wouldn't be so bad, since it is you I want, Jess," he replied, producing a winning smile as he stood and came round the table to take hold of both her hands. "No other woman means anything to me. Only you."

This conversation was getting them nowhere fast, and Jessica shook her head at him. "It's useless to talk about why our relationship has changed. The point is that it has, and it's never going to be the same again."

"Sure it is. You're just upset about last night, but you'll get over it," he whispered cajolingly, pulling her up into his arms to kiss her.

Jessica held herself stiffly, feeling nothing, nothing at all. Once, Brad's kisses had warmed and excited her, but now they didn't, and she gently extracted herself from his embrace. "Brad . . ."

"I think you should go home today," he interrupted, smiling down at her. "Once you've had a chance to think all this over, you'll realize you've just been exaggerating the whole situation. Nothing's changed. And I'll be finished here in a week to ten

103

days, and when I am, I'll come straight to you in Atlanta. We'll iron all this out. Just a little misunderstanding anyway."

"No, it's not just . . ."

"I have to run now, love. Sorry," he cut in, bending down to kiss her lips again. "Due in makeup. Have a nice flight and I'll call you in a couple of days."

"Brad," she called, but he was already several steps away. When he turned only long enough to toss up a hand in farewell, there was nothing she could do except return the wave, and watching him hurry out of the dining room, she released her breath in a long, heavy sigh. He hadn't taken what she had said seriously, and that meant they would have to have this same discussion again when he came to Atlanta. She didn't look forward to that, yet she couldn't feel angry at him for trying to hold on to what they had thought they had together. Instead, the emotion she felt was more akin to compassion. Brad seemed a little lost and confused to her, and if he felt that way, even subconsciously, it certainly explained his refusal to accept what she had tried to tell him. He might need her to provide some sense of security in his life. Yet she knew it would never be the same for them. Tears pricked her eyes. Somehow, she had to make him understand that, while at the same time assuring him she still cared deeply for him as a friend and would always be there should he ever need her friendship. Now, that was all she could ever offer him.

Jessica pressed her fingertips against her closed eyes, easing the burning ache behind them. Squaring her shoulders, she left the dining room, walked across the living room, and stopped outside the opened door to the study where Cade was working. After taking a deep breath, she stepped across the threshold, knocking quietly twice on the doorjamb to announce herself.

Cade looked up from the papers on the desk. Coal-black eyes traveled over her then met hers. A smile tugged up the corners of his finely carved mouth. "Morning," he said, his rich resonant voice as caressing as spring's first temperate breeze. "You just getting up?"

"No, I've been up for quite a while," she answered, stepping farther into the small room. Her heart did its peculiar little acrobatic act, as it always did when she saw him, and the memory of the moments they had shared last night in his room did nothing to calm her disruptive physiological response to him. Simply looking at him made her feel more gloriously alive, as if all her senses had miraculously become more attuned to every stimulus. Cade made her feel good, and once again she was tempted not to leave Bermuda while he remained here. Yet she would. She had made the logical decision and couldn't back out now. She had to have some time alone in order to put these new tumultuous emotions stirring in her into proper perspective. Returning Cade's smile, she curved her hands around the edge of the desk and added, "I got up early . . . to pack, actually. I've decided to fly home today, and I just wanted to say good-bye."

Silently rising up from his chair, he stood, tall, imposing, magnificently attractive and virile in khaki trousers and a navy crew-neck sweater. He came around the desk to her, his expression indecipherable, his dark gaze intent upon her face. "What time are you leaving?" he asked.

Not "why are you going?" Not "don't go; stay the next two days with me at least." Simply "what time are you leaving?" His easy acceptance of her decision distressed her, but she masked her feelings effectively, arranging her features in perfectly composed lines as she glanced at her watch. "We'll be taking off about an hour and a half from now. Since the storm's finally moved on, I was able to get a seat on the eleven thirty-five flight to Atlanta."

"I'll drive you to the airport."

"Thank's for the offer, Cade, but I've already arranged for a taxi to pick me up in about twenty minutes." The curve of her brow rose questioningly. "When do you think you'll be leaving here?"

"I'd planned to wrap things up with Brad by the day after tomorrow at the latest," he said, waving a lean hand toward the papers on the desk. "After I've explained some final details of the financial plan I've charted out for him, I have to fly to New York for a few days before getting back to Atlanta."

"Well, I think it's just as well that I'll be getting back there today. Living the good life on a beautiful island could easily become a habit with me, I'm afraid," Jessica said wryly. "I've gotten very lazy since I've been here, and all this idleness may have spoiled me for work forever."

"I don't think so, since your eyes light up whenever you talk about the magazine," Cade replied, matching her wry tone. "You'll really be happy to get back to work. In fact, I imagine you'll go into your office tomorrow and spend most of this weekend there too."

"Well, not most. I may go to the office for a while Saturday," she conceded, smiling somewhat sheepishly. "I expect to find work waiting on my desk. Since Peg's been out ill, things have been hectic. And this really wasn't the most convenient time to take a vacation, but I really needed it because it had been well over a year since my last."

"And this one didn't turn out quite the way you expected," Cade said, surveying her face closely. "Did it, Jessica?"

"That may be an understatement," she murmured, pondering everything that had happened to her in the space of eight short days.

"Is that why you're going home?" he asked, stepping closer, lifting her chin with one finger. "Are you leaving because of what Brad did yesterday?"

Secretly pleased that he was interested enough to finally ask that question, she looked up at him, but was far too unsure of what he felt for her to even consider telling him *he* was the main reason she was leaving. And since Brad's behavior was partially responsible for her decision, she instead answered evasively, "He really has changed . . . much more than I would ever have imagined he could. He used to be so different. Now he almost seems like a totally different person to me."

"And do you think he'll ever change back and become that other person again?"

"I guess he might."

"You don't sound very sure."

"I can't be sure. I can only hope he will."

"Maybe he doesn't want to. He could be quite content to go on the way he is now, and if that's true, you're hoping for something that probably won't happen," Cade said softly, his hand slipping around her slender neck to curve light against her nape. "You can't regain the past, Jessica. You have to live with the way things are now."

"I know," she murmured, glancing at her watch again and breathing an inward sigh when she saw how quickly time with Cade passed. Although she felt it was wise to leave Bermuda now, she still longed to be with him, and those conflicting emotions battled within her as her wide blue eyes once more met his. She forced what she hoped was a convincing smile to her lips. "About time for my taxi to arrive. I'd better go watch for it. Good-bye, Cade, and thank you for showing me the island. You're a terrific tour guide, and I enjoyed going with you."

"My pleasure, Jessica. I'm only sorry you aren't going to wait until I could fly back to the States with you," he said, his low tone only half teasing despite the warm glow of amusement in his eyes. "Without me along, who are you going to get to hold your hand during takeoff and landing?"

"I never thought of that," she confessed, her smile widening. "I guess I'll just have to see if one of the flight attendants will hold it for me."

"And if none of them will?"

"I'll just have to shut my eyes and hang on to the armrests. It won't be the first time I've done that, I assure you," she said, surrendering to compulsion and stretching up on tiptoe to lightly

107

touch her lips to his right cheek before moving swiftly away from him. "I have to go now. Good-bye, Cade."

"Jessica, come here," he commanded gently, catching one slender hand in his, turning her back around as she turned away and drawing her slowly to him. Smiling lazily, he reached up to touch the flaxen arc of hair that grazed her temple. Then his strong arms were around her; his black piercing eyes were probing the lambent depths of hers as he lowered his dark head.

Laying her arms on his, Jessica closed her eyes as his lips descended, warm, firm, yet brushing the parted softness of hers more with tenderness than desire. When he released her without another word, she hesitated for a fleeting instant, then turned quickly and walked out of the study, unable to force herself to say good-bye again. She crossed the living room, increased her pace through the foyer, and opening the front door, stepped out onto the portico where her luggage awaited in a neat stack where she had left it.

Touching shaky fingers to her lips, taking a deep tremulous breath, she scanned the stretch of road winding along parallel to the house, hoping for a glimpse of an approaching taxi. Only a small truck puttered south, and after several moments she leaned against a white fluted pillar, staring across the lawn. Torn and battered palm branches lay scattered here and there upon the grass, and scarlet hibiscus petals littered the ground beneath beaten-down shrubs. The storm had come and gone and left its mark. And, to Jessica, it seemed the emotional storm she had been experiencing since meeting Cade had also left its mark on her, one that perhaps would prove indelible, even if she never saw him again after today . . . and that was a distinct possibility, one she had to face. Although Cade had mentioned he would return to Atlanta within a few days, he hadn't said a word about wanting to see her there. Maybe he had no desire to ever see her again. Maybe this was the end of it.

That mere thought created a burning constricting ache in Jessica's chest as she gazed beyond the bedraggled palms at nothing at all, wondering bleakly how she had allowed Cade to become so important to her in such a short time. But that didn't matter now. What had happened had happened. No matter how hard she tried, she could never look back and discover precisely why she had fallen in love with him.

CHAPTER SEVEN

Wednesday, six days after her return from Bermuda, Jessica searched through the various materials on her desk one more time, then gave up and beckoned her assistant, Lynn Bennett. "I could have sworn I saw the copy for January's issue sitting on this desk just this morning, but I can't find it now," she explained, thoughtfully tapping the eraser end of a pencil against her cheek. "I hope you know where it is."

"Sure do. I have it."

"Oh, good. For a minute there I was wondering if I had accidentally tossed it into the trash," Jessica joked. "Well, how does it look? It has been proofread, hasn't it? Any major problems we need to correct?"

Lynn shook her head. "Nothing drastic so far."

"Great. You finish going over it carefully; then I'll only have to give it a quick glance." Jessica patted a small stack of manuscripts. "I need to start editing these articles for the March and April issues anyway."

"Speaking of the March issue, Roy Campbell called this morning while you were meeting with Joe. He wanted me to tell you he'll probably have to submit his March article a little late," Lynn said, grimacing. "He hasn't been feeling well."

"Oh?" A concerned frown nicked Jessica's brow. "I hope it's nothing really serious?"

"No. He said he thought it was just a touch of the flu or something like that. He's beginning to feel better."

110

"Then I'll give him a call in a little while," Jessica said, jotting down a reminder to herself. "If he's only going to miss making his deadline by a couple of days, there shouldn't be much of a problem."

Nodding, Lynn started to walk away but stopped short and turned back around. "Oh, by the way, I wanted to remind you that we're giving that baby shower for Lorraine right after work tomorrow. Since you're so busy, would you like for me to pick up your gift for her? I wouldn't mind. I have to go shopping tonight anyway."

"Thanks, but that's all taken care of," Jessica told her, a sparkle of enthusiasm lighting her eyes. "I brought a beautiful little lamb's-wool sweater set back from Bermuda for Lorraine."

"You really loaded up on the loot while you were there, didn't you? I'm surprised they ever finished checking you through Customs," Lynn kidded, then touched fingertips just behind her ears, her smile suggestive. "And I've been meaning to tell you that the perfume you brought me is really dynamite. Jim says I'm utterly irresistible when I wear it."

Jessica grinned. "Well, I'm glad it's having that effect. I thought it was a lovely fragrance," she said, but her grin slowly faded to nonexistence as she recalled she had been with Cade when she purchased the perfume. And as that set off a series of memories of all the hours they had spent together, she scarcely noticed when Lynn left the office. Looking out her window at the Atlanta skyline, Jessica heaved a deep sigh. Although she had been home six days and had to assume Cade was also back in town, she still hadn't heard from him and was becoming more and more afraid that she never would. She had known it might turn out this way, but immediately after returning from Bermuda, she had had good reason to think he would soon contact her. After all, he had said he wanted her, and she, in turn, had responded to him in a way that must have made it fairly apparent that the desire was mutual. Almost from the beginning of her vacation she had preferred his company to Brad's, and although

111

she had tried not to make her growing affection for him appear too obvious, he could hardly have failed to notice that she enjoyed being with him. So if he never contacted her, it couldn't be because she had discouraged him. It would simply mean he hadn't been nearly as interested in her as she believed or he had simply tired of waiting for her to resolve her situation with Brad. And it was those thoughts that had become predominant during the past two days while she had waited and hoped for the phone to ring and for Cade's voice to speak to her from the other end. She had waited in vain, however, and the initial hope she had felt began fading fast.

Dragging her gaze from the window, she shook her head as if to reassemble her thoughts and rouse herself from her reverie. She uttered a little self-derisive curse beneath her breath. This wouldn't do. She couldn't continue to allow things as inconsequential as perfume to remind her of Cade. During the past two days she had managed to think about him less often, but still she hadn't reached the stage where she could banish all thoughts of him completely from her mind, at least while she was at work. Yet she would reach that stage eventually; she was determined. She was too proud to let a man who cared nothing about her monopolize her thoughts both night *and* day. The nights alone were bad enough.

Resolutely squaring her jaw, Jessica forced Cade from her mind temporarily and instead concentrated on the work at hand. Taking the first typewritten article off the stack of manuscripts on her desk, she sat back in her chair and began to read, pencil in hand.

She had just turned to the fourth page when the telephone rang, then rang again and again. Glancing across the hall and seeing that Lynn's closet-sized office was unoccupied, she sat up straight and reached toward the phone, picking up the receiver only a fraction of a second before she saw that Lynn had dashed back to her desk and was answering the call too. Their hellos were almost simultaneous, and Jessica was about to hang up when the male voice at the other end stilled her hand.

"Jess, is that you?"

It was Brad.

"Yes," she replied, dropping the pencil onto her desk and smiling across the hall at Lynn who immediately got off the line. Resting one elbow on her desk, chin in her cupped hand, she looked with some regret at the article she hadn't yet finished reading but asked with genuine interest, "How are you, Brad?"

"Fantastic," he came back exuberantly. "We're having a little celebration here. Shot two long difficult scenes this morning without a single retake. And, believe me, that's cause for celebration."

Obviously nothing had changed. Jessica smiled wryly. "Congratulations. And does that mean everything is going pretty smoothly?"

"It's absolutely phenomenal how it's all clicking together now. We can't seem to do anything wrong. Christie and I have about decided that storm we had was the turning point. Maybe it washed away some bad vibes or something. Before, we were running into so many setbacks and the producers were giving us a hard time, screaming at us to get back on schedule. But now, it's all going great. Like I told you, this movie's going to be a tremendous box office hit. I just feel it."

"I'm glad, Brad," Jessica said softly. "I'm looking forward to seeing it."

"And you'll be one of the first who does. You'll be at the opening with me," Brad declared. "So how are you doing? Did you have a nice flight? I've been planning to call you since Saturday, but every time I started to, something came up and I couldn't. Sorry, Jess."

"It's all right; I understand. And I'm fine. I had a very smooth flight home."

"And now you're back slaving away on that magazine again."

113

"I don't consider it 'slaving away.' I enjoy my work, and you know it."

"That's what you've told me," Brad responded blithely. "By the way, Christie wanted me to say hello for her."

Jessica smiled. "Tell her hello for me too."

"Hey, have you seen Cade yet? He left here a couple days after you."

"*Cade?*" Jessica repeated, her heart leaping up at the mere mention of his name. "No, uh . . . I haven't seen him, but that's not surprising. Atlanta's a big place. I don't expect to just run into him. Besides, he planned to fly to New York for a few days after he left Bermuda."

"He changed those plans. Flew back to Atlanta from here instead."

"I see." A solid heaviness settled in her chest, and she pressed one hand against her forehead briefly as perfectly dismal understanding engulfed her. Now she knew that Cade had been back in Atlanta for several days rather than only a couple, yet he still hadn't gotten in touch with her. Obviously, he didn't intend to. And the last of her remaining hopes died a painful death. She took a long, deep breath. "Well, even so, I haven't seen him. It's not likely we'll run into each other anyhow."

"I know, but I'm sure you'll be hearing from him soon. I asked him to take you out to dinner for me when he got back."

Jessica stiffened, humiliation and dismay darkening her widened eyes. "For heaven's sake, Brad," she said tersely, wondering at his lack of perception, although perhaps she shouldn't have. While she had been in Bermuda, Brad had been so enthralled by his new life-style he really hadn't appeared to notice how much time she spent with Cade. Shaking her head, which was beginning to ache throbbingly, Jessica tightened her fingers around the receiver as she muttered, "I wish you hadn't asked him to do that."

"Why not? Don't you like Cade?"

Don't you like Cade? Closing her eyes, Jessica moaned inwardly. Brad's question was so ridiculous it was almost funny. But she didn't feel at all like laughing. "Yes, I like Cade," she said dully instead. "It's just not necessary for you to arrange dinner dates for me. And didn't it ever occur to you that Cade might have things he'd rather do than take me out? You shouldn't have imposed on him by asking him to."

"He didn't act like he thought it was an imposition."

"Maybe not, but he is a busy man and I doubt I'll hear from him."

"Oh sure you will. He . . ."

"Brad, I can't talk much longer," Jessica interrupted gently, unwilling to discuss Cade further. "But I'm glad you called. It's great to hear that the filming's going so well."

"And that's the real reason I phoned—to tell you things are going so smoothly that we expect to wrap it up here by Monday," Brad announced almost expectantly. "You know what that means, don't you? It means I'll be seeing you very soon, and we'll spend the entire time I'm in Atlanta together. How's that sound? You're not still mad at me, are you, baby? I didn't like letting you leave Bermuda miffed at me like you were, but what else could I do? I couldn't just walk out in the middle of filming."

As Jessica breathed a silent sigh, her shoulders drooped a bit. "No, Brad, I'm not mad at you, but you're going to have to start thinking seriously about what I told you before I left Bermuda," she said firmly. "If you do, you'll realize everything I said makes sense."

"Oh ho, you *are* still mad or you wouldn't keep on talking this way," Brad taunted lightly, chuckling, obviously refusing once again to take her seriously. "Jess, baby, this is all a lot of nonsense, and I want you to stop worrying. Nothing's going to split us up."

"Brad, this isn't something we can discuss on the phone," Jessica murmured, running her fingers through her hair, wishing he would stop lying to himself and simply accept the truth. "We'll have to wait until you get here to talk all of it over again."

"Maybe. You'll probably realize before then that you're just making mountains out of molehills."

"No, Brad, I . . ." Her words broke off. She knew it was useless to try to reason with him at the moment and longed for the conversation to end. "I don't mean to be abrupt, but you know how it is when you call me at work—I don't have much time to talk, so unless there's something else you wanted to tell me . . ."

"No, that about does it, so if I don't get another chance to call you, love, I'll see you very soon."

"Soon," she echoed, then returned his lighthearted good-bye and was relieved when a click on the line signaled the broken connection. She hung up the phone and reached for the article she had been editing, but when she tried to start reading once more, she was unable to concentrate on the typed words. On edge, she strummed her fingers on the desk top, wishing Brad hadn't called, wishing he wouldn't go on being so unrealistic, and wishing most of all that he hadn't mentioned Cade. If he had been back in Atlanta four days and hadn't yet contacted her, it was highly unlikely he ever intended to. But it crossed her mind, then settled there, that perhaps she should be glad he hadn't called. Since he hadn't, he apparently hadn't allowed Brad to impose upon him, and she was grateful he at least didn't feel obligated to take her out to dinner. That very idea made her cringe and blush hot with humiliation. Much as she wanted to see Cade, she would rather never see him again if he only sought her out because Brad had asked him to.

"Oh damn," she muttered crossly, tired of the tedious turnings of her mind. Snatching up the manuscript one more time, she was determined to force herself to concentrate. Resolve lifted her chin as she mumbled, "Cade Hunter's obviously forgotten all about you, so you just forget about him."

And for a long while, through sheer willpower, she succeeded.

After dinner that evening Jessica took daffodil bulbs and a

trowel outside to the narrow plots of earth she had cleared on each side of the front steps of her small brick house in one of the older residential sections of Atlanta. After moving back some distance to get an overall view of the steps and the sprawling evergreen shrubs that flanked the front of the house, she decided to plant the bulbs in concentric circles. Visualizing how fresh and lovely they would look, yellow blossoms bobbing atop strong green stalks when they bloomed next spring, she dropped down onto her knees in the dirt and began digging.

It was a lovely evening, warm yet with a slight nip of autumn in the air. The huge fat globe of the sun sinking in the western sky shot its warm light through a band of clouds lacing the horizon, coloring them a fascinating shade of pinkish-peach, and a light breeze rustled through the flame-red drying leaves of the red maples that bordered Jessica's street. Next door, her neighbor was mowing his lawn, and the scent of freshly cut grass drifted toward her. Humming, she tucked the first of the bulbs into the ground, pressed it down to eliminate any air pocket beneath it, then covered it over with clay soil which she had earlier enriched with sand and humus. Reaching for a second bulb, she slipped the trowel into the earth again.

Gardening relaxed her. She had loved puttering about in a garden since the age of five, when her maternal grandmother had poured a few round radish seeds into her small hand and told her to drop them individually into the shallow furrow she had made in the dirt with the end of a hoe. When the green leaves had poked up about five days later, she was thrilled as only a five-year-old can be, and thus had begun a love of growing things that had never diminished, which was why she rented a house instead of an apartment. A yard was essential. There she could plant trees, flowers, shrubs, and also have a small plot of vegetables in back. Gardening filled her with serenity. She found a very basic sense of peace when she prepared the soil, planted the seeds and fledgling shoots, then tended them with loving hands until they reached strong healthy maturity, bursting with new life.

117

And even when the span of existence was brief, there was the promise of rebirth in another season. The cycle was never-ending, and a certain tranquility could be found in simply being involved in the regeneration year after year.

Humming still, Jessica planted one last bulb in the plot to the right side of the steps, then got up and moved to the left. In the setting sun, shadows lengthened and she worked a bit faster, wanting to finish before the darkening curtain of twilight descended around her. Lulled by the muffled roar of her neighbor's mower, concentrating totally on her task, she was unaware that she was no longer alone until a pair of black leather shoes suddenly stepped into her field of peripheral vision. Caught off guard, she gasped softly, and wide eyes darted up over long legs clad in navy trousers, lean hips, tapered waist, and a broad chest covered by a pale-blue-colored sweater up to a wonderfully familiar dark face.

"Cade," she said softly, her heart responding to the sight of him in a delirium of joyous rapid beats. Frozen on one knee, she was nearly transfixed by the dusky black eyes that met hers directly. "How did you know where . . ."

"You're in the phone book," he answered the question correctly, although her voice had trailed off before she finished asking it. Towering over her, he slid his hands into his pockets. "I tried to call earlier, but there was no answer. Working late?"

"A little. But I might have been out here when you called. I had a quick dinner as soon as I got home then rushed outside," she explained, managing to control the breathlessness that threatened to catch at her voice. With lissome grace she rose to her feet, the knees of her faded jeans smudged with dirt, the sleeves of her western shirt rolled up above her elbows. Pulling off her gardening gloves, she smiled up at him.

"Well, this is a surprise," she added. And it was. This afternoon she had nearly given up on ever seeing him again, but now here he was, wreaking havoc with her emotions, although he might not know it. With all the aplomb she could muster, she brushed the excess soil off her knees, glancing at the silver Jaguar sedan now parked at the curb. "I didn't even hear you drive up. My neighbor's mower drowns out all other sound."

"Since I had a meeting in this area anyway, I decided to swing by here and see if you'd gotten home yet," he said, his low-timbred voice as warm and dangerously caressing as always. "I didn't think you'd mind if I just dropped by."

"Of course I don't. I'm glad to see you," she said honestly, though carefully concealing exactly how glad she felt. Looking back down at the flower bed, she slipped the gloves on again. "Let me just plant these last three bulbs; it won't take a minute, then we'll go inside."

Nodding, Cade took a quick glance around while she knelt down once more and busily applied the trowel to the soft earth. "Nice place," he pronounced after a moment. "I like your house."

"A modest little bungalow but one with limitless potential—that's how the realty agent described it to me before she brought me out here," Jessica told him, smiling wryly. "Not that she had to hard sell me after I saw it. Even though it's tiny, it's affordable, and more important, I have a yard for flowers, shrubs, even a vegetable garden."

"And obviously a very green thumb," Cade added, admiring the banks of rose-colored daisy mums that bordered the flagstone walk to the front steps. "These are beautiful, Jessica."

"And they'll go on blooming until the first frost," she said with much enthusiasm while covering the final bulb. Getting up, trowel in one hand, she lightly dusted off the legs of her jeans with the other, then gestured toward the front door. "Please come in, Cade." Preceding him up the short flight of brick stairs and across the diminutive porch, she went inside, leading him into the living room, where she switched on the light.

"Ah, the botanical gardens outside aren't enough for you, I see," Cade commented, his slow smile teasing as he surveyed the abundant greenery. "You had to turn your home into a greenhouse too."

"Oh, don't exaggerate," she chided good-naturedly. "I don't have all that many plants in here. Besides, since I've been living by myself, it's seemed more important to have something alive and growing around me. You know what I mean. You must have plants in your house too. Most single people do."

"I have a few, but I also have a year-old Labrador retriever who thinks she owns me and never loses an opportunity to let me know she's very much alive. She demands a great deal of my attention."

"I think that's a talent most dogs are born with," Jessica said, smiling as she waved him toward a chair. "Sit down while I put this trowel and my gloves away. Then I'll get you a drink if you'd care for one."

"I wouldn't mind. Scotch is fine, if you have any."

"Coming right up," said Jessica on her way into the kitchen. "I'll get some ice."

Instead of sitting down, Cade followed. Leaning casually in the doorway between the hall and kitchen, he watched her deposit gloves and trowel in a small utility closet, wash her hands, then take an ice bucket out of a cabinet. In the glow of the overhead light, her hair shimmered pale gold, its soft smooth texture almost seeming to call out for his touch. But Cade remained where he was, his dark gaze following as she moved about the room and roaming over her slender shapely form. Because he had felt she needed some time alone after her departure from Bermuda, he had waited longer than he had wanted to before coming to see her. This evening, however, he had decided the wait had lasted long enough, and now that he was with her again, he was even more intrigued by her than he had been. He knew how responsive she could be, yet he also knew there was a certain reserve in her, a torrid inner passion she had never fully exhibited with him. And it was that complete abandoned response that he was ultimately seeking. Wanting to reach out and pull her into his arms, he straightened and started toward her.

Hearing him move, Jessica turned her head to give him a faint but genuine smile. "I'll just be another minute," she said, twisting the plastic ice tray and tumbling the crystalline cubes into the bucket. After setting a tumbler and a wineglass on the counter, she stretched up on tiptoe to reach for the bottle of Scotch on the top cabinet shelf but only succeeded in pushing it back beyond the grasp of her fingers. She sank back down on her heels. "Cade, would you mind getting that?"

After bringing the bottle down, he remained beside her as she dropped several ice cubes into the tumbler, poured in the Scotch, and mixed it with water. Sidestepping him, she opened the refrigerator and took out a bottle of chilled white wine, pouring some into a glass for herself. When she handed Cade his drink then picked up her own, he inclined his head toward the row of fat ripening tomatoes lined up on her windowsill.

"Homegrown, I presume," he said. "In your own garden."

"I've really had a bumper crop this year. The vines are still producing. I'll give you some to take home when you leave, and you have to accept them. It's one of the house rules here. Anyone who visits me goes home with tomatoes. Agreed?"

"Agreed. I wouldn't think of refusing anything you want to offer me."

"I bet you say that to all the girls," she retorted, responding to the glint of amusement in his black eyes by laughing softly up at him until suddenly everything changed between them, and the very air in the kitchen seemed charged with electricity. Laughter died in her throat the same instant the amused glint evolved into a warm glow of desire. When he took a step closer, her pulses began to thud in a wild erratic frenzy, and she moved back a step, maintaining some distance between them. The scene had altered too swiftly. And she wanted him to touch her too much, was afraid that her response would prove almost wanton if he did. After six days alone without him she needed a little time to once

121

again become accustomed to the devastating effect he always had on her. Playing for that time, she moved past him, heading toward the doorway. "Let's sit in the living room. It's much more comfortable in there."

It wasn't, actually. Seated on a floral-printed cushion of the airy rattan sofa a few moments later, Jessica sipped her wine and looked over the rim of the glass at Cade, who sat at the other end, seemingly relaxed, his long muscular legs stretched out. Yet, she had a strong feeling he wasn't nearly as relaxed as he seemed, and in that moment he reminded her of a powerful panther, capable of pouncing with lightning speed when she least expected it. *Which was a ridiculously fanciful notion to have.* Cade simply wasn't the pouncing type. He had much more finesse than that. Yet she *had* always suspected that there was a certain potential for ruthlessness in him, evidenced perhaps by his carved features and the straightforward self-confident glint in his obsidian-black eyes. He was strong-willed, purposeful. If he couldn't achieve an objective with finesse, was he capable of just taking what he wanted when he wanted it? Or was she simply being overimaginative? She couldn't be sure, despite the fact that he had never attempted to take from her anything she wasn't willing to give. He was passionate, yes, even demanding in his passion, but he seemed to know he could gain much more through his considerable powers of persuasion than he ever could through use of force. Still, he was something of an unknown quantity, and as she sat twirling the stem of her wineglass between her fingers, his dark narrowed gaze wandering over her was more than a little unnerving.

Aided by an intrinsic source of self-control, she managed an easy unperturbed smile and said conversationally, "I guess you've been very busy since you got back to town."

"Fairly," he answered, then took a small swallow of his drink. "I still had some work to do on Brad's investment portfolio, and I took on two new clients."

The curve of Jessica's brow rose. "Oh? But you told Christie

122

that you didn't have the time to take on any new clients right now."

"To tell the truth, Brad was right about the reason I said no to her," Cade stated without apology but with a hint of amusement in his low tone. "I wouldn't mind having Christie as a client. But I decided to pass when she mentioned making large contributions to her guru. He may be everything she thinks he is, but if he isn't . . . well, suffice it to say I'd rather have clients who want to contribute to more established charities, the ones that can prove donations are put to good use."

Grinning, Jessica nodded. "Can't say I blame you."

"And how about you? You said you worked late tonight, but have you been doing that since you got back from Bermuda?" Cade asked. "Or was there less work than you expected waiting for you?"

"Less than there could have been but certainly enough to keep me busy for the next few days catching up."

"Too busy to have dinner with me tomorrow night?" he inquired casually. "Or could you manage to set aside a little time for that?"

"It depends," she replied candidly, unable to forget her phone conversation with Brad. "Are you asking me to dinner because that's what you want to do or because Brad asked you to do it?"

"*Ah.* He told you about that?" Cade's eyes captured and held hers, searching the azure depths with dark piercing intensity. A half smile moved his hard mouth. "And what do you think my reason is, Jessica?"

"I think you're probably asking because you want to," she admitted, practically lost in his hynoptic gaze. "I doubt anyone can manipulate you, especially someone you don't especially like . . . like Brad."

"I don't dislike Brad, Jessica," Cade said, his tone sincere. "He can be very likable."

"But he isn't always, is he?"

"He's never been anything but pleasant to me."

"You're being evasive and very diplomatic, although it's perfectly obvious that you and Brad are as different as night and day."

"That doesn't necessarily mean I dislike him, and you know it. I don't have to respect his life-style to like him."

"I know he must often seem very shallow to you," Jessica murmured regretfully. "He wasn't always this way. If you could have known him before, you . . ."

"Yesterday's over. It's now that matters."

"I know that and I know how much he's changed. But, in a way, that can be explained. Brad's life has never been a very secure one. That's probably why it's so important to him now to try to fit in and gain everybody's approval."

"Why try to justify his behavior?" Cade asked brusquely, a barely perceptible tightness hardening his strong jaw. "That won't help make it different."

"I'm not trying to justify anything. I'm just trying to explain that Brad's past may have a great deal to do with the way he's reacting to sudden fame and fortune now. You said yourself that it's easy for some people to get swept up in all the glamor, and maybe Brad's just very susceptible. He grew up without parents, and I think we have to try to understand how that may have affected him."

"Many people have to grow up without parents, Jessica," Cade said, both his tone and expression gentling slightly. "I'm sure that did affect Brad; any child is affected in that situation. But if Brad could cope with that particular disadvantage a year ago, why would he suddenly be unable to cope with it now? You must know his childhood probably has almost nothing to do with the way he's changed recently. It's more likely he got a taste of life with the beautiful people and simply liked it. Supposedly, it's an easy taste to acquire."

"Obviously too easy," she murmured. "Ah well, it is his life. He has the right to live it the way he chooses. But later he might . . ."

"Enough about Brad. I didn't come here to talk about him," Cade interrupted firmly with a rather impatient flick of one wrist. "Now, how about dinner tomorrow night?"

"I accept," Jessica said, Brad forgotten as renewed excitement mounted in her. A faint smile graced her lips as she looked at Cade. "But what time did you have in mind? We're giving one of the women at the office a baby shower after work tomorrow, and I don't want to miss it. Would eight o'clock be all right with you? That'll give me time to come home, change, and meet you somewhere."

"I'll pick you up here at eight."

"Fine." Glancing at the tumbler he placed on the glass-topped table before them, she lifted her brows questioningly. "Could I freshen your drink for you now?"

"No, thanks. But you can come here," he commanded softly, catching her off guard once again as the arm he had draped over the back of the sofa moved down and his large warm hand curved around her slender neck. Exerting light persuasive pressure against her neck, he was urging her to him, and when she held back momentarily, his coal-black eyes issued an intriguing challenge as he shook his head. "Oh no, I let you escape in the kitchen earlier, but there's no escape for you now. Come here, Jessica."

Hot tingles shot up and down her spine when in one swift fluid motion he moved toward her and drew her toward him, bringing them together in the center of the sofa. Breathing quickly, she looked up at his lean tanned face, ready for his kiss now and knowing instinctively that he wasn't about to take no for an answer anyhow. And the fiery demanding glint in his eyes heightened her need to be close to him. In that moment she could almost feel the potent power of desire mounting in him, and it drew her, making her careless to the possible consequences, compelled by ages-old instinct. Love and passion intertwined and bonded together in her, never again to exist as separate entities. And in one soul-shattering instant as they looked at each other, she knew she would probably soon be eager to do anything he asked of her, simply to be able to share that loving passion with him. The realization both excited and disturbed her, evoking a feeling of vulnerability only he could unleash in her. In the sudden hushed silence of the room, while her hands floated up to rest on his broad chest and his fingertips swept lightly over her face, exploring every feature, she was nearly ready to risk everything just to remain near him.

"Jessica," he whispered, parting her softly curved lips with the stroking edge of one long finger. "My sweet Jessica."

"Oh Cade," she whispered back, trembling as his hand skimmed around her waist to the small of her back. "Why didn't you come sooner?"

A somewhat triumphant smile touched his hard mouth as he brushed a feathery wisp of sunny hair back from her right temple. "Why do you ask that?" he murmured, his gaze intent. "Have you missed me?"

"Yes," she confessed compulsively. "When Brad told me you . . ."

"You're going to forget about Brad," Cade growled roughly. "I'm going to make you forget about him once and for all."

If he only knew he had already done that. . . . But Jessica could hardly tell him the truth, and even if she had been willing to, he gave her no chance. Before she could do or say anything, he brought her close against him. Then both his arms went around her, hard-muscled and strong, and his mouth descended on hers, insistent yet incredibly gentle. At the first touch of his firm warm lips, Jessica was lost in a maelstrom of sensations that quickened deep within her and radiated outward. Suffused with wild warmth, she arched against him, clasping her hands together around his neck as he swiftly bore her down onto the cushions, his lithe body issuing its own unmistakable demands when he lowered himself beside her. Still kissing her, he turned her onto her side, unbuttoned her shirt, and slipped fingers beneath a bra strap, lifting it off her shoulder to drop down around her upper

126

arm. When his lips left hers, she made a soft disappointed sound and ran her hands feverishly beneath his sweater over the broad smooth expanse of his back. A breathless pleasured gasp escaped her as his mouth found the frantic pulsebeat in her throat then grazed her collarbone and climbed with the teasing lightness of fluttering butterfly wings up along the gentle slope of her shoulder. She drew her nails gently over his back, her entire body catching fire as his tongue traced erotic designs on satiny skin.

"Oh God, you smell delicious, taste delicious," he muttered huskily, his lips taking swift possession of hers again, long fingers tangling in her silken hair. "I could devour you."

At that moment she felt the same about him, unable to get close enough, unable to touch enough, unable to find satisfaction even in the lengthening deepening kisses they shared. A hard knee glided between her thighs, parting them, and she entangled her shapely legs with his, moving sinuously, delighting in the undeniable proof of aroused masculinity that surged rigidly against her. A shudder ran over Cade, and she wrapped her arms around him, tenderly catching his lower lip between her teeth, dancing tiny provocative nibbles over the sensuous curve of it.

With a low groan, Cade pulled away slightly and tilted her head back. "Look at me," he said coaxingly. "Open your eyes."

She did and encountered the hot smouldering embers of nearly intolerable desire in his. "Cade," she breathed, her fingertips seeking the hard nub of his nipple while his hand roamed over the swell of her breasts down to curve with warm pressuring demand over her firmly rounded buttocks.

"You know what I want," he whispered, imprisoning her gaze. "I want us to make love right here, right now and all night long. And I think that's what you want too."

She could never have said no to him, yet she couldn't say yes either, and saying nothing at all, simply looked at him torn between passion and a natural need to avoid what might ultimately cause her pain.

"God, Jessica, you're trying to run away from me again," he

uttered, his deep voice unusually strained. Releasing her, he lifted himself up easily to stand beside the sofa. "I think you're going to have to make up your mind soon because next time I may not let you get away. I'm only a man. You'd better remember that. I don't know how many more of these little episodes I can take."

Jessica reached out toward him. "Cade, I . . ."

"Tomorrow night at eight," he said and walked toward the front door, closing it quietly behind him.

CHAPTER EIGHT

The following evening, after dinner in a charming French restaurant on Peachtree Street, Jessica and Cade returned to his car. After she settled into the front seat, he closed her door, then went around to slide in beneath the steering wheel, inserting the key into the ignition. As she wrapped her mohair shawl more snugly around her to combat the chill nip in the autumn night air, he watched her.

"It's still early yet and my place isn't too far," he said, unbuttoning the coat of his charcoal-gray pinstriped suit. "We can spend the rest of the evening there in front of the fireplace in my den."

"Umm, a nice crackling fire. Sounds terrific," Jessica murmured agreeably, smiling at him as he switched on the engine and almost effortlessly swung the silver Jaguar away from the curb and out into the traffic. The soft city lights dappled the car's interior and cast a lilac hue over the skirt of Jessica's royal-blue silk dress.

As Cade turned onto Highway 20, heading east, she drew in a long breath and relaxed comfortably in the seat, happy and contented. Despite the unsatisfactory way last night had ended for both of them and the underlying sexual tension that was always there between them, their dinner together had been highly enjoyable. Conversation had been interesting and lively, and as always, Cade had been a witty, knowledgeable, and exciting companion, as willing to listen attentively to her opinions on various topics as he was to share his. Sometimes their respective opinions were widely different, but he never attempted to dismiss hers as if they were of no importance to him or anyone else. He cared about what she thought and showed it, and that respect for her as a person was one of the many reasons it had been so easy for her to fall in love with him.

And she certainly felt like a woman in love now, almost light-headed in the grip of a strange exhilarating joy. Basking in the warm inner glow Cade nearly always evoked in her, she gazed out at the ribbon of highway stretching out before them as they left the heart of the city far behind. Except for the muted swoosh of the tires and the soft uninterrupted music coming from the tape player, the night seemed to cocoon them in a magical quiet. Turning her head, she surveyed Cade's profile silhouetted in the lights of the dash, and when he apparently noticed her observing him and glanced with a smile in her direction, she smiled back.

"I didn't know you lived this far out of town," she commented as they passed the Covington interchange. "It must be nice out here, just a short distance away from Oconee National Forest."

"I like it. My grandmother's place was really out in the country, and I guess I developed a need for more breathing space than I could have living in town."

"You've mentioned your grandmother and your sister several times to me," Jessica said curiously. "But you've never told me anything about your parents."

"Unfortunately, I don't remember that much about either of them," he softly replied. "They both died by the time I was seven, within a year of each other, and my grandmother raised Barbara and me."

"Cade, I'm sorry. I wish you'd told me before," Jessica murmured, reaching over to briefly touch his shoulder, then bringing her hand back to rest in her lap as compassion and some guilt caught at her heart. "If I'd known, I wouldn't have . . . Oh hell, I feel really bad about this. It must have been painful for you every time I mentioned the fact that Brad had to grow up without parents. Why didn't you shut me up by telling me you did too?"

"Because my childhood has nothing to do with Brad's. People sometimes react quite differently to the same set of circumstances."

"Well yes, but . . ."

"I do think I understand Brad much better than you realize."

"I guess you do . . . in a way," Jessica conceded pensively, nibbling a fingernail. "But like you said: people react differently. And maybe, although you lost your parents too, you just grew up stronger than Brad. And he was an only child. At least you have your sister."

"Yes, I do," Cade agreed flatly, then added, "but Brad has you."

Had me, Jessica might have corrected but didn't because she realized what he had said was true. Brad did have her in a sense and always would, although no longer the way he imagined or expected her to belong to him. That had been irrevocably changed, yet she knew intuitively that he could always count on her—should he need her, she would be there to try to help him. There would always be a special place in her heart for him, although at that moment her heart was aching for Cade. In her mind's eye she could see him as a boy: missing his parents, feeling lost without them, perhaps trying valiantly not to show those feelings or let them beat him down. Scalding tears filled her eyes, and she tried to blink them back, then ducked her head, knowing he would hate to even suspect she was crying for the little boy he had been.

"I'm really sorry about your parents," she repeated after a moment, managing to maintain a clear steady voice. "So sorry it had to be that way for you and Barbara."

"Jessica, *honey,* you're so tender-hearted," Cade said, perceptively interpreting her feelings even though she had tried to hide them from him. Reaching for her left hand, he brought it over

131

to rest on his muscular thigh, covering it with his own, playing his thumb idly over her fingertips. For a second he glanced at her, gave her an indulgent smile, then turned his attention to the highway again as he left the interstate at the next exit and turned right. "But rest assured that Barbara and I were well taken care of and happy. Gran saw to that."

"She must be a wonderful woman. Would . . . you tell me more about her? About all I know now is that she lives in the country and makes fantastic peanut butter cookies."

Cade laughed softly. "That she does, but there's much more to her than that. For one thing, she doesn't fit that old stereotype of a grandmother. She's not round or rosy-cheeked with her hair done up in a bun. Gran's a rather statuesque woman with loosely curled salt-and-pepper hair framing a surprisingly unwrinkled face. She's very spry for her age and very outspoken, always ready to stand up and say what she thinks is right even if her stand doesn't happen to be popular. But then, she's always been that way. My grandfather died about five years after Barbara and I went to live with them, but I can remember him telling me how proud he was of her because she had the courage to stick to her convictions. Well, he could still be proud of her. She hasn't changed."

"She sounds like a beautiful person," Jessica said quietly, stroking her fingers lightly against his hard thigh. "A very strong woman."

Turning onto a narrow blacktopped secondary road that wound through the wooded, rolling Piedmont hills, Cade nodded. "Gran is strong-willed and would only take so much nonsense from Barbara and me. I can remember more than one rainy day when she and I would decide it would be tremendous fun to bicker incessantly, and Gran would finally send us out to the barn to do it. Of course, we'd stop as soon as we got out there. It's no fun for children to bicker unless they have an audience, and Gran knew that."

"Wise lady."

"Very wise indeed and very loving," Cade said, turning his head to look at Jessica again. In the dim light of the dash, his lean face was shadowed, his expression unreadable. "So you see, you have no reason to be upset. I didn't have a deprived childhood."

"I never imagined you did," she told him honestly. "But there must have been times when you really wanted your . . . when you were terribly lonely?"

"All of us are lonely sometimes. That's not a feeling exclusively reserved for those of us who are technically orphans. I'm sure you've had your lonely moments too."

"Yes," she admitted, but now wasn't one of them. As Cade lifted her hand to his mouth, grazing firm lips across her sensitized palm, she felt so much a part of him and experienced an unbelievably warm sense of belonging that filled her so completely that there was no room for loneliness to creep in. And that is part of what love is all about—finding that one person with whom life can be totally shared and made exquisitely complete.

An abiding love inundated Jessica while Cade brushed kisses of fire over the pulsebeat in her wrist. She curved her fingers against his face, lightly tracing his left cheek.

"It's a good thing we're almost at the house," he murmured, his warm breath caressing her skin. "If we weren't, I might be tempted to pull off to the side of the road and make love to you right here. And I don't think we'd be comfortable in these bucket seats."

"You have a one-track mind, Mr. Hunter," she chided laughingly, detecting the teasing note in his deep melodious voice. "You think of nothing besides lovemaking."

"Damn, you've guessed my secret," he countered, laughing also as his lips trailed across her palm one last time before he released her hand to place his on the gear shift between them.

Slowing the Jaguar, he turned onto an asphalt drive that followed a rise of a gently sloping hill into a copse of trees. Her interest highly piqued, Jessica sat up straighter and peered ahead. In the beam of the headlights a long sprawling house appeared, its cedar and stone exterior blending so complimentarily with the surrounding landscape that the structure seemed a natural part of the woods.

"Oh, I like this," she said as the car rolled into the circle drive in front of the house. When Cade braked to a stop, cut off the motor, and got out to come around and open her door, she accepted the hand he offered, then stepped out onto the asphalt, smiling up at him. "You just told me you had a place away from town. But this is so secluded it's more like a mini-estate. What are you? Some sort of country squire?"

"With less than four acres of land I don't qualify for the gentry," he replied wryly, slipping long lean fingers between hers to more firmly clasp her hand and draw her into the soft light cast by the wrought iron post lamp. He looked down at her. "But it's home and I'm happy here."

"How could you not be?" Looking all around, Jessica pointed to a clearing beyond the east end of the house. "Do you realize how big a garden you could have over there? You'd even have enough room for a nice patch of corn and maybe some . . ."

"I promise I'll let you plan a garden for that spot, but let's do it in the daytime, not tonight," Cade said, amusement edging his deep voice as he turned her toward the front door. "Right now, we'll go inside and start that fire I promised."

Before they could proceed more than a couple of steps along the stone walkway, a sudden commotion in the woods to the left of them caught her attention and brought her to a halt. Something in the shadows of the trees was scurrying through a carpet of rustling oak leaves, and before she could speculate aloud on what it might be and before Cade could tell her, a sleek golden Labrador burst out of the woods and bounded across the lawn. Her entire body awriggle, long legs prancing, she torpedoed straight for Cade, gutturally moaning a welcome while gamboling all around him. She wiggled ecstatically when he leaned down to stroke her head.

"Hello, girl," he murmured while removing two burrs from the animal's glossy coat. "I see you've been out in the fields carousing again."

"Oh, Cade, she's a lovely dog," Jessica said enthusiastically, bending down to scratch behind silken ears and receiving the rapid swish of a wagging tail on the stone walk as thanks. Turning her head, she grinned up at Cade. "And she's very sweet. I can hardly believe she's as demanding as you say she is."

His darkly slashed brows lifted sardonically while a fond smile tugged upward on the corners of his mouth. "You just don't know her well enough yet. Once she knows you really like her, she'll show you how much she expects to be pampered. She's a pro at using that sweet disposition of hers to get exactly what she wants."

"And what intelligent dog wouldn't? What's her name?"

"Georgia. Gran started calling her that when she was a puppy, and it stuck."

Watching as Cade opened the front door and Georgia slithered between his legs to rush into the house, Jessica laughed softly and stepped into the lighted entrance foyer with a wise nod of her head. "I'm beginning to see what you mean about her. She doesn't waste time waiting to be invited in, does she?"

After Cade took her shawl and put it down, neatly folded, on the deacon's bench beneath the mirror on the right wall, she glanced around. The interior of the house was as aesthetically pleasing as the exterior. The parquet floor was highly buffed, the patina of the rich dark wood as simply elegant as the cream walls hung with paintings accented by brightly splashed colors. Smiling her approval, she walked into the spacious den to the left when Cade indicated with a gesture that she should precede him. There was a huge stone fireplace located at the far end of the room and a rust and tan sofa along with the matching love seat to its left formed a right angle facing the hearth. A well-used and obviously comfortable brown leather chair to the right of the sofa also faced in the same direction. It was a cozy arrangement in what could have been a chilly, overlarge room. Between two large front windows, a built-in bookcase contained several small sculptures and local craft objects along with, naturally, many books. Heavy cut-glass decanters sat atop the oak lowboy to the right of the double-door entrance.

Her eye caught by the expanse of homespun draperies that covered much of the room's left wall, Jessica walked over and parted them slightly, discovering that they concealed double glass doors and a spectacular view of the woods beyond.

"What a wonderful place to live," she murmured, turning back to Cade, who stood in the center of the room, the sides of his coat flipped back, lean hands on narrow hips. She made a sweeping gesture. "To think you have such beautiful scenery right outside your windows *and* enough room for a huge garden too. I'm impressed."

"As you were meant to be, my dear," Cade responded, the wicked inflection in his deep voice as exaggerated as the lustful glint in the black eyes that wandered suggestively over her. "I brought you out to my secluded love nest for the sole purpose of seducing you with wine and soft music before a blazing fire. And I knew that when you recognized the gardening potential of that clearing, you wouldn't be able to resist me."

Jessica laughed. "My, you can sound villainous. You almost had me believing what you were saying was true."

"Maybe it is," he countered, his low tone disturbingly provocative. "How can you be so sure I didn't bring you out here strictly to seduce you?"

"I don't know. I guess I just trust you."

Comically, Cade threw up his hands. "The worst possible thing a woman can say to man. Now you've ruined all my plans. I can't take advantage of this situation when you stand there and tell me you trust me."

"Sorry. Better luck next time," she quipped, grinning as Georgia trotted into the den and plopped down in a sprawl on the plush area rug before the fireplace. "It wouldn't have worked out anyway. We're not alone, and I'm sure you wouldn't have wanted your dog to witness your treachery."

Casting a feigned baleful glance at Georgia, whose sleek head was already nodding as her eyes drifted shut, Cade motioned Jessica toward the sofa. "Sit down. Even if most of my plans have been ruined, we can still have a fire."

Fighting a smile, she tilted her head to one side. "Maybe you don't think it's worth going to all that trouble now?"

"No, no, it's all right. I promised you a fire," he said, still pretending to be tremendously disappointed. "And I always keep my promises."

"You see, that's one of the reasons I know I can trust you," she shot back, eliciting his slow lazy smile in response. She sat down on the sofa, watching as he shed his coat then stripped his tie out from beneath his crisp collar, tossing it over onto the leather chair. He undid his collar button, vest, and cuffs, rolling the sleeves of his white shirt up just below his elbows, exposing hard-muscled forearms. When he sank down onto his heels on the hearth, beginning to arrange wood chips and kindling on the grate, her blue eyes warmed with love as they roamed slowly over him.

His lighthearted banter had enhanced his attractiveness, a good sense of humor being a seductively appealing quality in any man. Jessica felt a fleeting desire to reach out and stroke her thumb across the faint laugh lines that crinkled the corners of his eyes. Yet she didn't, wanting to relish this opportunity to simply look at him to her heart's content. Taking in his clean-cut profile, the casual sweep of his thick dark hair, and the redolent power conveyed by his well-defined muscles, she could sense the core of inner strength in him, another of those seductively appealing qualities in a man.

Cade was so very different from Brad, and she was glad he seemed as happy as she was to spend a serene evening like this. Although she was certainly not antisocial and knew Cade wasn't either, there was much to be said for the quiet times two people could share together, and Brad, especially now that he had changed, would have been bored to tears sitting in front of a fire with no one except her to talk to. Both men grew up without parents, but it seemed to Jessica that was the only similarity between them. Cade had become a mature man, self-confident and caring, while recently Brad seemed to have reverted to some rather boring stage of adolescence, showing little consideration for others, always anxious to impress his "peer group," and buying all the required status symbols that came and went as the latest rage. To Jessica, it was saddening. Some of the like and respect she had felt for Brad all her life had faded. Although she could still love him in her way, it was a love entirely different from the kind of love she longed to give to Cade. That was a woman's love, all-consuming and all-exclusive. Yet, did Cade even want what she would so willingly give him? That was the question that too often repeated itself in her brain, and she could find no answer to it, not that an answer would have changed anything. She loved Cade whether or not he wanted her to.

Lost in thought, actually staring at Cade as he added small slender logs to the kindling on the grate, it took her a moment to rouse herself from her reverie when he turned his head to look at her. She produced a smile and spread her hands apologetically. "Sorry. Daydreaming, I guess."

"Why don't you bartend while I get this fire going," he suggested, inclining his head toward the lowboy across the room. "Over there."

"Light on the Scotch as usual?" she inquired, after getting up and going over to open the door of the low oak table. She took out an unopened bottle of Chivas Regal. "And over ice?"

He nodded. "You'll find chilled white wine in the refrigerator too."

"Oh, I think I'll just have a ginger ale."

"Little coward," he admonished softly from across the room, trying to suppress a slow smile but without succeeding when she

138

looked over at him, somewhat bewildered. He shook his head chidingly. "And you just finished saying you trust me."

"Oh, but I do. I simply had enough wine with dinner and prefer ginger ale now," she said, wrinkling her nose at him. "Where's the kitchen?"

"Down the hall to your left."

Ignoring his lingering grin, she left the room. When she returned some minutes later with ice and poured drinks for both of them, he had a small fire going and was sitting on the sofa, waiting for her to join him. Carrying two tumblers, she walked around the sofa and stopped short, biting back the burst of laughter that arose in her when she saw Georgia. On the rug, the dog had rolled over onto her back, her golden head thrown to one side, one amazingly long gangling leg pointing straight up.

"My Lord!" Jessica exclaimed softly, suppressed laughter dancing on her lips. "Do you think she's dead?"

Chuckling, Cade shook his head. "Just resting comfortably."

"How did she ever get herself into that position? She must be some kind of contortionist."

"Attribute it to the muscular flexibility of the very young."

"Muscular flexibility is one thing; this is something else. That dog must be made of rubber."

"She's worn herself out chasing rabbits she has very little chance of ever catching. Tired as she is, she could probably sleep in any position."

"Obviously," Jessica agreed, handing his glass to him, too fleetingly experiencing the tingling electric shock of excitement that charged through her when Cade's pleasantly rough fingertips grazed her own. Taking a throw pillow from the sofa, she placed it on the rug beside his feet and sat down upon it, slipping off her black leather pumps. Happily wriggling her toes, she sat back against the sofa and sipped her ginger ale while gazing at the fire blazing up to engulf the larger logs on the grate. The flames licked and swayed, first iridescent blue, then yellow-orange, then red, as the different kinds of kindling and wood chips crackled and were consumed. Warmth flowed across the smooth stone hearth, pleasantly toasty as it enfolded Jessica and Cade.

Sighing contentedly, she watched the dancing blaze and luxuriated in Cade's nearness. When he stretched out his legs, crossing his ankles, she put her glass on the table at the end of the sofa and turned sideways toward him, resting her arms on the edge of the cushion, her chin on her clasped hands. "Umm, this is nice," she murmured drowsily, a smile soft on her lips as she looked at him. "The perfect way to spend a chilly autumn evening."

Nodding agreement, Cade put his own glass aside and reached out to run his fingers through her shining hair, the heel of his hand rubbing slowly against the delicate curve of her jaw. The leaping flames were reflected in the depths of the dusky black eyes that wandered over her face as he unhurriedly sat up straight and leaned toward her.

When Cade blew on her hair, stirring wispy tendrils and tickling her scalp, delightful sensations scampered along Jessica's spine and her breath caught inaudibly in her throat with the quickening ripples of sensual elation that fluttered through her. She loved his touch and loved to touch him. Curving a hand over one strong taut thigh, she shifted herself slightly on the pillow and lifted her face, needing to see his.

A slow sensuous smile etched faint indentations in his cheeks beside his mouth as he looked deeply into her blue eyes. The ball of his thumb feathered back and forth across her softly curved lips again and again as he lowered his dark head with deliberate slowness, as if to make her wait for the kiss she so badly wanted. At last only his magnificent black eyes and carved features filled her vision, and her heart thundered in her ears. Her eyelids flickered shut as she raised her mouth to his. The taste of his warm lips on hers was more intoxicating than any wine could have been, and as a certain warming dizziness swirled through her head while weakening her limbs, she was glad for the support of his hands that lightly clasped her shoulders.

Their lingering kisses subtly altered, became more impassioned and more intoxicating for both of them. Feeling enslaved by Cade's mouth, tempting him with her own, Jessica skimmed her hand up his leg over the flat plane of his abdomen, undoing two buttons of his shirt, her caressing fingers seeking heated bare skin. Their lips met and parted time after time, coming together in each successive kiss with increasing urgency as if they hungered for each other. He played with her mouth and she was as playful with him, inflaming his senses with tiny nibbles, inviting all his passion by the ardor of her response to him. Large hands tightening on her shoulders, Cade tenderly caught the full curve of her lower lip between his teeth, tugging her mouth open to the tongue that tasted and explored the honeyed darkness within. And when the tip of her own tongue skittered seductively along the edge of his, the demanding pressure of his lips graduated with swift, awesome intensity.

"*Jessica,*" he groaned, his breath caressing her overheated skin as he scattered kisses across her cheek. Lifting her up onto her knees, he pulled her between his thighs, bringing her much closer to him. Steel-muscled arms enfolded her. A hand in her hair, cradling the back of her head, he tilted her face up, and his hard mouth swooped down with heady insistence to take marauding possession of hers again.

She swayed against him, her arms winding around his neck as his wandering hands molded the gentle curving of her hips. He buried his face in the scented thickness of her hair, then brushed it back behind her ear, seeking the tender lobe with tiny nibbling bites, his gently closing teeth ravishing the sweet morsel of flesh. Softly, she moaned. Shattering thrills cascaded through her, and her fingertips eagerly outlined the strained muscles of his shoulders and the tendons of his neck. The clamoring need to be much much closer to him flowered deep within and rushed to fill her entire being with longing. And when he bent his head and

141

pressed a burning kiss against the beginning swell of one breast, scorching her skin through the sheer, fine fabric of her dress, she trembled and caught his face between her hands.

Lowering himself onto the thick plush rug, Cade swept her against him so that she was half reclining across his thighs, her head resting in the crook of his supporting arm. For a long moment he simply looked down at her, his black gaze conveying hot passion tempered by an indescribable tenderness. He pushed a tousled crescent of hair back from her left cheek, sensitive fingertips lingering on the sensitized contours of her ear. When a tremulous sigh of pleasure parted her lips, a small disarming smile played over his.

Through the thick fringe of her lashes, she searched his beloved face, her azure eyes softly luminous and heavy-lidded with drowsy sensuality. She drew the flat of her hand in lazy circles over his shirtfront, able to detect the slight acceleration of his strong thudding heartbeat. Curving her fingers across his nape, she raised herself while drawing him down, seeking his mouth.

"Kiss me," she whispered, teasing his lips with hers, the resilient fullness of her breasts issuing an invitation as warm feminine flesh yielded warmly to the firmer expanse of his chest.

It was an invitation he couldn't refuse. "Sweet. You're so sweet," he uttered roughly, his arms tightening around her as their mouths met in a series of countless deepening rousing kisses. His hands roved over her, exploring, caressing, lining every shapely contour of her slim body as if he meant to consign every detail of her form to memory.

Reveling at his touch, adrift in a hazy cloud of loving desire, Jessica opened his shirt completely, baring his chest to the brush-strokes of her fingers and the gentle playful tugging of her nails catching fine dark hair. Evocative whispered endearments filled her ear, and she whispered her own enticing messages back, losing all remaining powers of reason, capable now of experiencing the most soul-wrenching womanly feelings. Yearning to be nearer still to him, she curled her thighs tightly against his right side and, lowering her head, lazily teased and tormented his nipple with her tongue and teeth.

Now, it was Cade who trembled as a violent shiver ran over him. *"Temptress!"* he muttered, his voice low, his tone urgent. "God, I want you."

Jessica breathed in sharply as she was suddenly borne down onto the rug, left to lie there gazing up at Cade as he knelt beside her to strip off his shirt. He tossed it aside, muscles rippling in his shoulders and arms and the glow of the fire bronzing his dark skin. Caught up in a need more intense and gripping than she had ever known, she reached out her hands to him, disappointed when he caught them both in one of his . . . but not disappointed for long.

Cade came down beside her, turning her toward him, reaching around her to lower the back zipper of her dress. With infinite gentleness he drew first one arm from its sleeve then the other and pulled the bodice down to drape round her narrow waist. He began to tug the dress even lower.

"Help me," he commanded softly.

And she did, lifting her hips just enough for him to slip the silk from beneath them. Even when he removed the dress completely and she was left in the briefest of undergarments and her lace-edged ecru slip, she felt no fear, only a spellbinding sense of inevitability. Tonight seemed meant to be, and she did love him, much more than she had ever loved anyone before. Extracting one hand from his, she skimmed it over his left shoulder, massaging, caressing, beckoning him to her with coaxing touches.

"Cade," she breathed, a hint of an inviting smile fleetingly trembling on her lips. And as he slowly, relentlessly, drew her to him, she very lightly raked the tips of her fingernails down along his arm, feeling his muscle contract in their wake. Then his heavy hand claimed her waist and hers glanced over his broad back as their lips melded together again in near-intimate devouring kisses that conveyed the fever rising in both of them.

Her mouth opened wider to the persuasive pressure of his, and it was as if her every nerve ending had come keenly alive to each stimulating kiss and touch and huskily spoken word. When Cade pressed her back down onto the rug and leaned over her, his tongue making erotic forays into the hollow at the base of her throat and over the fiercely drumming pulsebeat above, she held him nearer, quivering as wave after wave of piercing sensation rushed through her.

"Yes," she breathed. "Oh yes."

"You're a delight, such an irresistible delight." Raising his head, Cade gazed down at her, and when a prolonged sigh and movement across the room caused her eyes to widen and dart in that direction, he took her chin between thumb and forefinger and turned her face toward him again. "It's only Georgia turning over in her sleep. She hasn't proven to be a very effective witness to my treachery, has she?"

"Are you being treacherous, Cade?" she asked softly. "Maybe we can't call it that because I'm being too cooperative."

Smiling indulgently, he shook his head. "Not *too* cooperative. Perfectly cooperative. Do you mind very much that you are?"

Losing herself in the comforting warmth of his gaze, she smiled rather tentatively in response, answering his question without words.

"Jessica, are you sure this time?" he murmured unevenly, passion flaring hotly in his eyes. "I think you'd better be because I'm not sure I can let you go even if you decide you're not."

The intent in his deep voice made her heart seem to do a crazy little somersault against her breast, but she continued to look directly at him. "What are you telling me, Cade?" she inquired, lifting a hand to cup his jaw. "That maybe I trust you too much?"

"Jessica, I didn't bring you out here tonight determined to seduce you," he replied, a wealth of tenderness gentling his features. Then he smiled. "But I have to admit that when I'm with you, the thought of seduction is never far from mind."

"At least you're honest," she whispered, love for him dissipating all inhibitions and even uncertainty for the time being. Laying her hands over his shoulders, she urged him closer and voiced the words she had previously been unwilling to say. "Cade, I'm sure this time."

And as his arms came round her and she went into them most willingly, the thought that she might someday regret this night occurred to her for only an immeasurably brief instant. Then it was gone and nothing mattered except that moment and Cade and all the love she had to give to him.

CHAPTER NINE

Cade undressed her slowly and completely before the blazing fire. The glow from the flames which deepened the bronze tone of his skin glimmered pearlescently over the satin smooth surface of hers, and Cade's eyes traveled unhurriedly over her. Although she was undeniably lovely, she was not the prettiest woman he had ever seen, yet she possessed an inner loveliness that made her by far the most desirable he had ever known. And that faint aura of reserve that clung to her and that, during times like these, seemed almost to border on a certain shyness, simply intensified his already raging need to know her as intimately and completely as a man can know a woman. Holding a tight rein on nearly intolerable desires, he waited to touch her. His dark gaze drifted up from her lusciously curved body to meet hers, and although he half expected her to look away with some uncertainty, she surprised and delighted him with a softly sensuous smile.

"Jessica," he said roughly, watching the swift rise and fall of firm full rose-tipped breasts and feeling the involuntary flutter of muscles beneath the hand he lightly ran across her flat abdomen. When she languidly stepped her fingertips over his chest, clearly meaning to heighten his desire, he gave her a rakish smile, the expression of his features teasingly wicked as he captured slender fingers in his and raised them to his lips. Intelligent, perceptive black eyes imprisoned hers as he whispered, "You're an incredibly sexy lady. Did you know that?"

"I only know that you're an incredibly sexy man," she countered, visually exploring his face while his white even teeth nibbled the pad of her thumb then the mound of flesh at its base. The centralmost core of warmth inside her burst into flames, and it was as if fire ran through her veins, weakening her limbs and drugging her to the point of total relaxation. The vulnerability she felt as his intent gaze drifted over every inch of her nakedness became an erotic pleasure she had no will to resist. She liked him to look at her, liked the way he made her feel as he did, liked the sweet anticipation that rushed over her when she saw the promise of passion-to-come in his eyes. And she liked to look at him, was compelled to look at him, her bemused gaze fixed on the coppery smoothness of his skin, underlaid with subtly contouring muscle that conveyed power. Most of all she liked to touch him and did, stroking his lean sides, kneading and massaging his back while he placed a strand of lingering kisses upward along her inner arm, setting wildfires on highly sensitized skin.

His rousing lips skimmed the ball of her shoulder, and she moved closer and kissed him, her mouth sweet, warm, and opening invitingly to the dizzying responsive pressure of his hardening lips. His firm, fiery hands coursed over her, defining every curve and line of her bare body as if she were a mystery he was compelled to solve. His touch was gentle yet potently insistent, and she moved sinuously beneath it, the tip of her tongue tantalizing his. On fire for him, she brought his large hands up to her breasts, moaning softly when his strong fingers played expertly over the mounds of alluring soft flesh. Wrapping her arms around him, her own hands caressing his shoulders, back, and hips, she watched through half-closed eyes when he lowered his head and began tracing kisses over the creamy slopes of her breasts into the shadowed, scented hollow between. Jessica gasped softly with pleasure and felt the faint curving of his answering smile against her skin. Obviously intent on arousing her desire to its most feverish limit, he cupped her breasts in his hands, the balls of his thumbs moving lightly back and forth and round and round her nipples, immediately teasing them into erect nubbles, irresistible morsels that invited the touch of his lips.

Scarcely able to breathe, she cradled the back of his head in one hand, her fingers tangling compulsively in his thick vital hair when he lazily flicked his tongue over and around first one nipple then the other again and again until the piercing sensations rushing through her became almost too exquisitely keen to bear. Her free hand pressed into the small of his back, fingertips slipping beneath the waistband of his trousers, and when he took one firm aroused tip between his teeth, gently nibbling, pulsations as hot and stirring as electrical charges invaded her.

"Cade," she whispered breathlessly, crashing waves of quickening desire washing over her, making her feel that she was too swiftly spinning headlong out of control. Intuitively, she curled her fingers into his nape.

His lips loitered on her breasts, stenciling fiery patterns which she felt would forever remain to brand her skin. Her every soft sound, every movement of her body, and her every responsive touch on him seemed to incite him to more soul-searing caresses. He scattered kisses over one straining tumescent peak then closed his mouth round it, capturing the throbbing flesh between roof and tongue, tasting sweetness, possessing her with a slow drawing pressure that took her breath away completely for several heavenly seconds.

"Cade," she gasped, pleasure soaring to nearly intolerable levels in her. "You're . . . driving me crazy."

"But that's what I want, my sweet Jessica," he whispered relentlessly, lifting his head to look deeply into her sapphire eyes. "I want to make you as crazy for me as I am for you."

Then he sought the ivory fullness of her breasts again, his lips and teeth and tongue doing wonderfully sensual things to her, stoking the fires raging deep within her into white-hot flames. She felt helpless, at the mercy of a man who apparently meant to show her no mercy, who was expertly sweeping her up to the moment of complete surrender. So fast—everything seemed to be happening so fast, yet she could not prevent her hands from moving caressingly over him and when, finally, his mouth met hers again, she seemed to literally melt against him as strong arms enfolded her. The hard pressure of his questing lips was echoed throughout the length of his body, and ignited by the very virile essence of him, she held him tight, her own lips clinging to his.

A hand slipped between her raised knees, parting them easily. Forsaking her kisses, Cade moved to kneel between them, yet when he started to lower his dark head, she turned hers slowly from side to side on the thick rug.

"No," she whispered, but her breathless voice made the word sound more like yes. And when his lips feathered along her inner thighs, the tip of his tongue leisurely sketching her skin, she was lost. Her love for him and her swiftly rising need to give it became everything; in that moment, nothing else had meaning. Surrendering to herself and to him, she kneaded his broad shoulders, quivering with the invasive physical joy that accompanied each of his successive kisses.

"Jessica," he uttered unevenly, rising up to gaze at her. "I want to touch you all over."

A faint smile trembled on her lips. "And I want you to."

"Come to bed then," he said, rising lithely to his feet, dusky coal eyes aglint as he extended a hand to her. "Come to bed with me, Jessica, and I may never stop touching you."

Hoping right then that he never would, she placed her fingers against his palm without hesitation, allowing him to draw her up beside him and pick her up effortlessly in his arms. As he carried her from the den down a long corridor, she nuzzled her face against his neck, inhaling the faint hint of lime after-shave that mingled with the clean male scent of him. She felt half-dizzy, as if caught up in a glorious fantasy. Yet the arms holding her, the hard chest she lay against, were undeniably real, and with the mere thought of the closeness she was about to share with Cade, she was engulfed by a tidal wave of fierce emotion that made her

149

senses swim. As if through the hazy flashing scenes in a dream, she was being borne away toward an inevitable conclusion from which there could be no escape.

At the end of the corridor Cade carried her into his large bedroom. Lamplit, decorated in warm earthtones of sand, russet, and cinnamon brown, the room had its own stone fireplace and was furnished with antique mahogany pieces simply and elegantly designed. Jessica saw this in an instant. Then the surroundings were forgotten as Cade lowered her to her feet beside his wide bed. That feeling of utter vulnerability rushed over her again, seeming to draw all her body heat to the surface of her skin as he extended her arms out from her sides and simply looked at her for a breathtaking eternity of time. His black eyes devoured the gracefully sweeping lines of her slender curved body, wandering over lightly tanned limbs and shoulders and over ivory skin in places never kissed by the golden rays of the sun. Unaccustomed to such an intimate appraisal, Jessica stood immobile under his ravishing gaze, her heart fluttering wildly, her legs growing agonizingly weak. Yet even as she felt exposed and in danger, erotic thrills began skittering up and down her spine.

"You're so lovely," Cade said huskily at last.

His words, the sound of his voice spun their own golden threads into a hynoptic spell weaving itself around her, and she was trembling by the time he brought her hands to his belt. She unbuckled it, her fingers shaking slightly then fumbling at the button on the waistband of his trousers. With an indulgent half smile, he gently pushed her hands aside and completed the task himself, quickly stripping. Reaching behind her, he tossed back the bedcovers then swept her up in his arms to lie her down on the mattress. The smooth percale sheets cooled her overheated skin but only for an instant before renewed warmth suffused her while she gazed up at him towering beside the bed. Her gaze flickered over him, fascinated by his superbly fit, sun-browned body. A moment later, when her eyes met his, she moved over toward the center of the mattress, her hand issuing an invitation as she trailed it across the sheet beside her.

Cade came down next to her on the bed, shunning the sheet she started to draw up over both of them. His large hand covered hers, demanding with gentle pressure the release of the percale. She let it slip from her fingers into his, her heart skipping several beats when he unceremoniously tossed it down toward the foot of the bed again and shook his head.

"We don't need that and you won't be cold, I promise," he said softly, supported on one elbow beside her, stroking her hair. "Besides, I need to see all of you. You're exquisite, Jessica."

Smiling tremulously, she caught his wrist and drew his hand to her mouth, grazing tiny kisses across his palm. Emblazing passion flared in his jet eyes, and when he withdrew his hand from hers to turn her onto her side toward him, she moved pliantly beneath his masterful touch, running her fingers through his hair when his sought the curve of her hip. They lay looking at each other for several long moments, gazes locked, searching, and for her it was as if he were taking her very soul into his keeping. Loving him with every fiber of her being, she caressed the firm line of his jaw, and when a lean finger brushed coaxingly under her chin, she tilted her head back on the pillow, smiling a secret woman's smile when he bent down and kissed her neck.

"Oh Cade," she breathed, shivers of delight running over her as he nibbled gently on her skin. "You really enjoy making me crazy, don't you?"

"You know how I've been feeling for weeks. You've always made me crazy," he murmured, his warm breath drifting into her ear as he took the fleshy lobe between his teeth. "And you're still making me crazy right now."

"I'm trying my best," she teased, reveling in her ability to arouse him as she moved closer and skimmed her hands over his chest. Alive with sensual excitement when he responded by impelling her back flat onto the mattress, she rested shapely arms across his broad shoulders as he leaned over her.

"I want all night in my bed with you, Jessica," he whispered roughly, rubbing the edge of his thumb back and forth across her lips even after they parted with her swiftly indrawn breath. His scorching gaze roved over her, from the tips of her toes to the top of her head. "I want to touch every inch of you, kiss every inch of you, and I want you to touch and kiss me too."

"*Cade,*" she whispered back shakily, her own desire fueled by his words. Pulling him down toward her, raising up slightly, she brushed her lips ardently over his. "Oh yes, Cade, start now."

"Where? Here? And here?" he asked softly, spanning the peaks of her breasts with a brushstroking thumb and forefinger, a slow triumphant smile gentling his features as the tips rose hard and tight beneath his touch. His palm played in tormenting circles over one while his long fingers explored the texture and perfect round shape of the other, leisurely toying with her. When she lightly moaned, his mouth caught up the soft sound as his firm warm lips claimed hers. He trailed his fingers between her breasts over her flat midriff and abdomen and down, the heel of his hand pivoting too fleetingly over her promising feminine warmth.

The brevity of that near-intimate touch made it no less electric and no less arousing. The throbbing ache deep within her intensified, and as Cade's hand glided up to her waist, she came up swiftly into his arms, her own twining around him. The feel of his taut naked body enthralled her, and she arched against him as he held her hair aside and his lips sought her nape. His caressing breath wafting over such tender skin bedazzled her senses and frenzied her every nerve ending into heightened receptivity.

"Oh, kiss me," she gasped throatily into the hollow of his shoulder. "Kiss me now and never stop."

His response was swift and evocatively impassioned. "God, I want you," he groaned, lifting his head and tilting hers back until his lips hovered just above her own.

Murmuring satisfaction when his mouth descended on hers,

Jessica moved with fluid grace when he turned onto his back, taking her with him. Relaxing, her breasts straining against his chest, she cupped his lean face in her hands, playing the tip of her tongue over one corner of his mouth then the other, teasing him.

"Tormentor," he uttered, turning again, bringing her beneath him, one long muscular leg pinning both hers as he leaned above her, capturing and holding her gaze. A rather wicked gleam of amusement illuminated his black eyes. "I think I'll prove to you that two can play this game."

"But you've already done that," she protested laughingly. "You've been playing the game all evening."

"Oh no, I've been seducing you. Remember? That's very serious business, at least to me," he teased. "But if you want to play games for a while . . ."

"Cade, you devil, stop it." She almost giggled, twisting beneath him and trying to free herself from the hand that caught hold of both her wrists and pinned them down above her head on the pillow. Silent laughter shook her as she squirmed and pulled and, in the end, all her efforts to escape were futile. Finally, she was still, surrendering to his superior physical strength. Yet the mischievous glimmer remained in her eyes as they looked deeply into his. "All right, all right, you win. I concede."

"Too late. No concessions allowed. When you start a game, you have to finish it," he declared mercilessly. Holding her captive, not allowing her to touch him, he leaned down to fain deliberately tantalizing kisses over her neck and creamy shoulders. His lips loitered on her skin, his tongue tasting, his teeth nibbling, seeking the hollow at the base of her throat, the flesh that hardened over her collarbone, the inviting rounded curve of her breasts.

Jessica's breathing quickened, laughter giving way slowly to quiet sighs of delight as his marauding mouth explored her, grazing across her abdomen, feathering along her thighs, then returning to the slopes of her breasts once again. A tremor shook her, and when he lifted his head to look at her, her soft drowsy eyes met his, detecting the waning of amusement and the resurgence of hot desire in the mysterious black depths. As if spellbound, she couldn't avert her bemused gaze.

"Cade, I . . ."

"I think this is a game we both win," he said unevenly when her voice trailed off into silence. "Don't you?"

"Yes," she answered breathlessly. And when he suddenly released her hands, they floated down not to resist him but to caress him as she nodded. "Yes, I do."

"Jessica," he whispered, poised over her, his lithe body taut and dangerous with the tightly coiled sexual tension in him. "Tell me what you want."

She caught her lower lip between her teeth. "You know what I want."

"Tell me," he persisted softly. "Say it."

"Why? Because you won the game?"

Smiling enigmatically, he shook his head. "No. We both won the game. I just want to hear you tell me what it is you want now."

"*You,*" she confessed compulsively, love for him overpowering even pride, her fingers adoringly tracing his carved features. "I want you. I want you to touch me, kiss me . . . love me."

"Oh, I intend to," he promised, touching her face, brushing back her tousled hair. Lowering himself down beside her, he gathered her to him, murmuring into her ear, "I've been waiting for this night."

She had been too, all her life, and she gloried in every moment of it. Unhurried in his lovemaking, Cade patiently transported her from plateau to higher plateau of pleasure, each one more erotically keen than the one before it. He possessed her lips with such tender insistence that she ached for his kisses and returned them with an ardor that equaled his. His hands roamed over her, caressing her with fire, and she could not get enough of touching him, her fingers instinctively guided as she wonderingly explored him. Her shapely legs entangled with the long length of his, and as his body responded with potency against the tender skin of her abdomen, she found herself moving sinuously against him. And when his mouth commenced devastating forays, probing her legs, even the tips of her toes, then the flesh and bone structure of her back and the rounded swell of her hips, she burned with a fever only he could cool and turned over, her own mouth beginning to eagerly explore him.

A low groan rumbled up from deep in Cade's throat as she flicked her tongue over the erect nubs of his nipples. When her lips grazed lower, he softly, half teasingly, growled and turned her beneath him, pressing her down into the softness of the mattress while his mouth closed with moist pulling pressure around the rose-tipped rise of one breast then the other. Holding her fast, he played a hand over her breasts, and his lips, his teeth, and tongue teased in turn the delectable aroused crests.

"Oh yes, Cade, *yes*," she gasped softly, entangling her fingers tighter in his thick hair. "Never stop."

But he did. Yet even as his mouth came up to cover hers, a hand parted her thighs and desire, instead of abating, ignited in a searing column of fire. She made a soft moaning sound as his fingers sought her warmth, feathering against her, charting secret valleys and ridges, exploring her with such intimate questing caresses that she felt almost faint with pleasure. Cade's touch was exquisitely arousing, evoking fluttering sensations that rippled through her flesh. Her breathing became more shallow, more rapid. She grazed her nails down the center of Cade's back as the piercing sensations mounted in intensity. Her mouth seemed to meld with his.

"Jessica, you're so sweet," he said gruffly, plundering the honeyed lips that yielded eagerly to his. "So very sweet and warm and giving."

She was ready to give, needed to give everything of herself to him, but he waited to take what she offered so willingly. Obviously intent on preparing her body completely for the ultimate intimacy, he continued kissing her, caressing her, exploring every inch of her.

Jessica had never felt so alive and awakened and receptive to every stimulus. Her love for Cade and his tenderness toward her combined with his expert seduction of her senses to make her wild for him. Whispering his name again and again, she rubbed a silken smooth thigh slowly up and down between his, her heart leaping with joy at the depth of his response. As he made a low hoarse sound, his lips possessed hers more demandingly and he arched her closer to his hard powerful body. Her hands trailed down over him, beginning their own rousing exploration, touching everywhere, caressing him, enticing him.

And Cade was far from immune to her touch. With every breeze-light stroke of her fingers, his kisses became more impassioned, more insistent, though still tempered by a very real tenderness. At last, he buried his face in her hair, his lips moving over the delicate shell of one ear as he whispered, "I *want* you, all of you."

". . . want you too," she whispered back, pulses hammering in her temples. When he raised his head, her eyes flickered open. His dark well-loved face filled her vision. The broad shoulders bending over her blocked the lamplight; his cleanly chiseled features were shadowed, yet the expression in them was, for once, readable. Although the unfulfilled needs raging in him seemed to have tightened his strong jaw, there was a gentleness in his eyes and the set of his lips that made her love him so much that she felt nearly stunned by the extent of her feelings. Smiling softly, she lifted a hand to touch the dark hair that had fallen forward across his forehead.

His answering smile was warm, and he kissed her again, slowly, coaxingly, as if he wished to still any lingering apprehension. In truth, there was very little, and as his firm hands on her began to explore even more intimately, it was the ache inside her that could not be stilled. Returning his kisses, she pressed close against him, but that was not close enough to satisfy either her needs or his.

"Cade," she murmured, her soft sigh signaling total surrender.

He looked down at her. "Yes?"

"Yes," she breathed, slowly sliding her thighs apart in response to the subtle persuasive pressure exerted by his hand. Yet when Cade moved directly over her, she instinctively stiffened.

"Honey, don't go all tense on me," he coaxed, his deep voice nearly whispering. Kneeling between her parted legs, he bent down to brush a kiss across her lips. "Try to relax. I'll help you. I want this to be as good for you as it will be for me."

"Cade, I . . ."

"Don't talk; kiss me."

She did, her lips soft and warm on his. Then his mouth was seeking the fullness of her breasts and her abdomen, his tongue drawing circles around her navel until rising warmth allowed her to become pliant and yielding beneath him once again.

His hands held her waist and glided beneath her hips to arch her upward. His black eyes searched the dark blue depths of hers. His lips on hers muffled the sound of her swift intake of breath as he moved and their bodies merged.

Jessica pressed her nails into the muscles of his back then wrapped her arms more tightly around him as inner warmth slowly blossomed open to receive and welcome him. Patiently, tenderly, he immersed himself in her, and the emptiness she had previously felt ceased to exist, although the need for absolute completion was not yet assuaged. Yet as his lips caressed the soft shape of hers and his tongue opened her mouth while his kisses deepened and lingered, the sheer joy that came even with partial fulfillment almost brought tears to her eyes. Adoring him, she breathed a long tremulous sigh, lost in the exquisite filling ecstasy of his possession. Her hands stroked his broad back, and when he kissed the side of her neck then the hollow beneath, she nuzzled her cheek against his.

"Jessica, honey," he said, his tone hushed. "I . . ."

157

"Don't talk," she murmured, smiling as she gave his own words back to him. Gazing into his dark eyes, she recognized the desire in their depths and needed to see the fiery glint of unbridled passion again. Clasping her hands over the small of his back, she urged him nearer. "Don't talk, Cade; kiss me."

His mouth moved close above hers, but he allowed her to make that first contact of flesh against flesh which she soon did, parted lips catching the lower curve of his, brushing with maddening slowness back and forth as she kissed him many times before his self-control snapped. His firm taking lips came down on hers, lightly twisting their softness as he began to move within her.

"Yes," she gasped, moving with him, meeting each successive gently stroking thrust of his hard body with increasing eagerness.

"God, you're warm," he uttered, his breathing ragged. "So wonderfully warm."

"So . . . are you," she answered haltingly, joy consuming her as he whispered her name like an endearment.

Cade was an aggressive lover yet capable of indescribable patience and gentleness. He was demanding, evoking ardent responses from her which he so obviously needed, yet he elicited her full participation in their lovemaking with the utmost finesse. His mouth, his hands, his body conveyed a warmth that induced incredible pleasure in her, and she did respond with an abandon that was sometimes wanton. She couldn't give her love in spoken words but gave it generously nonetheless, holding little back.

Adrift in a realm of delight where only the two of them existed, they were borne upward together in a slowly swirling mist of shared pleasure, higher and higher, reaching for the heights. As increasingly keen sensations rushed hotly through her and those deep plunging flutters he created came closer and closer together, finally merging into a continuous piercing tide, she cried out softly and wrapped herself closer to him. With a sunburst of ecstasy that radiated undulating heat waves, completion came. And when she soared up to and over the rapturous finely honed pinnacle, she clung to Cade as he joined her there, no longer capable of gentleness, taking in full measure as much pleasure as he was giving.

Afterward, Cade pulled the top sheet up over both of them as they lay together, limbs entangled, sharing one pillow. Physically spent yet replete, she burrowed her head in the bowl of his shoulder and settled more comfortably in the arm that cradled her to him. Even now, with desire satisfied and her love for him expressed silently, she didn't want to stop touching him. A small hand moved languidly across his hair-roughened chest, fingers drawing lazy circles on his warm damp skin until he caught them in his and pressed them against his lips. When he nibbled each sensitized tip in turn, she tilted her head back to look up at him, a sleepy smile curving her mouth. The warm inner glow she felt was mirrored in luminous eyes. Her golden hair was gloriously tangled, and faint rose color tinted her cheeks.

Cade's dark eyes seemed to search over her every feature as he smiled back almost indulgently. "I wonder if you realize how beautifully wanton you look right now."

She laughed softly. "I guess I should. That's how I acted, isn't it? Did you mind?"

"Hardly," he murmured, chuckling. "To be more specific, you were certainly worth waiting for."

"So were you."

His gaze suddenly narrowed, surveying her more intently. "Jessica, I didn't . . ." he began, but the words broke off and he shook his head. Brushing her hair back from her face, he kissed her forehead. "You'll stay the night."

It was a statement rather than a question, but Jessica nibbled her bottom lip with some uncertainty. "Maybe I should go home now. I have to go in to the office tomorrow morning and . . ."

"I have to go in too."

"I know. That's what I mean. We both do."

159

"I want you to stay the night."

And really wanting that too, more than she could say, she at last nodded and drew him closer to touch her lips to his. "I'll stay then," she told him. "But I'll have to get back home early enough to change clothes before work. I can't walk into the office in a silk dress. I like to keep my personal life private, and that would be like raising a flag inscribed with the words: I Spent the Night with a Man."

"I see your point." Cade grinned. "I'll wake you early enough to get home and change clothes, I promise."

Smiling secretly at the knowledge that the man she loved would be awakening her the next morning, she snuggled closer against him, protesting softly when he got out of bed to switch off the lamp. But then he was back beside her again, and her eyelids began to flutter shut, closing completely after a few moments. Basking in the warm afterglow of both physical and emotional contentment, she drifted toward sleep.

It couldn't have been very much later when she found herself reluctantly struggling out of the depths of a wonderful dream. A small frown nicked her brow as she felt a soft touch on her forearm, then another, then the flutter of warm breath over her skin. Her eyes flew open. She gasped. Someone was hulking over her and it wasn't Cade; she knew that. He didn't hulk, and besides, he was sleeping peacefully next to her in the bed, one heavy arm flung possessively across her waist.

"Oh my God," she breathed inaudibly and started to prod him awake as she lay there stiff as a board, staring up at the threatening form that loomed over her. But, as she squinted and her befogged brain began to function more efficiently, she suddenly realized what she was seeing. This was no dangerous intruder. In fact, that very thought now struck her as hilariously funny and laughter bubbled up in her, causing her entire body to shake as she tried not to laugh aloud and disturb Cade. Her efforts, however, were to no avail. Soon she felt Cade stirring beside her, the muscular arm round her waist tightening to pull her to him.

"Jessica, honey, what's wrong?" he asked somberly, cupping her face in one hand. "You're not crying?"

"No. Why should I . . . *No.* I'm . . . laughing. It's so funny." She gestured toward the edge of the bed. "Look, you'll see."

Glancing that way, immediately seeing the hulking shape beside her, Cade shot up straight in the bed. "What the hell?" and reached back to switch on the lamp atop the table on his side. Then, low laughter rumbled up in him too as he shook his head disbelievingly.

Beside Jessica, lapping over the bed's edge, Georgia sat on her haunches, head hunkered down, silken ears drooping low, mournful brown eyes accusing as she observed them. She looked for all the world like she had been terribly ill-treated and wanted everyone to know how utterly dejected she was.

Jessica reached up to stroke her head. "I believe she's feeling very left out."

"That very well could be, but I'm afraid she's just going to have to live with that feeling," Cade declared, fighting laughter as he swung off the bed and strode toward the opened door, issuing a command for Georgia to follow.

Feigning total deafness, the dog plopped down on the bed, burrowing her soft nose between Jessica's arm and body, obviously attempting the old "ostrich with its head in the sand" trick. Unfortunately, it worked no better for her than it does for ostriches, and when Cade repeated the command, controlling the amusement in his voice this time, the dog lifted herself up, heaved a long heavy sigh, and moved slowly, at a snail's pace, off the bed.

"All right, girl, out you go," Cade said, leading Georgia out into the hall.

"You're not going to throw that poor sweet thing out into the cold cold night?" Jessica called after him. "Are you?"

"She'll survive," he called back wryly. "If she doesn't want to go back to chasing rabbits, she has her own door into the basement. Contrary to what she believes, she'll be fine."

"Quite the little actress, isn't she?" Jessica commented several minutes later when Cade returned, turned off the light, and got back in bed beside her. "Ever thought of getting her into television?"

"No one would hire her. Too melodramatic," he said, draping an arm around her waist, drawing her back against him, his long body curving close against hers. "I'm sorry she woke you. I should have remembered she was in the house and closed this door."

"Oh?" Jessica murmured, an unpleasant thought popping into her mind. "Then this has happened before?"

"Sure, many times," he replied matter-of-factly, causing tiny splintering pains in the very center of her chest until he qualified his quick answer. "Georgia hops on this bed, any bed, every chance she gets."

Jessica shook her head. "No, I meant has she ever come visiting, like she just did, when . . . someone else was here with you?"

After several moments of silence, Cade murmured against her ear. "Why do you want to know?"

"No special reason," she lied. "Just curious."

"Hmm. Well, the answer's no; this hasn't happened before. You're the first woman ever honored with an unexpected night visit from Georgia."

In the dark, Jessica smiled secretly, more relieved than perhaps she should have been. After all, his answer didn't necessarily mean there were no other women in his life. She was certain there had been others and maybe still were, yet intuition told her he wasn't seriously involved with anyone. Hopefully, intuition wasn't misleading her, but if it was . . . well, it was a little late to start fretting about him being involved with another woman now, considering what had happened. Tonight, she had committed herself with love to Cade, and at that moment she couldn't regret what she had done. Later, she might. But now, lying close to him, she couldn't find it in her heart to be sorry for simply giving love that had needed badly to be given. Content in the circle of his arm, warmed by the heat that emanated from him, she relaxed and closed her eyes.

CHAPTER TEN

Cade didn't have a chance to wake Jessica the next morning because she awoke before he did. Perhaps because she was accustomed to sleeping alone and unaccustomed to his bed, she opened her eyes early when the pale gray light of dawn came streaming through the loosely woven window curtains. Turning carefully beneath Cade's arm, not wanting to disturb him, she lay facing him, softly bemused blue eyes wandering over him. In sleep he looked somewhat younger, somewhat vulnerable, his angular features relaxed, his lips parted slightly as he breathed. The crescents of his thick black lashes lay over sun-browned skin, and a night's growth of beard shadowed his jaw.

Jessica lay very still, simply looking at him. The feel of his naked body against her bare skin was a joy, and the mere remembrance of the night they had shared caught at her breath. When the memories began to arouse desire, however, and she almost succumbed to the temptation to wake him up with kisses, she grinned ruefully to herself. Better get up. Much as she would have liked to spend all day right here with Cade, she had to go to work.

Slipping quietly from the bed, she found a terry robe in Cade's closet, tied it loosely around her, then padded out of the room and down the long hall. In the den she felt rather deliciously naughty having to gather up her clothes from the floor, especially considering how far from the area rug some of them had been tossed. A sensuous smile curved her lips as she picked up

164

even her shoes and returned to the bedroom, silently entering the bath adjoining it. After straightening her clothes and laying them out neatly, she wrapped a towel Turkish-style around her head and stepped into the shower.

For a minute or so she turned beneath the soft warm spray, then reached for the soap, rubbing it briskly between her hands to work up a rich foamy lather. Humming, she started lathering her legs and arms, but her hands stilled, her eyes widened, and her humming faded into silence when the glass shower door suddenly opened. His bronze body bare, Cade stood outside, coal-black eyes traveling with disturbing slowness over her. Caught off guard by his unexpected appearance, she struggled to swallow, abruptly self-conscious of her own nakedness despite all that had happened last night between them. Her hands moved uncertainly.

"Cade, I . . ."

"Jessica, you're actually blushing a little," he interrupted her softly with an indulgent half smile as he stepped into the shower enclosure with her and closed the door. Moving beneath the spray, close to her, he laid his hands on her shoulders while the water cascaded gently over both of them. "I never would have imagined you could still feel shy with me, after last night."

"I'm not . . . shy," she murmured, trying to slow her silly heart's trip-hammering beat and trying not to smile back at him as she shook her head. "Cade, this is crazy. We can't take a shower together now. You know what will happen if . . ."

"Indeed, I do. That's why I'm joining you," he stated with an unabashed grin, brushing his thumbs along the sides of her neck. "When I woke up and found you gone, then heard the shower running, I couldn't resist coming in here with you."

"You'll just have to resist," she argued though without much real conviction. "We both have to go in to work today, so we really don't have time for . . . this."

"We have plenty of time. For this and this and this," he countered, lowering his head to kiss her shoulders, the curve of

her breasts, and the shallow hollow of her navel. "It's still ve
early, Jessica."

When he straightened and his hands encircled her waist, s
pressed hers against his chest. "It is early but . . . I can't go
to the office so tired that I fall asleep at my desk."

His dark brows lifted; amusement lighted his eyes. "Sure
you're not saying that I exhaust you?"

"Of course not. It's just that we didn't get to bed until late l
night."

"But that's not true," he said, his smile lazily wicked. "Actu
ly, we went to bed very early."

"But not to sleep."

"No. And sleep is the last thing on my mind right now to

"You're incorrigible," she chided halfheartedly, still fight
a smile and dropping her hands away from his chest when
realized her fingers had automatically begun stroking him
wish you'd be serious about this."

"Oh, but I am," he vowed, backing her up against the t
wall, placing a hand on either side of her. "I'm being
serious."

"No, you're . . ."

He halted her words with a slow simmering kiss that co
her lips apart, then ended.

Shaken, she looked up at him. "Cade," she began breathle
"This is crazy, so cra—"

He interrupted her with another slow kiss, one that ling
long enough for her lips to begin moving beneath his befo
broke it off.

"*Crazy,*" she whispered, her voice weakening.

Cade kissed her again.

"Crazy, crazy, crazy," she muttered before her warm pa
lips touched his again and again. Defeated, warmth sprea
through her, she rubbed her hands over his chest, and tiltin
head back, gazed up at him. "You're a corrupting influen
hope you know that."

There was not one whit of guilt in his answering smile. "Not corrupting, surely? Don't you think I'm just helping you to learn how to relax and live life to the fullest?"

"And go in late to work in the process."

"Does it matter just this once? I doubt you've ever gone in late before. One time isn't going to be the end of the world."

"No, but . . ."

"If I am 'corrupting' you, it's only because you don't give me much choice," he went on, ignoring her protest, cupping her chin in one hand. "You know how much I want you."

His piercing black eyes seemed to impale the softness of hers, and suddenly a look of intimate understanding passed between them. She moved into his arms, and if he was seducing her, he was either doing a very effective job of it or she was making it very easy for him. Whether it was either way or both, Jessica couldn't really care at the moment. All that mattered was Cade, the love she felt, and being close to him. Wrapping her arms around his neck, she relaxed against his trim virile body as the water splashed on his shoulders and ran in rivulets between them. He kissed her shimmering damp shoulders, the length of her neck, and the line of her jaw. When her lips sought the touch of his, he drew her close, arching her against him as he kissed her many times, encouraged by her responsiveness until at last his tongue opened her mouth, grazing her inner cheek, tasting all her warmth.

Trembling with desire, needing to experience last night's ecstasy again, Jessica allowed her hands to drift down and curve over his hips, and if he had taken her then and there with the water rushing over them, she could have responded uninhibitedly.

But he didn't. Moving her beyond the reach of the spray, he took up the soap and with unhurried lingering strokes began to cover her body with fresh-scented lather. His hands glided over her shoulders, down her slim straight back, and over her hips. He spread the soapy foam around and across her midriff and abdomen then up to her perfectly rounded breasts. His fingers lingered on taut full flesh, tracing seductive patterns in the frothy layer of soap on the rising slopes, round and round, up to the instantly aroused peaks his thumbs began to play with.

His touch, the mere sight of him so close to her inflamed her senses. Her eyes swept over his powerful bronzed body, taking in every detail of his overt masculinity. A soft breathless sound broke from her when he gently squeezed one erect nipple, and her hands swept eagerly down his arms, her fingertips enamored of his muscular contours. Her wandering gaze drifted up to meet his.

"Cade," she murmured.

"You're so lovely," he said huskily, his mouth descending onto hers, tenderly seeking, evocatively insistent.

A moment later as he bent down to cream her long shapely legs with soapy lather, Jessica stroked a hand over his damp dark hair while one of his eased upward between her thighs. He touched her everywhere, his fingers lightly caressing most-secret places, making her ache for him as she had ached last night. Breathing quickly, Jessica entwined her fingers in his hair until he handed the soap to her, spoken words unnecessary between them.

Ministering to him became its own arousing experience. Her hands found delight in his broad shoulders, back, and chest. Crisp dark hair tickled her palms as she lathered the length of his long legs upward past his thighs.

"Jessica, come here," he groaned, hard hands clasping her waist to bring her up and fast against him, then skimming possessively over her back as he whispered against her mouth. "You feel like the finest warm satin. I love to touch you."

"I love to touch you too." *Because I love you,* her heart cried out, but uncertainty locked those words deep inside her. And she could only hope she could voice them at some future time when she would know that what he felt for her was as deep and lasting as her feelings for him. Until that time, if ever it came, she would give her love in the only way she could.

"Come back to bed with me," he coaxed, his breath swirling warm into her left ear while his arms tightened around her. "This is delightful, but it's just not enough for me. I want much much more."

As did she. Her heart was ruling her head, and the physical demands her body was exerting had everything to do with what was in her heart. Where Cade was concerned she seemed to lose all strength of will, but it didn't matter. Nothing seemed more important than surrendering to her own inner demands and to the ones he made.

"Yes, take me to bed, Cade," she whispered falteringly, overcome by emotion and sheer unadulterated love. "That's what I want."

And when he guided her beneath the misty shower spray, sluicing water over every inch of her to rinse the soap away as she did the same for him, Cade plied her with ever-deepening kisses that literally stole her breath away. After turning off the faucets, he stepped from the shower, holding her hand as she followed. Despite the steamy fog that veiled the bathroom, she shivered slightly, and he enfolded her in a plush russet towel he brought down from the shelf of the bath closet.

"Better?" he inquired quietly, tucking one end beneath the edge over her left breast. "Warmer now?"

"Very warm," she confessed.

"You'll be even warmer soon," he promised, watching her deft hands as she draped another towel around his waist. When she finished tucking it securely about him, he opened the door, lifted her up in his arms with little effort, and carried her across his room to his wide bed. Lowering her down onto the mattress, he sat on the edge beside her, using a corner of her towel to blot-dry the droplets of water remaining on her shoulders and neck. Leaning down, he lightly kissed her lips.

"Don't go away," he murmured, then got up and walked back

to the adjoining bath. When he returned to her a few moments later, a bottle of unscented skin lotion in his hands, he moved onto the bed astride her, smiling as he slowly peeled the towel away from her languid body.

Jessica didn't protest when he turned her over onto her stomach and began massaging her back. As he applied the light lotion to her skin, she could almost feel it soak into her pores and a wonderfully relaxing warmth brought a glowing tingle to her entire body. Acquiescent, attuned to every stroking movement of Cade's hands, she closed her eyes and reveled in the sensations he was creating in her. There wasn't an inch of her he didn't touch, and an uncontrollable inferno raged through her. Yet, long after he had turned her over onto her back again and continued his rousing massage, she wanted, needed, to pleasure him. When he put the lotion on the bedside table and lay down next to her, she reached for the bottle, tilting her head questioningly as he stilled her hand.

"No?"

"Next time," he said softly, easing the bottle from her fingers, replacing it on the table, then pulling her to him. "How about tonight? Are you busy?"

She shook her head, happiness welling up in her. At least she meant more to him than just a one-night stand. She had prayed she did but hadn't felt positively sure of that until now. Hope burgeoned up in her as she lay gazing at him, seeing some affection for her in his eyes and feeling it in his tender touch. For the moment it was enough for her, that and remaining close to him. She feathered a fingertip along the faintly etched creases beside his mouth. "No. I'm not busy tonight."

"You won't decide you should work late?"

"On a Friday? Never, unless absolutely necessary."

"Dinner, then?"

"At my house this time, all right?" She smiled. "I can promise you something special."

"Oh, I know that," he murmured, a teasing grin moving his mouth. "You little vixen."

"I didn't mean it that way," she protested primly, pretending shock at his innuendo. "I meant something special for dinner. Like lemon sole, maybe."

"Sounds delicious . . . but not as delicious as you," he countered, a hand descending on one shoulder to press her flat down into the softness of the mattress. His thumb lifted her chin, exposing the slender length of her neck to a strand of hot nipping kisses before he raised his head again to look down at her. His grin had faded. His gaze conveyed an unmistakable passionate intent as he lightly pressed his thumb against her chin, parting her lips. "I still want you so badly. Good as last night was, I want you now as much or more than I did before."

"Show me," she invited in a hushed whisper, arms floating upward to encircle his shoulders, her mouth seeking the flexed contours of his chest. The tip of her tongue flicked over his warm, tawny skin. "Show me. Hold me, Cade. Love me now."

"Yes. I'm going to. I may never let you out of this bed," he warned softly, his knowing hands beginning to journey over the curves and planes of her smooth bare body.

When the mouth that had taken swift possession of hers strayed downward to follow the fiery trail his hands had blazed, desire burned out of control in Jessica and she moved voluptuously against him, heightening his passion and thereby her own.

It became a time out of time when the seconds, minutes, even hours, lost all meaning, and much later, when fulfillment embraced both of them, Jessica was too captivated by sheer ecstasy and love to even imagine that she might live to regret giving herself irrevocably to him.

Early Saturday evening Jessica finished dressing for dinner out with Cade. Standing before the full-length mirror in her bedroom, she surveyed the hemline of her ivory-colored square-necked dress, then stepped closer to the glass to examine her face. She wrinkled her nose at her reflection when it crossed her mind that she even looked somewhat different now that she was intimately involved with Cade. Surely that sort of fanciful notion was the result of an overactive imagination. Or was it? Scrutinizing her features more closely, she did seem to detect a subtle difference in her mouth, as if the shape of it had become more sensuously soft, and there was also a dreamy luminosity in her eyes that hadn't been so noticeable only two days ago.

"You *are* love-sick," she told herself, then shrugged. Of course she was. It was only natural for her to be after spending two breathtaking nights with Cade. She had loved him before, but what she felt now defied description. During the past two days she had begun to understand the phrase "walking on air" because she sometimes felt that was precisely what she was doing. Being with him Thursday night at his house and last night here at hers had left her somewhat giddy, and she was enjoying every minute of it.

Smiling, excitement dancing in her eyes, she executed a pirouette before the mirror, watching her softly shirred skirt twirl prettily around her legs. As wonderfully dizzy as she felt already, she halted after two complete turns and glanced at her watch. She had gotten dressed too early. Cade wasn't coming until eight, another hour away, but she had jumped the gun simply because she had been missing him since he had left her this morning to attend to business. Luckily, she had brought work home from the office, which had kept her occupied most of the day, but now it was done and she had the next sixty minutes to kill.

Never one to be at a loss for something to do, she went into the living room and picked up the historical novel she was currently reading. Curling up at the end of the sofa, she opened the book, scanned the page for her place, and became immediately engrossed. For the next several minutes the Revolutionary War raged through printed pages, but when someone suddenly

172

knocked on Jessica's front door, the war was forgotten, the heroine and hero were forgotten, and she closed the book with a bright smile. Cade had come early.

Smoothing her skirt, touching her fluffy hair, she walked across the room, unlocked the door, and immediately opened it, but as she did, her smile froze on her face.

"Jess, baby, surprise," Brad said, flashing her a smile as he strolled across the threshold and lifted her off her feet to swing her once around. Then putting her back down, he stood before her, beaming. "Yeah, you're surprised all right. I knew you would be."

"Surprised" was hardly the word for it. "Distressed" more aptly described how she felt. During the past two days especially, she had scarcely given Brad a thought, except to remember vaguely he was due in Atlanta Monday, and that had made it easy for her to postpone thinking about exactly what she wanted to say to him about the two of them. But now he was here, and Cade would soon be arriving. . . . For two or three seconds that seemed to last much longer, Jessica simply stared at Brad, but finally she took a deep breath and made her mind work. She could handle this situation.

"Brad, what . . . I mean, yes, I am surprised," she said at last, smiling rather wanly. "I thought you'd be here Monday."

"That's what you were supposed to think," he declared, rocking back on the heels of his Gucci loafers. "I just told you that so you'd be surprised when I flew in today instead."

"Oh. I see," she murmured, wishing he had told the truth in the first place so she could have been better prepared for this. But he hadn't and that was that. She moved one hand slightly. "Well, you've obviously finished filming."

"Wrapped up my last scene today."

"And Christie?"

"She finished too. But hey, don't I get a kiss?" Brad asked, his smile still flashing while he threw up both hands then reached

173

out to pull her to him. After kissing her, he led her by one hand to the sofa. "Let's sit down. I want to talk to you."

"Good, because I want to talk to you too," she said quietly, poised on the edge of a cushion. "Brad, I . . ."

"Hey, relax," he cut in lightheartedly, clasping her shoulders to move her back on the sofa. "I think you'd better have something behind you because I have another surprise."

"Another . . . surprise?"

"It's fantastic news. You'll love it," he declared enthusiastically, putting his arm round her. "I've rearranged my schedule, Jess, and I have the next month free, and I mean completely free. You and I will be able to spend every minute of it together. We . . ."

"But, Brad, I . . ."

"I've decided we'll take off for the Caribbean, maybe island-hop instead of staying in one place. We'll lounge around in the sun, soaking up the rays, just the two of us. Now, how does that sound? Terrific, huh?"

Jessica looked at him, dismayed, realizing he hadn't even begun to think this idea out logically, and that boded ill for the rest of the discussion she must have with him. Dreading the next few minutes immensely, she shook her head. "How could I possibly be away from work for a whole month even if I wan—"

"You quit your job, that's how," he replied much too carelessly. "You can do that, Jess. I've told you I certainly make enough money to take care of you."

Stiffening, Jessica sighed impatiently. Brad wasn't just being unreasonable now; he was being impossible, and she could already see that talking seriously with him tonight was going to be no easy accomplishment. Slipping from beneath his arm, she rose to her feet. "Excuse me just for a minute," she said. "I'll be right back."

Smiling weakly when Brad nodded, she walked across the living room into the hall and down to her bedroom, closing the door behind her. She had hoped she could finish talking to Brad before eight o'clock, but of course that had been wishful thinking in the extreme. Much as she longed to see Cade as soon as possible, she knew now that she was going to have to call and ask him to come by a couple of hours later. He was the one she wanted to be with, yet it was her responsibility to make her feelings perfectly clear to Brad. The break between them must be clean and quick, and she must make it right now, tonight.

Sinking down on the edge of her bed, she reached for the phone after finding Cade's office number in the book. On the eighth ring she started to hang up, thinking Cade must be at home or on his way to see her, but suddenly he answered.

"Oh hi, Cade. It's Jessica," she began hastily. "I'm sorry but something's come up here and . . ."

"Here too, as a matter of fact. I was about to call you," he announced. "I've gotten bogged down here with something unexpected that must be straightened out right away, and I'll be tied up for several hours. I won't be able to make it tonight. Sorry."

"Oh," she murmured, adding *hell* under her breath. Now there was no use asking him if he could come to see her about ten. He had already ruled that possibility out, so instead of having to wait to see him, she wasn't going to see him at all. With a rueful quirk of the lips, she pushed her disappointment aside. "I'm sorry too."

"It's an unfortunate situation," Cade agreed, then asked her to wait as he spoke to someone in the office with him. He came back on the line. "Listen, I called Pete in to help me work on this, and I need to explain everything to him. I'll call you later."

"Sure. Okay. Bye," Jessica said hurriedly and hung up, letting him get back to his emergency. After replacing the phone on the bedside table, she stood, sighing. This evening wasn't turning out the way she had imagined, and disappointing as it already was, it wasn't over yet, not by a long shot. She still had to contend with Brad. Squaring her shoulders resolutely, she returned to the living room.

"Brad, listen to me," she said earnestly, rejoining him on the sofa. "We really do have to talk."

"About our trip?"

"There isn't going to be a trip, and you have to know that."

"Don't give up so easily, Jess," he persisted. "Oh, I know you won't quit that job of yours, but you can probably talk them into giving you a leave of absence. If you want, I'll talk to your boss myself."

"Brad," she repeated more emphatically, then paused, affection for him causing her to revert to softer tones as she spoke the truth. "There isn't going to be a trip because I don't want to go to the Caribbean with you. Obviously you didn't believe me in Bermuda, but you have to now. It's over, Brad. I still want you to be my friend because I love you. But I'm not *in* love with you."

"Jess, baby, you're not still on this kick, are you? Just because you got a little miffed at me . . ."

"Stop it," she said flatly, elbows on knees as she leaned toward him, meaning to make him finally accept the truth. "I'm not miffed at you. I'm simply not in love with you. And I don't think you're really in love with me. You certainly didn't act much like you were four months ago or while I was in Bermuda."

"Jess, I . . ."

"No, let me finish. I thought about us a lot while I was there and since I've been back, and I think our 'romantic' relationship really hasn't been very romantic for a long time. It was just sort of a habit. Both of us were so wrapped up in our careers we didn't have time to develop romantic relationships with other people, so we just hung on to each other. Oh, I think we were in love once, as much in love as two teenagers can be," she said, smiling reminiscently. "After all, we had always been so close and we loved each other. When that physical attraction flared up suddenly when we were seventeen, we were automatically in love. Then we went away to different colleges and later you were in

176

New York in drama school and doing off-Broadway, and lately you've been in Hollywood or on location. We've seen each other just enough over the years to make us think that all that old feeling was still there between us. But it's gone, Brad. We lost it somewhere along the way. We're older and we've changed and we've gone back to being just friends again. I suspected that months ago, and my suspicion was proven right in Bermuda."

Brad stared at her, a brooding expression on his handsome face. "I hope you don't expect me to accept what you just said because I don't. It's ridiculous. You mean more to me than anyone else in the world."

"As a friend. Be honest, Brad," she gently urged. "Hasn't it been convenient for you to mention your 'fiancée back home' to stop other women from expecting a serious involvement with you?"

"Never, Jess, never," he swore, catching her hands in his, squeezing them. "How can you think I've been using you as a convenience."

His denial didn't ring true to her. She knew his act and didn't buy it. But that wasn't the main issue, and she quickly steered conversation back to what was. "Maybe you haven't used me as a convenient escape from other women," she conceded. "That's something only you know. But even if you haven't, nothing changes. It's still all over."

"Jess, baby, don't talk like that," he cajoled. "You can't really mean it. What would I do without you? I need you."

There was more sincerity in his words this time, and Jessica was filled with affectionate compassion. "Oh, Brad, I'm not telling you to get out of my life completely. I'll never do that," she assured him, patting his hand. "I'd be very unhappy without you in my life . . . as a friend. I need your friendship too. And Mom and Dad need you too. You're one of the family. That won't change just because our relationship has."

"I don't want to just be one of the family," he insisted vehemently, squeezing her hands tighter. "Dammit, Jess, I want *you*. I want to marry you."

"Do you really, Brad? You haven't pressed very hard for marriage all these years. Neither have I. I think that has to tell us something. At least, I *hope* you don't really believe you want to marry me because I'm not going to marry you. I know now that what we feel for each other, even what we felt for each other before, isn't enough to satisfy me."

"There's some other man!" Brad snapped angrily. "Isn't there?"

Jessica nodded, unwilling to lie to him. "Yes, there is. It's . . ."

"Don't tell me his name. I don't want to hear it," Brad interrupted somewhat adolescently, releasing her hands to grip her shoulders. "I don't care what his name is because he isn't important. And he's dead wrong if he thinks he's going to take you away from me."

"I'm not sure he even wants to," she replied, her expression growing rather wistful. "Take me away from you, I mean."

"Are you saying you're breaking it off with me for somebody you're not even sure wants you?" Brad questioned caustically, the short laugh that followed the words derisive. "What the hell's wrong with you? I thought you had some sense."

"That's enough," Jessica said tersely, irritated by his abusive comments. "I think you should go on to Mom's now and spend the night, and if you want to, we can talk more tomorrow when I come over for Sunday lunch."

"Oh no, I'm not waiting until tomorrow. We're together right now, and I'm not going anywhere until you realize *I'm* the only man for you. And I'm going to prove it," he muttered, yanking her to him, clamping his lips down on hers.

Even as his kiss gentled, attempted to become more seductively arousing, Jessica remained totally unresponsive, totally unyielding in his arms. Her mind wandered. Lynn had asked her once if Brad was as intense in person as he was on screen. Now

Jessica could have given her a definitive answer. No. He wasn't. Cade was intense. Brad only possessed the ability to appear that way when he was acting when, in reality, he was simply head-strong, at least lately. *Intense. Headstrong.* There was a vast difference between the two, and thinking of how much she loved Cade for his warmth and intensity, she broke away from Brad's romantically uninspiring embrace.

"You'd better go on to Mom and Dad's now. You know how tickled they'll be to see you," she told him, firmly stilling his hands as he tried to pull her to him again. "Brad, just go. Think about what I've said. If you want to talk some more tomorrow, we will."

"I'll love you forever, Jess, and I'm not going to let some other man ruin everything," he muttered, buttoning his immaculate tailor-made blazer. "You think about that tonight. For God's sakes, stop this nonsense and come to your senses."

"Good-night, Brad," she said flatly. "I'll see you tomorrow."

Without answering, he marched across the room but didn't slam the front door on his way out, for which Jessica was truly grateful. Tightness had gathered at her nape, bunching tendons and beginning to radiate pain into her temples. Closing her eyes, she curled up on the sofa for an indeterminate time but at last rose wearily to her feet, reaching behind her to lower the zipper of her dress as she walked to her bedroom. Her head ached; she wasn't going to see Cade. The most sensible thing for her to do was to go to bed.

Cade didn't call Jessica either Sunday morning or Sunday evening after she returned from an uncomfortable visit with her parents and Brad. He had been in a maudlin mood all afternoon, but she did have more hope now that he was beginning to consider seriously what she had said to him. And that was the only thought that cheered her when she went to bed Sunday night, wondering why Cade hadn't called and telling herself he had simply been too busy handling the emergency in his agency. Yet the very depth of love she felt for him made her feel uncertain, and she had to wonder also if perhaps there was some other reason she hadn't heard from him. *Maybe he was bored with her already.* Unable to bear that thought, she banished it from her mind, but even after it was at least consciously gone, she still felt exceedingly lonely.

CHAPTER ELEVEN

Jessica took her mother's call in her office early Monday afternoon. Before she could even finish saying hello, however, Mrs. Grayson began talking very rapidly, and as the rush of words poured out, a frown nicked Jessica's brow, etching deeper with each passing moment.

"No, Mom, I don't know where Brad is," she said when her mother at last paused for breath. "Didn't he say anything about where he might go when he left?"

"He just said he was going out. I thought he meant for a couple of hours. But he's been gone all night and morning, without even calling. I'm getting really worried that something might have happened to him. Do you think we should call the police and start checking the hospitals?"

"Maybe we won't have to do that if we just put our heads together and try to think of some places where he might have gone," Jessica said, her tone calming. "First of all, I guess it's possible he's flown on to California. He was pretty upset with me after our talk Saturday night, so maybe he just wanted to get away from here. Did he take his things with him?"

"Well, of course not, dear. If he had taken his luggage with him, your father and I would have known he was leaving town, and we wouldn't be worried about him now. Would we?"

"No, you wouldn't be. But that's not exactly what I meant. I was thinking maybe Brad came back during the night and got his things. Have you checked his room to see if his belongings are gone?"

"No. I mean, I looked in but I didn't really check. Hang on a minute," Mrs. Grayson said, her tone perking up a bit. "I'll go check now."

Waiting, holding the receiver between her right shoulder and ear, Jessica uttered a curse beneath her breath and broke the pencil she held in half. She tossed the two ends onto her desk top. Damn that Brad. Even if he was honestly upset by what she had told him Saturday night, he had no right to take out his feelings on her parents by allowing them to worry about him like this. He could have at least called them to let them know he was all right. But no, he was acting like he had the day of the storm in Bermuda, not bothering to consider anyone else's feelings, and Jessica realized if her mother came back to the phone and reported his belongings missing that she would want to put her hands on him, just to give him a good shaking.

That was not what Mrs. Grayson reported, however. Her voice shook slightly when she came back on the line. "Jess, all Brad's things seem to be here. I helped him unpack, and as far as I can tell, nothing is missing except the clothes he had on when he left last night. What . . . do you think it means? What do we do now?"

"It may not mean anything, Mom. And the first thing you should do is try to call all Brad's old friends, every one you can remember. I thought he'd lost touch with most of them, but there's a chance he ran into one last night or decided to look one up. So you start calling around and I'll try to get in touch with Cade to see if he's heard anything from Brad. You know, he's his business manager."

"I know. He's the one who was with you in Bermuda, the one you . . . I doubt Brad would want to get in touch with the man who's taking you away from him."

"Nobody's taking me, Mom. I made my own decision. Besides, Brad doesn't know it's Cade I'm involved with," Jessica explained patiently. "Saturday night, when I started to tell him, he refused to listen."

"Poor Brad. He's so hurt," her mother murmured. "Dear, I'm not trying to interfere in your life. And I suppose you know what you're doing but . . ."

"That's right, Mom. I know what I'm doing," Jessica cut in quietly but firmly, her tone alone putting an end to that particular useless discussion. She switched the receiver to the other ear. "Let's hang up now. You call Brad's old friends and I'll call Cade. I'll let you know if I find out anything, and you call me if you do. Talk to you later."

After replacing the receiver in the cradle, Jessica's hand remained on the phone as she stared at the slip of paper on her desk on which she had put down Cade's office number. Since she hadn't heard any more from him since Saturday night, she had been thinking all day about calling him. Yet she had been reluctant to do so. Assuming he hadn't called her because he was still tied up by his emergency, she hadn't wanted to interrupt his work. Now, with Brad being his new inconsiderate self, she had reason to call Cade, but oddly enough, she still felt reluctant. A vague uneasiness was stirring in her. *Why hadn't he called?* Surely he could have spared her a few minutes of his time, no matter how busy he was. Then again, he couldn't drop everything, especially during an emergency, just to phone her for a chat.

Those conflicting thoughts chased each other round and round in her mind for another half minute, until determination squared her jaw and she lifted the receiver. Although she felt insecure because she loved Cade and didn't know exactly how deep his feelings for her were, she was not so ridiculously insecure that she was afraid to phone him.

She didn't reach him. Out of the office, his secretary said, but due back about three thirty. When Jessica called again at three forty-five, however, he hadn't returned yet. Then he was back in the office but tied up in a conference call when she tried a final time at ten till five. Frustrated by not being able to contact him, and even more frustrated with Brad for causing her parents worry and herself inconvenience, Jessica sat strumming her fingers on the desk top. She had left Cade a message but decided at five o'clock not to wait for him to return her call. She would drive over to his office to see him instead. She wanted to know if he had heard from Brad because she could imagine how worried her mother was by now. Obviously, she had not succeeded in locating Brad by calling his old friends or she certainly would have called Jessica with the good news.

"Dammit, Brad, your second childhood's beginning to annoy me," she mumbled beneath her breath. And, after putting the work she wanted to take home into her soft leather briefcase, she left the building and went out to her car.

Cade's suite of offices was located in a monolithic steel and glass edifice on Decatur Street. She parked in the underground garage, then took the elevator up. When it stopped and she stepped out, she realized Cade's agency occupied the entire thirtieth floor. The decor was simple, understated, but warm, and she walked across plush beige carpeting to the woman sitting at the reception desk who directed her to Cade's private office.

There, she gave her name to his secretary, Mrs. Martin, who glanced down at the book on her desk and immediately began to shake her head.

"Oh, I don't have an appointment," Jessica told her quickly. "And I realize how busy Mr. Hunter is, but I do need to see him."

"I'll tell him you're here then," Mrs. Martin said, smiling graciously. "Please have a seat while you wait."

When the secretary excused herself and went into the inner office, Jessica settled down in a comfortable rose damask chair. She automatically started to select a magazine from a nearby table but had no chance to choose one because Mrs. Martin returned almost immediately.

"Mr. Hunter will see you now, Miss Grayson."

Smiling her thanks, Jessica rose and entered the spacious private office where Cade sat behind a mammoth teakwood desk. Simply seeing him after two long days made her happier, and she smiled as she walked toward him.

Glancing up from some papers on his desk, he briefly smiled in response, then observed her rather expressionlessly while waving her into a chair across from him. He inclined his head in a nod. "Hello, Jessica."

"Hello, Cade. I . . . won't keep you long," she said, seating herself, feeling somewhat disappointed by his dispassionate greeting. "I know how rushed you are while you have this emergency on your hands."

"No problem," was his casual answer as he leaned back in a black leather swivel chair. "We got everything solved late yesterday afternoon anyway."

"I see," she murmured. But she most certainly didn't and glanced down at her hands in her lap for an instant. His emergency was over, yet he still hadn't called her. *Why?* It was on the tip of her tongue to ask him, but she decided he would surely explain soon anyhow. She looked back up at him, smiled again. "Well, I've come about Brad. I mean, he's in town and . . ."

"I know he's in town."

"Then you've seen him? Oh thank goodness," she said with a sigh of relief, eyes brightening perceptibly. "What time today did you see him?"

"I didn't see him at all today," Cade said flatly, his darkly slashed brows lifting. "Was I supposed to for some reason?"

"No. I . . . uh, I'm a little confused. If you didn't see him today, when did you?"

"Early Saturday evening. He called from the airport and dropped by here to discuss a few business details before going to your place. I haven't talked to him or seen him since."

Momentarily, Brad was forgotten. Jessica's eyes widened with surprise as she looked at Cade. "Then . . . when I called you here

Saturday night, you knew Brad was at my house? Why didn't you mention you'd seen him?"

"I thought he'd probably already told you," Cade replied, getting up to walk around the desk and sit back on the edge before her chair. "Obviously he hadn't."

"No, he didn't say a word," she said, confusion written over her face. She eyed Cade speculatively. "His being there . . . That didn't have anything to do with you saying you had to work late, did it?"

"We did have something of an emergency here, but I could have seen you later," Cade explained, his expression and tone bland. "I thought you should see Brad instead and maybe you'd finally realize that what the two of you once had together is over."

"*Finally* realize! What are you talking about?" she exclaimed softly, more confused now than she was before. "If I hadn't already realized it was over, I . . . you and I . . . what's happened between us would never have happened. What kind of person do you think I am? Of course I know it's over with Brad."

"Then you'd better tell him that."

"Don't you think I've tried?"

"When I saw him Saturday, he acted as if nothing had changed between the two of you."

"Maybe he did, but I've tried to tell him different. I told him in Bermuda and again Saturday night, but he refuses to accept it."

"Maybe you're not very convincing," Cade suggested coolly, crossing his arms over his chest and staring down at her. "In fact, I would imagine you're not. Look at yourself right now. You're saying you know it's over with him, yet here you are, obviously trying to find him. You can't let him go and hold on to him at the same time."

"I'm not doing that. I'm looking for him because he's missing," she protested, her spine stiffening. "He left my parents'

186

house last night and still hasn't come back. My mother's worried sick about him."

"And are you?"

"A little, yes. We know he probably didn't leave town because he didn't take any of his things with him. That does worry me. If he didn't fly back to California, where is he and why has he been gone so long?"

"For God's sake, Jessica, he could be anywhere. You should know damned well he's capable of pulling stunts like this. He did it during the storm in Bermuda, didn't he? When are you going to stop pretending he hasn't really turned into an overindulged superstar who thinks mostly of himself?" Cade asked, black ice shards glinting in his eyes. "If you really know it's over with him, walk away. He holds on to you, but you're going to have to stop letting him."

"I'm not going to just tell him to get out of my life," she retorted. "I won't do that. I still care about him, Cade."

"I've been very patient with you, Jessica," he muttered, leaning forward to clasp her upper arms in his hands. "But my patience is wearing thin. And I've warned you before that I don't get involved in triangles. Understand? In other words, I won't share a woman with another man. While I'm involved with someone, I want her exclusively to myself. I'm odd that way."

His words seemed to stab directly into her heart, each one sharper and more painful than the last. He made their relationship sound so cold, so clinical, as if it were no different from many others he had probably had. *A* woman . . . *while* I'm involved . . . He certainly didn't make her feel very special in his life by saying he wouldn't "share *a* woman with another man." And it was obvious he didn't view their relationship as lasting or he never would have used the word "while." Intense disillusionment and hurt caused pride to gather in force in her, and she tossed back her head to glare coldly at him.

"Contrary to what you obviously think," she uttered frostily,

187

"I'm not a possession that can be shared. I'm not your damned piece of property. Do *you* understand that?"

"Perhaps 'share' was a poor choice of words," he replied sardonically, long fingers tightening around her arms. "Let me put it another way: good as you are in bed, my lovely Jessica, I can do without your considerable charms if you don't put an end to this nonsense with Brad because—I repeat again—I won't be involved in a triangle."

"You didn't seem to mind getting involved in one in Bermuda, although you said you wouldn't," she muttered between clenched teeth, flexing her shoulders to try to escape his hands, glowering at him when he wouldn't release her. "That was when I was still unofficially engaged to Brad, but that didn't stop you from doing your damnedest to seduce me."

"Not without a great deal of encouragement from you, I might add. Besides, it was obvious the first day we were there that you and Brad are totally wrong for each other," Cade said with infuriating calm. "I decided to be patient and give you time to realize that for yourself and break it all off with him. But you've had enough time now, and my patience has almost run out."

"Has it really?" she drawled, forcing herself to sound as calm and cold and uncaring as he had. "That's a pity. I thought we were getting along so well."

"You can't have it both ways, Jessica," Cade stated unequivocally, a hint of a sardonic smile touching his lips as he at last released her arms. Propped against the edge of his desk, legs outstretched and crossed at the ankle, he flicked back the sides of his coat, placing hands on hips while looking directly into her eyes. "Not with me, anyhow. Some men might be willing to share a woman. But I'm not one of them."

"You've made that very clear," she said tautly, blue eyes flashing defiance that she hoped adequately masked the intense disappointment she felt. She thrust out her chin. "And I quote: '*while* I'm involved with someone I want her exclusively to myself.' That was sufficiently blunt. How could I fail to understand

188

what you meant? And now that you've enlightened me, I'll leave."

"If you're really serious about ending it with Brad, just do it, Jessica," Cade counseled, catching her by one wrist when she quickly stood. "You may have to be forceful, for his own good."

"Thank you very much, Dear Abby. I'll certainly keep that advice in mind."

"Sarcasm doesn't suit you."

"And psychiatry's *not* your line."

Cade actually smiled. "No, it isn't. But I don't have to be a psychiatrist to realize that you may have to cut the string that ties you to Brad completely in two, for his sake. Stop being his security blanket and he might be forced to discover who he really is again."

"I have to handle this situation my own way. After all, I know him better than you do."

"Just try forgetting he's an orphan awhile. He may be using that to manipulate you. That's a fairly easy habit to get into. I used to try it occasionally myself, when I was a child."

Gazing at him, she chewed her lower lip. She could hardly tell him he knew nothing about being an orphan because, of course, he did. Yet he was different from Brad, who was a little lost and needed people rallying around him. Cade knew who he was and exactly where he was going, and he didn't appear to need anyone very much. *Not even her* . . . although she had hoped so much that he did or soon would. Icy fingers squeezed her heart, sending a twisting pain through her chest. She wouldn't think such debilitating thoughts now. There would be more than time enough to think later. With all the willpower her pride could muster, she regarded him serenely, trying to ease her wrist from his light grip.

"Would you mind letting me go now?" she finally had to ask, managing to keep her voice steady. "Mom's probably on pins and needles waiting for me to let her know if you've seen Brad."

"I want you to remember something, Jessica," Cade said softly, drawing her between his thighs rather than setting her free. "I want you like hell. I did in Bermuda and I still do. I'm sure you know that—but not if Brad stays in the picture."

When he cupped her chin in one hand and his warm lips descended to brushstroke over hers, she steeled herself, determined to be immune this one time to his touches and his kisses. Yet, even as she maintained an outward composure, she was filled with longing deep inside, a longing that was both emotional and physical. Distraught, she knew she had to get away from him. She took a backward step and immediately felt a chill seep through her, away from his warmth.

"Bye, Cade," she murmured, turning and starting toward the door. "I'm sorry if I bothered you."

"Jessica," he called after her as her hand closed around the door handle. When she looked back, he straightened before his desk, hands in the pockets of his trousers. "Maybe Brad's agent has heard from him. Have you called him yet?"

Her features arranged in a composed mask, she shook her head. "Not yet. I'll try to reach him when I get home. He should still be in his office, considering the time difference in Hollywood."

"If Brad does contact me, I'll tell him you're looking for him," Cade told her matter-of-factly.

Jessica only nodded. And since there didn't seem to be anything else for them to say to each other, she opened the door and left him, feeling that she was also leaving part of herself behind.

On Tuesday evening, when Jessica returned home from work, she found an unknown young woman awaiting her on the front doorstep.

"Miss Grayson?" the woman inquired as Jessica approached the house. "Jessica Grayson?"

"I'm Jessica Grayson. May I help you?"

"Libby Wheeler, *Atlanta Constitution*," said the reporter, extracting a small notebook and pen from the pocket of her jacket. "I'd like to ask you a few questions about Brad Taylor."

"Brad?" Jessica exclaimed softly, halting mid-stride, praying she wasn't about to hear that something had happened to him. "What . . . about him?"

"We have it from reliable sources that you've been making inquiries concerning his whereabouts and that it turns out that nobody seems to know where he is. Exactly how long has he been missing, Miss Grayson?"

"Why don't we talk about this inside," Jessica suggested, transferring her briefcase from one hand to the other. She walked up the front steps, unlocked her door, and ushered the reporter into the living room, gesturing toward the sofa while seating herself on the edge of the opposite chair. Clasping her hands together round her knees, she smiled politely. "I'm not sure we can actually say Brad is 'missing.' His agent and I just can't seem to locate him. But he has recently finished filming a movie in Bermuda, and I imagine he's tired. It's possible that he needed a rest and decided to take off on his own somewhere for a few days."

"Without telling anyone where he was going?" Miss Wheeler questioned skeptically. "Do you really think that's likely? Surely he would have told you about his plans, since you are his fiancée."

"No. I'm not," Jessica corrected. "Brad and I are close . . . friends, but even so, he doesn't always tell me all his plans."

"Then you're not really concerned about him at this time?"

"I didn't exactly say that. I would like to know where he is right now, and I'm hoping to hear from him very soon. That's about all I can tell you," Jessica said, regarding the other woman with some curiosity. "But may I ask how you found out I've been trying to locate Brad? Who are your reliable sources?"

"To tell the truth, I haven't the foggiest idea. I have a friend who works on the L.A. *Times*, and she was contacted by someone in Mr. Taylor's agent's office who said that he had disappeared while in Atlanta. So my friend called and asked me to check out the story. She gave your name and here I am." Libby Wheeler thoughtfully tapped the end of her pen against the notebook. "Since the agent leaked the story to the press, I guess he was looking for some free publicity for his client. In fact, I have to wonder if this entire 'disappearance' could have been contrived. In other words, a publicity stunt."

"Well, if it is, nobody bothered to tell me," Jessica replied coolly, then pressed her lips firmly together as hot indignation rose up in her at the very idea. If she ever discovered Brad had involved her parents and her in a seedy publicity stunt, she'd feel like kicking him to the ends of the earth and back again. But surely, even as much as he had changed, he wouldn't do something that inconsiderate. She refused to believe that of him and shook her head. "I don't think it is a publicity stunt, Miss Wheeler. I'm just hoping Brad will contact someone soon and end the mystery for all of us."

Nodding, Libby Wheeler closed her notebook and stood. "Thanks so much for talking to me."

"I'm afraid I wasn't a great deal of help," Jessica said, rising also to escort the reporter to the door. "This hasn't turned out to be a terrifically exciting story, has it?"

"It doesn't have to be terrifically exciting. Brad Taylor's a superstar," Miss Wheeler told her. "The public wants to know everything they can possibly find out about him. And there's a hint of mystery in this story. That will fascinate many readers. And besides, Taylor is a hometown boy who made it big. That makes him even more interesting."

"Yes, I'm sure it does. Well, if we're lucky, maybe Brad will show up and the mystery will be solved before you even have time to print your story."

"He'd better show before tomorrow's first edition then because the story will be in it." With a jaunty smile, Libby opened the door and stepped outside onto the small porch. "Thanks again, Jessica. I'll be in touch."

192

After exchanging good-byes with the other woman, Jessica slowly closed the door, then wearily leaned back against it, massaging her temples with her fingertips. Now, even the newspeople were picking up on Brad's "disappearance." Their interest would certainly do nothing to reassure her mother, and Jessica was already finding it increasingly difficult to sound upbeat when she talked to her parents. It wasn't easy to pretend she wasn't the least bit worried when, in actuality, she was becoming more concerned with every hour that passed. Brad had been gone two full days now and had contacted no one, at least no one Jessica had thought to get in touch with. And the fact that he had taken none of his belongings with him nagged at her constantly, becoming more and more frightening.

"Where are you, Brad? For God's sake, let someone know," she muttered aloud, moving across the living room into the kitchen. Taking a lamb chop from the refrigerator and preparing it for the oven, she wished she had someone with whom she could discuss her fears, perhaps allaying them simply by sharing them. She couldn't confide in her parents. Because of her father's mild heart condition and the already frazzled state of her mother's nerves, she felt compelled to put on a cheery face.

If only she could talk to Cade about her feelings. . . . Yet, she knew that was beyond the realm of possibility. In his office yesterday, he had proven beyond a shadow of doubt that he was unwilling to understand that it was impossible for her to stop caring altogether about Brad. And he had also proven, by his words and his tone, that she wasn't nearly as important to him as she had wanted to hope because she was helplessly in love with him. And that realization hurt too much for her to seek him out willingly. She would simply wrestle with her fears on her own.

There was no word from Brad either that night or all the next day. On the way home from work, Jessica made the decision and stopped at the police station to report him missing. Happily, the officer she spoke to reassured her to some extent by not being overly concerned. People frequently disappeared but usually turned up in a few days saying they had wanted to get away from everything and everybody. When she told the policeman that she and Brad had had a rather strong disagreement concerning a personal matter, he shook his head wisely. No doubt Brad had taken off somewhere to think things over. The officer did file a report, letting her know in no uncertain terms that he considered Brad a very important person, the local boy who had made it as a movie star.

Jessica went home and called her parents with the news that the police didn't consider Brad's so-called disappearance all that worrisome. After easing their minds a little, she said good-bye, then decided on a very light dinner. Later, when she had finished both soup and salad and was tidying the kitchen, she heard the knocking on the front door. Untying her apron, she crossed the living room, switched on the porch light, and stretching up on tiptoe, peered out one of the three small, high, diamond-shaped windows in the door. She dropped back down onto her heels, her heart seeming to plummet all the way down to her stomach before commencing a fierce thudding.

It was Cade standing on the porch. Her hand floated to her throat, which had suddenly tightened, then moved upward to smooth her hair nervously. Hiding behind a nonchalant expression, she opened the door.

"Hello, Cade, come in," she invited, sounding considerably calmer than she felt as she stepped aside for him to enter. "Here, let me take your coat before you sit down." When he shrugged off the tailored black leather jacket and handed it to her, she tried to ignore the faint but disruptingly familiar fragrance of lime after-shave that came with it. After hanging it on the walnut coat stand by the door, she motioned him to the sofa, her mind feverishly trying to reason out why he had come to see her after all the discouraging remarks he had made Monday.

Cade didn't keep her in suspense long. His black eyes flitted over her while she took the chair opposite the sofa and smoothed her indigo-blue skirt.

194

"I may have a lead on Brad," he announced, deep voice evenly modulated, gaze intent on her as her eyes widened. "I called his agent in Hollywood this morning, and he told me you had just phoned again because you still hadn't heard from Brad. I decided to put an investigator on it. He did some checking out at the airport and found a ticket agent who says she sold tickets early yesterday afternoon to a man who closely resembled Brad."

"Closely . . . *resembled?* If it had been Brad, wouldn't she have positively identified him. I mean, most people would recognize him," Jessica pointed out logically. "His face has become very familiar."

Cade nodded agreement. "But this man wore a hat and dark glasses, which makes positive identification more difficult."

"But didn't you say the man bought *tickets?* Why would Brad buy more than one?"

"He wasn't alone. There was a woman with him, Jessica," Cade said quietly, closely regarding her delicately featured face. "The woman had auburn hair and also wore dark glasses but, according to the ticket agent, she very closely resembled Christie Myerly. She could have been wearing an auburn wig as disguise."

"*Christie?*" A puzzled frown knitted Jessica's brow. "But . . ."

"Although the two people bought the tickets under other names, the agent was so sure they were Christie and Brad that she asked them outright if they were," Cade continued. "They denied it, even laughed off the suggestion fairly convincingly, but when the investigator talked to the agent today, she still couldn't believe it was a case of mistaken identity. In fact, she feels almost sure it was Christie and Brad she sold the tickets to."

"Tickets to where?"

"Miami. But they never showed up at the gate and missed the flight. Maybe if it was them, they changed their plans because the agent recognized them. They could have flown to Miami on another airline, or they could have decided to go elsewhere."

195

"Brad and Christie . . . imagine that," Jessica mused. And he had said he would love her *forever*. Forever simply hadn't lasted a very long time. Unaware of the rueful accepting little smile that flickered briefly on her lips then was gone, she nodded her head. "Well, I guess I shouldn't be surprised. They enjoyed working together and liked each other, so I think it's probably good that it turned out like this. Brad certainly has more in common with Christie recently than he does with me. They can understand each other."

"Yes, I guess maybe they can," Cade agreed tonelessly, irritated by the hint of regret he had detected in her voice, a sense of loss for what was gone now between her and Brad.

And Jessica had felt fleeting regret. Brad had been part of her life so long. They had planned a future together, a future that would never be. And it was a little saddening to let go of an old, once-cherished dream. Until a few months ago her life had been orderly and predictable. Then in Bermuda she had realized she could never marry Brad and had fallen in love with Cade and was now having to face the loneliness that came with knowing her feelings weren't reciprocated. In a relatively short space of time her entire life had changed, as if everything had been turned upside down. With Brad, she had felt secure. With Cade, she didn't. And the natural human yearning for security was strong enough in her to evoke a brief sadness because she had lost it. Yet, Cade's news had also made her feel free, free of Brad and a romantic entanglement that no longer had meaning. She was glad to know he was with Christie.

She gave Cade a somewhat tentative smile. "What made you decide to hire an investigator to try to find Brad?" she asked curiously. "Monday, when I told you he was gone, you didn't seem to think there was much to worry about."

"He'd only been gone one day then. When I read the article in the paper this morning, I knew you still hadn't heard from him. I thought I'd better look into the situation myself, called

Brad's agent, then the investigator. Brad is one of my clients. I felt a responsibility."

"I see." Jessica smoothed her skirt once more and clasped her hands around her knees. "But it turns out you were right Monday. There wasn't much to worry about, was there? Nothing, actually. Brad's just playing the free spirit again. Mom and Dad will be surprised but relieved to hear that he's with Christie."

"I knew you'd want to know what the investigator found out," Cade said, rising to his feet.

He was leaving. Although Jessica hadn't expected him to stay a long time, she had hoped he would for a little while, and his obvious reluctance to be with her caused a hollow aching to radiate through her chest. Perhaps he had only been using her attachment to Brad as an excuse not to see her again. Perhaps he had simply become bored with her. A two-night stand instead of a one-nighter—not much difference. Masking her feelings, she also stood.

"Thank you for coming by. I—" she began, but the telephone ringing halted her words. She hesitated, then lifted one hand to keep him where he was. "Could you wait just a minute while I get that? It might be Mom. I'll have her hold on."

Jessica dashed into the kitchen to the cheery yellow wall phone by the cabinets. In the middle of the fourth ring she answered but barely had a chance to say hello before the caller started speaking. She gasped softly at the unbelievable words she began to hear, and as the muffled male voice continued, her entire body started trembling. Then before she had a chance to say anything at all, the man hung up, and she fumblingly replaced the receiver. Woodenly, she left the kitchen, hand to her mouth.

"Jessica?" Cade murmured, striding across the living room to take her by the shoulders. "What is it? What's wrong? Who was that on the phone?"

"A man," she said, her voice raspy as her hands came up against his chest, fingers tightly clutching his shirtfront. She

197

stared up at him, face almost white, eyes wide with near panic. "H-he said he's . . . holding Brad for ransom. Oh my God, Cade, somebody's kidnapped him!"

CHAPTER TWELVE

"What?" Cade exclaimed, strong fingers tightening over her shoulders. "Jessica, this man, what else did he say?"

"Oh God, we thought he was safe but he isn't. He isn't!" she cried, scarcely hearing the question put to her, gripped by a horrible fear. "It wasn't Brad the ticket agent saw. *That* man has Brad and he's threatening to . . . Oh, I can't believe this is happening. It's too awful."

"Come sit down," Cade murmured softly, slipping an arm round her waist and guiding her to the sofa. Sitting down beside her, he took both her hands in his. "Take a deep breath, then tell me everything the man said to you."

"He s-said . . ." she began, but her voice was so quavery that she took another shuddering breath and started anew. "He said that he has Brad and he'll be safe as long as I do exactly what he tells me. He wants money but said he'd call later to tell me how much and when he wants it. He said Brad told him to call me because I would know who to go to for the money—meaning you, I'm sure."

Cade nodded, his expression grim. "Did he say how long he's been holding Brad?"

"No. But I guess he's had him all this time we've been waiting to hear from him. That's why we haven't heard anything."

"Not necessarily. If he'd had Brad that long, he would have made the ransom call before now. It could be that Brad has been out on the town for the past couple of days. Maybe this man saw him, recognized him, and decided to abduct him. If that's how it happened, the police might be able to find people who saw Brad around. If they know where he was last seen, they could pick up some leads on who might have him," Cade reasoned, lean fingers tightening around her smaller ones reassuringly before releasing them. He stood. "And this could even be a hoax. Someone could have read in the newspaper about Brad being missing, got your name from the article, and decided to exploit the situation."

Hope brightened Jessica's eyes. "You think . . ."

"I don't *think* anything. Just running through the possibilities, even the slim ones," he said candidly. "All I know is that we have to call in the police. I'll do that now."

With a jerky urgent movement, Jessica caught him by the hand. "No, you can't call them! He warned me not . . ." Her voice broke. She looked up at him, her features drawn, and nodded. "Of course you have to call them. I know you do."

"Yes," he murmured, then strode away into the kitchen to use the phone there.

Nearly four hours later the police had come and gone after a crew had come to connect trace-back and monitoring equipment to the telephone line. Now a van was parked across the street from her house. Inside, a policeman waited for her phone to ring and surveyed the immediate vicinity, watching for anyone who looked or acted the least bit suspicious. The surveillance made Jessica feel somewhat less helpless. Something was being done; that was a comfort in itself.

Exhausted by sheer tension, she poured coffee for Cade and herself and carried it into the living room on a black enameled tray. Even so, the cups rattled in the saucers because her hands were still shaking, and after Cade took his coffee, which had sloshed over a little, she put hers down on the table at the end of the sofa, deciding it would be prudent to let it cool a little before she risked spilling it on herself. Clasping her fingers together on her lap, she gazed at Cade. He was being so supportive, and for that she would be eternally grateful. Despite everything he had said to her Monday, despite his opinion of Brad, which wasn't always complimentary, and despite his obvious lack of deep feeling for her, he *was* here now that she needed him. Strong in a crisis—another of those qualities that had made it so easy for her to fall in love with him.

Apparently noticing how intently she was observing him, Cade returned her gaze over the rim of his coffee cup while he took a slow sip. His dark eyes narrowed as he replaced the cup in the saucer and put them on the table next to hers.

"The police will turn something up," he said with quiet confidence. "They know what to do in situations like this."

"I know. And I know we had to call them," she murmured, pushing her love for him into a far corner of her mind and trying to close a door on it in order to concentrate on the danger Brad was in. Her hands fluttered uncertainly. "But do you think the kidnapper has any way of knowing we did?"

Cade's broad shoulders rose and fell in a shrug. "It's possible he or an accomplice is watching the house. The police did come in unmarked cars, but if someone is watching, it was probably obvious that the authorities had been called in. I doubt that came as any surprise to the kidnapper."

Jessica gnawed her bottom lip. "Then you don't think they'll . . . do anything to Brad because I called the police?"

"I wish I could say no, but I can't," he answered candidly. "People capable of something like this are totally unpredictable. We can only hope they realize they'll have to prove Brad is okay before they have any chance of collecting the ransom. We don't know for sure they have him and that he's all right. We have to be given some proof."

"The next time the kidnapper calls, I'll insist on talking to Brad," Jessica said, at last reaching for her coffee and having several sips. The hot liquid warmed her going down but would soon have a stimulating effect, and she knew she certainly could do without that, tense as she was already.

201

"Have any brandy?" Cade asked, as if reading her mind. "I think that would do both of us more good than coffee at the moment."

"Brandy's a great idea. I think I have some in the cupboard," she told him, smiling weakly and standing. "I'll get it."

"Just point me in the general direction and I'll take care of it," he said softly, rising lithely to his feet also. He motioned her back into her chair. "You sit back down and try to relax."

"That's the problem: I can't. I think I'd feel less jittery if I did something."

"We'll get the brandy together then," he acquiesced, catching her hand in his to usher her into the kitchen.

While Jessica brought out two small snifters, Cade located the brandy behind the Scotch on the topmost shelf. After he had poured fairly generous amounts for her and himself, he returned the decanter to the cupboard, and that was when the shrill pealing of the telephone shattered the quiet in the kitchen to jagged pieces.

Jessica's eyes darted up to meet Cade's, and the expression that suddenly settled over his lean features was warm enough and supportive enough to calm some of her fear. She walked to the yellow phone, lifted the receiver, and answered clearly, her voice amazingly steady, her tone even.

It was her mother calling. "I know it's late, but I didn't think you'd be in bed yet," Mrs. Grayson began, words tumbling over themselves in their rush to get out. "I'm just about walking the floor over here, and I . . . I know this is a foolish question. You would have let me know if you had . . . But I still feel like I have to ask you if you've . . . heard anything from Brad?"

Jessica's chin wobbled. Tears filled her eyes, one crystalline drop spilling over to catch in the fringe of her lower lashes. When Cade stepped in front of her, handing her a neatly folded square of white linen handkerchief, she dabbed at the teardrops, then tried to blink the lingering moisture away. Clutching the handkerchief in one hand, she decided it was useless to tell her mother the honest truth. "I was just about to call you, Mom," she said, telling a half-truth instead, relating the report Cade's investigator had given him.

"I declare," her mother said when she had finished, resorting to that old Southern euphemism she sometimes employed when immensely surprised. "I have to say I never expected Brad to be this irresponsible. He could have told one of us he was running off with this Christie what's 'er name."

"Myerly," Jessica repeated. "Christie Myerly."

"Yes, yes, Myerly. I've seen her in some movie, I think. Is she the one with the raven-black hair and exotic eyes, the one who reminds you of Cleopatra?"

"One and the same," Jessica said, trying valiantly to keep her tone light enough to be believable. "I met Christie in Bermuda, Mom, and I liked her. I think you would too."

"Maybe so, but I do wish Brad had told us what he was up to," Mrs. Grayson said sternly, disapprovingly, clucking her tongue against the back of her teeth. Then she sighed with relief. "Well, at least we know he's okay now. And he must not be too upset because you told him you weren't going to marry him."

"I hope he isn't," Jessica managed to say evenly before her throat clamped tightly on her and images of Brad, bound and gagged somewhere, filled her head. Relieved when her mother said she might be able to sleep now and was going straight to bed, she said good-bye and hung up.

Cade stepped in front of her when she turned away from the phone. A lean forefinger lifted her chin. "Why didn't you tell her, Jessica?"

"What good would it do for my parents to know Brad's been kidnapped? And you said there's a chance this could be a hoax, so I don't want to tell them anything. There's nothing on earth they can do about it except worry themselves crazy. Dad has a heart condition, and Mom would panic. No. I think I should try to keep this from them. Maybe I won't have to tell them until this nightmare's all over and Brad's been found safe," she said hopefully before uncertainty shadowed her face. "If something were to . . . *happen* to Brad, though, I don't know how I'd explain not telling them."

Cade had no answer to her dilemma, but understanding of it gentled his gaze. Taking both brandy snifters in one hand, he indicated with a gesture that she should precede him into the living room. They talked quietly for a while about tactics the police might possibly employ to find Brad and apprehend his abductors and about how Cade would be able to arrange the money if and when a ransom demand was made.

It was well past midnight when utter exhaustion overtook Jessica. Weary to the bone, feeling her head was too heavy on her slender neck, she had a final sip of brandy and smiled tiredly when Cade removed the glass from her hand.

"I think you should go to bed," he suggested, brushing a tendril of golden hair back from her left temple. "Tomorrow will probably be a long, hard day. You need to rest."

"I know. But I'm not sure I'll be able to go to sleep."

"You have to try, and you might as well try right now," he persisted gently, standing and reaching back down to pull her up before him. He turned her toward the door that opened onto the hallway, his hand curving into the small of her back exerting coaxing pressure. "Go to bed, Jessica."

"But . . ."

"I'll be out here finishing my brandy until you've had a chance to go to sleep. Then I can let myself out."

"But you don't have to stay. Thanks for offering, but it really isn't necessary," she insisted, turning to look at him. "I'll be all right by myself. And I know you're tired too and want to get home."

"I can wait. Besides, if I don't stay awhile, you might sit up all night worrying. I'd rather know you're getting some sleep before I leave."

"Oh, I'll go to bed, I promise. I'm feeling too tired to sit up, so you really can go home and . . ."

Touching a fingertip to her lips, he silenced her. "Don't be so damned independent," he said sternly, his expression somber. "Stop arguing with me and just go to bed. I'll let myself out later after you're asleep."

Realizing he fully intended to stay and too tired to resist any longer, she shrugged, sighed softly, and walked out into the hallway. "Good-night, Cade," she said back over her shoulder, hearing his low response as she went into her bedroom.

Ten minutes later, after brushing her teeth and getting into a nightgown, Jessica got into bed beneath the covers. The moment her eyes closed, however, thoughts of Brad being held prisoner in some dank, dirty place filled her head. She bit her lip and turned her head from side to side on her pillow. This entire situation was insane. People she knew simply did not get kidnapped. But Brad's life had changed, and he was no longer like most other people she knew. He was a celebrity who earned a great deal of money, and one of the prices he paid for success and fame was becoming a target of maniacs. At that moment it seemed far too high a price to pay, and she wondered if, wherever he was, he was thinking the same thing. Or was he simply furious about the predicament he was in? Brad had a temper that could flare hotly out of control on occasion, and she could only hope he wouldn't be foolish enough to provoke his captors into violence. *Something else to worry about.* Ghastly images depicting what could happen to Brad bombarded her brain until she cursed beneath her breath and resolutely erased the mental pictures. Such thoughts only made her crazy and did nothing to help Brad. He would be all right. He would be found safe. Cade was right; the police knew what they were doing, and she tried to cling to the very unlikely hope that he hadn't really been kidnapped at all, that this was only a cruel hoax. It was a hope however that offered little comfort because if he hadn't been kidnapped, where was he?

Lying on her side, she opened her eyes and gazed out the opened door and down the darkened hallway, seeking the shaft of light that spilled out from the living room. Cade was there, and that knowledge did help ease some of her anxiety. Although it hadn't been necessary for him to stay, it was comforting to have him close by, at least for a little while. And as she stared through the darkness at the beacon of light, her eyelids became heavier and heavier.

The letter arrived in the mail the next afternoon. Jessica had stayed home from the office after calling in to say she didn't feel well, and although she had tried to occupy some time with the work she had brought home in her briefcase, she didn't have much success at it. She was unable to concentrate on anything except the telephone, which could ring at any second but didn't. By midafternoon the never-ending silence seem to pulsate throughout the house, making it even more difficult for Jessica to focus on the article she was editing. Although Cade had spent all morning waiting with her, he had left the house after lunch on urgent business and wasn't back yet. She missed him not only because she loved him but also because his mere presence right now was reassuring.

When Jessica heard the postman's footfalls on her front porch, then the light thunk of mail dropping into the metal box, she quickly went to open the door, grateful for any distraction from that mockingly silent phone.

Two bills, three pleas for contributions from political organizations, and an envelope bearing no return address and her own in tiny printed letters. Jessica ran a fingernail beneath the envelope's flap, opened it, and withdrew a folded sheet of paper on which words cut from magazines had been pasted. Her heart dipped; she took a quick short breath, eyes rapidly scanning the page which read: YOU CALLED THE POLICE. ANY MORE STUPID MOVES AND YOU'LL NEVER SEE THE MOVIE STAR AGAIN.

Jessica felt as if her stomach had somersaulted then tied itself in painful knots. Someone *was* watching her house and did know that the police were investigating the case. Had it been a stupid move to agree with Cade about contacting the authorities? By doing so had she made things worse for Brad? She shook her head. Especially until she knew beyond all doubt that someone had Brad and he was all right, she was wise to play by established police rules, so no, it hadn't been a stupid move—it had been the only move she could make. If Brad had been abducted, he was in danger, and only the police were qualified to handle that sort of situation.

And this letter might provide them with some clues. As she held the sheet of paper carefully by one corner, it rustled in her shaky hand. She looked out the window across the street at the omnipresent dark van, then realized she didn't dare take the threatening note to the officer on surveillance. Obviously, someone was watching the house, and she didn't want to draw their attention to the van, in the slim hope the spy hadn't realized the significance of the vehicle yet. Instead, she gingerly placed the letter on the coffee table and went to call the lieutenant in charge of the case.

About five minutes later Cade returned, and shortly thereafter Lieutenant Flanders arrived in an unmarked car. After he left to take both envelope and note back to the station to be thoroughly examined, Jessica sank down onto the sofa.

"It never occurred to me that they might send a letter. I wasn't expecting that," she said, explaining her trembling hands when she noticed him observing them. "I expected the phone to ring but it hasn't, and it's after four o'clock already. Cade, why don't they call?"

She repeated that question around ten thirty that evening. Tucking stockinged feet and jeans-clad legs beside her on the cushion of the chair she now sat in, she twirled a strand of hair round and round one finger. Propping an elbow on the armrest, she dug her chin into the cup of her hand and cast a perplexed glance in Cade's direction.

"I don't understand," she murmured. "The kidnappers obviously want money, so why don't they tell us exactly how much so we can get it for them? It doesn't make sense for them to wait. Why don't they just call?"

"I have a feeling they won't call tonight. Deliberately making you wait to hear from them may be part of the plan," Cade answered, long fingers steepled beneath his chin. "The longer you have to wait, the more frightened and upset you become, which they might believe will make you more cooperative when you finally are contacted. Besides, they undoubtedly know the phone's tapped."

"Animals. *Worse* than animals," Jessica muttered caustically. Then something akin to supplication darkened the blue eyes that lifted to meet his. "You really don't think we'll get a call tonight?"

"I'd like to say yes, but I can't. The kidnapper or kidnappers know we wouldn't be able to raise the money tonight. Why call now then? They can wait until tomorrow morning and put you through a few more hellish hours."

"*Damn,* I feel so helpless."

"Precisely how they want you to feel. There is something you could do to thwart that plan," Cade suggested, leaning forward on the sofa, arms lying over muscular thighs, hands hanging loose between his knees. "You could go to bed right now and try to get some sleep. And I think that's what you should do, Jessica. You look very tired."

"I guess I am. I slept last night, but not very restfully," she admitted, nibbling a fingernail. "I had such vivid crazy dreams."

Cade nodded, dark carved features overlaid with solemnity. "All the more reason for you to get to bed early tonight."

"I know. You're right."

"Want some brandy to relax you?"

She smiled softly at him, loving him for the tender consideration he was showing. But she shook her head. "I think I can get by without the brandy. Maybe I am tired enough to go to

208

sleep right now. And that will give you a chance to go home. I know you must want to."

His face tightened; his eyes narrowed and cooled. "I'm not going home tonight knowing someone's out there watching this house," he stated unequivocally. "You're not staying here alone. I'm staying with you."

"Oh, but you don't have to do that. I'll be fine. The police van's just across the . . ."

"And no one's watching the back of the house," Cade reminded her pithily. "The police can't spare another officer to do that. And we're dealing with a very dangerous person or very dangerous people. How do you know someone won't break in to deliver the ransom demand face-to-face? You don't. And I'm not taking that chance. I'm staying."

Jessica tensed. She longed for him to stay with her yet knew it would be a mistake to let him. She shook her head. "Cade, you've done enough already. I can't thank you enough for being as supportive as you've been, and I don't want to cause you any more inconvenience."

"You have a spare bedroom," he said flatly, ignoring her words as if they had never been spoken. "Why don't you show me where it is?"

"But you . . ."

"I'm not leaving you alone here," he almost growled. "Now, stop arguing and accept the fact that I'm staying all night tonight and every night until this is over with."

"For heaven's sake," she uttered wearily, wishing he would stop tormenting her like this. She wanted him to stay. He had been kind, but kindness had its limitations, and she knew he had gone past the limit. The desire to be kind had become a feeling of responsibility. After all, Brad was his client and she was the one the kidnappers were expecting to extort money from and he felt obligated to stand by her to the very end. Well, that wasn't good enough for her. She needed much more than a sense of obligation from him. And since he was unable to give more, she wanted nothing at all. If she could only be with him because he felt responsible for her, then she would rather be without him. An intrinsic pride ran too deep for her to accept what amounted to nothing more than charity. Gathering that pride around her like a protective mantle, she took a deep breath and shook her head.

"Go home, Cade," she said with quiet dignity. "You have to. If you don't, what about Georgia? You can't leave her out there with nobody to look after her."

"She's not nearly as fragile as she thinks she is. She can get into the basement, and I called a neighbor earlier who promised to go feed her. Tomorrow, I'll pick her up and take her to Gran's until this is over. You don't have to worry about her, and neither do I. And I'm staying here."

"For God's sake, Cade," Jessica muttered between clenched teeth. "I don't *want* you to stay here."

"That's too damned bad." Cade's hands shot out, closed around her delicately boned wrists, and merciless despite her sharp surprised gasp, he pulled her onto her knees between his thighs before him. His fingers entangled in her silken hair. His hard black eyes glinted, piercing hers. "Get this straight, Jessica," he uttered harshly. "Either I stay here with you every night, starting now, or I'll call your parents and tell them what's happened so one of them can come stay with you."

"I don't believe you," she retorted tersely. "You wouldn't do that."

"No?" he drawled, his deep voice deceptively calm. "Try me."

A strangling constriction squeezed her throat while she looked up at him, recognizing the stony determination that hardened the planes and contours of his dark face. She had suspected he could be ruthless on occasion, and now he was proving that suspicion correct. He felt he should stay with her, and he intended to stay, regardless of her objections. But she didn't want him that way! It was far too humiliating to know he was only standing by her because he felt he should. Resentment and defensive anger flushed her cheeks and flashed in her eyes as she struggled to twist her wrists free of his viselike grip. But her efforts to escape were in vain, and she glowered at him.

"Let me go," she demanded heatedly. "Right now, Cade."

"I presume your parents' phone number is listed in the book?" he taunted, turning a deaf ear on her demands. "Or would you like to save me the trouble of looking it up by just telling me what it is."

"You're not going to call them. And you don't need to stay with me. I'm not a helpless female who has to have someone around for protection. For pity's sake, I've lived alone for a long time now, and I'm used to taking care of myself."

"But you're not used to dealing with lunatics who go around kidnapping people, and I'm not leaving you alone here to deal with them now," Cade uttered, his words clipped and ice-edged. His hands moved upward from her wrists to grasp her upper arms, fingers pressing warningly into her firm flesh. "So you decide, Jessica. Do I call your parents, or do I stay here myself?"

"But I'm saying it isn't necessary for anyone to stay," she said, lowering her tone, trying to reason with him. "Besides, the kidnappers would be crazy to show up here."

Cade uttered a stridently explicit curse, one she wouldn't have cared to repeat, and a muscle ticked impatiently in his tight jaw. "Anybody capable of kidnapping probably is crazy, Jessica. That's exactly what I'm getting at."

Jessica opened her mouth, snapped it shut again, and pressed her lips firmly together. She really couldn't argue with such logic.

"What's your decision?" he asked flatly. "Do I call your parents, or do you stop being ridiculously stubborn?"

His steely gaze convinced her he meant every word he said— he would call her parents and tell them what had happened to Brad unless she gave in and agreed for him to stay with her. It was practically emotional blackmail, and there wasn't anything she could do to combat it. He had the upper hand. She was defeated. This particular battle was a victory for him, and as that realization settled heavily in her, she sank back tiredly on her heels, nodding.

"I'll show you to your bedroom," she said simply, rising gracefully to her feet the moment he released her.

To his credit no triumphant gleam appeared in his eyes. He merely accepted her decision with a brief nod, stood, and followed her along the short hall to the room directly across from her own. She went in, looked around quickly to be certain he had everything he needed, then pointed out the bathroom at the end of the hall. There was a heavy silence between them, one that made her infinitely sad and nearly brought tears to her eyes. But perhaps that was because she was already overly tired and overwrought. Or perhaps it was because she loved him too much and he didn't love her at all. Whatever the reason, Jessica suddenly longed for the sanctuary of her own room where she could deal privately with her roiling emotions. Disturbed by the watchful gaze she could almost feel burning on her, she stepped to the doorway.

"I hope you'll be comfortable in here," she murmured, her clear eyes wandering slowly over Cade's tanned face then meeting his. "I'm sorry I don't have pajamas or even a robe to offer you."

"I'll manage without," he said, moving away from the side of the bed toward her, his expression indefinable. He stopped about three feet from the door, hands sliding into his trouser pockets. "Why don't you want me to stay, Jessica?"

Because it hurts my pride, she could have answered truthfully, but that was a truth she didn't want him to know. It would too clearly reveal her feelings for him. She offered him a partial truth instead. "I just know that staying will be inconvenient for you."

"I'm more flexible than you obviously realize," he told her, a semblance of a smile brushing his mouth. "I stayed here last night and didn't find it extremely inconvenient."

"Last night?" The curve of Jessica's brows rose. "But you said you'd let yourself out."

"I did. Early this morning before you woke up. To tell you the truth, I fell asleep on the sofa while finishing my brandy."

Jessica wasn't at all sure she believed that. More likely he stayed the night because he had felt the same obligation he was feeling now. But she pretended to take him at his word and only said, "The sofa couldn't have been very comfortable."

"I think I will prefer the bed," he replied dryly.

"You'll find extra blankets in the closet if you need one," she said, moving out into the hall. "Good-night, Cade."

As he said good-night, she walked across to her own room, deliberately maintaining a leisurely gait, but once she was inside and had closed her door behind her, she lifted shaky hands and pressed them against her forehead for a second. She almost wished she hadn't already had her bath. A nice hot soak in the tub might have proved relaxing right about now. And she certainly needed something to relax her. Falling asleep was going to be no easy accomplishment with Cade just across the hall.

Jessica did fall asleep, however, lulled by the sound of the shower running. Tired as she was, she tumbled into a dreamless darkness, conscious of nothing until some time later when the ringing of the phone on the table beside her pierced the silence of the night and screamed shrilly in her ears. She shot upright in bed, heart pounding almost painfully. A phone ringing in the middle of the night was frightening enough, but now the harsh peals were dreadful, ominous sounds. Throwing back the covers, she jumped out of bed and was staring at the telephone about to pick up the receiver when she heard Cade's door open. Then hers did and he stepped into the room.

Raking a hand through tousled hair, she glanced anxiously at him, then scooped up the receiver and answered but had to restrain herself from slamming it back down after only a few seconds. "Oh damn, a wrong number! Can you believe that?" she softly exclaimed, spinning around to face Cade after hanging up.

Anguished frustration lay over her face. "Tonight of all nights, why did someone have to call here by mistake?"

"Maybe it wasn't a mistake," Cade suggested, gently sweeping a hand over her hair. "It could have been the kidnappers just harassing you, trying to put more pressure on. Did anyone say anything? Or did they just hang up when you answered?"

"Someone mumbled 'wrong number.' "

"But you didn't recognize the voice as the same as last night's?"

"It was too vague and far-away-sounding." Jessica heaved a sigh. "It could have been anybody."

"Hopefully, whoever it was won't call back again tonight," Cade said, his fingers massaging the bunched tendons that lay along her nape. "Do you think you can go back to sleep now?"

"I think so, since I only feel half-awake anyhow," she murmured. But suddenly while she was looking at him, the fact that he was clad only in white briefs registered in her mind. There was a little hitch in her breathing. Although she had seen Cade wearing nothing at all, this moment with him seemed more fraught with danger than any other time ever had. She wanted him so much, needed him so badly, and they were alone in the house, and even though she knew she should resist him, she doubted she would be able to if he chose to take her in his arms. Those thoughts ran together in her head as his touch on her neck seemed to sear her skin and his warm proximity heightened her senses. *Nonsense! You can resist him,* common sense screamed at her.

But common sense was wrong. When Cade whispered her name caressingly, she could practically feel all hope of resistance rapidly melting and made one last feeble effort to defend herself from her own traitorous body and heart.

"It's . . . the middle of the night," she began haltingly. "I guess we should go back to bed."

"I think we should," he quietly concurred, black eyes drifting over her delightfully curved body which was covered but not concealed by a clinging powder-blue nightgown that flared out prettily around her bare, slender feet. Leaning down, he brushed warm lips across her cheek. "But this time we'll go to bed together, Jessica."

Still warm and drowsy and very susceptible, she felt as if she were adrift in misty dream. Entranced, she allowed Cade to pull her to him and was at once swept up and lost in loving desire. "Cade," she whispered.

"It's what we both want," he muttered huskily, linking kisses around her neck in a gossamer chain that seemed to bind her to him and claim his right of possession. "At least it's what I want, and I think you do too."

"Yes. Oh, Cade," she breathed, taking that one step that brought her close against him, her hands gliding over his broad chest and fingers playing over fine dark hair. "It is what I want too."

His arms went around her, their iron-hard strength tempered by endearing gentleness. He arched her slender body, bringing her nearer still. "I *need* you, Jessica, and I want you right now."

"Then kiss me," she demanded, bare shapely arms winding invitingly around his neck. "Really, really kiss me."

"*Honey,*" he whispered triumphantly, crushing her to him. "Lovely Jessica."

Then his lips were on hers, as sensuously firm and burning as she remembered, and she felt totally alive again after days of feeling oddly numb and very incomplete. She fervently returned his kisses, fully curved lips playing with the enticing shape of his, freely offering warmth and sweetness to the tip of the tongue that licked over them. Her own tongue flicked lazily against his, teasing, provoking, encouraging a rougher more impassioned taking of her mouth.

With a muffled exclamation, Cade complied. Hardening lips lightly twisted hers, as if he might devour them. He widened his stance, large hands curving over the gentle swell of her hips holding her fast against him, demanding her recognition of his intolerably aroused masculinity.

Jessica moaned, head spinning, body aching, soul longing for love's precious completion. All pliant and warm in his embrace, she moved a slender thigh against his pulsating rigidity, reveling in her power over him as he responded, pinioning her harder against him, lifting her so that the tips of her toes scarcely grazed the floor. Their lips melded together, eager, seeking, coming together again and again. Their desire fused in overwhelming passion, on and on upward in a never-ending cycle of take and give. Singeing sparkles of fire ignited and imploded deep within her, and the searing heat blazed a path of longing. She was flung upward in a swirling hot space, far beyond all ability to reason, transported to a mystical realm where nothing at all mattered except feelings. Cade wanted her; she needed him.

When Cade turned and dropped down onto the edge of her bed, pulling her between long strong legs, Jessica caught his face between her hands and smiled languidly down at him. She slowly traced his lips with her fingertip.

"Enchantress," he whispered, capturing the tip between his teeth, nipping tenderly. "You're doing everything you can to seduce me."

"It seems like you're the one who's seducing me," she countered, her voice softly caressing. "It's always you."

"Is it really?"

"I think it is."

"Maybe it's a case of mutual seduction."

"Maybe it is," she admitted, touching the tips of his thick black lashes.

His hands circled her waist. He drew her to him, his lips lingering on her flat abdomen, igniting her skin through the sheer gown. He kissed the length of her thighs, her midriff, then the rounded curve of her breasts in enclosing circles to the peaks. The tip of his tongue played idly over and around the hardening tips until the fabric of her gown was damp and clinging to the peach-tinted crests, outlining burgeoning nipples that he soon possessed with lips and tongue and teeth.

Jessica was trembling violently when he pushed the narrow corded straps of her gown off her shoulders and put her away from him.

"Take it off," he commanded coaxingly. "I want to see you, all of you."

She smiled sensuously, adoring the glow of passion in his eyes, adoring him. Enjoying his penetrating gaze, aroused by it, she skimmed her right hand down her left arm, easing the gown straps off with slow, seductive intent. Her left hand skimmed her right arm, and when those straps too were off, only her firm breasts held the bodice of the gown in place. The neckline was slipping, slipping very slowly, exposing more and more fully the rounded curve of ivory flesh, until the tops of her breasts were revealed to him and the fabric was clinging only precariously to the peaks. Before the gown could fall of its own accord, Jessica slipped her thumbs beneath the top edge and began lowering it, deliberately unhurried, making him wait, making her own pulses race with the erotic thrills that rushed through her. Her body burning under the white-hot intensity of his gaze, she peeled the garment downward, ever downward, past her hips then allowed it to drift from her fingers and float to the floor around her feet in a silken whisper. Watching Cade, she stepped out of it, clad only in lace-edged panties.

"You're driving me crazy. Come here," he murmured, his voice appealingly rough as he reached out, his hands pulling her to him. When her fingertips slid beneath the elastic of the panties, he gently moved her hands away and eased his own fingers beneath the waistband instead, shaking his head. "Let me do that."

Jessica complied gladly. Standing before him relaxed, she touched his hair, fascinated by the clean vital feel of it between fingertips as he bent down, removing the last remaining barrier of her clothing. Straightening, he looked at her, taking in the

217

satin sheen of her skin and exploring visually the enticing shape of her body. His hands roamed upward, cupped the sides of her breasts as he leaned forward and pressed his lips into the scented hollow between. His breath caressed the soft, yielding flesh of her breasts. He trailed a strand of kisses around her narrow waist and over her abdomen and down the length of one thigh then back up again, lips lingering here and there, tongue etching tingling patterns on her skin.

"Cade," she whispered, pressing against his shoulders, urging him backward on the bed. She came down above him, tawny hair tumbling forward like a silken curtain to frame her face. Following the delicate arching of her back with one hand, he smiled lazily up at her, enfolding her in his arms when her mouth lowered and sought his. Their lips touched and parted, touched and parted, each successive kiss intensifying their hunger for each other and inducing a raging fever that soon consumed both of them. Keenly alive, wildly in love, she was lost in him, lost in the potent power of his body beneath her own. She moved sensuously against him. Her hands frolicked over his chest, his face, his ears, his neck, as lightly as the touch of a kitten, and his response heightened her delight in her own femininity.

His breathing quickened. His heart beat strongly, steadily but fast under her straining breasts. His rambling hands followed her shape, squeezing and caressing, stoking the fires of her desire and making her arch closer to him.

A low groan came from deep in his throat, and in one swift fluid motion he turned over, moving her beneath him and around on the bed until her head was resting on a pillow. He stood off the bed for a moment, stripped naked, then joined her once again, dusky eyes conveying passionate intent as they imprisoned hers.

Gazing up at him, she ran fingertips along one muscular arm from shoulder to hand. "Touch me," she beckoned. "Everywhere."

"Yes, I'm going to touch and kiss every inch of you," he

promised. And he began with her breasts, large hands covering them, his questing fingers probing taut rounded surfaces, his possessive mouth partaking of her tender flesh. Caught up in a never-ending rush of sensations that became more and more keen and deeper, she explored him, delighting in the contours of his muscles and his imposing male strength. She could have gone on touching him forever and being touched by him. This was their world, their pleasure shared in the giving of her love and his tenderness, and it was all exclusively theirs.

"Jessica," Cade whispered into her ear. "My lovely Jessica."

And she was his. She knew it. He might not understand that fully, but she did, and she couldn't at that time feel any regret. Love was too strong a force for her to hope to suppress, especially when she could be this close to him, could feel his hands moving freely over her, and sweep her own hands freely over him.

"You make me feel so good, Cade, so alive," she said softly and was rewarded with a lingering rousing kiss. Softly shaped lips nudged and nibbled his in return, and she wound her arms around him as the weight of his upper body bore her down into the mattress.

"You have the smoothest skin," he murmured, appreciatively running a hand along her side, her waist, and the curve of her hip and a line of her thigh. He turned onto his side and pulled her over to face him. His palm sought her left breast and moved in slow light circles over the crest until it was tipped by a surging hardness, which he swiftly took into his mouth.

Jessica gasped at the moist tugging pressure being applied to her sensitized flesh, and as the tip of his tongue began to flick over and around the nipple, she moved feverishly, moaning. Her breath was coming rapidly when he at last raised his dark head.

"Sweet, you're so sweet," he said against her parted lips. "You taste so good."

"How good?" she asked, smiling mischievously and caressing

219

his face as she looked up into his black eyes. "As good as your grandmother's peanut butter cookies?"

"Better." Smiling back, he tapped the end of her small straight nose with a fingertip that trailed down to outline her lips. "You taste much better than even Gran's cookies."

Catching that fingertip between her teeth, she nibbled. "Ummm, you taste good too."

"How good?" he countered teasingly but gave her no chance to answer as, with a wicked grin, he flipped her over onto her stomach and began to rain kisses over her back, showering them along her spine over her hips along the backs of her thighs and calves. Even the soles of her feet were kissed and the tips of her toes individually. Sensations like tiny electric shocks ran riot over her, yet much as she delighted in what he was doing, she needed something more too. Rolling over onto her back, she reached out to him.

"I want to touch you too," she explained, spellbound by the look of passion in his eyes as he lowered himself to lean on elbows above her. He slipped his fingers through her hair, fanning it out in an arc of shimmering gold on the pillow. Clasping her hands round the back of his neck, she drew his face closer to hers. Their lips touched, softly parted, playing and parrying then clinging together in ardent mutual demand.

It was that way with them, hot, consuming, totally beyond resistance. A few caresses, a few kisses, were all that was needed to sweep them up toward an inevitable end. Gloriously adrift in that sense of inevitability, Jessica lazily entwined her long shapely legs with his and caught her breath when he forcefully arched her against his potently aroused body. Her hands charted the powerful structure of his broad back, the smooth trimness of his waist, the narrow tautness of his hips. Her lips sought the strong sunbronzed column of his neck, the line of his jaw, and the corners of his mouth while he, in turn, masterfully brought her ever closer to the highest pinnacle of physical awareness. Every nerve ending was awake and tingling and receptive.

"Sometimes I think I'll never be able to stop touching you," Cade muttered, voice muffled in the thickness of her hair as long fingers spread open possessively across her bare abdomen. "I always want more and more."

"Never stop then," she breathed, pressing kisses into the hollow of his left shoulder. "I never want you to."

His mouth descended on hers. "What a sexy little wench you are."

"You really think so?"

"Hmmm, and I'll prove to you just how hot-blooded you can be," he promised, parting her smooth thighs with a slowly gliding hand.

Unrushed, bathed in soft mellow light, they found delight in each other, sharing the wonder of most exquisite intimacy. Alone together in the swirling mist of mutual desire, the rest of the world forgotten, they created experiences that Jessica suspected she would never want to experience with any man except Cade. With him she was freed of all physical inhibitions, and nothing they wanted to do together went beyond the limit because there simply was no limit. Her love, knowing no boundaries, enabled her to respond with all the inherent passion in her. By silent mutual agreement, they prolonged the pleasure, allowing it to graduate slowly in intensity until the ecstasy they brought to each other became everything and all to both of them. They made the night unforgettably sensuous as they learned each other, taught each other, and aroused desires in each other so powerfully awesome they defied description.

Considerably later, when the fire that engulfed both of them swept out of control, Cade's warm demanding lips plundered the sweetness of hers before he whispered. "I can't wait any longer. I want you so much."

"Take me. Love me," she whispered back, and as his hand stroked the tender skin of her inner thighs, she parted her legs wider for him.

Cade moved between them, black eyes searching the depths of

hers as he gently lowered himself upon her, making her his, filling emptiness with hard, pulsating need and groaning softly as he himself was enclosed in her warmth. He heard her corresponding moan of pleasure, saw the pleasured smile that flickered on her lips, and was fascinated by the soft light that brightened her dreamy blue eyes. And even as they began to move together in a perfect rhythm that slowly but surely increased in tempo, his gaze held hers.

Unable to look away from those dark eyes, searching their mysterious depths, Jessica clung to him, winding herself closer, ever closer, moving with him, meeting every slow stroke of his hard body with eagerness and unspoken love. Emotion burst forth in her, pure and abiding and filling her to overflowing as she gazed up at him and saw the intense passion conveyed by his tightened features suddenly tempered by a warm, slow smile.

"Cade," she sighed, her answering smile tremulous as she urged him closer still, warm lips grazing his.

"Lovely. You're so lovely," he murmured, a hand beneath her rounded hips squeezing gently. "And tonight you're mine."

She always would be. In her heart she suspected no other man ever would mean as much to her as he did. He was that special one, the one she had waited for even before she had known she was waiting. And as he demanded everything of her, she gave gladly while taking from him as together they were transported level by exquisite level, closer and closer to the supreme heights of rapture. And when completion came for both of them, piercing sensations dashed in continuous waves through her, ebbed, then crested in finely honed peaks once again, she caught the edge of her finger between her teeth, muffling her soft sweet cry of ecstasy.

Cade breathed her name. Holding him tight, she kissed him, feeling the thunder of his heartbeat against her yielding breasts. A few minutes later, as they lay together in the tangle of sheets, she drew his encircling arm closer round her and rested her hand lightly on his chest. Cade reached over to switch off the lamp, enveloping them in soft darkness.

"So far, this certainly beats staying on the sofa," he teased, brushing a kiss against her tousled hair. "I prefer being in your very comfortable bed."

"It's the firm support mattress that makes all the difference," she replied wryly, smiling as she cuddled closer to him and closed her eyes.

It was nearly dawn when Cade awakened to Jessica's touch. For a few moments he pretended to still be asleep, but a hint of a rueful smile soon flitted across his lips in the gray semidarkness. She was enchanting, bewitching, and as he felt her small light hand move in slow circles over his chest, he couldn't resist her. A bare breast brushed his arm, and he moved with sudden swiftness to pull her over on top of him, his lips taking possession of hers and capturing her soft surprised gasp.

"You're very sneaky," she chided softly a moment later, resting her forehead on his shoulder. "I thought you were still sleeping."

"You mean you weren't trying to wake me up?"

"I didn't say that," she confessed. "Waking you up is exactly what I wanted to do."

"And now that you've succeeded, what do you have in mind?" he whispered suggestively, hands roaming over her naked back. "Tell me."

"Why don't I just show you instead," she countered and began dancing kisses along his neck and up into the hollow below his left ear, teeth and tongue playing with the fleshy lobe, her warm breath caressing his skin. Although she realized he was already strongly aroused, she sought to stoke the fire of his passion until it was a raging blaze in him.

Since the moment she had awakened beside him, she had needed to be this close to him once again, to become lost in her love, and to believe if only for a while that his need of her was as deeply intense as hers was for him. Now, as she kissed and caressed him, displaying a natural talent for seduction she had never really known she possessed, she was not at all sorry she had awakened him. This was their time, and she only wished it could continue forever, knowing as she did, deep inside, that it might be all she ever had with him.

CHAPTER THIRTEEN

When the telephone rang at ten forty the next morning, Jessica sprang for it. She answered, listened a moment, then nodded at Cade, her eyes widening as the muffled male voice at the other end made the long awaited ransom demand. She paid close attention to everything he said, but the instant he fell silent, she gripped the receiver so tightly her knuckles turned white.

"Before I even think of raising the money you want, you're going to have to let me talk to Brad," she said, sounding convincingly stern although her stomach was fluttering wildly with fear. "I won't pay the ransom until you give me some proof you have him and that he's all right. I'd be a fool if I did."

A string of expletives and threats filled her ear and she winced, some of the color washing out of her face, but as Cade took one long stride toward her, she lifted a hand and inclined her head to let him know she was able to cope with the kidnapper herself. When the obscene man on the line wound down, she clenched her jaw and insisted once more that she would have to speak to Brad personally before any amount of ransom would be considered.

"But how do I know you haven't already harmed him?" she asked after the kidnapper abused her with gutter language again. "That's the condition. No ransom until I know Brad's alive and well."

"Forget it," the muffled, faraway answer came back. "We

aren't going to let the movie star talk to you or anybody else. No way."

"You'll have to or . . ."

"If you don't come up with the money, something nasty's going to happen to him, you coldhearted bitch!"

"I'm not sure something nasty hasn't already happened," she reiterated, struggling to swallow past the tightening constriction in her throat while she gathered up all her courage and added, "Either I talk to Brad or . . . you can forget the whole thing."

The kidnapper cursed her again, then sullenly agreed to the condition and slammed the phone down in her ear, making her flinch.

"You son of a . . ." Her voice cracked and she shook her head impotently, tormented blue eyes seeking Cade's face when he gently eased open her fingers, took the receiver from her hand, and replaced it. Wrapping her arms around her waist, she sank down onto a chair. "Do you think I kept him talking long enough for the police to trace the call?"

Reluctantly, Cade told her he doubted she had. "The conversation probably just seemed to last longer than it actually did," he added, towering over her, his hands clasped behind his back. His voice lowered. "I know that wasn't easy for you—demanding to talk to Brad before considering paying the ransom. But you sounded amazingly convincing."

"Should I have? Was it the right thing to do?" she questioned urgently. "What if . . . Oh God, if it was a mistake and Brad is . . . I'll never be able to forgive myself."

"Jessica, it was the only thing you could do," Cade reassured her, his expression grim. "The police know how to handle these situations, and they advised you to insist on speaking to Brad."

She gestured helplessly. "I guess, but . . ."

"Did the kidnapper give you any idea when he might call back?" Cade asked, and his question seemed prophetic as at that exact moment the phone rang shrilly again.

Yet when Jessica hastily answered, it was only the police

officer in the van who confirmed Cade's doubts. He told her the conversation with the kidnapper had been too brief for the call to be traced and advised her to keep the man on the line longer the next time he phoned.

"Unfortunately, that's much easier said than done," she muttered after relaying the policeman's message to Cade. Pressing her fingers against her temples, hoping to ease the throbbing ache that was building there, she shook her head again. "And I have a feeling this man we're dealing with isn't stupid. He's probably a maniac, but that doesn't mean he isn't cunning. He's not going to chitchat on the phone with me while the police track him down. Probably the thought of three hundred thousand dollars will keep him from getting careless—that's the ransom he wants. Do . . . you think you'll have trouble raising that amount?"

"It'll take some time, but I've already begun converting some of Brad's assets to cash," Cade said, stepping behind her, his hands coming up to lightly massage the tension-tight muscles along the back of her neck. His fingers expertly stroked and kneaded while the melodious cadence of his voice hypnotized her. "Relax, Jessica. You need to relax."

And she tried, but before the warmth of his soothing touch could penetrate flesh and bone, a loud, sharp rapping on the front door caused her to stiffen once more and jump up from the chair.

"It may be the lieutenant," Cade offered, walking with her into the living room. "He did say he'd want to talk to you when you got another call."

Nodding, Jessica went to the front window and peeked out through a crack between the draperies. When she saw Libby Wheeler standing on the porch her hand lifted as she started to knock again, her heart fell, and before she could close the drapes back, Libby glanced in that direction, saw her looking out, and waved cheerily. Jessica was trapped.

"Oh no," she breathed, turning to Cade. "It's the newspaper reporter. She's here about Brad, and the lieutenant told us to say nothing to the press about the kidnapping. How am I going to answer her questions? I've never been much of a liar, and she's going to know I'm not telling the truth."

"Improvise. Tell her anything you have to that you think she might believe," Cade cautioned. "I'll back you up, don't worry."

Reassured to some extent, Jessica went to the door and opened it, valiantly producing a welcoming smile. "Libby, hello, this is a surprise. Please come in."

"I decided to take a chance and just drop by to see if you were here," said Libby, stepping into the house, still squinting as a result of the bright sunlight beaming down outside. "It's a workday, I know, but I was in the neighborhood."

"Great timing. I woke up this morning and decided to take today off," Jessica lied, glancing from Libby to Cade and maintaining her smile. Yet as she started to introduce the two, the reporter made that social amenity unnecessary.

Hand extended, Libby Wheeler stepped toward Cade. "Mr. Hunter, isn't it? Cade Hunter?"

Taking the woman's hand firmly in his, he nodded and smiled politely. "But I'm afraid you have me at a disadvantage."

"Libby Wheeler, the *Constitution,*" she explained. "I used to cover the financial beat, and I have a terrific memory for faces. How's business these days? Is your financial counseling agency still expanding?"

As Libby suspiciously cut her eyes from Cade to Jessica then back once more to him, Jessica could just imagine what she must be thinking: an editor of a regional magazine couldn't earn enough money to make many investments and certainly not enough to warrant a house call by the president of one of Atlanta's most prestigious financial counseling firms. And if that was what she was thinking, she was correct, so Jessica could only try subtly to convince her that her relationship with Cade was strictly personal, thereby allaying suspicion that Brad was his client. Libby seemed to be an extremely intelligent young woman. It might take nothing more than the fact Brad was missing and his financial counselor was somehow involved in trying to locate him for her to put two and two together and eventually, after further digging into the story, come up with a feasible answer to the mystery—a kidnapping. Jessica couldn't take a chance on that happening. The police had advised her strongly to keep news of Brad's abduction out of the press, fearing public disclosure would generate countless false leads and greatly hinder their attempts to locate and safely rescue him.

That thought foremost in her mind, Jessica invited the reporter to be seated and, as she settled herself on the sofa, deliberately sat down on the arm of the easy chair Cade took. Without actually touching him, she sought to convey an aura of intimacy between them by appearing completely relaxed, and after bestowing a warm slow smile on him, she turned her attention to Libby Wheeler.

"What can I do for you today, Libby?" she asked, crossing slim ankles and casually draping her arm over the back of Cade's chair. "I assume you're here to follow up on your story about Brad?"

Libby nodded. "Exactly. Have you heard from him?"

"Not directly, no."

"But now you do know where he is?"

"Not precisely. I have a general idea," Jessica told her, unwilling to utter an out-and-out lie for fear it could be too easily proven false. Instead she repeated the story she had told her mother, insinuating that Brad had gone off somewhere with Christina Myerly. When she had finished, she shrugged lightly, hoping she appeared suitably unconcerned. "So it looks like Brad just wanted to get away from it all for a while. I can understand that."

"I'm not sure I can," Libby replied, busily jotting in her notebook, then questioningly spreading her hands. "I mean, I understand Brad Taylor wanting to go off and relax somewhere after making a movie. But I can't really understand why no one knows exactly where he is right now. I've contacted his agent, and he doesn't know precisely where he is. No one knows, not even you, Jessica, and you're an old trusted friend."

"Even the closest of old friends don't tell each other everything, Libby," Jessica countered with what she hoped was a convincingly resigned and unworried smile. "I imagine Brad just didn't want to tell anyone, even me, where he was going and who he was going with so the gossip sheets wouldn't get wind of his relationship with Christina Myerly."

"The gossip sheets don't need confirmation to print their stories. They make them up as they go along," Libby said, lips twisting disparagingly. "And I'm sure a celebrity like Brad Taylor realizes that, so I still don't understand why those people who are the closest and dearest to him don't know exactly where he is right now and apparently haven't heard a word from him."

Jessica shrugged once more. "I wish I had more information to give you, but I don't. If you're looking for some explanation for Brad going away like this without telling anyone exactly where he was going, I guess I can't help you. I've told you everything I know."

Obviously not convinced, the reporter turned a speculative gaze on Cade, who had intelligently contributed nothing to the conversation thus far, acting for all the world as if Brad was someone personally unknown to him. But Libby was too persistent a personality to let even his remarkably convincing lack of interest thwart her natural curiosity. She eyed him hopefully.

"By the way, Mr. Hunter," she began, pen poised on a page in her notebook. "Does your agency handle Brad Taylor's financial affairs?"

In response, Cade gave her a slow easy smile but shook his head. "The names of our clients are strictly confidential, Miss Wheeler."

Provided with neither a blatant lie she could disprove nor the truth which could have prompted further questions, Libby smiled ruefully. "A very evasive answer, Mr. Hunter."

"It wasn't meant as an evasion. It's simply a fact that the names of our clients are confidential."

Temporarily outmaneuvered, the reporter turned to Jessica once again. "You obviously feel there's good reason to believe Mr. Taylor is simply off on a holiday with Miss Myerly. Then may I quote you as saying you're no longer concerned about his 'disappearance,' although you still haven't heard directly from him?"

"I don't recall saying that. Maybe I've given you the wrong impression," Jessica answered calmly, feeling it would seem too suspicious for her to act as if Brad's exact whereabouts no longer interested her. "It does look like Brad is probably with Christie Myerly right now, but I would still feel better if he got in touch with me."

"Maybe I'll see if I can track Miss Myerly down," Libby mused, tapping the point end of her pen against her notebook. "If I find her, I should find him."

Jessica smiled. "I've already tried that. Christie's agent has heard from her a couple of times this week, but she hasn't told him where she is or who's with her. He says she could be with Brad or she could be in seclusion with her guru. Apparently it isn't unusual for her to be very secretive."

"But she has been in touch with someone. Mr. Taylor hasn't. I wonder why."

"So do I," Jessica replied as naturally as possible. "And when I do finally hear from Brad, I plan to tell him that the next time he goes off on an impromptu vacation he should try to remember to let someone know where he is."

"Umm, odd that he hasn't done that this time," Libby mumbled almost inaudibly, as if she were thinking aloud. Then she flipped her notebook shut and stood but continued to examine Jessica's face rather speculatively. "Well, I suppose that about covers everything for now, but you will contact me if there's any news about Mr. Taylor, won't you?"

"Of course, glad to." Getting up, Jessica escorted Libby across the living room where the reporter paused to exchange good-byes with both Cade and her. When she at last left the house, Jessica closed the door behind her and leaned back against it, worry darkening her eyes as she looked at Cade. "How suspicious do you think she is?"

"Enough to keep her on this story," was his quiet, candid answer. "I'm sure she feels there are too many unanswered questions and will try to dig around for the answers."

"I just hope she doesn't notice the van parked across the street. If she discovers the police are involved, she probably won't have too much trouble figuring out the whole situation."

"She may not notice it this time. But if she comes back and sees it parked there in the same place again . . ."

Cade didn't finish that statement; there was no need for him to. Jessica understood only too well what he was saying and suddenly could no longer stand still. "Damn, this is all we need," she muttered. "If news of the kidnapping gets out, Brad may be in even more danger than he already is."

"It could complicate matters," Cade admitted, reaching for her hand and stopping her when she started to pace by him. "Try not to worry too much about the press though. Maybe before Libby Wheeler or anyone else can find out anything, everything will be over."

Would it ever be over? Jessica was beginning to wonder. Sometimes, she felt she had been entrapped in a never-ending nightmare, and it seemed like forever since she had received that first call from the kidnapper. While she stood looking down at Cade, she knew he was trying to offer her some comfort, and she longed to accept it by flying into his arms and being as close to him as possible. Yet, she didn't dare do that because she had decided earlier in the morning that she must try to put some distance between him and herself for the sake of her own emotional well-being.

Awake before him, she had gone into the kitchen to make coffee, and alone with her thoughts, she had been forced to accept the distressing realization that the glorious hours she had spent with Cade last night had made her love him even more. And she was no masochist. Loving him more would ultimately mean worse pain for her when their relationship, tenuous as it was, no longer existed. If only she could detect some strong sense of commitment to her in him, she could probably risk heart and soul for the chance they might have a future together . . . but she didn't. Once she had, but that had been before he had demanded she eliminate Brad totally from her life *while* she was involved with him, connoting the temporariness of their relationship. She also knew she probably wouldn't have ever heard from him again if Brad hadn't been kidnapped. Now he was here with her merely out of a sense of responsibility. Not enough, not nearly enough to assuage her intrinsic self-respect. She needed more from him, more than even the passion that flared so easily between them. Last night had proven they still shared an overwhelming mutual desire, but then again, she had been available and very willing. He was only a man, and he had always admitted he wanted her physically as much as she knew she wanted him.

As unbidden memories of the night suddenly and insidiously filled Jessica's head, a part of her needed badly to take whatever happiness she could find with Cade for however long it lasted and damn the consequences. Yet, another part of her, pride most likely, bridled at the very idea, and she thought she might never be able to forgive herself if she allowed him to use her then cast her aside like an old shoe when he was no longer interested. Self-esteem was the victor in this particular battle in the war of conflicting emotions, and she knew now had to be the beginning of the exorcism of him from her heart. She had to start backing away. Gazing down into his magnetic coal-black eyes, even as she ached to reach for whatever joy she could have with him, she mustered all the inner strength she possessed and slowly extracted her hand from his.

"Maybe you're right," she murmured, taking a backward step away from him and turning her back. "Maybe the press won't find out what's really happening. I hope so, because if they plaster the news of Brad's kidnapping all over the newspapers and television, Mom and Dad will . . ." She broke off, swiping the sweep of flaxen hair back from her forehead. "Oh God, I'm so worried about him!"

Cade didn't answer, but that didn't surprise her. What could he possibly say that would ease her concern? And, glancing over her shoulder, she saw him stretch out his long legs, lean his head back against the back of the chair, and rub his eyes. He looked nearly as weary as she felt.

"I'll make another pot of coffee," she said softly, then trudged into the kitchen.

Lieutenant Flanders, a tall portly man with prematurely gray hair who looked more like a career politician than policeman, arrived approximately fifteen minutes later. He stayed for the late lunch Jessica insisted on preparing simply to have something to do to occupy her hands, and he was still there when the kidnapper phoned again about two o'clock. Both he and Cade stood close by as she gingerly lifted the receiver from the cradle and answered.

"You wanted to be sure we have the movie star and that he's safe," the muffled voice rasped. "Okay, baby, here he is to tell you so himself."

Holding her breath, Jessica heard a chair scraping in the background, followed by a few indistinguishable sounds, then quick breathing.

"I'm all right," another, very familiar voice gasped. "I'm okay, really. You . . ."

"Brad! Brad!" Jessica cried, recognizing the voice immediately but receiving no response as she called his name except for the sounds of a struggle on the other end of the line. She clenched her hand so tightly her nails dug painfully into her palms. *"Brad!"*

"Now you know he's safe," the first cold voice came back. "So maybe you're ready to listen to what I've got to say?"

234

"You hardly let him say anything," she protested vehemently. "Put him back on. I want to ask him . . ."

"No way," the kidnapper snarled. "You think I'm stupid? I know the cops are trying to trace this call, so I'm going to make it short and sweet. Three hundred thousand in unmarked bills, small denomination. Nothing bigger than a twenty. You got that straight, baby?"

"Yes . . . but it might take a little time for us to raise that much. Three hundred thousand is a lot of money."

"Not to a movie star," the man retorted snidely. "And you've got twenty-four hours to get it. That's all. Got that? I'll be in touch, baby."

"But wait," Jessica called out, but too late. A loud pop assaulted her ear as the phone was slammed down at the other end. She winced, then shook her head at Cade and the lieutenant. "He hung up."

Flanders grimaced. "He didn't stay on the line long enough for us to get a trace," he told her before a brighter expression appeared on his rather patrician face. "But I assume Taylor did have a chance to say something to you?"

Nodding, Jessica repeated the too-brief, breathless message.

"And you're absolutely sure it was Taylor you heard?"

"Oh yes, I recognized his voice."

"It couldn't have been someone impersonating him?"

"No, it was Brad. I'm sure it was," she assured him. "I'd know his voice anywhere."

Starting to pace back and forth in the kitchen, Lieutenant Flanders nodded. "All right now, what about the ransom? Did he say anything about when and where he wants it delivered?"

"Not where. But he told me we only have twenty-four hours to raise the money."

Flanders looked at Cade. "How about it? Can you get three hundred thousand together in one day?"

"Tomorrow's Saturday, and that might make things a little more difficult, but I should be able to manage it," he answered.

"There's a cash account to draw on, and I've been making arrangements to sell some bonds."

"The kidnapper wants unmarked bills," Jessica added. "Nothing larger than a twenty."

Cade nodded. "I'll get right to the office and try to finalize all the arrangements this afternoon."

"I'll walk out with you," Flanders said, falling in step behind him when he started out of the kitchen. "I want to take the tape of that last call down to the station where we can give a listen to it carefully. Never know, we might pick up some background noise that would help us pinpoint the general area where Taylor's being held."

"I did hear a few sounds in the background," Jessica said, her expression becoming hopeful. "Do you really think you might get a clue to where Brad is?"

"It's a long shot," the lieutenant conceded, shrugging. "We might not hear anything that will help us, but then again, we might. There's always that possibility. I'll certainly contact you if we find anything of interest, Miss Grayson."

She expressed her thanks, and after the policeman stepped out of the house, Cade paused in the doorway, looking down at her, and she lifted her eyes up to meet his, breathing a sigh. "I wish there was something I could do besides just sit here and wait," she said somberly. "I feel so helpless."

"Now might be a good time for you to get out of the house for a couple of hours," he said softly, raising a hand to lightly stroke her hair. "The kidnapper's not at all likely to call back for a while, and you need to get away. You've been cooped up here too long."

It was a tempting suggestion. He was right. She was beginning to feel as if the walls were closing in, but that was more a result of high anxiety than a genuine case of cabin fever. She wasn't sure going out would make her feel a great deal better. Besides, she felt compelled to stay close to the phone just in case. Sighing once more, she shook her head. "No, I guess I'll just stick around here. I know you're right and the kidnapper probably won't call again today but . . ." She threw up her hands uncertainly. "He *could* decide to let Brad say something else to me. You know, urge me to cooperate with the man or something."

"I doubt that'll happen, Jessica," Cade murmured, dropping his hand and moving farther out the opened door. "I'll be back as soon as possible."

"Could . . . would you give me a call if you're going to be very late?" she asked hopefully, then produced a somewhat sheepish smile. "I just don't think I could stand it if I had to start wondering where you were too."

"I'll call," he promised.

After watching him take the front steps two at a time and lope out to the Jaguar sedan then quickly drive away, Jessica went back into the house. Because she had already tidied the kitchen, she simply wandered through the rooms, looking for something to do to occupy both hands and mind. After several fruitless minutes she stopped by her desk in the living room and stared at the work she had gotten Lynn to bring over earlier in the day. An article about home gardening in Georgia was atop the stack, and a slight glimmer of hope appeared in her eyes as she sat down and pulled the thin manuscript to her. She picked up a pencil, determined to lose herself in work for at least a little while.

Cade was late returning that evening, but because he did call Jessica, as promised, she knew not to expect him until after nine. And when he did arrive, greeting her with a nod and a smile, her spirits were immediately lifted.

"Does that mean what I hope it does?" she asked, her own answering smile brightening. "You were able to raise the money?"

"Almost all of it. We need ten thousand more, but I should be able to arrange that in the morning without any problem."

"I didn't realize you'd be able to do it so quickly," she admitted, following him down the hall and stopping in the doorway of the guest room. She watched while he shed both charcoal-gray coat and vest and placed them on the chair with his burgundy tie, which he had stripped off as he walked into the house. "That's such a lot of money. How did you manage to get it together?"

"We knew there was going to be a ransom demand," he explained, unfastening his collar button and the one directly beneath it. "I'd already set some of the procedures in motion which saved us time today."

"Thank heaven. Now I hope and pray that horrid man will call tomorrow and tell me where to deliver the ransom. Just think, maybe by tomorrow night this time . . . Oh God, I wish it would hurry up and be over."

"He probably will call. The longer this takes, the edgier he must be getting too," Cade told her, gaze narrowing as he noticed the faint violet crescents beneath her eyes. He fluttered a fingertip over delicate skin. "You look tired, Jessica."

"So do you, a little," she replied, trembling inwardly at his touch while managing to show no outward response. "And you must be hungry. I have a treat for you, my own original world famous beef stew. You'll love it."

"I'm sure I would if I hadn't already had dinner—if you can call what I had dinner," he said with a wry grimace. "I'm not even sure you could call it food. My secretary ordered something in for me. I think it was supposed to be corned beef, but I have a feeling boiled shoe leather would have tasted better."

Jessica softly laughed. "Sounds absolutely horrid."

"Horrid is too mild a word for it. Jackie's never failed me like that before, and if she ever does it again, I may be tempted to have her arrested for trying to poison me," he joked. "At the very least, I may forget to give her a Christmas bonus."

"Why not just let her eat what she's ordered," Jessica suggested, amusement dancing like tiny candle flames in her eyes. "If you really want revenge, that should do it."

"Hmm, yes, the perfect punishment," he agreed, chuckling. "What a devious mind you have, Jessica."

"Thank you," she answered outrageously, grinning as she bobbed him a curtsy. "But if that's all you had for dinner, you probably didn't eat much. You must still be hungry, so how about some of that stew now?"

"Maybe later. Better give me a chance to recover. I was busy and not really thinking about what I was doing. I had a few bites of the sandwich, and that was enough to put me off all food for a few hours."

"I think you're exaggerating, and I also suspect you're going to tease Jackie about this for some time to come."

"I may mention it once in a while. Jackie looks especially nice when she blushes."

"Oh?" Jessica questioningly tilted her head to one side. "Why didn't you tell me you have this thing about women who blush? I never knew that about you."

"Maybe you should have. After all, you blush very prettily sometimes too."

"I do? Oh, I doubt it. I've never been much of a blusher."

"No, you don't do it often. But there have been some rare occasions," Cade said, his deep voice lowering. "Occasions when I've seen a little darker pink rush into your cheeks, Jessica."

Her smile became tremulous then faded completely as his did while he stepped closer to her. Suddenly, the banter they had been exchanging became something far different, something that would have set off danger signals in her head had she been thinking rationally. But she wasn't. For several intense moments she wasn't actually thinking at all. Perhaps she was too tired to or perhaps she was simply too much in love to be sensible except erratically and this didn't happen to be one of the sensible times. Feeling as if she were drowning in his eyes, she was unable to look away from him or move beyond his reach when he took her left hand in his and lifted it to his lips, slowly kissing each fingertip in turn before seeking her cupped palm. Her pulses quickened, and still she couldn't drag her gaze from his clean-featured, suntanned face. Even when his free hand stole around her waist to the small of her back and he pulled her nearer, she continued to look up at him, incapable of offering resistance. All her fine resolutions made in the morning were lost and forgotten in evening's magic spell.

Cade said nothing. Penetrative and perceptive black eyes held hers while he raised her chin with one finger. When her hands drifted up to graze over his white shirtfront, his dark head lowered; his lips descended.

Jessica's eyes fluttered shut as he kissed her, drew back, then kissed her again, repeating the process over and over until each light kiss was both a delight and a torment. His body heat seemed to radiate through her skin and underlying flesh into the very marrow of her bones, and she felt as though she were melting in the warmth as she inhaled his faint lime scent. Her tenderly parted lips met the firm curve of his as his hard body elicited the exploration of her hands, which flowed over his back, fascinated by the subtle tracing of flexing muscle. Her mouth opened to his, and when the pressure of their kisses increased with dizzying swiftness, she moved closer. Her warm round breasts yielded to his more muscular flesh, and she thought he must be able to feel the riotous beating of her heart against his chest as her arms wound upward round his neck.

Cade pressed her tightly against him. His fingers glided through her hair, entwining in soft silken strands to tilt her head back and to one side, exposing the pulse in her throat, one side of her neck, and the hollow beneath her left ear to his hot branding kisses.

Shiver after shiver plunged through her, making her tremble, weakening her limbs, and sending waves of wildfire blazing through her. Unmindful of both past and future, concerned only with the present and the consuming love she felt for this special man, she urged his warm taking mouth to hers once more, initiating a series of deepening searing kisses. She only felt totally alive when with him; she knew it. Only then did everything in the world become more vitally alive and more exquisitely meaningful. She was only human; she wanted to live life to its fullest and to find every gram of joy in it. How, when Cade made her feel more joyous than she ever had, could she deny herself the ecstasy of being with him? For a long while, she couldn't. Her heart ruled her head, and she reveled in sheer happiness that came with being enfolded in his strong arms, forgetting anything or anyone else existed. His hands riding over her, following every enticing curve and line, burned her skin through the denim of her jeans and the cotton of her shirt but warmed her with delicious pleasure at the same time.

It was only as Cade undid three of her buttons and those hard hands cupped the weight of her breasts, lean fingers shaping rounded curves, and only as he bent down to seek the firm flesh with bruising lips that reality began to intrude on the dream she was dreaming. His hands dropped down over her hips, arching her against his hardening thighs, and she felt the potency of his desire. The dream began to splinter. She knew what Cade wanted, knew what she needed—another night together like last night had been, scorching with passion, filled with sweet delight. But if she spent another night like that in bed with him, she also knew she would awaken in the morning loving him even more than she did right now. Somewhere it had to end, this continuous cycle of lovemaking and deeper loving, each one leading to the other again and again, every full cycle making her more dependent on the way she felt when she was with him. Fear of the pain she still had to face when he left her for good washed over her, and she was suddenly too afraid to risk making his final leave-taking even more traumatic for herself than it already promised to be.

"*No*. Cade, no, I . . . can't," she whispered, a sob rising in her throat as she pushed away from him. She swallowed past it, held it down, and glanced up at him. "I'll make you a drink," she uttered, then turned and was gone.

Guilt? Had that been guilt darkening her blue eyes that had darted up to meet his, only to be concealed by quickly lowering lashes? Raking a hand through his hair, Cade turned away from the empty doorway, his jaw hardening. Was Jessica feeling guilty because while Brad was being held for ransom somewhere, she was making love with another man?

Uttering an indecipherable curse beneath his breath, he strode over to the bedroom window and stared out at the clear autumn night sky. His dark gaze hardened. He had meant it when he told her he wouldn't share her with Brad. He still meant it. And she said *she* wanted this entire situation to be over. Well, so did he. He wanted to be able to walk away from her and forget her completely. . . .

In the kitchen Jessica leaned her forehead against the cold, smooth surface of the refrigerator before finally opening the freezer to take out ice. When she went to the counter, as she emptied the cubes out into the bucket then reached for the Scotch on the cabinet shelf, she told herself repeatedly that it was best this way. Somewhere along the line the break had to come, and it was better for her to make it now than to wait breathlessly for Cade to make it later. Yet she wondered how much longer she could bear to live in the same house with him, needing him and knowing he wanted her. Their relationship should have been simple, but it wasn't at all. She wanted too much from him, and he wanted too little from her. And she knew she would be the one to pay the highest price for that irreconcilable difference.

CHAPTER FOURTEEN

A few minutes past six Saturday evening Cade removed the last of the money from his office safe and placed it in the navy canvas tote bag atop his desk. After rearranging several of the neat stacks of bills, he zipped the bag shut and looked at Jessica, who stood beside him. Her troubled azure eyes met his for an instant before she glanced at her watch.

"Maybe I should go early," she suggested solemnly. "I'd hate to get tied up in traffic."

"I know, but leaving around six twenty will give you more than enough time even if traffic is heavy," he assured her. "Don't you agree, Lieutenant?"

"Oh sure, you should get there well before seven if you leave at twenty past," answered Flanders as he hovered nearby. "Frankly, I don't want you arriving too early so you won't have to sit out there alone in the dark and wait very long. We'll be watching you of course. Sheriff Gregg will post deputies around, but they'll be keeping their distance, and you'll be on your own."

Although Jessica nodded, a small frown creased her brow. "After the kidnapper calls me out there to tell me where to go next, I'm sure he's going to suspect I'm being followed. And he said it would be bad news for Brad if he even saw someone who *looked* like a policeman."

"Oh, he'll be watching for us at the drop site, no doubt about it," the lieutenant admitted. "But we'll be very inconspicuous, I promise you. You'll hardly even know we're there."

"But what if he spots you anyhow? Maybe no one should follow me. Maybe I should just go alone, drop the money wherever he tells me so he can pick it up then release Brad."

"That's the problem. There's no guarantee he would release him even after being paid the ransom," Cade reminded her quietly, intently surveying her face. "We've talked about this already, Jessica, and you agreed that we have a better chance of finding Brad if the police follow you and wait until the man picks up the money at the drop site, then follow him, hopefully to Brad."

"I know I agreed, and I still understand that's really the only sensible plan," she said, laying her hands over the top of the tote bag and squeezing tightly. "But now that it's time to put it into action, I'm afraid we could be making a terrible mistake."

"I think that's natural. We're all a little nervous right now," Cade said, his long fingers briefly brushing hers as he checked the bag's clasp. "But this can't be as much a mistake as letting you go deliver the ransom alone would be."

"I know this is difficult for you, Miss Grayson," Lieutenant Flanders commiserated. "But Mr. Hunter is right. This is the safest way for you and Brad Taylor. And we're going to take care not to do anything that would further endanger him. As I said, we'll be inconspicuous."

"I'm sure you will, Lieutenant, and I know you both are perfectly right . . . but . . ." Jessica's words trailed off into silence. It was useless to voice her uncertainty and niggling fear again. This was simply one of those desperate situations in which any action taken entailed great risk. As long as Brad was in the hands of a conscienceless degenerate, there were going to be no easy answers. Breathing a silent sigh, she checked her watch once more. Eighteen after six. She looked up at Cade. "I think I'll get started now."

The three of them took the elevator down to the underground garage. Stopping by Jessica's car before going to his own, Flanders gave Jessica an encouraging nod. "While you're out there beyond the city limits, you'll be under the sheriff's jurisdiction and the FBI's, since they're called into any kidnapping after twenty-four hours. But I still see this as my case, and I want Mr. Taylor found safe and his kidnappers caught, so I won't be far away from the action. Good luck, Jessica."

Always a very formal, somewhat staid man, he had never called her by her first name before, and she smiled warmly at the change, returning the nod. "Thank you, Lieutenant. I know it will make me feel safer knowing you are out there somewhere watching what's happening."

As the policeman fidgeted with the knot of his tie, then hurried away, Jessica turned to Cade, checking the time again while he put the bag he had carried down from his office into the front seat of the Citation. A moment later, when he closed the door and walked her around to the driver's side, she extracted her keys from her purse, trying to ignore her shaking hands.

"Well, this is it," she announced unnecessarily, waiting as he opened the door for her. "I'll see you in a little while."

"Jessica," he murmured, lightly catching her by the elbow to stop her when she started to get inside the car. He released her arm but only to reach out and tap the end of her nose with one fingertip. A semblance of a smile touched his carved lips. "Remember to be careful. Don't decide to try to play the heroine out there."

Shaking her head, she smiled faintly in response. "I won't. I'm really just a coward at heart."

"Sure you are," he drawled disbelievingly. "Just don't get the idea you might be able to save Brad single-handedly. You could end up in worse trouble than he's in."

"I know. I . . ."

"You may be dealing with someone who can be very violent."

"I realize that."

"Then you just make the drop and drive away. All right?" he persisted. "Let the police handle everything after that."

"I plan to. My goodness, what brought on this sermon?" she

asked too cheerily, sweeping a hand toward the canvas tote bag and foolishly attempting to lighten the atmosphere. "Are you worried about me or about all this money I'm carrying?"

"Not funny at the moment," he replied shortly, obviously in no mood for weak humor. He helped her into the car and leaned down to look in at her while she fastened the seat and shoulder belts. When she finished and turned her head to face him, his piercing black eyes locked on hers. "I mean it, Jessica. Be careful."

"I will," she promised, warmed more than she should have been by his concern. After all, he or anyone else would be concerned about a veritable stranger in this situation, and she certainly couldn't consider herself a stranger to him. It was only natural for him to be somewhat apprehensive; even Lieutenant Flanders had shown he was to some extent. As she gazed at Cade's dark face, she suddenly banished all such thoughts and nodded. "I will be very careful. I'd never do anything foolhardy that might botch up everything. I'm too anxious for this to be over and done."

"All right then, I'll see you soon," Cade said flatly, straightening to close the door for her.

And after starting the engine and backing out of the parking space, Jessica glanced up in the rearview mirror and found Cade watching as she exited the garage.

Fifteen minutes later she had left the heavier city traffic behind. Interstate 85 stretched out toward the north ahead of her, seeming somewhat isolated despite the fact there was always some traffic. Gripping the steering wheel tightly with both hands, shivering in a lightweight tweed suit, she finally realized she hadn't turned on the heater and reached down for the control knob. Although warm air almost immediately began blowing over her feet and legs, she couldn't relax. A cold harsh prewinter wind was buffeting the car, and in the sky a band of brackish, threatening clouds scudded in ragged vapors over a faraway, frosty half-moon. The perfect night to be meeting a kidnapper.

Leaning forward slightly, Jessica glanced from the road up through the windshield at the cold, partially veiled moon, then turned her attention to the highway again at once, trembling. Tonight was eerie, and her heart pumped just a little faster, its beats heavier than they should have been.

She was frightened, to some extent for herself, but more so for Brad. If something went wrong, if she were unable to drop off the ransom or if the police intervened too soon or lost the kidnapper after he retrieved the money, what would happen to Brad? She didn't dare allow herself to really consider the possible consequences to him if everything didn't work perfectly for the next couple of hours. Gnawing her lower lip, she switched on the radio until the DJ's inane chatter threatened to drive her mad a minute or so later. She switched it off again, but the silence was nearly as unnerving as the rapid-fire voice had been. Her eyes were drawn momentarily to the canvas tote bag on the seat beside her.

Wherever Brad was, what was he thinking right now? Had he been told he might be set free tonight, that the ransom money had been raised, and that she had agreed to deliver it? Or was he trapped in some dark dirty place wondering what was to become of him, wondering when this nightmare was going to end . . . if it ever ended? The mere possibility that he might be feeling totally forsaken made Jessica want to cry for him. He could be weak sometimes; she had noticed that tendency more recently, and she could only say a little prayer that he had found the strength to bear up under the horrible strain of the past few days. When the police found him (and they would find him; they *must*), and if they found him in physically sound condition, she knew exactly where she would take him to spend the night—home, to her parents, who loved him like a son and would provide all the tender affection and initial pampering he might need in order to begin recovering from this ordeal.

With that thought in mind, visualizing how her parents would dote on him and make him feel truly safe once more, Jessica looked at the odometer and saw that she had driven seven miles past the city limits. Not too much farther to go. Unaccustomed to traveling this particular highway, especially at night, she started carefully scanning each passing road sign, her breathing accelerating rapidly when she at last spied the one she had been searching for. One Mile Ahead. A little more than thirty seconds later—½ Mile. Then more swiftly, the sign that proclaimed ¼ Mile Ahead. She slowed down slightly, more closely hugged the outer line of the right lane, and soon veered gently onto the widening lane that took her off the interstate.

Fingertips pressed against her mouth, Jessica followed the asphalt up the gently sloping incline that curved into the upper parking lot of the rest area. She drove past the wooden shed that enclosed on three sides a bank of vending machines that offered a variety of snacks and drinks to hungry and/or thirsty travelers and pulled up alongside the drive-by public telephone set on a pole backed by a line of thickly needled evergreens. She stopped and cut the motor, hoping no one would want to use the phone while she sat here waiting for it to ring.

Time dragged past. Jessica looked at both her watch and the clock in the dashboard repeatedly until it was six past seven, and still the telephone was dreadfully silent. She shifted restlessly, hands clenching and unclenching around the steering wheel. With the car engine off, the heater had ceased functioning, and as the chill driving wind whistling outside began seeping in, she started shivering again. Hugging her arms to her breasts, contemplating whether or not to switch the ignition key to the on position in order to turn on the heater for a few minutes, she heard the faint tapping against the front passenger window, thinking it was nothing more than the tip of a branch hitting the glass. But the tapping was too regular, too persistent, and soon it became louder, harder. Her heart stopped; her breath caught in a gasp, and she jerked her head around, a soundless moan rising in her throat when she saw the face distorted by a stocking mask staring in at her. *This wasn't the way it was supposed to happen!* He was supposed to *call* her with instructions at the rest area, not *be* here! But he was here and very well concealed among the low boughs of the trees.

A *nightmare.* It had to be a nightmare. But it wasn't; it was very real, and when the man jerkily motioned her to the window, she moved over the space between the bucket seats with leaden limbs, too stunned to feel afraid. A numbness was running through her, sapping all her strength. She could only stare at the flattened features of the face beyond the glass.

"Open the window," the face hissed.

And she did, letting in a blast of unseasonably frigid wind that she was barely capable of feeling. Somehow, she had enough presence of mind to lay her right hand on the canvas bag next to her. "I have the money," she told the stockinged face. "Right here."

"Hand it over then," the same muffled voice she had heard on the telephone spat out. And as she obeyed and gave him the tote, he added sharply. "It's all here? Three hundred thousand?"

"Yes, all of it," she said weakly. "But what about Br—"

Her words were cut off by the man's abrupt curse. "Cops! I warned you not to let them follow you!" He reached into the car and coolly flipped the switch of the overhead interior light so that it didn't come on when he jerked the door open. Jessica tried to scream, afraid no one could see what was happening, but her mouth had gone dry, and the sound she made wasn't very loud as she was grabbed by one arm and wrenched across the seat out of the car onto her knees in browning grass. Then she was being yanked to her feet and pulled between the overlapping evergreen branches.

"No! Wait, I . . ." she gasped to no avail, and while she was dragged away from her car, she instinctively looked back over her shoulder and saw the Georgia State Patrol car that had pulled into the rest area. Her heart was pounding. She felt faint. How ironic that a state patrolman had inadvertently stopped at this particular rest area at the worst possible time.

"It isn't what you think," she uttered breathlessly, trying to focus her eyes on the average height, well-built man pulling her after him, the man who was taking her . . . God only knew where. Intuitively, she balked, digging her heels into the ground. "Listen, please. That patrolman—it's a coincidence. He couldn't possibly know what's happening."

"Shut up," her captor snarled. "You're going to be my ticket out of here."

"You have the money. Run with it," she reasoned as best she could. "You have what you want. There's no need to hurt anybody now."

Even as she held back, resisted with all her remaining strength, she was pulled along parallel to the line of trees until, abruptly, a sharp pop as if from a twig snapping sounded above them up the hill. Seeming to panic, the kidnapper clutched the tote bag closer to him while shoving her backward.

"You blew it, baby," he hurled at her. "You blew it all!"

Jessica bounced against the trunk of a tree, her head smacking against it. She felt the rough bark against her left cheek and temple, and then she was falling, the ground rushing up at her, and as she tried to catch herself by grabbing for the tree, her foot caught on an exposed root. Her ankle twisted, and hot grinding pain shot up her leg. She collapsed onto the ground, the blow to her head causing sparkles of light to explode in her eyes, and with the breath knocked out of her, she lay on her side for several long moments, only half-aware of what had happened. The pain in her ankle shafting upward into her thigh finally roused her to some degree. She tried to get up but couldn't. Still dazed, her burning, throbbing ankle unable to bear any of her weight, she huddled beneath the low-hanging branches which provided surprisingly little protection against the penetrating wind.

Dimly, she heard a burst of shouting in the distance, men's voices barking out words she couldn't distinguish. Relieved that the police apparently realized the plan had gone wrong, she tried to stop shaking and calm down. But the slow deep breaths she started taking became quick shallow gasps of air when evergreen boughs rustled noisily, moved by something other than the wind, and footsteps crunching the carpet of brittle needles on the ground grew louder and louder.

Was it the kidnapper returning to grab her again and use her as hostage to escape the sheriff's deputies and the police? Heart hammering viciously, she shrank back against the tree trunk, hoping she wouldn't be seen. Keeping completely still, her lips tightly pressed together, she saw the dark form coming toward her, and had it not been for her injured ankle, she would have made a run for it then. It wasn't until the man was almost on her, his towering shape silhouetted in the dim light of the mercury-vapor lamps shining down on the parking area behind him, that she realized the kidnapper had carried the tote bag away with him after throwing her to the ground. But this man rushing swiftly toward her was carrying nothing and . . .

"*Jessica,*" he called.

That low-timbred, beloved voice calling her name was the most welcome sound she had ever heard. A half sob stuck in her throat, preventing speech as she scrambled forward and tried to get up, forgetting her ankle in the emotion of the moment.

"Cade," she gasped softly at last, reaching for him, stumbling when searing pain careened up her leg. She nearly fell and sank onto her knees on the ground, grasping the large hands that shot out toward her as she went down.

"Jessica, are you all right?" Cade asked urgently, dropping to his own knees before her. "What's wrong with your leg?"

"It's my . . . ankle," she answered haltingly, still breathless, still so glad to see him she could easily have cried. Her gaze fixed on his shadowed face. "I twisted . . ."

Suddenly a car engine revved up loudly and tires squealed on asphalt, spinning away as a second vehicle roared after in hot pursuit. More than one siren shattered the quiet night, wailing out danger and warning.

"Oh God, they didn't catch him!" Jessica softly cried, clutching the lapels of Cade's jacket. "They have to catch him!"

"They will," Cade said, his tone grim. "He can't get away from all of them."

"But if he does and he gets back to Brad, he might . . ." She couldn't bring herself to say the words, but what she meant was all too clear, and she could only stare over Cade's shoulder at the whirling flashes of blue lights that would soon disappear out of sight on the interstate. "Oh my God, this all worked out wrong, didn't it?"

"It'll be all right," Cade murmured, gently prying open the small fingers that gripped his coat, freeing himself to bend over her and lift her up in his arms.

"I can probably walk if you'll help me a little," she said automatically. "I can try."

"I'll carry you. The sooner we get you out of this wind and into your car the better," he said, frowning when she drew a whistling breath between her teeth as her ankle was jarred while he rose to his feet. "Do you think it's broken?"

"Probably just badly wrenched."

"You'll need an X ray. I'll get you to the hospital."

"But . . . All right," she acquiesced reluctantly, allowing her head to come to rest on his shoulder. "I guess there's nothing else we can do out here anyhow. But there must be some way to find out what's happening."

"I'll take care of that while you're having your ankle examined," Cade said, lowering her down to stand on the uninjured leg, his arm round her waist while he opened the car door. After helping her into the front seat, he gently assisted her as she swiveled around straight to place both feet on the floorboard, his fingertips lightly probing the injured area. "It's swollen already."

"I imagine it's just sprained," she murmured. And when he shut the door and walked around to the driver's side, she hastily rolled the passenger window back up. The frigid, gusting wind had cut through her clothes, chilling her to the bone, but it was

252

also delayed reaction that made her shiver so violently her teeth nearly chattered. As Cade got in the car beneath the wheel beside her, slipped off his coat, and leaned over to wrap it snuggly around her, her response to his kindness was overly emotional but natural under the circumstances. Tears welled up in her eyes; she blinked them away, but they came right back, and she accepted the handkerchief he handed her with a throaty word of thanks, shaking her head. "It wasn't supposed to work out this way. They were supposed to follow him to Brad, but now he doesn't dare lead them there. And if they lose him . . ."

"They won't lose him. Lieutenant Flanders is itching to get this man. He told me so in no uncertain terms on our way out here."

"Why did you come along?" Jessica turned her head to look at him. "I mean, I got the impression you'd be staying in town."

"There are times when it's impossible to simply sit and wait, and after you left the garage, I hailed Flanders down on his way out to follow you," Cade explained flatly, starting the car and pulling away across the now deserted parking lot. He had no choice except to continue north on the interstate, the same direction in which the kidnapper and pursuing police had headed. But by the time he left the highway at the next interchange and turned back toward Atlanta, they had seen no sign of stopped cars and flashing blue lights that would have indicated the chase had ended with an arrest.

It was more than two hours later that Jessica hobbled back into the hospital's emergency waiting room, her ankle wrapped, a crutch tucked under her arm. Her eyes darted around, searching for Cade. She hadn't seen him since nearly an hour ago when he had come to the examining room where she had been waiting to be taken to X ray. He had told her that, although the kidnapper had just been apprehended, there was no word on Brad yet. Certain there must be news by now, Jessica scanned the waiting room once more, but still she didn't see Cade. Unaccustomed to the crutch, she moved slowly between rows of molded fiberglass chairs, and about the time she reached the center of the room, Cade strode around the corner from the alcove where the public telephones were located. As he came straight to her, her eyes brightened with hope.

"Brad? They've found him?" she questioned eagerly. "Is he all right?"

"He hasn't been found yet. Apparently, the kidnapper isn't cooperating," Cade said, his candid black eyes meeting hers. "I was just on the phone to the lieutenant, and he wants you to come down to the station as soon as possible. Are they all finished with you here?"

With disappointment settling in her chest like a stone, she nodded. "Yes, everything's done, so let's get to the station right away," she insisted. She tried to hurry toward the glass double doors but discovered she could only hobble along, and as Cade slowed his pace in deference to hers, she gave him a worried look. "Can't they make him tell where Brad is? Couldn't they offer him some deal or something?"

"I don't know the details; I only spoke with Flanders for a few moments," he said, stepping ahead of her to push one of the doors open and hold it for her. "We'll just have to wait until we get to the station to find out exactly what's happening."

The fifteen-minute drive to police headquarters seemed to take at least ten times that long, but at last they arrived and were directed to Lieutenant Flanders's cubbyhole of an office. When the policeman looked up and saw them enter, he stood, his graying hair unusually rumpled. Beckoning them in, he swept a jumbled stack of paperwork to the side of his metal desk and waved Jessica into one of the straight-backed chairs in front of it.

"Sit down, please," he invited. "How's the ankle?"

"It's just a bad sprain," she told him, taking a seat. After Cade took the crutch and laid it aside then settled in the chair next to hers, her troubled eyes sought the lieutenant's, and she clasped her hands tightly together in her lap. "Has the man told you where Brad is yet?"

"No. That's precisely why I wanted to talk to you," Flanders stated, dropping back down into his own chair again. "The name of the man we arrested is Freddy Sims. That mean anything to you?" When she shook her head, he nodded. "I doubted it would. Now, out at the rest area tonight, during the time Sims had you with him, did he say anything at all that might help us locate Mr. Taylor?"

Jessica thought carefully and shook her head once again. "He didn't say anything that might help. In fact, he didn't even mention Brad."

Tapping his cheek thoughtfully with one finger, the policeman nodded. "I was afraid of that."

"Why don't you tell us exactly what's going on, Lieutenant," suggested Cade somberly. "For some reason you're obviously having trouble getting this Sims to talk to you."

"That's just the problem. Sims nearly talked our ears off for over an hour, but he told us nothing about Brad Taylor. He says he doesn't know anything because he never had Taylor in the first place. He swears he has no idea where he is and has never even seen him in person."

"Then he's lying," Jessica interjected, anger at this despicable, cowardly criminal mantling her cheeks in rosy red. "How does he dare pretend he doesn't know where Brad is? Of course he does! He's the same man who called me and let Brad talk to me, so he has to know where he is."

The lieutenant's shoulders rose and fell in a rather weary shrug. "Sims says that was a trick."

"But it wasn't. It was Brad! I'd know his voice anywhere."

"Sims doesn't deny it was Brad Taylor's voice, but he swears it was on tape, a tape he made at the Regency Theater during yesterday afternoon's matinee—a showing of *That Summer*, starring Taylor." Leaning on his arm across his desk, Flanders sighed. "I sent one of my men to the theater to check it out, and sure enough, in one of the scenes Taylor does say: 'I'm all right. I'm okay, really. You . . .' Exactly the same thing Mr. Taylor said to you yesterday, Jessica, although in the movie, he is saying it as he regains consciousness after a blow on the head."

Though *That Summer* wasn't her favorite of all Brad's movies, she now recalled the line nevertheless. But still . . . Her confused blue eyes sought Cade's, seeming almost to appeal for his help.

"I understand what you're saying, Lieutenant," Cade intervened, looking away from her toward the older man. "Of course, we've been aware of the possibility that this might be a hoax, but I still don't think we can be certain of that. Sims *did* make a ransom demand, and I assume he still had the money on him when he was arrested?"

"Oh yes. He's guilty of extortion, if nothing else," the policeman said, jumping up from his chair and beginning to pace back and forth behind his desk, hands clasped behind his back. "But Sims says he got the idea for the ransom from an item he read in the newspaper about Taylor being missing. He swears he thought it just might be an easy way to make a lot of cash."

"But, like Cade said, you can't be sure of that," Jessica softly exclaimed, her entire body tensed. "Sims could easily be lying. After all, I imagine extortion is a much less serious crime than kidnapping. He's trying to get away with what he's done. Surely you don't believe you can trust what he says?"

"Jessica, I'm not saying I trust him at all," Flanders told her, halting mid-stride in his pacing to regard her kindly. He shook his head. "But I have to tell you that Sims doesn't impress me as a very intelligent man. I wonder if he'd have the brains to plan a kidnapping and then be able to successfully hold someone captive, especially a well-known movie star, for several days without making somebody somewhere suspicious."

"Maybe he just got lucky this time," she said weakly. "And everything just worked out right for him."

"Maybe, but I have my doubts about that when I think of how he messed up tonight. Why didn't he call you at the rest area and direct you to an absolutely isolated back road somewhere, where any approaching car would have made him suspicious? Why did he try to grab the money at the rest area where he should have known we were watching you and where cars are always moving in and out?" The policeman sighed heavily. "Would a man who's smart enough to plan a kidnapping and to keep a victim hidden for several days make a stupid mistake like that? Sims has a record, but all his prior crimes have been strictly small time. He's never been involved in anything nearly as big as a kidnapping."

"But he must have kidnapped Brad," Jessica insisted. "If he didn't, then where is Brad and why hasn't anyone heard from him?"

"Maybe Sims isn't the only person involved," Cade spoke up. "Maybe he has an accomplice who planned everything and Sims simply botched it."

"Naturally, that's a possibility I'm not ruling out," Lieutenant Flanders assured them both. "I'm not going to consider this case solved until Brad Taylor is located. We'll continue the surveillance on your house and continue monitoring your phone, Jessica, in case there's another ransom demand. I intend to press on with this investigation; I mean that."

Then why, despite his honest assurances, did Jessica somehow feel as if she had just lost a trusted ally? Why, when her eyes sought the dark depths of Cade's, did she long to fling herself into his arms, seeking his comfort and his strength? Digging her nails into her palms, she restrained herself from doing that, but deep inside, she wondered fearfully how much longer she could go on enduring the horrible tension that came with not knowing what had happened to Brad. It was the uncertainty that was the most difficult thing in the world to bear.

CHAPTER FIFTEEN

Tuesday morning, three days later, Jessica swung her legs off the side of her bed, cautiously lowering her feet to the floor. Hoping to be able to discard the crutch, she stood up to test her ankle but immediately sank back down, uttering a mild oath, as pain lanced up her leg. The ankle was improved but still too tender to walk on, which meant she would have to continue hobbling around.

"Terrific," she mumbled, pulling her nightgown off over her head and throwing it halfway across the room onto the floor. Frustration had been mounting in her since Saturday night's ransom delivery debacle, and this morning especially, she felt like she would scream if she didn't get out of this house soon and get back to living life normally once more. Last night hadn't helped. Unable to sleep for hours after going to bed, she had tossed and turned so much that finally the covers were all tumbled and even the sheet beneath her had felt rumpled and uncomfortable. It had been necessary for her to get up and hobble around the bed, straightening the linens, but that hadn't helped much either. Sleep still hadn't come until a long time later. Now, her eyes burned and felt gritty, and there was an unpleasant little buzzing in her head due to lack of proper rest.

Trying to alleviate the physical malaise that gripped her, she dressed as quickly as possible in a denim skirt and white oxford blouse, then went into the bathroom to brush her teeth and wash her face. Afterward, she applied light makeup, mainly in an attempt to raise her spirits. When she left the bath a few minutes later, the guest bedroom door was open, and she found Cade in the kitchen sitting at the small round maple table, a cup of coffee in front of him as he perused the morning newspaper. He looked up when she entered.

"Morning," he murmured, watching as she moved to the counter to pour a cup of coffee for herself. "How's the ankle today? Any better?"

"It's getting there, I suppose. Maybe by tomorrow I won't need this," she told him, waving the end of the crutch off the floor a few inches while balancing on one foot. "I hope I won't, anyway. It's very inconvenient."

"At least the scratches on your face have faded," he observed laconically. "Now you don't look like you've been in a catfight."

Responding with a wry smile, she carefully carried her cup to the table but merely put it down instead of taking the chair across from him. "How about a nice big breakfast?" she suggested. "I'd be happy to make anything you want."

He shook his head. "Thanks, but no."

Jessica wished he had said yes. Making a large breakfast would have at least been something to do to pass a little time, but if he didn't want it, it was useless to make it for herself. She really only felt a bit hungry. Suppressing a sigh, she looked toward the counter. "Then how about those cinnamon buns I baked yesterday? Would you care for one?"

"Fine, but you sit down and I'll get them," he commanded, getting up and waving her toward the opposite chair. "Maybe if you hadn't come in here and baked yesterday, your ankle would be less sore now. You're supposed to stay off of it as much as possible, but you haven't been doing that."

"I can't spend all my time in the living room with my foot propped on a pillow," she replied flatly, lowering herself onto the seat. "If I'm not doing something, I feel like the walls are starting to close in on me."

"I know it isn't easy right now, but there are things you can do sitting down with your foot up. What about that work your assistant brought over?"

"I've finished it already. Lynn's planning to pick it up today when she brings more but . . ." Jessica sighed, her gaze lifting to meet his when he returned to the table with two small plates and the bread basket containing the cinnamon buns. While unfolding the linen cloth in which they were wrapped, she continued, "I can't keep up with all my work at home. There's so much I need to be doing at the office. I've explained to my boss why I haven't been coming in, but . . . Well, he says he understands, but he's not at all happy about the situation. I can tell by his cool tone of voice."

Cade's black eyes looked like chips of obsidian as a frown flew to his brow. "You're not afraid you might get fired, are you?"

"Oh no! At least I don't think I have to worry about that," she murmured, qualifying her first quick answer, an easily readable tinge of uncertainty shading her features. "But I just had a vacation, and with Peg still out on sick leave, I need to be at work."

"Maybe you should consider going back then."

"How can I until . . ." Jessica didn't finish because there was no need to elaborate on the question that was foremost in both their minds: when is another ransom demand going to be made? They had been awaiting a call from Sims's accomplice since Saturday night, but nothing whatsoever had happened, and while she felt she was well on the road to going crazy, she could sense the rising restlessness in Cade. And there had been that pall of tension that seemed almost tangible between them for the past two days. Sometimes, like now, they were able to escape it for a little while, but it always crept back up on them, usually heavier than before, like a smothering miasmic cloud hanging about their heads. Jessica hated it and knew he did too, but the nerve-wracking situation had them trapped, and she could see no way out of it until either it resolved itself somehow or the police located Brad. It was natural for them both to be feeling the strain because of this seemingly endless siege of waiting, yet she longed to ease some of the tension growing between them. It was soul-wrenching enough for her to be in the same house with him, loving him yet knowing he didn't love her. She didn't need the additional agony that accompanied the forced, stilted conversations that had been occurring more frequently during the past couple of days.

After taking a small bite of the cinnamon bun then washing it down her dry throat with a sip of coffee, she moved one hand rather hesitantly, saying, "I know this isn't any more pleasant for you than it is for me, Cade. But it has to be over soon."

He simply looked deeply into her eyes for several long breathtaking moments without speaking, and when he finally did, his comment didn't pertain to what she had just said. His searching gaze skimmed over her face. "Speaking of work, I have business I must take care of today. I'll be going into the office for a while this morning."

Wishing she could do the same thing and escape to her own office for at least a few hours, she struggled to swallow past the lump coming to her throat and nodded. Then, mentally chastising herself for feeling forsaken simply because he had to attend to business, she dismissed that silly emotion and, lifting the basket, held it out to him. "Another cinnamon bun?" And a natural pleased smile graced her lips when he accepted.

Less than an hour later, as Cade was adjusting the knot of his blue tie while he walked toward the front door to leave for the office, someone knocked. "I'll get it," he said sternly when Jessica started to reach for the crutch next to her chair. She sat back, and he went to answer the knock, stepping aside to admit Libby Wheeler into the house.

At the sight of the newspaper reporter, Jessica's heart sank. What she didn't need at the moment was someone grilling her about Brad, but she managed to appear unconcerned when Libby accepted her invitation and sauntered over to take a seat on the opposite sofa. Relieved as Cade returned from across the room to join the two of them, Jessica made no attempt to avoid the issue. She simply plunged right in, smiling politely at the other young woman.

"I assume you're here about Brad again?"

"Right. I've come because of a tip I've received," the reporter said, flipping open her notebook. "All of us in the news business have a few sources in the police department, a few people who leak information from time to time, and one of my sources has told me an incredible story about Brad Taylor's kidnapping. Is it true? Has Taylor been kidnapped?"

Sitting up stiff and straight in her chair, Jessica drew in a long, shuddering breath. Her eyes shifted from Libby to Cade then back to the reporter, and she forced herself to utter a flagrant lie. "Kidnapped? Brad? I'm afraid I have no idea what you're talking about."

Libby cast a dubious glance in her direction. "Then you're denying a man named Freddy Sims was arrested Saturday night after picking up ransom money you personally delivered?"

"Obviously your source didn't provide you with the entire story, Miss Wheeler," Cade intervened before Jessica could even open her mouth to answer. He casually smiled. "You're right about a couple of things. Mr. Sims was arrested Saturday night. And for a time there was strong reason to believe that Brad Taylor had been kidnapped. But now Sims denies ever having Brad and swears he got the idea to extort the money after reading your article about the disappearance."

"Then you're saying Mr. Taylor *hasn't* been kidnapped?"

"Maybe we'd be wise to reconsider the possibility that he's somewhere with Christina Myerly right now" was Cade's oblique reply.

"I see," muttered the reporter, seeming a little disappointed that such a potentially dramatic story had lost a great deal of its pizazz. But she was resourceful and didn't give up very easily. "And do you think Mr. Taylor might have engineered this 'disappearance' as a publicity stunt?"

"Maybe we'd be wise to consider that possibility too," Cade said, meeting Jessica's startled look with a bland expression. Resting his chin on steepled fingers, he nodded thoughtfully. "Yes, it *has* to be a possibility. Actors do want publicity."

"Enough to arrange a fake kidnapping?"

"I didn't say that," Cade responded calmly to the incisive question. "Even if the 'disappearance' is a publicity stunt, I'm sure Mr. Taylor never imagined someone like Sims would pretend he had kidnapped him in order to extort a large amount of money."

"But . . ."

"I'm sorry, but Jessica and I have already told you everything we know," he stated politely, rising lithely to his feet, an obvious indication that he regarded the interview over.

"Just a couple more questions," Libby persisted, although she did get up too, as if preparing to leave soon. "I'm curious, Jessica. What happened to your ankle?"

"I sprained it."

"How?"

"Oh, I fell."

"Could you elaborate a little?" Libby queried. "When you delivered the ransom money to Sims, did he attack you? Is that when your ankle was injured?"

"As I said, I fell," Jessica reiterated, telling the truth, just not all of it.

"Then Sims didn't . . ."

"I think Jessica would rather just put Freddy Sims out of her mind," Cade cut in.

Apparently deciding she had gotten all the information she was going to for the time being, Libby said her good-byes and left the house.

After Cade had closed the front door behind her, he turned back to Jessica. "I think you'd better tell your parents what's been happening before they read about it in the newspaper."

"I guess I don't have much choice," Jessica said, tight-lipped as she looked at him. "Why did you tell Libby all that?"

"She already knew about the ransom payoff and planned to write a story about it. We wouldn't have been able to convince her it wasn't true," Cade explained, coming back across the room to get his briefcase, which was on the coffee table. "I thought we might as well tell her the truth about Saturday night anyway, then try to play it down."

"I don't mean that. I mean why did you tell her all that about Brad's 'disappearance' maybe being a publicity stunt?"

"It's a convincing explanation for an actor being missing."

"Maybe too convincing," Jessica said shortly. "Libby may slant the story she writes and make it seem like Brad did arrange a fake kidnapping. If she does do that, a lot of people are going to believe it."

"Fine. Let's hope they all do. If Brad's disappearance is downplayed, it's less likely another Freddy Sims will come along and try to make the most of the situation."

"If that's what Sims did," Jessica answered, her voice lowering, her darkening eyes searching his. "Are you saying you agree with the lieutenant now and don't believe Sims ever had Brad. *You're* the one who suggested he had an accomplice."

"That's still a possibility. But you have to admit that it's one that gets slimmer and slimmer with every day that passes." Cade's answer was quick and curt, while something akin to impatience tightened his carved features. "If Sims has an accomplice who's holding Brad, why haven't we received another ransom demand?"

"I don't know why! Maybe this person is just trying to wear us down by making us wait to hear from him just the way Sims did. I don't know what's going on. I have no idea what makes people like that tick. I only know I don't want a newspaper story to give the police the idea that Brad planned all this to get publicity. If they get that idea, they'll stop looking for him."

"That idea's already occurred to Flanders, Jessica. He doesn't suspect Brad of arranging a fake kidnapping, but he is considering the possibility that the disappearance was nothing more than a publicity stunt and that Brad's safe somewhere right now. But of course he's continuing the search for him too."

"He is for now," she muttered, stunned by this news. "I can't believe the lieutenant could even imagine this might be a publicity stunt." Glittering sapphire eyes locked Cade's. "And what about you? Do you believe that too?"

"I see it as a possibility."

"Surely Brad wouldn't ever do that!"

Cade's darkly slashed brows lifted, casting a rather mocking expression over his bronzed face. "Wouldn't he, Jessica?"

"No, I don't think he would," she retorted wodenly, feeling betrayed. "And even if he did disappear for such an inexcusable reason, which he didn't, he wouldn't have let it go as long as this has. So, if somebody's not holding him hostage right now, where *is* he?"

"I wish to hell I knew," Cade said, jaw clenched, eyes narrowed as he regarded her irritably. "But I suspect more and more every day that if we could find Christie, we'd find him too."

Jessica turned away, unable to talk about this any longer. Weariness crept over her, and the pressure of tears that needed badly to be shed increased rapidly behind her eyes. Tightly squeezing together her linked fingers, she mumbled, "Didn't you say something about having to go to your office?"

And after Cade strode across the room and out of the house without another word, she rested her head against the wing of the chair and at last allowed hot tears to start sliding down her cheeks.

The sound of footsteps in the living room brought Jessica fully awake. Her heartbeat quickened with her realization that Cade was back. She sat up in bed, noticed the slant of the dim light coming in her window, and checked her wristwatch, eyes widening with surprise. It was nearly six o'clock, and Cade had stayed away the entire day. She had expected him back before this, and maybe if he had returned earlier, she wouldn't have slept so long. In the afternoon after she had called her parents, an emotional ordeal, and after Lynn had brought work by for her then left again, her headache had made her decide a nap was a good idea. But she had only meant to sleep an hour or so instead of three. Yet perhaps the extra rest had helped. Now her head no longer ached, and she felt human again anyway.

Lowering her feet to the floor, she sat poised on the edge of the bed and reached for the crutch as Cade lightly tapped on her door. One hand closed tightly around the tubular metal while with the other she smoothed her slightly tousled hair and softly told him to come in.

His eyes swept over her when he opened the door and stepped into the room. "Did I wake you?" he asked. "If you're tired, this can wait."

"No. No, that's okay. I had too long a nap anyway."

His coat and tie removed, his vest unbuttoned, Cade advanced toward her several steps. "I want to talk to you, Jessica."

"Oh?" she murmured, fresh tension plus some apprehension rising in her because of his serious tone. "What about?"

"This entire situation and the way we're handling it. It's time for a change," he said forthrightly, leaning his elbow on her bureau, his large brown hands loosely clasped. "I've just been with Lieutenant Flanders, and he's decided to discontinue monitoring your telephone and to pull his men off surveillance because he says it's useless to have someone out in that van waiting for a call that would have come by now if it was coming at all. He needs to assign his men elsewhere."

"I see." Jessica's grip on the crutch tightened. She should have been prepared for this, considering Cade's comments this morning, and in a way, she had been prepared. As she looked up at him, her chin lifted a fraction of an inch. "So, the lieutenant's just giving up on Brad?"

"The police will still be trying to locate him, but the investigation has been downgraded. It's no longer considered a top priority case. Flanders feels almost certain Brad was never a kidnap victim and that he simply went off somewhere."

"Does he *really*?" Concern darkened her eyes. "And I suppose you agree with him?"

"To the extent that I think it's time for us to stop sitting here and waiting for a call that isn't going to come."

"Then you don't believe Brad was ever kidnapped?" she asked tiredly. "You really think this is all some kind of publicity stunt?"

"I'm not sure of that; neither is the lieutenant," Cade said calmly. "But I do agree with him that it looks as if Brad just went off without bothering to tell anyone where he was going."

"And what if that's wrong? What happens to Brad?"

Cade met her anxious gaze directly. "I'm going to put the private investigator back on the search. The trail's colder now, but he has something to go on. He can go to Miami to try to discover someone who saw Brad, possibly with Christie, approximately a week ago, and if he does, he can go on looking from there."

"You think he just ran off with Christie and didn't let anyone know? I just can't believe he would do that, even now."

"For God's sake, Jessica," Cade growled, straightening to walk over to her, angry fire igniting in his eyes. "You know damned well he's perfectly capable of doing that."

"Maybe you think so, but he's not a perfect nitwit," she said succinctly, unwilling to consider the possibility that Brad had changed *that* much and had become that selfish and thoughtless. "I've known Brad all my life and . . ."

"The Brad you've known all your life isn't the same Brad you know now, and you realize that. You may not admit it even to yourself, but you know it. And this new Brad is capable of being very selfish and inconsiderate."

"Not *this* inconsiderate."

"Take the blinders off, why don't you!" Cade muttered harshly, hands planted on his hips. "Surely you haven't forgotten Brad showed a distinct knack for being inconsiderate in Bermuda when he didn't bother to call you during the storm."

"That was not exactly the same," she protested. "Then he was only missing a few hours, and this time he's been gone for well over a week. He just wouldn't stay out of touch that long."

"Wouldn't he?" Cade drawled sarcastically. "Maybe he's simply improved his talent for acting like a selfish little boy."

"I'll forget you said that," she said tautly. "You just don't understand what life has been like for him."

"*I* don't understand what it's like to grow up without parents?"

"That obviously didn't affect you the way it did Brad," she murmured, a tenderness for Cade that she didn't want to feel overpowering her for an instant. She pressed her fingertips against her forehead. "You're a strong man, Cade, but Brad's
. . ."

"Weak?" he finished tauntingly for her when her voice trailed off. "So you have noticed that about him."

Suddenly it was all much too much for her, and the misery welled up inside was threatening to make her burst into tears. And she refused to cry in front of this man. She shook her head. "I don't want to discuss this anymore."

"Too bad, because I have something else to say to you," Cade went on relentlessly, reaching down to grip her chin between thumb and forefinger. "You'll be wasting your time if you sit in this house waiting for a call from a kidnapper who doesn't exist. You have to go back to work, Jessica."

"Maybe you and the lieutenant are right to give up on Brad, but I can't risk it."

"So you'll risk losing the job you love instead?"

"That won't happen," she said but didn't sound terribly convinced, even to herself. "But if it does . . . what's more important, a job or someone's life?"

"The answer to that is obvious. But no one's life is at stake in this situation."

"I can't be as sure of that as you obviously are," she said, turning her head aside quickly to escape his hold on her chin. She stared morosely at her feet. "Don't you think I want to go back to work? I . . ." Close to tears, she pressed her lips tightly together, and overcome by frustration, confusion, and hurt, she stood too quickly and not cautiously enough. Her injured ankle struck the bottom of the metal crutch. Pain shot through her leg, and it began to collapse beneath her. "Oh dammit all to hell," she cried impotently, starting to struggle the instant Cade reached out and caught her, preventing her from falling. "Let me go. I can take care of myself; I don't need you to . . ."

"Don't you?" Cade whispered roughly, easily subduing her efforts to escape him and drawing her closer against him. "I think you do, and I know you can't take care of some things by yourself; we have to take care of them together. And it's been too long since we did, Jessica."

Her eyes darted up to meet his, and her heart seemed to leap up in her throat when she recognized the passionate intent in the glinting black depths. "Cade, *don't,*" she breathed, twisting valiantly in an attempt to be free of the muscular arms that bound her. But it was too late. Winding her hair around one hand, he tilted her head back and his warm lips descended onto the creamy skin of her neck. She gasped as wild sensations ran riot through her at that first caressing touch, yet aided by a core of inner strength, she continued to resist him. When the tip of his tongue flicked into the hollow beneath her right ear, she tried to jerk away, but he simply retaliated by dragging her arms around his waist and arching her against him. Aroused as he was, he took no time to undo her blouse slowly and instead tore it open so that three or four buttons popped off to land with a ping on the hardwood floor.

"No, Cade, no," she uttered softly, tremulously, when he bent over her and his mouth suddenly closed around the peak of one breast, warm and moist through the wispy lace of her bra. *"No!"*

"Oh yes, Jessica, yes," he raised his head to say. Then his lips were teasing the roseate nipple once more, bringing it to full erectness against the sheer, dampened fabric.

"Cade. Don't."

"I have to. God, I need you," he muttered, lowering her blouse from her shoulders, stripping it off her completely, then seeking the button on the waistband of her skirt.

"No. No," she repeated, but each breathless denial contained less conviction. The wicked weakness that was spreading through her legs had nothing to do with the fading ache in her ankle. He was masterfully kindling the fire of desire in her, and the rising flames were swiftly consuming all hope of resistance. She moaned softly when her skirt dropped down around her feet and his hands coursed over her, shaping her every curve, conveying his right of possession with each demanding yet gentle touch. Lost and knowing she was lost and not caring much anymore, she tightened her arms around his waist, hands sweeping lovingly over his broad back while he deftly removed the rest of her clothes.

When she was naked, the satin-textured surface of her skin shimmering in the early evening light streaming through the bedroom window, Cade put her from him, drawing her hands to the collar of his shirt. "Take it off," he commanded huskily.

And eagerly, she did, undoing the buttons slowly before easing his vest off, the shirt following. Then her fingers sought his belt buckle and soon he too was naked, his superb body bronzed in the glow of fading daylight.

Cade stripped back the bedcovers, picked Jessica up, and put her down in the center of the mattress. He leaned over her, stroking one hand between her thighs, parting her long shapely legs, then coming down between them, his hard mouth indescribably tender as he claimed the softness of her sweetly shaped lips.

"I've wanted to do this for days," he said hoarsely, kissing her eyelids, her temples, the shallow hollows beneath her high cheekbones. "I've been going crazy across the hall knowing you were in here alone in this bed. I want you so much. And you want me too, don't you, Jessica?"

"Yes," she confessed breathlessly, her hands molding his lean taut hips. "Yes."

"Then say it," he demanded urgently. "I want you to say it."

"Oh Cade, yes, I . . ." Pride made her bite back the word love, but she gave it nevertheless, parted lips invitingly brushing against his. "I do want you too. Hurry. Take me."

"Soon," he promised, devouring her mouth. "I'll have to soon, but first . . ." His hands and lips traveled all over her, and as she explored him as thoroughly, they drifted together into immeasurable delight.

Even the wondrous completion that came with her sweet surrender was not enough for him. Later he took her again, and this time their lovemaking was less urgent, less feverish, but no less satisfying for either of them. Knowing each other fully, intent on pleasuring each other, they prolonged the ecstasy, carrying it upward to its most dizzying heights until at last when they could bear to wait no longer, they were borne together to the keenest spire of piercing rapture and tumbled together over the peak into warm fulfillment to lie quiet and spent and deliciously replete, wrapped in each other's arms.

After Cade's slow, steady breathing signaled he had fallen asleep, Jessica lay awake, feeling no regret for giving her love to him once more, although she knew he would have left her already if this hadn't happened between them. He had, after all, given up on Brad, and that meant he would be able to leave her now. She knew that and didn't want to go to sleep, feeling intuitively that when she awoke in the morning she would find him gone forever from her bed, from her house, and from her life. And needing his warmth as long as she could possibly have it, she snuggled closer to him. Yet she simply couldn't regret the love she had given or the passion they had shared, though she knew that tonight had been the end.

CHAPTER SIXTEEN

Jessica's intuition was wrong. Cade was still in bed beside her when she was awakened at six thirty the next morning. Aware of him stirring next to her, she reached out to answer the telephone, its strident pealing reverberating in her head and making her heart race unpleasantly. Never knowing anymore who might be calling, she cautiously said hello and shot straight up in bed when she instantly recognized the voice speaking to her.

"Brad!" she gasped, clutching the sheet around her. "Are you all right? Have you been hurt? Where are you?" Listening closely to his almost inaudible response, she glimpsed Cade out of the corner of her eye sitting up beside her now, as tensed and alert as she herself was. Half expecting a stranger's voice to replace Brad's at any moment, she urgently asked him if he could tell her where he was, and he suddenly did, confusing her completely. "But how did you get there?" And when he answered by only pleading for her to come to him, then added a few more words, she tried to assure him she would get to him as soon as she possibly could, but he was mumbling incoherently and didn't seem to be listening. Then an abrupt empty silence filled her ear, and she raised her voice slightly. "Brad, wait! Don't hang up."

But he did anyhow, and a click followed by a dial tone caused her to reach for her robe while returning the receiver to its cradle. Compulsion nearly made her jump out of bed, but just in time, she remembered her injured ankle and stood cautiously instead, testing it. Although still tender, it wasn't unbearably

273

painful even as she rested her weight upon it. Hearing Cade move out of the bed on the other side, she took a step, then looked at him as he came around to her, careless of his nakedness.

"Where is he?" he asked tersely.

"The Hyatt Regency," she answered, wrapping her robe more tightly around her. "He sounded so odd, almost disoriented. He must have escaped from wherever he was being held and is hiding in the hotel. I have to go to . . ."

"I'll go with you."

"But you don't have to do that."

"I'm going, Jessica," Cade said grimly, starting toward the door. "And that's final."

"All right then," she replied, limping to the bureau to open a drawer. "I just thought you wouldn't want to go."

Halting mid-stride, Cade turned back to glare at her. "You thought wrong because I'm not about to let you go alone. I never totally ruled out the possibility Brad had been kidnapped. I didn't think he had, but maybe that was a mistake. And maybe he did escape his captors somehow. Or maybe this is a trap someone's trying to lure you into. I don't know. But just in case it is, I'm not going to let you walk in it by yourself. So let's get dressed and go."

Ten minutes later Jessica and Cade left her house in his Jaguar, the drive downtown seeming to last forever as they exchanged not a word. After parking the car and entering the hotel, Jessica hurried across the lobby, her limp more pronounced now.

"He couldn't remember his room number," she murmured to Cade as she approached the desk and gave the clerk the name.

They were soon being whisked up on the elevator to the twenty-third floor, and after locating Brad's room number, Cade knocked on the door while Jessica stood at his side, her hands clasped tightly together before her.

It was some time before the door opened onto the sitting room of a suite and Brad stepped into the opening with a crooked grin,

274

looking a bit bedraggled but not exceedingly so. And he certainly didn't appear to be injured. "Jess, baby, you did come," he muttered, reaching for her then moving aside when Cade brushed past him to stride into the sitting room. "And you brought Cade. How you doing, Cade?"

Without answering, Cade conducted a seemingly perfunctory search of the suite, and when he disappeared for a few seconds in the adjoining bedroom, Jessica looked around, taking in the clothes strewn willy-nilly on the floor and over the sofa. And she knew the truth even before Cade walked back into the sitting room, shaking his head to indicate no one else was there. Fighting the desire to slap Brad's hands away as they sought her waist, she simply turned from him instead and met Cade as he walked toward her.

"There isn't anybody else here," Cade told her expressionlessly, glancing at the other man. "I'll leave you alone with him."

"Maybe that would be best," she agreed, her sapphire eyes searching the black depths of his, then following him with longing as he left the suite and closed the door quietly on the way out.

Taking a deep breath, Jessica turned around and walked back to Brad, clenching her hands into fists at her side.

"What happened to your foot, baby?" he asked as she approached. "You're limping a little. How did you hurt it?"

"I'm going to ask you a question I doubt will make much sense to you," she declared, ignoring his as if he'd never uttered it, her glacier eyes flicking over him. "How did you manage to escape from the kidnappers?"

Taken aback, Brad stared blankly at her, his handsome face the picture of confusion. "Kidnappers?" he repeated, shaking his head. "I don't know what you're talking about."

"I had a feeling you wouldn't. So where the devil have you been the past ten days?" she exclaimed furiously, resentment exploding in her. "Tell me, Brad. Just where have you been?"

"Jess, baby, I can explain everything, if you'll give me a chance," he cajoled, his words slurring slightly.

"Are you on something?" she asked, moving closer to peer into eyes that did indeed seem a bit bleary. "You act like you . . ."

"Aw, come on, baby, I'm not on anything," he protested, starting to touch her then letting his hands fall limply into his lap when she brushed them away. "You know I've never been into drugs. I'm not now."

"I'd like to think you haven't done anything quite that stupid yet, but you're certainly acting . . ."

"I just had a couple drinks too many, that's all."

"It's seven in the morning," she caustically reminded him. "And you've already started drinking?"

"I'm still working on last night," he mumbled. "I haven't been to bed."

"And is that how you've spent the past ten days? On a binge in this hotel room?"

To his credit he did show some shame as he shook his head. "I just checked in here late yesterday. The rest of the time I was down in the Caribbean."

"Oh, island-hopping," she drawled with much sarcasm. "Alone or with Christie?"

"Well, you wouldn't go along, so I asked Christie to go with me. I'm sorry."

"I wouldn't have cared if you'd taken every actress you knew along if you had just had the decency to tell someone where you were going," Jessica retorted angrily. "How could you do that to Mom and Dad? You simply disappeared and left them here to worry themselves silly about you. What a despicable thing to do, Brad."

"I'm sorry they were upset," he mumbled but petulantly added, "but I thought it might be good for you to worry about me a little."

Almost of its own volition, her right hand shot up to deliver

276

a sharp stinging slap to his left cheek, and she didn't regret hitting him even as he gawked at her disbelievingly.

"You didn't have to do that."

"That's not the half of what I'd like to do right now. I feel the greatest urge to drag you over to that window and push you out. You wanted me to worry about you a little, is that it? Well, let me tell you exactly what you accomplished," she uttered, still seething and glaring at him as if she wished to do him great bodily harm. Omitting no details, she told him about the "kidnapping" and the ransom demands and delivery, ending with a pithy accusation. "Now, do you see what you did? You put me in a position where I had to deal directly with a criminal. I had to go out to meet him with the ransom money in the dark Saturday night, and he grabbed me, Brad! He started dragging me off with him. That's how I hurt my ankle. It happened when he threw me on the ground. But it could have been worse than that. He could have hurt me badly, even killed me, and all because you didn't bother to tell anyone where you were going or even that you were going."

"I just wanted to get away, after what you said to me. You wanted it to end between us and said there was some other man. How did you expect me to feel after that?" he muttered defensively. "And besides, it's not my fault somebody tried to get money from you by pretending to kidnap me."

"It's not your fault there are criminals in the world, but you're responsible for this one being able to exploit a situation you created. If you hadn't vanished without a word, there wouldn't have been a newspaper article about your 'disappearance,' and no one would have gotten the idea to try to extort money. So it *is* your fault. And you've gone much too far this time, Brad. I've had enough of you," she said, her tone unyielding. "It is time for me to cut the strings and let you try to get your act together again by yourself. Cade's been right about that all along."

"What's Cade got to do with us?"

"There is no 'us.' But Cade is the other man," she declared bluntly. "The man I told you about, the one I'm in love with."

"Damn him," Brad swore violently, fury flushing his face. "He's not going to get by with taking you . . ."

"He didn't take me. I went very willingly. And I've already told you that too."

Brad slammed his fist into the other hand. "If he expects to go on managing my money, he can just forget it."

"For God's sake, will you start acting like an adult again, Brad," she challenged. "I'm sure Cade's agency will survive very well even if you're no longer a client."

Brad stared her down. "Are the two of you . . . lovers?"

Meeting his eyes without apology, she nodded. "Yes, we are."

Brad's hands closed into tight fists. "But, dammit, Jess, you . . ."

"I love him, Brad, and I'm not at all sorry for what's happened." Turning, she started to walk away. "I'm leaving. I want to get to my office finally. I still have a chance of holding onto my job despite the days I had to miss because of what you did."

"Jess, wait!"

When Brad caught her by the arm, she calmly reached over and removed his hand, shaking her head with a faint regretful smile. "Sleep it off, then go see Mom and Dad. I'm sure they'll be able to forgive you even if I'm not."

"But, Jess, I . . ."

"You're an intelligent man, Brad. The trouble is you've started believing your own press," she said candidly. "You're not handling becoming a star very well at all. But I know you could become the person you used to be if you really tried to see beyond all the glitter. If you can do that, maybe we can be friends again someday. If you can't, I don't want to see you."

When he called after her as she walked across the room, she didn't answer. She simply opened the door, left him, and took the elevator down to the lobby. Cade was nowhere in sight, and after she stood looking around for him for several seconds, she was approached by the desk clerk.

"Miss Grayson?" he questioned, smiling when she nodded and handing her a set of keys. "Mr. Hunter asked me to tell you that he left the car for you and took a taxi to his office."

Closing her hand so tightly around the keys that sharp edges dug into her palm, she murmured her thanks, then walked outside. Generously, Cade had not wanted to leave her without transportation, but neither had he wanted to waste any more time on her or Brad and away from his business. For that, she couldn't blame him. She too was most eager to return to her own office. Yet, before she did that, she intended to leave Cade's car at his building, the keys with his receptionist. She and Brad together had certainly already caused him enough inconvenience.

When Jessica returned home from work that evening, she went as quickly as possible into the guest bedroom and to the closet. Looking inside, she half expected to find all his belongings gone, but they were still there, and some hope bloomed in her until she was able to suppress it.

"Ninny, just because he hasn't gotten his things yet doesn't mean he won't get them later," she mumbled aloud to herself. And with a crestfallen look on her face, she limped into the kitchen where she still was an hour later when Cade too returned to the house.

Tensing when she heard him let himself in the front door with the key she had provided him, she drew a ragged breath and tried to steel herself to what was inevitably coming as she opened the oven door, peered in, then shut it again. She looked up as Cade stepped through the doorway, loosening his tie, his coal-black eyes fixing on hers.

"I meant for you to keep the car," he said in way of greeting, the expression lying over his features indecipherable. "I didn't need it."

"I thought you might, so I took a taxi back here and drove the Citation to work."

Dark brows lifted. "You went into work today? But where's Brad?"

Jessica shrugged, opened the oven, and removed a cookie sheet which she placed on a cooling rack on the counter as she picked up the basket beside it. "I presume he's either sleeping off the too many drinks he had last night or he's with my parents." She turned to Cade. "You were right. He wasn't kidnapped."

"I was fairly sure he hadn't been after seeing him this morning," Cade flatly replied. "His tan hadn't faded, so I assumed he hadn't been held prisoner anywhere."

"No, he's been island-hopping in the Caribbean," she explained, took a couple of steps toward him, and held out the basket. "I have a surprise for you. Have a peanut butter cookie."

Cade glanced down then back up at her. Amazingly, his gaze hardened ferociously. "And just why did you bake these? You said you never would because you weren't willing to compete with Gran."

"I . . . I changed my mind. I decided . . ."

"If peanut butter cookies are your idea of a consolation prize, you're crazy," he said harshly, taking the basket from her to put it on the table next to them. With little gentleness he caught her by the hand and pulled her out of the kitchen along the short hall to her bedroom where he brusquely commanded, "Pack a suitcase. I'm taking you to my house right now. For the next few days or however long it takes, you can consider yourself the kidnap victim."

Jessica's mouth nearly fell open in disbelief, and she sank down on the edge of the easy chair by her bed and stared up at him towering over her. "I don't understand," she breathed. "You have to explain what you're talking about."

"Gladly," he muttered, strong jaw clenched as he leaned over her, hands gripping the armrests of her chair, imprisoning her. "I'm talking about keeping you with me for as long as it takes to drive Brad out of your mind forever. Now, do you understand?"

And suddenly she did. Joy erupted in her as he jerked away to drop down on the edge of her bed. Looking at his bowed dark head, tears of sheer happiness glimmering in her sapphire eyes, she knew what he was feeling. Oh, how she knew because of the uncertainty and fear she had felt day after endless day herself. Yet, even as she knew, she had to hear him tell her, needed to at last hear the words she had so long yearned to hear. She leaned forward in the chair, elbows on knees, unmindful of the mild throbbing in her ankle. "I'm not sure I do understand, Cade," she lied softly. "Why should you care if I forget about Brad since your relationship with me is only temporary?"

"I thought it was too. At first, I only wanted you, wanted to make you realize you couldn't be happy with Brad. You have nothing in common with him anymore, but you do with me, and I knew we could have something wonderful together. But you're right, I didn't expect it to last," he confessed, raising his head, a vulnerability in his black eyes that she had never before detected as they met hers. "I'm something of a loner, Jessica. Maybe because my parents died when I was only a child, I've been . . . afraid to let myself be really close to anybody. And I wouldn't admit to myself how close I'd become to you or how much you meant to me until Saturday night. When Flanders and I realized Sims had you and was dragging you away from your car, I . . . My God, I don't know what I would have done if something had happened to you."

"Why?" she persisted, her breathing quickening as she adored him with lambent eyes. "Tell me why."

"Because I love you," he said simply. "More than I ever imagined anybody could love anyone else."

"You big dummy, how do you think I feel about you?" she asked tearfully, going down onto her knees between his legs, her hands curving over his thighs as she smiled tremulously up at him. "It seems like I've loved you all my life."

281

"Are you sure?" he questioned urgently, emotion straining his deep voice as he cupped her face in his hands. "And Brad?"

"I gave him his final walking papers this morning," she said softly. "Unless he shapes up and becomes a real caring human being again, I can't even be his friend. And how can you even ask me about Brad? Surely you know you drove him right out of my mind a long time ago? After all, I was so willing to be your lover. Didn't you think that meant something?"

"I didn't know exactly what," he muttered, drawing the edge of his thumb over her lips. "You might have made love to me because you were disillusioned with Brad and knew you were losing him. You might have just been looking for someone to be close to for a little while. People make love for many different reasons, Jessica."

"I don't," she replied earnestly. "You're my lover because I love you so much I *have* to be close to you. I need you as much as I need to breathe, or at least it feels like it."

"Then marry me," he commanded, lifting her up into his arms, embracing her possessively. "Soon."

"Tomorrow, if you like." She accepted the proposal laughingly, wrapping her own arms around him. "As soon as possible."

Kissing her again and again, he whispered against her lips, "We'll live here or at my house, whichever you want."

Drawing back slightly, Jessica gave him a slow teasing smile. "Your house of course. Georgia would never forgive us if we didn't. And besides, you have that clearing in the woods that will make a fantastic gardening spot."

"If you're only marrying me for that, you'd be better off with Brad," Cade teased in return. "He's becoming a tremendously wealthy man and could buy you an estate where you could even have fabulous formal gardens."

"Do I care?" she retorted, caressing his broad back. "He could never make me feel as alive as you do, and to keep that feeling, I'd gladly give up gardening forever."

"God, I love you," Cade uttered huskily, his mouth descend-

282

ing warmly on hers before sweeping seductively across her cheek. "Bermuda for our honeymoon—where it all began?"

Joy welled up in her, and she nodded. "Yes, Bermuda, if you promise to hold my hand on the plane."

"I will if you promise to make me some more peanut butter cookies," he bargained, cradling her close against him. "Agreed?"

"Agreed. I'll bake them any time you want. Why do you think I baked some today? Because I hoped you'd like them so much you'd never leave me or would at least see me once in a while," she confessed, burying her face in his neck. "And you haven't even tasted them yet."

"Later. I'm more interested in tasting you right now." To prove his words he nipped and nibbled on one earlobe, smiling when an excited tremor ran over her. "Besides, I'm sure your peanut butter cookies are even better than Gran's anyhow."

"If they're not, you'd be wise to lie and say that they are," she warned, brushing parted lips over the strong pulse in his throat. "But, Cade, about Bermuda—I may not be able to get time off from work again for a while. The way things are at the office with Peg still out sick, they need me there."

"No problem; we'll just postpone the honeymoon for a few months."

"I hoped you'd say that. Some men wouldn't. They'd tell a woman to quit her job if it caused them any inconvenience."

"I'm not some men."

"Oh, I know you're not and I'm so glad," she whispered, snuggling nearer, "because you're the one I love so very much, and I think I might go crazy if you don't make love to me right now."

"My pleasure," he whispered back, unbuttoning her blouse then lowering his head. Warm firm lips caressed the swell of her breast while her hands on his back urged him closer to her.

They undressed each other slowly, pausing often to savor the poignant moments as anticipation mounted delightfully. Ever mindful of her ankle, he lowered her onto the bed and came down beside her across it, the bronze tone of his skin contrasting with the lighter pale gold hue of her own. His hands and lips coursed over her, lingering here and there while she thrilled him with rousing kisses and caresses. Fever rose in them, burning purely in consuming desire. At last breathlessly whispering her need of him, she arched upward against him. His body conveyed love and irrepressible passion, and as she received him, he sheathed himself in her warmth and filled her with his. They merged together perfectly, moving in slow heady synchronization, creating spellbinding emotion and sensation they both shared equally. That part of her he had felt she kept reserved, that love for him she had always felt compelled to conceal, was unfettered now, swelling up in a tumultuous tide of abiding passion that engulfed them in a maelstrom of joyous delight. And when fulfillment came, their ecstasy was more exquisite, more heavenly, more meaningful than it had ever been because of the words of love they exchanged without inhibition.

Considerably later, Jessica lazily stirred against Cade, floating a hand upward from his abdomen over his broad hair-roughened chest as she inquired, "Hungry?"

"Hollow," he admitted, brushing her hair from her eyes and smiling wickedly. "If we keep spending dinnertime in bed together, we're both going to starve to death."

"Hmmm, but what a way to go," she replied provocatively.

"Shameless wanton," Cade murmured with a deep-throated chuckle, watching as she rose gracefully from the bed to slip into her robe. He followed, stepping into the room across the hall for his own terry robe before joining her in the kitchen. For a moment he paused in the doorway, observing her every move, practically mesmerized by the way the light caught in her golden hair. Then he walked across the room to help her prepare an impromptu dinner, taking the salad ingredients she handed him from the refrigerator and placing them on the counter. His hands curved over her shoulders. With a loving smile, he pulled her to him, grateful that he had found her and that their life together was just beginning.

Jessica wound her arms tightly around him, holding him closer, knowing that as much as she was irrevocably his, he was hers too. They belonged together. They always had and they always would.

THE WILD ONE

by
MARIANNE HARVEY

bestselling author of *The Dark Horseman*
and *The Proud Hunter*

Proud, beautiful Judith—raised by her stern
grandmother on the savage Cornish coast—
boldly abandoned herself to one man and sought
solace in the arms of another. But only one man
could tame her, could match her fiery spirit,
could fulfill the passionate promise of rapturous,
timeless love.

A Dell Book $2.95   (19207-2)